Public Enemy

By Craig William Emms

Cold Fish Books

This novel is entirely a work of fiction.
The names, characters and incidents portrayed in it are
the work of the author's imagination or are used fictitiously

First published in Great Britain by
Cold Fish Books 2013

Copyright © Craig William Emms and Linda Barnett 2013

Craig William Emms asserts the moral right to
be identified as the author of this work

A catalogue record for this book is
available from the British Library

ISBN 978-0-9572168-4-6

All rights reserved. No part of this publication may be
reproduced, stored in a retrieval system, or transmitted,
in any form or by any means, electronic, mechanical,
photocopying, recording or otherwise, without the prior
permission of the Copyright owners

This book is dedicated to my best mate, the *real* Paul Gray, his lovely wife Claire and their four gorgeous daughters. Long may you all be happy.

Thank you to Barbara and Johnny for your help.

Also by Craig William Emms

ONE HEARTBEAT A MINUTE

HEART OF STONE

INTRODUCTION

Public Enemy is the second story in the John Smith series, following on from *One Heartbeat a Minute*.

In **One Heartbeat a Minute** we meet John Smith. He is an ex-Rhodesian and British Army Special Forces veteran who has fought in several brutal and bloody wars around the world including Afghanistan, the Falklands and the Gulf War. Smith has taken on guerrillas in Africa, terrorists in Northern Ireland and Libyan insurgents in Chad. He is a true warrior of the modern age... but has never been acknowledged as a hero...his work has been clandestine and "off the books". When he finally leaves the army, he is a broken and embittered man on the edge of insanity.

However MI6 refuses to leave Smith alone and his skills are put to use as an assassin, murdering enemies of the state in cold blood. Then, when he's of no more use to them, they frame him with the abduction, rape and murder of a little girl. They want to keep their dirty secrets to themselves and plan to have Smith locked away forever.

But John Smith is not the type of man to take such action lying down. He fights back, setting out on a rampage of death and destruction that shakes the establishment to its very core. Smith single-handedly takes on the system and leaves it in ruin. Then, his sense of vengeance finally satiated; he flees from the UK to find himself something that he has never had before: a life of peace.

ONE

Detective Chief Inspector Alan Davies was enjoying his packed lunch as he sat on a bench on the Thames Embankment, outside the Headquarters of the Secret Intelligence Service in Vauxhall Cross. The early summer sunshine blazed down, warming the exposed skin of his face and hands. As he closed his eyes for a few seconds, he daydreamed of a warm tropical beach and heard the sound of waves splashing on white sands, while a slight breeze waved the tops of the palm trees behind him. He was just about to sink his teeth into a ham sandwich when the call came through on his mobile.

"Yes? Davies here."

"Sir, it's Helen here. We have him! A customs officer recognised his face from the fliers that we sent out. He's at Heathrow!"

Davies's heart skipped a beat.

"Are you sure, Helen?"

"It's definite, Sir. It's Smith, without a shadow of a doubt!"

"Okay, calm down, Helen. How long ago was the alert raised?"

"Less than four minutes, Sir!"

"Where is he exactly?"

"He checked his luggage on to a flight to Tokyo, sir, flying with Japan Airlines from Terminal Three."

"Okay, Helen. Have you got a pen and paper?"

"Yes, Sir."

"Good, write this down. First of all ask – no - *tell* the

commander in charge of Aviation Security at Heathrow that I want Smith's plane to be stopped. Do not let it take off. Tell the commander there's a terrorist suspect waiting to board, and he's to get his team to keep tabs on him, but for God's sake don't mention Smith by name. If Smith realises there's something wrong and makes a break for it, I want him arrested, but they are not to make a move unless he does. Have you got that?"

"Yes, Sir."

"Next, get on to the duty officer of the SAS in Hereford and get the standby CRW team on their way to Heathrow as soon as possible. Make sure that their OIC understands the urgency of the situation. They can take a chopper to the nearest airport, wherever that is."

"Denham Aerodrome, Sir. It's a small airfield only eight miles north of Heathrow. I just looked it up on the internet."

"Good girl, Helen, you're a star! Get a couple of minibuses from the nearest nick to the airfield to pick them up and take them to Heathrow."

"Yes, Sir."

"Then I want you to call the Home Secretary and inform her about what's happening."

"Yes, Sir. Shall I tell her that you're on the way to Heathrow, Sir?"

"Yes."

He laughed out loud.

"I'll be breaking every speed limit between here and the airport. Tell the commander of Aviation Security that I'll meet him at Heathrow Police Station. I want to be there when we get the bastard!"

Less than forty-five minutes later, Davies raced his car into Heathrow, his tyres squealing as he swung a left on to the offramp just before the tunnel entrance to the central terminal areas. He continued speeding along the Northern Perimeter Road, pushing his BMW to the limit, until he sighted the police station opposite the Renaissance Hotel.

His brakes threw up a cloud of smoke as he screeched to a halt in front of the station. His car had barely stopped moving before he was out of it and running into the reception area. Two minutes later he was breathlessly introducing himself to the man in charge of Aviation Security, Metropolitan Police Commander Paul O'Brien.

"I'm Alan Davies, Serious and Organised Crime Agency, on attachment to the Secret Intelligence Service," he said, shaking the Commander's hand.

"Have we still got our man under surveillance?"

"Yes. He's still in the departure lounge at Terminal Three. We've got him covered by two CCTV cameras plus a couple of plain clothes detectives who have a clear line of sight to him. Our firearms officers are on standby."

"Good! Good! Any news from the SAS?" O'Brien glanced at his watch.

"The CRW team are on their way. Their ETA at Denham is twenty-five minutes."

"Excellent! Well, let's not let the grass grow, Commander. Let's have a look at the CCTV."

The command centre of Heathrow Police Station looked like the bridge of the USS Enterprise. Computer stations and monitors lined the walls on a long series of desks, and technicians sat before them on swivel chairs. Everyone in the room looked up as Davies and O'Brien made their entrance, and there was an electric feel to the air as they shared the DCI's obvious excitement. It was clear to everybody that something big was about to go down - it wasn't every day that the SAS and a hotshot from MI6 turned up in their little world. The commander of Aviation Security led Davies straight to a large monitor positioned in the centre of one wall. Davies craned his neck over the shoulder of the operative seated in front of it.

"Where is he?"

"Just there, Sir, sitting in the second row, reading a book."

The operative pointed at the screen.

"Can you zoom in a bit?"

"Yes, Sir."

The operative placed his hand on a joystick and pressed a button. The picture on the monitor blurred as the camera zoomed in quickly, then cleared again as it refocused. There was a clear shot of the suspect's head and shoulders.

"Just a little more please."

"Okay, Sir."

"There, that's perfect. Thank you."

"Is it your man?" asked the Commander as they stared at the face on the screen. The camera gave a clear shot of a man that looked to be in his late forties or early fifties, with short-cropped dark hair and a thick muscular neck. He was wearing a pair of reading glasses as he read a paperback. For just a second, the suspect looked up from his book and glanced around nonchalantly before returning to his reading.

"It is! I'm sure of it!"

"What now?"

"Ah! I would be grateful if you would give the Home Secretary a call, Commander. She's expecting it."

Commander O'Brien made the call in the privacy of his office and he was not a happy bunny. The politician thanked him in a patronising way for the help of his unit, then she broke the news that control of the operation was to be handed over to DCI Davies. The Commander argued the point that the DCI was, in fact, a lower rank. However it cut no ice with the Home Secretary.

"When the SAS team arrive at Heathrow, DCI Davies will take over command of the operation. You and your unit will place yourself at his disposal, do you understand?"

He didn't, but nonetheless he knew how to take orders, even when they appeared to be the wrong ones. He thanked the Home Secretary for her time and passed on his regards to the politician's husband. He might not have liked the situation he found himself in, but no way was he going to jeopardise his career.

The nineteen soldiers of the standby Counter Revolutionary Warfare team of 22 Special Air Service Regiment arrived in a characteristically low-key manner. Dressed in a variety of civilian clothes and looking more like ordinary men off the street than some of the most highly trained and professional Special Forces soldiers in the world, they exited their minibuses in the car park at the rear of the station and entered the building, carrying their gear and weapons in large black holdalls. The soldiers were directed into an empty recreation room to kit up while their officer was shown into the command centre.
"I'm Captain Westaway, in command of the CRW standby team."
The officer was a dapper man in his early thirties, lean, fit and with a face browned by a faraway sun in some other, warmer climate. He oozed a quiet self-confidence that immediately rubbed Davies up the wrong way.
"I'm Davies, SIS, and this is Commander O'Brien of Aviation Security. I'm in command of this operation."
The SAS Captain raised an eyebrow.
"So I've been informed. Must be an important deal for SIS to be involved?"
"Not at all, Captain, not at all. Just make sure that your men do as they are told and everything will be hunkydory."
Before the Captain could counter this slight on his men's professionalism, Davies turned to the Police Commander.
"Thank you for all of your help, Commander. I would be grateful if your people would withdraw from Terminal Three as soon as the SAS move in to take their places. You can tell your officers to leave the command centre as well."
"Certainly."
The Commander waved to his officers to leave the room.
"And if you could join them as well."
"Don't push your luck, *Detective Chief Inspector*!"
"I apologise if you feel put out, *Sir*, but this is an SIS

operation. It's classified."

"Very well."

The Commander stalked out of the room, obviously very annoyed.

"Prat," Davies said under his breath.

He continued in a louder voice.

"Right, Captain, let's give you a look at our target shall we?"

They turned to the CCTV monitor.

The man who sat reading a crime novel in the departure lounge had no idea that all of this activity was going on around him. Every few minutes he looked up from his book and glanced around, then lowered his head to read again, ignoring the hustle and bustle on the concourse as hordes of passengers made their way to departure gates or visited the duty free shops. He did not see the men who were slowly making their way to him. They were hard-looking men, even in their civilian clothing, and their emotionless eyes watched his bowed head with the concentration of a tiger stalking antelopes in the Indian bush.

DCI Davies and Captain Westaway were watching the CCTV monitor with almost the same intensity.

"Is there anything you can tell me about the target?" asked the soldier. "Is he likely to be armed? Is he dangerous? I really do not like to send my chaps in without a decent briefing beforehand."

"I'm sorry, Captain, but we've been after this man for months. It's imperative that your boys strike before he begins to get suspicious about the delay that we've imposed on his flight. If he decides to disappear we'll probably never get as good a chance to nab him again. It's possible that he's armed, but unlikely - he's already passed through the airport security scanners and they would surely have picked up any firearms. Anyway, he would have to be crazy to enter an airport with a weapon."

The soldier's brow creased up with a frown.

"Then do you mind telling me why it was thought necessary to call my team in from Hereford? Surely Aviation Security could have arrested the target?"
Davies looked at him sharply.

"Have you not been told, Captain? The target is too dangerous to be arrested by a bunch of flat-foots. He's possibly the most dangerous man in the country!"

"But if he's unarmed...?"

"Listen to me, captain. The man that you can see here is highly intelligent and resourceful. He is also highly trained in just about every method of armed or *unarmed* combat. Your job is to *eliminate* the target, Captain, not to arrest him."

The soldier stared at Davies with a look of distaste on his face.

"Well if those are your *orders*, Davies, I'm afraid that I will be disobeying them!"

"What?"

"Despite what the tabloid press may say about *my* regiment sir, we are *not* a bunch of gun-toting assassins."

"You'll damn well do as you are ordered, Captain!"

"No. I will not. My men will happily arrest this target for you, but no way will we 'eliminate' him. This isn't America, Davies, and you are not in the CIA!"

"Listen to me, Captain. This man is wanted for at least six murders, possibly many more, including the cold-blooded killing of a Crown Court Judge! Plus, he has carried out several terrorist attacks in the UK."

"I don't give a flying fuck what he's done. He will be arrested unless he proves to be a threat to any of my team."

"This was the same bastard that totally destroyed the Police National Computer at Hendon last year, and its back-up server! Not to mention blowing up the National DNA Database in Birmingham! We've been searching the world for him and here he is at last. We are not going to let this bastard walk away now that we've got him!"

Westaway looked at the DCI coldly.

"Do you mean that this is *John Smith*?"

"Yes I do."

"Jesus fucking Christ man! Why didn't you inform me of this right away, before I sent my chaps out there? You do realise that Smith was one of us, don't you?"

"Of course I do, but so what? As far as I'm concerned he's a criminal and that's that."

"That's fine you silly bloody little man, but there are chaps in my team who might have served with him in the past. He only needs to recognise one face and ……. *poof*! Smith will be gone and you'll never bloody catch him. He may be a criminal to you, but in the regiment he was a legend in his own lunchtime. Positively the best Close Target Reconnaissance man we've ever had. I understand that he was treated abominably by you and your cronies once he was on civvy street, after a lifetime of serving his country in some of the worst conflicts that the world could throw at him. He's a bloody hero to some of our guys!" Davies was fuming at being spoken to in this way and was about to throw the Captain a stinging riposte when the radio's loudspeaker announced that the 'target' was making a move. Both men instantly switched their attention to the screen in front of them.

The target stood up and stretched his stiff muscles, before placing his paperback down on the chair and walking off. In the command centre a voice came over the speakers.

"Hello Sunray, this is Two Zero Alpha. Tango One is on the move, over."

Captain Westaway spoke into the microphone, casting a foul look at Davies as he did so.

"Sunray. Wait one, over."

He turned to the DCI.

"Well, what's it to be, Detective Chief Inspector? Do you want us to take him into custody or not?"

Davies fumed, "Yes. Do it!"

"Sunray. Keep Tango One in sight. Once he's clear of potential bystanders, take him down. Be aware that the target is highly dangerous. I say again, be aware that the target is highly dangerous, over."

"Two Zero Alpha. Roger that. Are we cleared to use lethal force if necessary? Over."

"Sunray. Affirmative, I say again, affirmative. But only if it's necessary, over."

"Two Zero Alpha, wilco, out to you. Hello all callsigns, close on Tango One. Wait for my go, out."

Davies and Westaway intently watched the action unfolding in the departure lounge. First of all the target joined a queue in one of the duty free shops where he purchased a small bottle of water. Then he slowly ambled through the crowd, all the time with the SAS teams following and steadily closing in. After a while he broke away from the crowd and made his way towards the toilets.

"Two Zero Alpha to all callsigns, Tango One is heading for the men's toilets. Two One and Two Two, take up positions where you've got a clear view of the toilet doors in case he clears us and makes a run for it. Two Three, you're in reserve. Wait by the exit to the departure lounge. We're going to go in and take him, wait out."

"If this is your man," said Westaway, "then he's just made a very stupid mistake. He's got himself into a position where there is only one exit."

The two men huddled over the monitor, watching with bated breath as four figures detached themselves from the hundreds of travellers passing through the concourse. The figures homed in on the toilet doors like four guided missiles, and hands could be seen straying under their jackets as they felt for the hand-grips of their pistols. Then, just as they converged in two well-rehearsed pairs, all hell broke loose. The toilet doors banged open, and the space they once occupied suddenly filled with a teeming mass of men all dressed in the same red and white striped rugby shirts. The large group of drunken rugby supporters surged past the undercover soldiers, jostling them to one side, as they shouted, sang and cursed with happy abandon.

"Hello all callsigns, this is Two Zero Alpha. Stand down. Wait out."

The team leader waited until the drunken supporters had passed his men and had got well into the concourse before signalling to the rest of his four man 'brick'. They then moved forward through the toilet doors.

In the office DCI Davies grinned widely, apparently having recovered from his earlier irritation. Turning from the monitor, he slapped the SAS captain on the back.

"We've got him now! We've finally run the bastard down! Hah!"

The captain's hard face remained inscrutable as he replied:

"Yes. We've got him now." However he didn't seem as happy as his companion.

A few minutes of silence passed.

The DCI and the captain tried to avoid each other's gaze as their minds wandered over the 'what ifs' and the 'if only' that all such men suffer at moments like this. A loud burst of static screeched through the speakers, followed immediately by:

"Hello Sunray, this is Two Zero Alpha. Tango One has been apprehended. I say again, Tango One has been apprehended. No trouble, over."

A stunned silence replaced the noise of the transmission for a few seconds. Then Davies leaned down and pushed the button beneath the monitor, his mouth pressed up against the microphone, spittle spraying from his lips.

"Bring the bastard to the police station!"

Twenty minutes later all of the joy and happiness had fled from Davies's face as he looked into the eyes of a very frightened man standing before him with his hands handcuffed behind his back.

"Who the hell are you?" Davies almost screamed into the man's face, scaring him even more.

"My.....my...name's Daniel Hatchet!"

"Shit! We've got the wrong fucking man! He looks like him, but it's not him! Shit! Shit! Shit!"

"So," said Captain Westaway, doing his very best not to smile at Davies's cock-up, but failing miserably, "I take it we can let Mr Hatchet go then?"

"Yes, yes. Let him go."
Westaway leaned in close to the DCI and spoke softly into his ear.

"Rather lucky that we didn't just 'eliminate' him really, don't you think?"
Davies glared at him.

TWO

7th June
Abuko Nature Reserve, The Gambia

At almost the same moment, nearly three thousand miles to the south of Heathrow Airport, Paul Gray was sitting on a bench in the field station gallery that overlooked the crocodile pools in Abuko Nature Reserve in The Gambia.
    Early afternoon in this tropical West African country was one of the hottest times of day and Gray could feel the sweat dripping down his neck and soaking into the collar of his T-shirt. He loved this place - there was a wonderful sense of peace here, even amongst the backdrop of loud and extravagant wild bird and animal sounds and the occasional group of noisy white tourists climbing the wooden staircase to gaze out over the pools. He let his mind wander as he watched a pair of giant kingfishers that were perching in the old cabbage tree off to his right, their heads pointing downwards to the surface of the pool, waiting for that tiny glimmer of silver that would herald a chance to catch their next meal.
    He suddenly shook himself as dark memories began to intrude into his thoughts, as they always did, no matter where or when. There were just too many of them. He swore softly to himself: *Fuck off and leave me in peace!* It sometimes worked, but not often.
    "Hello, Mr Paul," said a voice to one side and he almost jumped, startled by the man who had silently sidled up to him.

Fuck it! he thought. *I'm getting too old and too slow. I would never have let anybody sneak up on me when I was in the regiment. I was always so alert to any danger, and always in control.*

He turned his head to the African who had spoken, a smile lighting up his face as he recognised the man.

"Hello, Ousman."

The Gambian smiled back. He was short and slightly built with a round open face. He looked smart in his tan uniform shirt and trousers.

"*Somuley?*" (How is your family?)

"*Ebebejay.*" (They are fine.)

"*Kori tanantay?* (How are you?)"

"*Tanantay.*" (I am fine.)

"*Tilo kandito backay.*" (The sun is hot today.)

"*Tilo kandito backay, backay,* the sun is way too hot today."

"Not too hot, three hot!" Ousman laughed at his own joke.

"Your *Mandinka* is getting very good, Mr Paul."

"Thank you, Mr Bah, I've been practising."

"But you know, if you look at my face you can see that I am a whiter black, my hair is straight and my nose is straight. You know what this means here in The Gambia?"

"Yes I do, Ousman. It means that you are a *Fula* man."

"That's right! Can you talk *Fula?*"

"Just a little Ousman. *Nmbata?*" (How are you?)

"*Jamtan!*" (I am fine.)

"*Tanala?*" (How's the family?)

"*Jamtan!* (They are fine!) Very good Mr Paul, you'll soon be a Gambian man like me!"

"No, no, Ousman, I'm an English Man and England is..."

"...the best country in the world!"

The two men laughed at this joke, which was often shared between them.

"Damn right, Ousman."

"Yes. England good, Gambia no good!"
They laughed again.

"Are you going to the animal orphanage, Mr Paul?"

"Yep, thought I'd take a stroll up there today. See how the hyenas are doing."

"Ah, *Bookie*, they very big animals, *Bookie*."

"Very big, with very big teeth."

"Like my first wife!"
They laughed again.

"I will walk with you? Malang, he want me to buy cold Coca Cola for him."

"Okay, that would be great Ousman."

The walk took them along a winding path through the reserve's gallery forest. The shade from the huge trees with their buttressed roots was very welcome in the searing heat. A troop of grey-green callithrix monkeys passed by them, searching the forest floor for fallen fruits and insects. They were followed closely by a lone Maxwell's duiker, a tiny blue-grey antelope whose short tail was wagging furiously backwards and forwards as if powered by clockwork. The duiker was trailing the monkeys so that it could grab any half-eaten fruits they dropped to the forest floor. Overhead, another troop of monkeys, the much larger red-and-black coloured western red colobus, crashed through the topmost branches of the trees. Tiny babies clung perilously to their mothers' bellies as they fearlessly leapt the huge distances from tree to tree. And all the time the air was filled with the startling cries of western grey plantain-eaters and red-billed hornbills.

After a few hundred yards the dense forest canopy gave way to more open Guinea Savannah woodland and the sun blazed down on them. The sporadic patches of shade where the branches of the trees met over the path were plagued by swarms of tsetse flies. These insects gave both men powerful bites on their exposed skin. As soon as Paul and Ousman broke into the sunshine again, the tsetses dropped away behind them. Flocks of Senegal wood hoopoes and laughing doves kept them company as they walked companionably along. Occasionally, bushbuck antelopes, much bigger than their duiker counterparts and with their red fur covered in a handsome patchwork of white spots and stripes, crashed away into the bush when the two men surprised them by walking around a corner in the path. They also sometimes saw nile monitors (huge lizards that were over a metre in length) stalking the path looking for anything that they could overcome and eat. Brightly coloured butterflies and sunbirds fluttered on either side of them, feeding on the nectar of the orange and pink flowers of lantana flowers. Small orange-bodied and blue-headed agama lizards scampered away from their feet and ran up the trunks of the trees to watch them as they passed. *African wildlife*, thought Paul, *is just like the African people themselves - loud and brightly coloured.*

After an enjoyable but extremely hot walk that took them about half an hour, they emerged into a pleasantly shaded area that contained two small kiosks. Sitting inside one of them was a young African man who grinned widely as they approached.

"Hello, Mr Paul. Hello, Ousman."
"Hello, Yayah," said Gray in return.
"How are you today?"
"Fine, fine. How are you Mr Paul?"
"Fine, fine. Just very hot."
"Yes, it is too hot today."
"Yayah, it's always too hot in The Gambia."
"No, it is three hot!" laughed Ousman.

They all joined in, laughing at his joke, even though they had heard it many times before.

Gray brought Ousman, Yayah and himself small bottles of Coke that were stored in a chest freezer in the kiosk. There was no mains electricity connected to the animal orphanage area, but the drink bottles were kept cool by slowly-melting bags of ice that were delivered each morning. Ousman and Paul took a seat on a wooden bench in the shade and were joined by Yayah. They sat chatting while they sipped at their cool drinks.

Fifteen minutes later they heard the sound of a vehicle parking, followed by the muted bang of closing car doors. From the car parking area a short white man in a smart suit, followed by an African in a dark uniform, approached their island of shade. Yayah leapt up from the bench and disappeared back into his kiosk as the pair walked up to it, both of them nodding in friendly greeting at Paul and Ousman.

"Good afternoon," the white man said.

"Hi," Paul replied.

"Could I have two cold Sprites please?" the man asked Yayah.

Once the bottles and some money had changed hands, and Yayah had opened the bottles for them, the two men approached the bench.

"Mind if we join you?"

"Feel free."

Paul gestured to the bench beside him. They did so, the white man passing one of the bottles to his companion.

"My God, but it's a hot day!"

"It certainly is."

"Are you here on holiday?" the man asked Paul.

"Nope, I live here."

"Really? I thought I knew all the ex-pats in The Gambia but I'm certain that we haven't met before."

"I spend a lot of my time out in the bush. I don't really mix with the other ex-pats," Paul replied evasively.

"That's a shame. They're really quite a jolly lot - lots of colourful characters amongst them."

"I can imagine."

"I should really introduce myself. I'm Eric Williams, the British High Commissioner to The Gambia. This is Buba, my driver."

He indicated his companion, who grinned at Paul.

"And you are...?"

"Gray. Paul Gray."

"Pleased to meet you, Mr Gray."

"Likewise, Mr Williams."

"Please call me Eric. We don't stand on formality out here," he smiled.

"Pleased to meet you Eric. Just call me Paul." He smiled back as they shook hands.

"I'm supposed to be meeting the Director of the Wildlife Department here, but I don't suppose he'll be on time."

"He'll be operating on GMT," said Paul.

"GMT?"

"Gambian Maybe Time."

They shared a laugh and Ousman piped up.

"Doctor Bojang, he no good!"

"The Director, really?"

"He bad man, very corrupt!"

"Oh, I see. Well never mind. I haven't got any money to spare for him from my budget anyway."

Paul decided he'd make a move and stood up.

"It was good to meet you Eric. I must be on my way now."

"Ah, right. Good to meet you too."

He also rose from the bench and the two shook hands again.

"Look, old chap. We have a bash on in a week's time at the High Commission. You must come to it and meet some of the other ex-pats."

"Maybe."

"Well, give your address to Buba, and I'll make sure that an invitation is delivered to you. You'll enjoy it. Free food and plonk, and very good company. Anybody who's anybody will be there. We're celebrating the Queen's birthday, so you'll have to come along."

His friendly enthusiasm was catching and Paul broke into a smile.

"Okay. I'll be there."

"Excellent! I'll look forward to seeing you!"

THREE

7th June
Abuko Nature Reserve, The Gambia

The man now known as Paul Gray was better known to the British authorities as John Smith, although even this wasn't his real name - not the one he was born with. Sometimes even he couldn't remember that name - it was such a long time since he had used it. During the last thirty-odd years he had operated around the world using dozens of different names. Sometimes he thought that he was just a shadow, a man with no real name or past. He certainly had no family or friends that he could turn to to prove his sanity.

John Smith was six feet two inches tall with broad shoulders and a straight back. He was in his early fifties - showing mostly in the lines of his craggy face and the grey that was spreading throughout his once dark hair. His hair was long, pulled back from his tanned face and held tight by an elastic band in a ponytail which hung down his back. His long rangy legs and arms were still well-defined with muscle, not the heavy balled muscle of a weightlifter but the long smooth muscles of an athlete. These muscles now drove his legs forward as he hurried back down the path towards his parked car at the entrance to Abuko. The sun was rapidly sliding below the horizon, and he knew that he would only just beat the darkness of the twilight that would come with its customary tropical swiftness.

Shit! he thought to himself as his long legs ate up the ground in front of him. *Shit! That was fucking bad luck to run into the High Commissioner, and after all of these months of trying to keep out of the way! Shit!*

John Smith was a wanted man. He was an ex-soldier who had served in the Special Forces of two countries - Rhodesia and Britain, though the former was as a British spy working for the Secret Intelligence Service. He had served in wars and conflicts around the world, from the terrorist war in Northern Ireland through to the First Gulf War against Iraq. He was rough, he was tough, and he was a cold-hearted killer when he had to be. He had once been tortured and of course, he had cracked and given his torturers everything that they wanted. It didn't matter to him that everyone cracked in the end. It didn't matter that it had taken an "unheard of" three months to break him. As far as John Smith was concerned, he had cracked and had been broken, and therefore he was worth less than the shit on the bottom of a shoe.

Lots of thoughts were spiralling through his head, as they always seemed to be - though you would never have guessed the turmoil that constantly went on behind his cold coal-black eyes, so well did he hide it. There were the dark deep memories that were always with him of course, thoughts of that bastard Russian's cold, calm voice, whispering into his ear *"Just tell me what I want to know, John. I'll make the pain go away if you talk to me. Tell me John."* There were the memories of fire-fights and he often felt the fear that he had felt as a younger man, as a tight ball in his stomach, as he imagined the 'crack' and 'thump' when a round flew by his ear. Sometimes he remembered the intense pain of one such round, fired from a Mozambican Kalashnikov AK47, as it had sliced through his groin, taking muscle and bone with it. Often he thought of his ex-wife and his two sons, not boys anymore, but fully grown men now, with lives of their own. He wondered what they were up to these days. Were they married? Did they have children of their own, his grandchildren? Did they ever think about their dad? He doubted it. These thoughts led in turn to much more recent memories. Memories of sitting helpless in a courtroom, accused of something that he had not done, his subsequent escape in which he killed, with his bare hands, the two guards who had been taunting him. The killing of the Crown Prosecution Service Prosecutor, the detective sergeant and the judge that had helped to set him up, and of course the bullet that he put into Harry's head from his tree-top perch. Harry had been the head of the Increment, a top secret section of the Special Intelligence Service that carried out assassinations and other 'off the book' and deniable operations. *Fucking Harry!* he thought. *He would have bollocked me up sideways for talking to Eric Williams. He was a stickler for keeping out of sight and out of mind - a typical fucking SIS spook! I hope he's rotting in hell, the bastard!* The last person he had murdered had been the former chief of the Secret Intelligence Service. He had been the last link in Smith's chain of command and he was the last person alive who knew Smith's real name. With him gone and with the destruction of the Police National Computer and the National DNA Database, both of which he had blown to bits, John Smith had felt that he was finally free enough to leave everything behind and to make a new life for himself far away. And so, here he was living in The Gambia under the name of Paul Gray.

Abruptly his thoughts turned once again to his present dilemma. *Damned if I do and damned if I don't.* He knew that he would be taking a chance if he turned up to the Queen's birthday celebrations. He might run into one of the High Commissioner's staff who dealt with fugitives on the run from UK law, or someone might have their curiosity piqued by seeing him, or by talking to him. There were all sorts of possibilities that entered his head, none of them pleasant. *I could just send my apologies and tell them that I've come down with malaria, or something, and not go.* But deep inside he knew that that would only prolong the inevitable. He was known to the authorities now. He wasn't as faceless and nameless as he had been only this morning. How long would it be before someone got curious enough to run a check on him, or put his description through the Police National Computer? *Ha!* he thought with a smile. *They won't be doing that for a while. I fucked them up pretty well when I blew that sucker to Kingdom come! Ha!*

He reached his car just as the last rays of the sun touched the horizon. Sitting inside he thought - *time to move on. I'll go to the damned party, but meanwhile I'll book a flight out. Where to though? I've always fancied the West Indies. Tobago looks nice.* He looked around as darkness enveloped the forest. *Shame, I was beginning to like it here.*

FOUR

10th June
Vauxhall Cross, London

"What the bloody hell were you thinking? Ordering the SAS team to 'eliminate' Smith! I've had the bloody colonel of the regiment on the phone berating me for a full half hour about how his men are professional soldiers and not bloody assassins!"
Sir Rupert Giles glared across his desk at Alan Davies and Helen Wright, who were standing like naughty school children before an angry headmaster.
"And you dragged the Home Secretary into it!"
"I..." started Davies.
"Don't! I don't want any bloody excuses! You and Wright have been seconded to us from SOCA for one reason, and one reason only."
"I know, it's just..."
"Quiet! I'm not bloody interested! Your job is to locate John Smith. Locate him. Not bloody well start World War Three!"
He visibly restrained his anger before carrying on.
"Okay, so this was definitely not our man today?"
"No Sir, although he looked very much like Smith."
"Well, we're not in the game of killing bloody doppelgangers. How close are you to locating Smith? Have you got any leads at all?"
"None, Sir. We've gone through the usual channels of putting wire taps on his family and former friends, and

his two sons are under twenty-four hour surveillance in case he shows up."

"Is there any likelihood of that? I thought that he was estranged from his family?"

"His younger son has had two daughters, Sir. They are Smith's grandchildren, so there's always a chance that he will turn up to see them."

"Mmmm, a bloody small chance if you ask me. How would he find out about them for a start?"

"When they were born, we put notices about the births in the local newspapers, acting as anonymous well-wishers. But there's been no sign that Smith has read them."

"Do you think he's hiding locally?"

"Not really, Sir, I just thought it would be worth a shot."

"Mmmm. What else have you got going?"

"Well we've recovered several photographs of Smith from other sources after he blew up the PNC. Copies of these have been given to every man and woman in the UK Border Agency, Customs and Excise and Airport Security. Every port, airport and the Channel Tunnel have been alerted, and every police officer in the country is aware of his description. We have also been in touch with every SIS officer in all of our overseas diplomatic missions. I believe it's just a matter of waiting and biding our time. He's got to turn up sometime. Meanwhile we are tracing every person that has ever been in contact with Smith, whether they are ex-military or civilian. Someone, somewhere must have an idea about where he's gone to ground."

"Mmmm...*'no man is an island'*, eh?"

"Exactly, Sir."

"Right, well keep at it, Davies. Just remember that your job is to locate Smith. We'll carry out the arrest. No more bloody talk of eliminating him. Is that understood?"

"Yes Sir, understood."

"Anything else that you need from the Firm, Davies?"

"Just one request, Sir. If we could harness your men from the Increment, I believe that we'd have a better chance of getting Smith, Sir."
Giles gave Davies a hard stare.
"The Increment no longer exists, DCI Davies. We are an intelligence-gathering agency and like our comrades in the SAS, we do not carry out assassinations. We operate entirely within the law of the land. Even the idea of a self-governing internal group of cold-blooded killers is abhorrent to me and to the Service."
"Sorry Sir, I jus..."
"Never mind. Your job is to find John Smith so that he can be arrested and brought to justice. That is all. Don't let me detain you any longer."
"Yes, Sir. Thank you, Sir."

Sir Rupert Giles KCMG CVO OBE, Chief of the Secret Intelligence Service, sat back in his expensive leather swivel chair after the two police officers had left his office. He gave them two minutes to clear his outer office and then pressed the intercom button to his personal assistant.
"Heather. Is Donnelly in the building?"
There was a slight pause while she looked up the daily duty roster.
"Yes Sir, he is."
"Good. Send him up to me directly, will you?"

Five minutes later a short heavy set man in his early thirties entered the office. He was dressed casually in jeans and a sweatshirt.
"Good afternoon, Chris. How's the new man settling in?"
Chris Donnelly sat down at a gesture from his boss.
"Are we being taped, Sir?"
"No. We don't want an official record of our conversations, do we?"
"No, Sir, we don't. He's settling into his new flat, Sir, glad to be out of prison of course."

"I expect he is. A life sentence with no option of parole must be hard on a man. I take it that he is fully aware of all the conditions of his release?"

"Yes, Sir. No problem there. He's happy to get on with the job."

"I bet he is."

"He's champing at the bit to get hold of Smith, sir."

"Yes, I can imagine. It's quite personal to him."

"That's right, Sir. As you're aware, it was Smith that took out his younger brother in Belfast twenty years ago. He'll be happy to exact his revenge, sir."

"Excellent! I presume that he hasn't lost his touch whilst he's been languishing in jail?"

"No problem there, Sir. I've had him working hard since we got him out."

"Just make sure that he doesn't get up to any of his old tricks again. The last thing we need is for it to become public knowledge that the firm is employing an ex-IRA hitman to do our dirty work for us!"

"There's nothing to worry about there, Sir. He fully understands why he is out of prison and what he has to do if he wants to stay out of prison."

"Good. It may be some time before Smith shows himself again. Make sure that your team keep running their surveillance on our tame policeman from SOCA. As soon as he locates Smith I want our Irish friend to get to him first. There mustn't be any cock-ups on this one, Chris. Do a good job and the Increment will be yours - permanently."

"Don't worry, Sir. We'll get him and it will all be kept under wraps."

"I trust so, Chris. I don't care what this Smith character has done in the past - he might very well be a bloody war hero, for all I care. Just remember that he murdered my predecessor, shot him dead right in front of his wife! The Firm never forgets, and it never forgives!"

"He's as good as dead already, Sir."

"Excellent."

FIVE

14th June
Fajara, The Gambia

By the time the day of the Queen's official birthday celebrations arrived, Paul Gray had already made his preparations and set his escape plans into operation. He was booked on to a Monarch flight to Gatwick in two days' time; this was the shortest route as there were no direct flights from The Gambia to the States or Caribbean. His new documents had been retrieved from his stash sewn into the bottom of his travelling suitcase, and his new disguise was ready to be adopted on the day that he left. He'd even grown the beard that he would need to trim down to a goatee. He would be travelling under the name of David Keller - yet another false name which he had used a long time ago in Latin America while working for the Firm. Luckily he had kept all of the passports, driving licences and other documents up to date. These documents had originally been issued to John Smith by the SIS and were, to all intents and purposes, genuine papers issued by the British authorities. He had no problem with using them again as he knew that no written records of his work in the Increment had been kept, or of the aliases that he had used back then. The only people who could have recalled those names - Harry, once the head of the Increment, and Sir Thomas Sewell MBE, the ex-chief of SIS - were both dead and six feet under.

Once he landed in London, Keller would rent a hotel

room somewhere, change identity once again, and then get on a plane to Tobago ready for a new start under a new name in a new place. He would be clean away from The Gambia. All he had to do now was to get through this evening's celebration without arousing anyone's suspicions.

He took a local taxi to the residence of the British High Commissioner along Atlantic Road in Fajara. As he approached the residence with a few other guests, he could see that it was set in a fantastic location; perched on the cliff-top and with a wonderful view of the sea and the coastline. Once in the large and spacious hallway of the obviously well-appointed house he was directed by a smiling Gambian maid to the guest book, which he dutifully filled in and signed.

This is the last time I sign anything in the name of Paul Gray, he thought to himself, with just a touch of sadness. The last few months in The Gambia had been some of the most peaceful he had ever known in his life. He had had a chance to face his ghosts and start to get in touch with himself again.

He joined the short line of people snaking into the rear garden of the residence and looked up ahead to see the High Commissioner welcoming everyone personally with a handshake and a smile. As the line moved quickly forward he realised with a start that there were bright lights on the High Commissioner. He could just see a television crew with a camera and a baffled microphone off to one side, obviously filming the guests arriving.

Shit! What's the TV doing here? he glanced around, trying to keep the rising panic from his face, but it was too late - the queue was snaking behind him as well. There was no way that he could make a break for it without raising suspicions. *Shit!* he thought. *I'm bloody well trapped!*

As his turn came to shake the hand of Eric Williams, Gray tried to hide his face from the camera by pretending to study a small statue on one side of the hall. However his face was caught full on by the camera when Eric leaned forward, smiling pleasantly, and gripped him by the shoulder.

"Ah, Paul. I'm very happy that you could come tonight! I told my wife that you had been hiding yourself away from us and she is *dying* to meet you. Any break in the monotony of being a diplomat's wife is welcome - especially if she has a man of mystery to talk to!"

"I look forward to talking to her, Eric," said Gray, hoping that his smile didn't look too false, and thinking: *If you and your lady wife knew who I really was you'd probably be wetting your pants right now!*

He manoeuvred himself, as quickly as he could, out of the glare of the TV camera lights, and pushed himself into the throng of party-goers that was crowding the lawns. He spotted a row of trestle tables set up to one side acting as a bar, and made his way over to them thinking: *God, I need a drink!*

Behind the tables, which were filled to capacity with bottles and glasses, was a row of a smartly dressed Gambian waiters. Catching the eye of one of them above the noisy crowd that had gathered around the bar, he shouted for a cold 'Julbrew' lager and the waiter poured him one from an ice-cold bottle.

"*Jerejeef*" (Thank you), he said, guessing correctly from the returned smile that the man was from the *Wolof* tribe.

He took a sip of his beer and began to drift slowly to the edge of the crowd, nodding in passing to several people who caught his eye as he made his way.

"You must be our mysterious Mr Gray!"

A small hand caught the sleeve of his suit and he looked down to find a very handsome middle-aged woman looking into his face and smiling.

"I am indeed."

He smiled back.

"And you must be Mrs Williams!"

She laughed at his deduction.

"Is it that obvious that I'm the wife of a diplomat?"

"Not at all."

"Good," she said, sliding her arm through his in a friendly way and diverting his drift back into the throng.

"Come on. I'll introduce you to some of the guests and you can tell me all about yourself along the way."

SIX

14th June
Broadstone Farm, Essex

In the barn of a semi-deserted farm in Essex, two men stood together. One was Chris Donnelly, the acting head of the Increment. The other was a small, wiry and very compact man who held a pistol lovingly in his hands.

"Feckin' hell, but this is a sweet wee gun."

"It certainly is. It's a P228 SIG Saur semi-automatic pistol, a lighter and more compact version of the P226, which is the preferred personal weapon of the SAS."

"Ah well, if it's good enough for those Brit bastards, then it's good enough for me."

"This particular version is actually the P228R, which has an extended barrel and external threads to accept a suppressor."

"Ah, a silencer, eh?"

"That's correct. The weight of this pistol without the suppressor is eight hundred and twenty five grams. It has a five inch barrel and a box magazine that holds thirteen 9mm *parabellum* rounds."

"Ah, '*si vis pacem, para bellum*'."

"Sorry...?"

"Do you not be knowing your classical Latin, Chris? It's amazing what you get to read when you're whiling away your life in a prison cell. A literal translation would be: 'If you wish for peace, prepare for war'."

"How very apt."

"Can we be shortening the introduction? I'd rather be having a go with this sweet wee thing."

"Go ahead. This barn is sound-proofed and a couple of my men are stationed outside to keep away the curious."

And to stop me from shooting you and having it away on me toes, the Irishman thought to himself, smiling. He adopted the standard two-handed firing posture, the gun fitting his hands as though it was made for them as he casually aimed along the pistol's iron sights. Gently he squeezed the trigger. The bang of the firing pistol was not as loud as he remembered it, but it had been several years (courtesy of HM Prison Services) since he'd heard the sound of a discharging firearm.

The two men walked forward over the short distance to the cardboard target that leaned against a wall of hay bales. Donnelly peered forward at the neat hole that marred the otherwise undamaged target.

"Not a bad shot, if you were actually aiming for his kneecap?"

"Ah, but it's been a while."
The Irishman grinned.

"Just need a wee bit o' practice!"

"Right. Well let's start with your stance shall we? That could do with some improvement, and from now on you'll always put two shots into the target, not one. We call it 'double-tapping'."

"Ah, just like the SAS, eh?"

"That's right. After a couple of weeks of practice you'll be as good a shot as anyone in the SAS."
The small Irishman threw off his pretence at being the charming Irishman, and his pale blue eyes narrowed at the thought.

"Perfect, considering the murdering bastard that you want me to kill."

SEVEN

14th June
Fajara, The Gambia

The party had gone amazingly well. His host's wife, whose name was Mary, had turned out to be very good company and had steered him around the guests with a fine mixture of kindness and good humour, making him feel truly welcome and valued. Mary introduced him to a great diversity of people, from ex-pat car mechanics and builders trying to scratch themselves a living in The Gambia, through to Gambian government Secretaries of State. Along the way he had met lots of people that he'd rather not have met, such as the Chief Constable of the Gambian Police Force and the Director of the Gambian Secret Service - the National Intelligence Agency. He watched their eyes and their faces with the careful observational skills that he had learned over a lifetime of danger and conflict, but had not once seen a flicker of recognition or suspicion. He was quite sure that no one thought of him in any other way except as the retired and divorced ex-college lecturer that he pretended to be.

The bloody television crew was a pain though. He constantly tried his best to dodge the attention of their roving camera lens throughout the evening, but he knew that his face had definitely been caught on camera at least a couple of times. At one point he was even introduced to the BBC producer in charge of the crew, who turned out to be from the 'Panorama' programme. Apparently they were going to do a show about the worldwide celebrations of the Queen's birthday. Paul asked when the show was likely to go on air and the producer put his mind at rest when he said "in a couple of months' time". He would be long gone by then.

After this encounter (and a few more Julbrews) he managed to relax and began to enjoy himself. It had been a long time since he had been able to fully relax in anyone's company but he found to his surprise that the ex-pats he met were a fun-filled, laughing bunch of nutcases and he appeared to fit right in with them. It was not without a little sadness in his heart that he left the party with the drunken and giggling rearguard well after midnight.

As he sat in a taxi on the way back to his lonely compound he reflected that it was sad that he wouldn't be able to stay on in this lively, friendly country. When he finally turned into his bed in the small hours of the morning, it was with the thought that he'd never be able to make a lasting relationship with another human being again. He'd always be on the run and on the move, shifting from one place and identity to another, until the day he died - or was finally caught.

If his heart hadn't already been killed thirty years ago by that fucking Russian interrogator, he would have cried. As it was, he was asleep as soon as his head hit the pillow.

EIGHT

16th June
Banjul International Airport, The Gambia

David Keller looked like a man in his early forties - a full ten years younger than John Smith, or Paul Gray. He wore a casual light grey suit with an open necked shirt from which could be glimpsed a gold chained pendant resting on a hairy chest. On the middle finger of his left hand he wore a large gold signet ring. His face was smooth shaved except for a short black goatee beard and moustache. He had jet black hair which was trimmed neatly to collar length, covering his ears. To top it all off, he wore a pair of those narrow and heavy framed glasses that are all the rage these days. If you didn't know who or what he was your first impression of him would be of a slightly ageing wide boy who had a bit of money to throw around – he was obviously not married and probably preferred the company of young women with loose morals. He even walked with the short stepped rolling cockiness that you would have expected of this type of man. He spoke to the plump, young woman behind the Monarch Airlines check-in desk at the airport with the easy familiarity of a dyed-in-the-wool womaniser, and elicited a few giggles and smiles from her with his flirtatious manner as he checked in his luggage.

You never would have guessed that inside the head of this shallow looking man he was constantly evaluating and processing every person that he saw in the large airy concourse of Banjul International Airport. His eyes flicked from face to face, taking everything in, searching for the least signs of recognition or subterfuge. He was an expert at this and had learned the hard way what signs to look for. When he found none, he still didn't relax or let his guard slip. He had no illusions about how much danger he was in. International air travel was not the carefree affair it had once been, and the danger from terrorists had multiplied security checks on travellers' severalfold over the last decade or so. If he was ever going to be picked up by the authorities, it would probably be as he travelled through an international airport.

He decided to wait until the last possible minute before passing through the gate into the departure lounge, where his passport and boarding pass would be checked again. He knew from experience that there would probably be a small crowd of latecomers that he could mingle with - and any slight advantage was worth the effort it took.

He sat down at a table in the small restaurant come bar in the middle of the airport concourse and ordered himself a burger, fries and a coke for lunch. Then he settled back into his chair. As he waited for his meal to arrive, he let his gaze wander. He studied the throng of people in the concourse, looking for anything that might be out of the ordinary or unusual.

There was the usual eclectic mix of people in the airport. The tourists leaving the country after a holiday were easy to pick out. The vast majority of them were white and they spoke in a range of languages from Swedish to German, though most of them were English. They usually had bright red skin from too much time spent in the sun and were bathed in a glistening sheen of sweat, still not used to the heat after a week or two in the African sun. Unusually for holidaymakers in an airport, very few of them were accompanied by children. This was probably due to the long-lasting race-memory that Africa was too dangerous a place to bring children to.

There were also a lot of well-to-do Gambians who

had homes and families in both The Gambia and Britain and who were used to travelling between them. Some of these were wearing the typical African costume of a loose *burnoose* of brightly-covered material with either open flip-flops or pointed shoes. Many of the younger ones wore expensive-looking strictly European styled clothes. Other Gambians in cheap suits were probably minor government officials going overseas for a conference or to further their education in a college or university.

The ex-pats stood out a mile from the rest if you knew what to look for; well-tanned skin and a very relaxed attitude to travelling. They were dressed casually in shorts and either open shirts or T-shirts.

Scattered in small groups throughout were the local Lebanese business people. These men and women had been born in The Gambia and lived their lives out there, forming a very close-knit and distinct community. They ran just about every medium or large business in The Gambia from shops in Banjul that dealt with cloth, supermarkets and fast food joints, through to the large import-export companies that supplied the country with just about everything that it needed. The women were usually well dressed and turned out, while the men looked like Mafia hitmen in dark suits and expensive shades.

Amongst all of this mix, was a host of typical Gambians. Some of them were there to see off or welcome back relatives or friends, but most just seemed to be hanging around for the heck of it. There were also the Gambian officials - men and women in the blue uniforms of the police or customs, the tan uniforms of the Immigration Department or the European styled suits of airport officials. The concourse was a mass of seething, sweating humanity that ebbed and flowed backwards and forwards around the static and mostly tranquil island of the restaurant where David Keller sat and ate his lunch.

One person eventually caught his eye as acting out of step with the rest. This was a tall and thickset Middle Eastern type, possibly Lebanese. Keller noticed him because he looked slightly nervous and furtive as he checked his luggage in. He constantly swept his eyes around as though watching for someone observing him and at one point he caught the eye of an African man standing well behind him in the queue, and both nodded imperceptibly to each other. Keller's professional eye and instinct noted that the African, possibly a Gambian, looked distinctly nervous as well. He watched them carefully as they checked in and then blended in with the crowd as they made their way towards the departure gate. It had been obvious from the look they gave each other that they knew one another, yet they remained apart as they passed through the gate to the departure lounge and out of sight. *Perhaps they're drug smugglers*, he thought to himself, *and scared of getting caught*. They had not shown any interest in Keller, so he dismissed them from his mind as he continued to scan the concourse. Drug smugglers were two a penny flying from Africa into Europe. There was always some silly bastard prepared to risk a few years in prison for a huge profit.

Fuck them.

NINE

16th June
Broadstone Farm, Essex

"Okay, let's take a break from practice. Make the pistol safe and put it down. You can have a smoke for a few minutes and then we'll do some more unarmed combat." The Irishman unloaded the pistol and placed it on a table that was stacked with small boxes of 9mm rounds and pistol magazines. He vigorously shook his right hand to ease the pain in it, then fished out a roll-up and lit it.

"BeJaysus man, but you're a hard taskmaster, so you are. I'm getting a blister on me hand from all this feckin' shooting."

"Practice makes perfect," Donnelly quoted as he began to straighten up the old blue gymnast mats covering one part of the barn's floor area.

"True, very true. At least I can hit the target fairly regular now."

"Yep, another ten days or so and you'll be getting fairly tight patterns."

"Another ten days and my hand will hurt so much I won't be able to toss meself off!"
He grimaced as he peered closely at his hand and then shook it again to ease the cramp.

"Not my area of expertise, I'm afraid."

"And there was me thinking what a right wanker you are."

"Very droll. Now put out the fag and get over here.

We're going to go through the standard hand and arm blocks again."

"Again?"

"Yep. You know the old saying. 'Prior Preparation and Planning Prevents Piss-Poor Performance'? By the time I'm finished with you, you'll be a mean, lean, killing machine."

"Aye, either that or a poor wreck of a man with sore hands and no strength to wank!"
He tossed down his cigarette and stamped on it. Then, looking up at Donnelly, he suddenly grinned and rubbed his hands together.

"Perhaps this time I'll get to land a fair old punch on yer smug feckin' face!"

"Give it your best shot," replied the SIS man impassively.

TEN

16th June
Somewhere over the Atlantic Ocean

At that moment David Keller was dozing and daydreaming as the Monarch Airline Boeing 757 cruised at over twenty thousand feet on its way to England.

I wonder how many times I've been up in an aircraft during my life, he thought. *It must have been thousands of bloody times. I've flown in just about everything from old Dakotas to modern Jetstreams, and almost every make of bloody helicopter there is. At least I don't have to jump out of this one!* He half opened his eyes as a pretty female flight attendant walked past his seat, and he studied her shapely legs and rear end as she made her way up the aisle.

He'd had a bit of a shock when he made his way to his seat. He was looking for his seat number 22D, and when he eventually found it he also found himself looking straight into the eyes of the BBC cameraman who had been at the Queen's birthday bash two days ago sitting in the seat right next to his own. He remembered then that he and the cameraman had shared a few friendly drinks together towards the end of the evening. As he broke eye contact with the guy and reached up to push his hand luggage into the crowded overhead locker, a moment of panic almost overwhelmed him. *Fuck it! Does he recognize me? How the hell do I explain my radical change of appearance to him?* Luckily, when he glanced down again he could see that the guy was searching through the in-flight magazine with a bored look on his face. Keller slipped into his own seat with a mumbled "Hi" that the guy returned half-heartedly. It became obvious that there was no sign of recognition there at all. Perhaps they had both been too drunk, or perhaps his disguise was that perfect that he just didn't register in the cameraman's memory. Either way, it was with immense relief that he settled down and began to unwind after the scare.

Keller glanced at his watch. They were just over three hours into the flight now, another two and a half hours should see the 757 circling over London for a landing.

It was then that something caught his eye.

At first he couldn't make out what had made the hairs on the back of his neck stand up, but then it became clear. The thickset and nervous-looking Middle Eastern man that he had spotted at the airport earlier and the African man that he had seen at the same time had both stood up about six rows in front of him. In what looked like a concerted and well-rehearsed move they both started walking quickly forward towards the front of the plane.

All of Keller's instincts suddenly came alive. Quickly he glanced around the cabin and to his consternation he saw other pairs of black African men stand up in a similarly determined way to the first two. From his viewpoint on an aisle seat towards the centre of the cabin he had a clear view along the full length of the aircraft and he could see that there were now four pairs of men, all acting in a remarkably similar way, one pair moving to the rear and three moving forward.

Suddenly there was a piercing scream from behind him as one of the Africans grabbed hold of a female flight attendant in the aisle. As Keller's head whipped around he saw a flash of light reflecting from a steel blade that the man swept up to her throat. Momentarily, Keller half rose in his seat but then there were a lot more screams from the front of the plane as the other men acted in the same way, grabbing at the attendants who were up there. All hell broke loose as the two hundred and forty-odd passengers began to realise that something bad was going down and the noise became deafening as shrill screams and shouts rent the air. Panic spread like a wildfire through the aircraft. Some passengers stood up and spilled into the aisle and others just stood and pointed at the action. All of them were terrified and it was some minutes before any sense of order began to return. Keller had sat down again once he realised that there were too many of the bad guys to handle. The bad guys themselves had succeeded in pushing all of the frightened cabin crew onto the floor of the cabin by the flight deck. Two of them had then kicked in the unlocked flight deck door and were scuffling with the flight crew out of sight. Meanwhile the other six men began to stalk down the aisle restoring order. In their hands they held long evil looking knives and they slashed at the heads of any one giving them even a hint of trouble. Some of the braver passengers made a grab at them as they passed but were soon pushed back roughly into their seats, faces oozing from bloody wounds.

    Remarkably, within just ten minutes it was all over. The two male flight crew and their six female colleagues from the cabin crew were trussed up and kneeling on the aircraft's floor. The hijackers had gained control and the passengers were now experiencing shock and fear following the initial bloody violence, and cowered away from the big black Africans who were stalking aggressively up and down the centre aisle. Keller settled down in his seat and bided his time.

ELEVEN

16th June
Vauxhall Cross, London

DCI Davies and DC Wright sat at their respective desks in the tiny office that had been allocated to their team in SIS headquarters at Vauxhall Cross.
    Team – my arse! thought Davies as he stared across his desk at the tiny window, with its bombproof glass and its view of smoke-stained rooftops. He doodled with his pen on a pad of paper. *There's just the two of us! How in the hell are we supposed to catch Smith with just the two of us? He could be anywhere, living like a free man without a care in the world while I'm cooped up in this bloody broom cupboard, watching my career slip slowly down the bloody drain!* He glanced across at Helen. *At least she's here with me.* He thought, his eyes drawn to her ample cleavage as she concentrated at reading something on her laptop. *I really must make an attempt to fuck her. I know that she's up for it, silly cow.*
Helen looked up at him as though reading his thoughts, her face reddening as she caught his eyes on her chest, embarrassed at her boss's overt appraisal.
    "There's something here that might be of interest, Sir," she blurted out.
    "Yes? What is it?" the DCI replied in a bored and uninterested tone as he finally moved his eyes upwards to contemplate her face. *My God, he thought. But she is quite a looker! Why haven't I noticed before?*

"It's a note from the Deputy High Commissioner in The Gambia, Sir. He's replying to our request for information on anyone that's new to them."

"Where the hell is The Gambia?"

"It's a tiny country in West Africa, Sir. It used to be a British colony until the 1960s and is well known as a tourist destination now. My brother went there a couple of years ago and said it was really nice apart from the hassle he got off the local teenagers."

"Hmm. Sounds absolutely wonderful. What's the note about?"

He couldn't keep the sarcasm out of his voice, making Helen's face go even redder.

"Well, apparently a new face has turned up in the country. An ex-pat by the name of Paul Gray. He's been there about five months."

Suddenly Davies's interest was roused.

"Five months? That would tie in nicely with Smith. Do they give any more info on this Paul Gray? Any photos?"

"No photos, Sir, but there is a brief description - he's male, approximately one hundred and eighty five centimetres tall, broad-shouldered, in his early fifties. He has long dark but greying hair always tied into a ponytail and black eyes."

"Black eyes? That could be our man."

Davies shuddered as he remembered looking into Smith's cold black eyes when they had arrested him for the rape and murder of that young girl. He remembered the fear that he had felt then as the man had looked at him with no emotion at all. *Smith was a cold-hearted bastard.*

"Get back on to the Deputy High Commissioner and ask for more info on this Gray character. Especially photographs if they've got any. I want to know exactly when he arrived in the country, where he came from, what he does, who his friends are and where he lives. Meanwhile get onto the Border Agency and get them to search their passenger lists for all flights to The Gambia during January. Oh, and get on to the Passport Office and see if they can locate his documents. There must be a photo with them, as well as an address and next of kin."

He knew better than to get too excited. They had already been through this process half a dozen times over the past couple of months when information had turned up on various suspicious characters, and they had all come to nothing. Still, you never knew. It only took one lucky break, and maybe this was it. He rubbed his hands together and smiled once again at Helen. If this was the break that they had been waiting for, perhaps he would celebrate by taking her out somewhere and then getting his leg over. His smile expanded into a wide grin at the thought.

TWELVE

16th June
Somewhere over the Atlantic Ocean

Time seemed to slow down on the flight, and the passing of the first hour after the hijacking seemed to last half a lifetime. It became clear to Keller that the black Africans who were now in complete control of the aircraft were not Gambians as he had at first assumed. He recognised the language that they spoke readily enough - Arabic – north African Arabic from the heavy accent. When he heard two of them utter under their breadth *'Allahu Akbar'*, it confirmed that they were Muslims. The thickset Middle-Eastern man had disappeared from view, and Keller assumed that he was a pilot as he had gone on to the flight deck and not returned.

The passengers were handling the hijacking remarkably well, Keller thought. Most of them were sitting back and watching the unfolding events with big wide eyes. Keller knew through experience that this was a sign of deep-rooted fear. However, the initial panic had passed with only a few casualties.

The only sound that was allowed in the cabin by the hijackers was the low sobbing of a few passengers. Any attempt by the passengers to talk to the hijackers, or with each other, was ruthlessly and violently stopped with threats and punches. An uneasy peace had settled on them all.

Keller was the first to spot the beginning of the trouble. He saw the group of five English tourists sitting a couple of rows ahead of him on the other side of the aisle. He watched as they dipped their heads in unison and he heard their low, whispered conversation. He could feel the tension rise palpably amongst the group as he watched them. He wanted to tell them to cool it and not be so fucking stupid, but knew that it would have been pointless. The men were young and looked as though they could handle themselves in a ruck, but he guessed that they wouldn't stand a dog's chance against the hijackers. The North Africans were probably trained in some way, and anyway they had fanaticism and *Allah* on their side - never mind their long, sharp knives. He knew that it would be an unequal match, despite being a courageous one. For a moment he thought of joining in, but something told him that this was not yet the time for action. So he sat and watched as the drama unfolded in front of him, and felt the coldness that he knew so well settle around his heart.

The group of Englishmen waited until one of the North Africans walking up the aisle was almost level with them. With a loud shout, probably more to bolster their own courage than to frighten the terrorist, they rose in unison from their seats and went for their lone opponent. The first of them made a mistake when he grabbed the African's knife arm. The man simply flicked his wrist against the weak spot of the man's thumb, lifted his arm and swung the knife down in a glittering arc that slashed against the Englishman's face. The tourist-come-hero screamed as the blade bit deeply into him and he fell back against the others behind him in the confined space. Within seconds the big African had moved forward and stabbed another of his attackers in the shoulder. He was quickly joined by two more terrorists who with more stabs, slashes and violent kicks subdued the would-be heroes. Pandemonium took hold of the passengers again as a crescendo of terrified screams and shouts broke out at the renewed and bloody violence. The rest of the hijackers tramped up and down the aisle, forcing people back into their seats with a rain of punches and threats, until eventually the panic settled down again.

Keller had quietly watched the action, his mind coldly assessing the hijackers' response to the attack. He was impressed by what he saw. These were men not unlike himself, he realised: men who were used to violence and bloodshed; men who had dealt out death before. The terrorists coolly tied the arms of the Englishmen behind their backs and pushed them at knifepoint up to the front of the aircraft, where there was a wide space in front of the galley. They were forced on to their knees looking back down the plane towards the terrified passengers, each with a hijacker positioned behind them holding them by their hair so that their faces were pushed upwards. All of the Englishmen were bleeding from wounds.

A minute or so later the heavyset Middle Eastern man emerged from the cockpit. He stood and looked down at the captive Englishmen, then raised his head and looked back down the aircraft at the passengers.

"Do not be stupid!" he shouted. "My men are soldiers of *Allah*, and they will not hesitate to fight in His name."

There was an eerie silence throughout the aircraft.

"Now you will see what will happen to anyone that opposes us in doing His work! *Allahu Akbar!*"

"*Allahu Akbar!*" his men shouted in reply as they drew their knives across the exposed throats of the kneeling Englishmen.

Spurts of bright red blood arced up and splashed across the passengers in the nearest seats, who tried in vain to cover their faces from the hot and sticky shower. Screams broke out again.

"Silence! Silence!" screamed the leader of the hijackers. "Silence!"

This time it took longer before order was re-established and quiet again descended upon the aircraft.

Keller had been so engrossed in watching the exhibition of brutality that it took him a minute to realise that the guy sitting next to him was crouched down and holding a small palm camera over the headrest of the seat in front of them. He jabbed him sharply with his elbow.
"What the fuck do you think you're doing?" he whispered.
The BBC cameraman looked up at him, but didn't lower the camera.
"What's it look like? I'm filming the bastards!" he whispered back.
"I can get an exclusive on this that'll be worth a fucking fortune!"
"Not if they catch you at it, you daft prat. These fuckers will cut your throat as soon as look at you!"
The cameraman sat there for a second more, contemplating what Keller had said.
"Yeah, yeah. You're right, they would an' all. It's not worth it."
He lowered the camera quickly and shoved it back into the voluminous thigh pocket on his trousers.
"Cheers, mate."
"No worries. Just don't be a dickhead until I tell you to be, alright?"
He smiled at the cameraman who looked back at him with a confused look on his face.
"What do you mean?"
"You'll see my friend, you'll see."

THIRTEEN

16th June
Vauxhall Cross, London

Helen's laptop beeped, indicating that an e-mail had arrived. Her fingers flew over the keyboard as she quickly opened it.
"Here we go, Sir. Here's the info from the Passport Office in Peterborough."
Davies got up heavily from his chair and skirted around his desk until he stood behind her. He had a quick look down at her cleavage before moving the focus of his concentration to the screen. Helen scrolled down the scanned-in document.
"His full name is Paul James Gray. Date of birth 15th September 1959. Place of birth Dorridge, West Midlands. His address is down here as 15 Temple Road, and his occupation is stated as a college lecturer."
"Probably a bloody paedophile. Where's his photo?"
Helen clicked on the document's attachment and a face sprang up on to the screen, filling it.
"Fucking hell!"
Davies's voice rose in amazement.
"It's him. It's fucking Smith!"
Helen looked a little more doubtful. She remembered the fiasco at Heathrow when her superior had been so sure that he had got Smith at last. She also remembered the rollicking they had received from the chief of SIS.
"Are you sure, Sir? I know he looks similar to Smith,

but not that much. The shape of his face is fuller."

"It's him I tell you! Look at his bloody eyes. They're as black as night. I'd recognise them anywhere. That's definitely him!"

Helen was still not sure, but she felt the excitement course through Davies's body as he leaned against her to get a better look at the screen.

"Right, make this a high priority. I want everything there is on this man! Get on to SOCA and get someone to visit the address he's given. I'll bet you a tenner that he's never bloody lived there! And chase up the bloody Deputy High Commissioner in The Gambia. I want everything they can find on Paul bloody Gray, and I want it now!"

His face lit up as he started to pace up and down in the confined space.

"We've got him, Helen! We've got the bastard!"

Helen watched him warily. She was glad that he was happy, though worried that he might be wrong and jumping the gun again. However, she still felt her heart flutter just a little at seeing him so animated again, reminding her why she felt so much for him. His sharp voice brought her back from her innermost thoughts.

"Come on Helen! Move yourself! Now that we've found him we'll have to bloody well catch him, won't we? Don't just sit there daydreaming!"

"Yes, Sir!"

FOURTEEN

16th June
Somewhere over southern Europe

Keller studied the eight terrorists carefully. He watched their movements and sought out weaknesses that he could exploit. Did this man look more nervous than the others? Was this one left-handed? He watched them very carefully to see if any of them shared signs of recognition with any of the others passengers: a nod here; making eye contact there. He knew that sometimes a favourite trick of hijackers was to have a few men concealed amongst the passengers, just in case. He didn't see any signs of this but he didn't rule it out in his mind. These men were extremely well disciplined. It didn't seem likely that they would give anything away.

Over the next hour and a half he watched the terrorists settle into a routine. Getting into a routine in this sort of situation was always a mistake, making it easier for an opponent to fight back. Yet these guys didn't seem to know this golden rule.

The aircraft was narrow and long, with one main passenger cabin extending from behind the flight deck with its associated toilets and galley. This was a charter flight and therefore there was no separate first class or business compartment. The passengers' seats were in pairs either side of a narrow aisle that was just under a metre in width. The hijackers positioned one man at the rear of the cabin, looking forward. Another was in the middle of the cabin about six rows of seats behind Keller's own position. Two men were out of sight on the flight deck and the remaining four men were stationed at the front of the plane, guarding the bound crew and looking back through the cabin. The hijackers seldom moved, watching the passengers closely for any sign of rebellion.

"I don't understand it," whispered the BBC cameraman sitting next to Keller.

"What's to understand?" Keller whispered back, trying not to move his lips and give himself away. "These guys are Islamic terrorists. They've hijacked the aircraft. That's it."

"But why? What are they going to do now?"

"Use your imagination, mate. They're either going to hold us hostage in return for something; or they're going to…"

He thought better than to finish the sentence.

"Or what? What are they going to do?"

Keller could sense the growing fear and panic in the man.

"You remember the Twin Towers in New York?"

"Yeah sure, but what…shit! You don't mean that they intend to crash the plane?"

His voice had begun to rise.

"Ssshh! That's a distinct possibility, but keep your fucking voice down. I don't want them to catch us talking."

"But shit, man, that means we're all dead! Why isn't anybody doing anything about it? I mean, there are only eight of them and there're a couple of hundred passengers. Why doesn't someone do something and stop them? We could easily overpower the bastards."

Keller couldn't help but smile slightly.

"Okay, mate. Go on then, why don't you have a go at them?"

"What me? I'm not a bloody hero. Why should I get myself killed?"

"Exactly, mate. That's what everyone else is thinking. They're either hoping that it will all go away or they're waiting for someone else to have a go. Human nature, mate, that's all it is."

"Shit! We're fucked then, man."

"No. Not yet. There's always a chance."

"What sort of chance?"

Keller turned slightly to look into the man's eyes.

"There's always the chance that some fucking idiot - who should know better - will take the terrorists on and kill them all."

Keller's coal-black eyes bored into his and the man felt himself shrink away from that cold stare. He thought that those eyes were as cold and dead as a shark's, and he shivered involuntarily. Keller smiled again.

"Now shut the fuck up while I plan how I'm going to do it."

FIFTEEN

16th June
Vauxhall Cross, London

"SOCA's on the line, Sir. A DS Jones from Birmingham."

"Thanks, Helen."

Davies picked up his extension and spoke into it sharply.

"DCI Davies, here."

"Hello, Sir. DS Jones from West Midlands SOCA. I've had a couple of my lads pay a visit to the address you gave us. I'm afraid that it's just an old couple that live in the house. They've never heard of a Paul Gray."

"Thanks, Sergeant. Believe it or not, that's just what I wanted to hear! How long have they been living there?"

"Getting on for thirty years sir. They have two grown-up daughters who have both gone off and got married. The man is a retired pet shop owner and his wife used to do the books for him. They seem pretty well off. Neither of them has a police record."

"Did your lads show them the photo I faxed through?"

"Yes, Sir. No reaction from the old couple. They didn't show any signs of recognition."

"That's just what I hoped, Sergeant. Even so I want you to give them the full works. Get a search warrant and go through their house with a fine-toothed comb. Arrest them on suspicion of aiding and abetting and give them a drilling down the local nick. Also, get a warrant to access their bank and phone records."

"Are you sure, Sir? My lads said that they seemed okay. Just a normal run-of-the-mill retired couple."

"Yes I am bloody sure, Sergeant!"

"Okay, Sir, whatever you say. Can you give us any idea what it's all about? Be a devil to get a warrant without some info, Sir."

"Don't worry about that, they're a threat to national security. Get a warrant signed off with the Counter-Terrorism Act. Give the Magistrate my number and I'll fill him in if he needs it."

"Okay, Sir. I'll have to clear it first with my boss though."

"Don't worry about that either. I've already had a word with Commander Edwards."

"Okay, Sir. We'll get on with it then and let you know if we find anything out of the ordinary."

"Good! I don't expect that you will, but we have to try."

"Okay, Sir. Bye."

"Yes bye, Sergeant, and thanks again."

"No problem, Sir."

SIXTEEN

16th June
Somewhere over Western Europe

"Can you take still pictures with that video camera of yours?" Keller asked the man sitting next to him.

"Yeah, of course. This is a cutting-edge camera, man. I don't carry around any old shit!"
He sounded indignant.

"Good. Does it also have a flash then?"

"Yeah, man."

"Is it fully charged up?"

"Yeah, man. But why? I ain't gonna take their fucking pictures for them!"

"Just get it ready to flash, mate. When I tap your leg I want you to set the flash off."

"No way, man. They'd fucking kill me like they did them other poor bastards!" Keller looked at him and his whisper was low and menacing.

"You don't have to worry about upsetting these fuckers. What's your name?"

"Terry."

"Well, Terry, like I said, you don't have to worry about upsetting these fuckers. What you have to do is worry about upsetting me. Now get the fucking camera ready to flash when I tap your leg."

"Okay, okay, man! Don't go getting upset! If you want me to use the flash, I will! Just stay cool, man. Stay cool!"

"Just be ready. How long does it take to recharge after flashing?"

"About half a second, man."

"Good. Because I may want you to flash it a couple of times. Then when I shout '*Now!*' I want you to set it off in the bastard's face."

"Whose face?"

"You'll know when I shout. Just be ready to go when I tap your leg. Got it?"

"Yeah, man. I'm cool."

"Good." Keller smiled at him. "Look, Terry. We're all going to die if we don't do something. Help me and I promise you'll be a fucking hero. Okay?"

Terry half-smiled back and swallowed nervously.

"Yeah, man. I get it. A fucking hero. If they don't kill me first!"

"Let me worry about them."

16th June
Vauxhall Cross, London

The phone rang. Helen picked it up and listened for a moment.

"Sir, it's the British High Commissioner to The Gambia."

"Thanks, Helen. Put him through please."

"Hello Detective Chief Inspector Alan Davies here."

"Hello Davies, Eric Williams here, High Commissioner to The Gambia. My Deputy has just informed me that you are possibly interested in one of our ex-pats, a Mr Paul Gray?"

"That's right, Sir. Paul James Gray. We understand that he's a resident in The Gambia."

"Yes he is. He seems to be a nice chap. I met him myself about a week or so ago and my wife spent some time getting to know him at the Queen's birthday bash a couple of days ago. Can you tell me what you want him for?"

"Afraid not Sir, it's a matter of national security."

"Oh dear, that sounds rather ominous. Is there anything that I can do to help? My deputy has already visited Gray's compound to try and get some more information on the fellow. But I'm afraid that he didn't meet with much luck. Apparently Mr Gray left his compound in his vehicle first thing this morning and has not been seen since."

"Is that usual behaviour for Gray, Sir?"

"Afraid I can't answer that one, old boy. As I said we've only known of his existence for the last week or so. It was only sheer luck that I ran into him in the first place."

"Okay, Sir. I'm going to request that a couple of operatives be sent out to you so that they can keep his house under surveillance. With any luck they'll be able to get the first available flight out there."

He glanced up at Helen, who read his thoughts.

"It leaves Gatwick at six tomorrow morning, Sir," she said, quickly consulting her notes.

"Did you hear that, Mr Williams? They should be with you around about midday. Would it be possible to have them met at the airport?"

"No problem at all, Davies. I'll get my driver to pick them up and take them wherever they want to go."

"That's great, Sir, thanks. Would it also be possible for one of your staff to keep an eye on Gray's house in the meantime? Perhaps your deputy, sir?"

"Again, no problem. About time he made himself useful! Do you want me to inform the Chief Constable of the Gambian Police Force?"

"No Sir, definitely not! I'd like to keep this in-house at all times, Sir, purely on a need-to-know basis."

"I say, it all sounds rather exciting!"

"It is, Sir. We've been after this man for a long time and this is the first solid break that we've had!"

"Jolly good. I'll have my deputy go back to Gray's compound. Please let me know if there is anything else I can do to help."

"Thank you, Sir, you've been most co-operative. There's just one thing before you go though, sir."

"Yes?"

"Tell your deputy to be very careful, Sir. Paul Gray is a killer and a terrorist. He's a very, very dangerous man, Sir."

"Okay, thank you. I'll be sure to pass that on. Well, bye for now. I hope you catch your man, Davies."

"So do I Sir, so do I."

As he put the receiver down, Davies looked across the room to Helen again.

"He seems like a nice chap. I wish they were all as helpful as he is! I suppose we'll have to make an appointment with the chief to get his okay on the extra manpower?"

"It's all in hand, Sir. I've already had a word with his PA and let her know that we might need to see him at short notice. She's okayed it, Sir."

"Dear Helen. What would I do without you?" he smiled.

She blushed.

SEVENTEEN

16th June
Over the English Channel

Keller looked at his watch. By his reckoning, there were about forty minutes to go before they would be arriving at Gatwick. A quick glance out of the window revealed the sparkling lights of London lighting up the dark landmass of England in the distance. *This is it.* He thought. *It's now or never. If I leave it too late we'll be going into a dive and we won't have time to pull out.* He had no doubt in his mind about what the terrorists were planning. Even so, getting ready to launch yourself into a deadly fight is not the normal way for a human being to behave, no matter how many times he had done it before. He whispered to Terry:

"Get ready with the flash."

He closed his eyes and tried to clear his mind of the dreadful fear that he felt was eating up his belly and which he knew could paralyse his attack before he even started it, if he let the terror take over completely. He took deep, even breaths to oxygenate his blood and slowly he began to clench and unclench the muscles in his body. He'd sat still for far too long and he needed to warm his muscles up if he was to move fast and with any fluidity. He knew that what he needed to do now was to use maximum aggression and speed, and that once he started on this course of action he would not be able to stop until either he had won or was dead. He felt the adrenaline start to flow through his body and he began to think of all the bad things that he normally tried not to think about. Harry. The SAS. The SIS. The pain. The killings. The shame. The guilt. He gave these thoughts free rein to invade his mind and slowly he felt the familiar rage begin to build up. He welcomed it into his mind. He embraced it. He needed the rage to see him through the next few minutes. And the hatred and the fear. He felt the rage and hatred and fear grow within him like a cancer until he was ready to explode.

    He tapped Terry's leg.

16th June
Vauxhall Cross, London

Twenty minutes after receiving the phone call from Eric Williams in The Gambia, Alan Davies and Helen Wright found themselves once more facing Sir Rupert Giles, Chief of the Secret Intelligence Service, across his desk. They stood in silence while Sir Rupert read through their hastily thrown-together report. Eventually the Chief looked up.

    "This is very interesting, Davies. And you say that it's definitely your man this time?"

    "I'm almost certain, Sir. The passport photo of Paul Gray is the giveaway, Sir."

    "Mmmm. That's what you thought last time. I hope you get a better result with this show."

    "Yes, Sir."

    "Okay. What do you want from me Detective Chief Inspector?"

    "I need a couple of operatives to go out to The Gambia, Sir and put his house under surveillance."

Sir Rupert sank back into his chair and was silent for a few moments as he stared at Davies, making him feel distinctly edgy. Then he moved, tossing the report back to Davies across the desk.

    "Okay. You've got them. Get a briefing note set up for the operatives and I'll have them sent out a.s.a.p. Give the details to my PA on your way out."

"Thank you, Sir," said Davies, taking the hint and moving towards the door.

Sir Rupert waited a few minutes until the police officers were clear of his outer office, then he pressed the intercom to his personal assistant.

"The job in The Gambia that Davies has just told you about," he started. "Put Donnelly and his Irish friend onto it. I want them both out there as soon as possible, so have a word with the airline and make it happen. Everything on this job is now a high priority."

"Yes, Sir Rupert. Have you any instructions for the team, Sir?"

"No. Donnelly knows what he's got to do. Just make sure that he knows the man he will be looking for is John Smith. Oh, and make sure that they are armed. Clear it with customs so that they can take their firearms with them on the plane."

EIGHTEEN

16th June
Somewhere over southern England

Terry jumped and the camera's flash popped, creating a bright white light for just a millisecond.

Fifteen feet behind Keller, Mohammed Abbas, the terrorist on station there, whirled around from where he had been watching the passengers in the rear of the cabin. Something had caught the corner of his eye. What was it? He looked out over the rows of seated passengers but he didn't see anything unusual. He switched his gaze to his comrades at the front of the aircraft but they were talking amongst themselves in low voices and looking away from him, not paying attention as they should have been. He looked around once again, then gave a mental shrug and turned back to face the rear.

"Remember. When I shout '*now!*' let the flash off right in his eyes."

Keller's whispered voice was like ice. He tapped Terry's leg, which was shaking with fear, and '*pop*' went the flash again.

The terrorist behind them whirled around again. He was sure that he had seen something this time. A bright white light. He looked at the passengers, but again couldn't see anything suspicious. Slowly he started walking forward, peering into the laps of the passengers on either side of the aisle as he went.

Keller gently released the catch on his seat belt. His

whole body began to tense like a coiled spring as he waited. By his shoulder he sensed rather than saw the terrorist as he quietly moved forward up the aisle. Then, out of the corner of his eye, he saw the North African pause and look down at Terry's lap. He saw the camera that Terry held tight in his sweating fingers and swooped forward, one hand outstretched to snatch at it.

"Now!" shouted Keller.
Terry shoved the camera into the terrorist's face and the flash exploded right in front of the man's eyes. Then everything happened at once. The terrorist blinked, half blinded as the flash caught him. Terry screamed with shrill fear and Keller moved like a striking snake. His body rose from his seat as his muscular arms looped upwards and curled around the back of the terrorist's neck. Then using his full bodyweight, Keller forced himself back and down into his seat while his arms dragged down the head of the terrorist with sickening force. The rapidly-moving head came into contact with the hard, unmovable wing of the chair back and Keller heard the crunch of snapping teeth and felt the first hot spots of blood shower his face. Then he forced himself to half rise again, using the powerful muscles in his legs and his back. Just as suddenly he fell back, dragging down the terrorist's head and forcing it to smash into the seat back again. This time he pulled down so hard and so fast that he felt the man's neck snap under the impact and heard the grate of bone as the vertebrae separated. He instantly threw the man's helpless body into the aisle, grinning insanely as he heard the breath rasp out of his enemy's body. He wasn't dead yet, but he would be in a minute in two. Just to make sure, Keller leapt upwards from his seat and stamped down hard on the African's face. He felt the satisfying crunch of bones disintegrating under his heel.

For a second or two everybody on the plane except Keller - whether they were a passenger or a hijacker - froze at the unexpected and extreme violence. Keller used the momentary shock to snatch up the long blade from the dying terrorist's hand and look quickly up and down the plane, judging the distances to the other terrorists. Then once again pandemonium broke out as everyone seemed to start shouting and screaming at the same time. Keller leapt forward up the aisle towards the group of hijackers at the front of the plane. The noise of two hundred people screaming in the confined space hit him like a solid wall of sound.

One of the hijackers at the front was braver and moved more rapidly than the others. Screaming unintelligible abuse in Arabic at the sight of his dying comrade and the insanely grinning man rushing up the aisle towards him, he shot forward to meet him head-on. His long-bladed, wickedly sharp knife weaved patterns through the air as he rushed to the attack. Then, just as the two of them were about to crash into each other, Keller threw himself headlong down the aisle, rolling underneath the man's outstretched knife and slamming upwards with his own blade. The ten inches of slightly curved steel stabbed into the terrorist's soft belly and sank almost up to the hilt in his flesh. Keller used the powerful muscles in his legs to force his own body upwards and ripped the blade up and into the man's breastbone as he rose. For half a second the terrorist stood looking down in disbelief at the huge gash in his own belly, and then he opened his mouth to scream, but found that he only choked on a gush of bright red blood. Keller viciously twisted the handle of the knife in his hand, slicing through more muscle, arteries and innards as he angled the blade upwards towards the man's heart. A coil of grey intestine plopped from the open wound and slithered down to the floor. Keller glanced behind him to see another terrorist rushing up the aisle towards him, and then looked forwards to see yet another man coming at him from that direction. Coolly, he yanked out the blade from the dead terrorist's body and stepped back one pace before placing his foot in the open wound and kicking the dead man's body up the aisle into the path of the terrorist advancing from that direction. Then he whirled around, knife at the ready to face the man behind him, just as he felt the searing coldness of the terrorist's blade slice into the muscles of his own back and the heat of his own blood splashing onto the back of his trousers. He slashed out at the man's eyes, forcing him to stagger backwards to avoid the blow, and as he did so the passenger sitting in the seat just behind the terrorist leapt forward and wrapped his beefy arms around the big African, immobilising the terrorist for a second or two. Keller jumped forward, deftly reversing the knife in his hand and slamming the blade into the terrorist's throat. He ripped it towards himself so that the blade sliced through skin and muscle in a shower of blood that gushed like a fountain and soaked his clothes to the skin.

    Almost immediately Keller felt another searing flash of sharp pain as the other terrorist, having disentangled himself from the body of his comrade in the aisle, opened a long slash along Keller's exposed back with his blade. Keller roared with rage and hate as he whirled back to face this new attacker and slashed forward with his own knife. He opened the terrorist's arm to the bone, forcing him to drop his weapon. He then reversed the blow to send the point of the blade crunching into the man's temple. Keller screamed abuse and twisted the handle of the blade yet again, turning the man's brain into mush and glaring into his eyes as he watched them rapidly glaze over in death. Then he stooped down, let the terrorist's inert body fall forward across his shoulder and with a renewed roar of hatred he spurted forward, throwing the body before him into the faces of the remaining hijackers, following on, right behind it.

NINETEEN

16th June
Somewhere over southern England

The basic rules of warfare echoed through Keller's brain as he charged forward up the aisle - *maximum aggression - keep up the pressure - take the fight to the enemy - never let up until the fight is won*. He was covered from head to foot in blood - most of it not his own - and he screamed in challenge as he went.

The two terrorists left alive in the passenger cabin were not as brave as their colleagues that were lying dead in the aisle. They backed away rapidly from this screaming white devil who was covered in blood, his face split by an insane grin and his black eyes blazing like the pits of hell as he charged towards them. Before they knew it Keller was barging into them. He thrust the body of the dead terrorist which had been draped over his shoulder into their faces. This forced them back into the bulkhead of the galley behind them. All three men desperately stabbed and slashed at each other, blades ripping through flesh on both sides, sending more blood spurting through the air, filling the confined space with its sickening sickly-sweet stink.

Keller managed to force one of his opponents off balance so that he fell backwards into the laps of the first row of passengers. One of the passengers instinctively grabbed at the man and they started wrestling, giving Keller the second or two that he needed to divert his full attention to the remaining hijacker. He attacked with undiminished aggression and within moments he had opened a slash in the terrorist's shoulder which made him drop his knife, arm in pain. Keller finished him off with a stab to the throat.

    Just as Keller turned on the balls of his feet to attack the remaining terrorist, the aircraft lurched to the side as it went into a tight turn. Keller went with it, caught off balance, and at the same time he felt a knife blade stab deep into his back. One of the terrorists who had been out of sight on the flight deck had emerged on hearing the racket in the cabin, and seeing Keller's exposed back he had thrust forward with all of his might, aiming at his heart. The same movement of the aircraft that had thrown Keller off balance had also caught the terrorist so that his aim was put off and his blade went into Keller's lung rather than his heart. Keller screamed with pain and rage, whirling around so fast that the terrorist's hand was ripped from the knife's handle, leaving it sticking grotesquely from the wound. Keller stabbed his own blade into the man's groin and then ripped it upwards with all of his strength, opening a large crimson slash in the man's abdomen. Meanwhile, the terrorist wrestling with the passenger in the first row of seats had battered his opponent with the hilt of his knife and had leapt back into the attack with the desperation borne of absolute terror, grabbing hold of Keller forcing him backwards. Keller smashed his forehead on to the man's nose again and again until he released his grip, then he brought his knee up into the man's groin, pushed him away and slashed across his throat with the blade, opening up the flesh down to the spine. Keller stood there for a few moments, sucking in huge gasps of air and looking around for someone else to fight and to kill, snarling like a wild beast with his hatred and rage. The adrenaline was burning through his veins and his heart was hammering away in his chest.

    Slowly he came to his senses as he felt the incline of the deck and realised that the aircraft was settled into a shallow dive. He grinned at the battered face of the English passenger that had wrestled with the terrorist, and picking up a discarded knife from the floor he handed it to the man, hilt first.

"Cut the flight crew free," he said, his voice rasping from all the screaming he had done. "There's only one of the fucker's left."

TWENTY

16th June
Over London

Keller stumbled to the smashed in door of the flight deck and looked inside. The last of the terrorists, the tall, thickset Middle Eastern man, was standing there blocking the way to the pilots' seats. He had a grim look on his face and his knife was held low – he was ready to fight. Behind him, through the cockpit windows, Keller could see the lights of London rapidly growing brighter as the plane continued its dive. Without hesitation he flung himself forward at the man, using his bodyweight to bowl him over, both of them tumbling to the floor in a mess of flailing limbs and knife blades. The terrorist came out on top, twisting his body so that he got his knees either side of Keller's belly - but not for long. Keller stabbed the man in the side of his chest and at the same time, with enormous effort, he twisted his own body and forced the terrorist to fall to one side. Then Keller was on top, the long blood-soaked blade held in both hands while he tried to force it downwards into the man's face. For a minute or more they struggled together. The terrorist stabbed upward, thrusting his blade deep into Keller's abdomen. Then he let go of the knife so that he could use both of his hands to push upwards on Keller's wrists, trying to force away the blade that swayed above his face. But Keller was not going to give in. He ignored the gush of fresh pain that shot through him from the knife in his guts, and shifted his bodyweight forward, leaning onto his own blade as it slowly inched closer to the terrorist's face. He saw the blade touch the man's left eyeball and could smell his fear as the terrorist's bowels let loose, filling the cabin with the acrid stink of piss and shit. The terrorist was babbling now in absolute terror.

"Don't kill me! Please! Don't kill me!"

Keller leaned forward more, forcing the blade downwards, puncturing the man's eyeball in a gush of clear fluid and then slipping into the eye socket. He felt the blade slicing into the bone at the edge of the eye socket, then abruptly the man's resistance ended and Keller almost fell forward, the long blade stabbing down and into the man's brain so hard that he felt its sharp point go through the skull at the back of the man's head and bury itself into the floor of the flight deck. The terrorist's body convulsed a few times, but he was already dead.

Keller collapsed forward on to the dead man, his will to fight suddenly leaving him. He heard the pounding of the blood through his veins and gasped in a great chestful of air, ending in a rasping cough that brought blood into his mouth from his punctured lung. He felt feet scramble past him and heard the pilot's voice barking out orders to the co-pilot.

"Quick! Switch off the autopilot and send out a mayday! We're diving fast! I've got to bring up her nose or we're fucked!"

Keller's will to fight had gone, but not yet his will to live. He struggled up on to his knees, his head swimming with the pain and slowly pulled the knife blade out of his stomach with yet another gush of blood. Then he looked forward, nothing now but a helpless onlooker as he watched the two pilots fight their own panic and the aircraft's controls. The pilot was pulling back with all of his might on the stick, willing the plane to come up with the effort. His right hand shot down and slammed the throttle forward, instantly increasing the aircraft's speed and filling the cockpit with the screaming of the engines.

"Are you fucking nuts?" The co-pilot glanced across. "You're making us dive faster!"

"We need the power to pull up!"

"Oh fuck!"

This last exclamation came as the co-pilot looked out of the cockpit at the lights of London rushing up at them.

"Fuck! Fuck!"

Keller saw a huge building suddenly filling the view from the cockpit's window; a massive square set, solid looking building rushing forward towards them at an unbelievable speed. The pitch of the engines drowned out any other expletives as the nose of the plane slowly began to rise and the building got closer and closer. Then after an almighty crash that shook the entire plane and a terrible grinding-scraping sound that seemed to last forever, they were above it and pulling up, up, up. The lights in the building's windows disappeared and were replaced by the cool stars of the night sky.

"Fucking hell! But that was close! Shit!"

"Did you see what that building was?"

"No! I was too busy trying to miss it, you daft bastard!"

"It was Buckingham fucking Palace!"

"What?"

"We've just knocked the roof of Buckingham Palace!"

"Fuck!"

"I hope we don't get sent to the Tower for that."

They both dissolved into hysterical laughter, relief flooding them at the nearness of the miss.

Keller couldn't join in, even though he wanted to with every fibre of his being. Instead he staggered to his feet, looked down at the corpse at his feet with its head pinned to the floor, and the handle of the knife sticking out of the dead man's eye socket. He turned and took a few steps back toward the main passenger cabin. The pain of his wounds was intense now that the adrenaline was wearing off. He could feel his life-blood pumping from his body, and his brain seemed to be spinning inside his skull. He stumbled a few more steps, felt an immense weariness and weakness take hold of him and pitched forward on to the floor, unable to break his fall with arms that felt as heavy as lead.

He heard a woman's voice shouting out "Somebody help me! Help me, please!"

He felt himself turned over and an arm go behind his head to cradle him. His vision dimmed to a dull, glowing red. A man's voice replaced that of the woman's.

"It's okay, love. I'm a paramedic. Get the first aid kit."

He felt hands moving over his body, skilful, knowing hands.

"Shit, he's been stabbed all over. He's got internal bleeding!"

Keller struggled to sit up, but his feeble efforts didn't raise him even an inch. The blood-red before his eyes began to darken to a deep crimson.

"It's okay, mate, just lie back and relax. You'll be alright."

He felt everything dim: his vision, his hearing, the pain. It all began to fade away.

"Shit! He's going!"

The darkness overwhelmed him and suddenly he felt fine, like being wrapped in warm cotton wool. He felt his will to resist slipping away. As he sunk into a deep warm pool the last sound he heard as just a whisper was:

"Shit! He's gone. He's dead."

Then there was nothing but silence and blackness.

TWENTY-ONE

16th June
Redhill, Surrey

Monday night at the Emergency Department of the East Surrey Hospital in Redhill wasn't, of course, their busiest night of the week, but it was busy enough. There had been a steady stream of patients arriving all evening but during the last half an hour the figure had tripled due to the usual mix of alcohol-related incidents. The waiting room was packed with a variety of bleeding and drunken patients. The poor woman at the reception desk was facing a constant barrage of abuse about everything from the long waiting times to the lack of seating. The ED nurses and doctors were rushed off their feet with every sort of case, from broken noses sustained during drunken brawls through to young binge-drinking girls suffering from alcohol poisoning. Staff Nurse Susan Elphick could have done without the telephone call that came in just after midnight.

She left the relative peacefulness of her office and stood in the open area by the cubicles. She had to raise her voice to be heard over the noise of a young girl who was retching and screaming as her stomach was pumped and washed out.

"Can I have your attention, please!"
The members of staff within hearing distance instantly recognised the tone in her voice. They knew that an important announcement was about to be made and called

to other staff members who hadn't heard the shout to join them. Soon there was a gathering of anxious-looking doctors, nurses and even porters around the staff nurse.

"Thank you," she said. "I've just had a call from the police. Apparently there has been a terrorist incident at Gatwick Airport and I've been advised to call a Major Incident Alert."

The small crowd erupted into a dozen questions aimed at the staff nurse.

"Quiet please. Quiet! Thank you! As of now all other emergencies will be redirected to the emergency departments of the Princess Royal and Croydon University Hospitals. The ambulance service is laying on a fleet of ambulances and minibuses to take away the less serious casualties in the waiting room."

After this announcement, there was a spontaneous if somewhat tired smattering of applause and many happy smiles amongst the staff. They were starting to get fired up at the thought of dealing with an emergency rather than the normal day-to-day routine.

"However, we shall still be stuck with the serious cases that are already here. I want all of you who are dealing with casualties at the moment to finish off their treatment as soon as possible. The rest of you start getting ready for a major influx of casualties from Gatwick. Come on ladies and gentlemen, let's clear the decks!"

She clapped her hands together to emphasise her last words and the staff dispersed to their various jobs, talking to each other in excited voices. Just like anyone else finding themselves in similar circumstances, the professional health service workers felt a little buzz of adrenaline coursing through their veins. In the next few hours they wouldn't just be simple bystanders - they would be a major part of unfolding events.

Twenty minutes later the first of several ambulances arrived, with sirens howling and blue lights blazing, from the incident at Gatwick. The ED team flowed into action with their usual efficiency.

The first casualty through the doors was a stretcher case covered in blood. As they wheeled him through the almost deserted waiting area the paramedic gave his information quickly to the consultant ED doctor, leader of the clinical team.

"Multiple stab wounds and slashes with massive loss of blood and probable hypovolaemic shock. He's tachycardic and his stats are almost negligible. His blood pressure is very low. Apparently he has been resuscitated three times already by another passenger who happens to be a paramedic. The casualty is about forty, forty-five years of age but I've no idea what his name is. He's been unconscious since we picked him up about five minutes ago."

"Okay, thank you. Do you know if he's a terrorist or a victim?"

"I've no idea, doctor. I don't think anyone knows what's going on. It was absolute bloody chaos at the airport and apparently the hijacked plane was a blood-bath. We weren't even allowed on board. Armed police and soldiers were running all over the place. I heard the cops are sending over a security team though."

"Well that's good news at least. Okay let's get our patient into *resus* and see if we can stabilise him. He's in a mess though, I don't hold out much hope. Are there many more casualties coming?"

"About three dozen walking wounded from what I could make out. Mostly knife wounds by the look of them, but I don't think there's any as serious as this one. Mind you the morgue's going to have a busy night. I saw lots of body bags being carted off the plane."

"The whole world's going crazy."

"Sure is, Doc."

"Staff Elphick. Can you take a sample and get his blood type as soon as possible please and make sure we get plenty of blood for the emergency transfusion. I don't think he's got much left, the poor sod!"

"Right away, doctor."

"Okay. Let's see what we can do for him shall we?"

TWENTY-TWO

17th June
Gatwick Airport, Surrey

At four o'clock that same morning a bleary-eyed passenger was just checking in for his flight at Gatwick. As he lifted his small carryall onto the scales he cast a look at the pretty woman behind the counter.

"BeJaysus luv, how do you manage to look so beautiful at this godforsaken time in the morning?"
She smiled back at him but didn't answer.

Trying another tack, he asked "What's all the activity about? There's an awful lot of rozzers about the place, so there is."

"There was a hijacking on a flight last night! The airport was closed for a couple of hours."

"Bloody hell! What happened?"

"No one seems to know yet, and of course nobody will tell us anyway. We'll have to watch the telly when we get home to find out about it!"

"Ah, isn't it always the way? Here you are only yards from the action and you'll have to wait for the BBC to tell yer what happened."

"We're always the last to find out!"

"Will ye be going straight home after your shift then?"

"Yes."

"Back to the warm embrace of your husband then?"
She smiled at him again.

"No. He'll be off to work before I get back. He's on the early shift this week." She smiled again. "He's a traffic policeman."

"Ah well, that's a shame. There's just no justice in the world. You such a pretty lass and married to a rozzer! What is the world coming to?"

He grinned at her as he walked away towards the entrance to the departure lounge.

Five minutes later he approached the Border Agency officer on duty.

"I believe you're expecting me?"

He handed over his passport and the officer opened it.

"Yes, sir, we are. Your colleague has already passed through and asked me to tell you that he'll be waiting for you in the smoking area."

The Irishman nodded his thanks and started to walk through the gate.

"I'm sorry, sir, not that way. I've been told that you are to go around the metal detectors sir."

"Ah, of course. Silly me!"

"If you'll just wait a moment, sir, I'll get someone to escort you through the staff entrance?"

"Okay. Thanks very much."

He thought to himself how different this all was from every other time that he had ever passed through an airport.

I could get used to this.

Chris Donnelly was sitting enjoying a quiet cigarette in the smoking area when the Irishman walked up and sat down next to him.

"Top of the morning to yer."

"And good morning to you. Are you set?"

"I sure am. Got my wee baby right here."

He patted the pistol in his shoulder holster with affection.

"Good. Let's hope that this isn't a false alarm and that you get to use it."

"And I'll say a few Hail Marys to that emotion!

Where the hell is The Gambia, anyways?"

"West Africa. Apparently they used to call it 'the white man's grave'."

"Well let's be praying that it's John Smith's grave and not ours, eh."

"Amen to that."

TWENTY-THREE

17th June
Downing Street, London

Just two hours later the Prime Minister brought the emergency meeting in the Cabinet Office Briefing Room (COBR) to order.

"Good morning, ladies and gentlemen. I'm sorry about the early hour and I realise that most of you have been dragged from your beds to attend this emergency meeting." He smiled at the group gathered around the large table before him.

"I know that most of you will only have heard rumours about the incident last night and have not had time to hear the full facts yet, so I suggest that we start the proceedings with a briefing by Sir Hugh Metcalfe. Sir Hugh?"

The Chief Constable of the Metropolitan Police looked up from his notes and cleared his throat before speaking.

"Thank you, Prime Minister. Before I start it's important to note that the incident occurred less than six hours ago, and as of yet we are not in possession of the full facts of the matter. However, this is what we've been able to piece together so far. At approximately six o'clock GMT yesterday evening, a Monarch Airlines charter flight took off from Banjul International Airport, bound for Gatwick."

"Excuse me, Sir Hugh," interrupted Sir Rupert Giles, Chief of the Secret Intelligence Service. "Isn't Banjul the main airport for The Gambia?"

"Yes, Sir Rupert. It is. Is there something that SIS knows that we don't?"

"No, no. Not at all. It's just a coincidence. The Firm's interest in the country has nothing to do with Islamic terrorism. Please carry on."

"Thank you, Sir Rupert. As I was saying, this charter flight was due to land at Gatwick sometime between midnight and thirty minutes past. It appears that eight men, who have been positively identified by the other passengers as Muslims, hijacked the aircraft whilst en route. We do not as yet have the timings for this. The terrorists were armed with long bladed knives but no firearms."

At this point he reached into a brown paper evidence bag on the table and withdrew a see-through polythene bag. Inside the polythene bag was a large, wickedly curved knife that was encrusted with dried blood.

"This is one of the weapons in question. We are in contact with the Gambian authorities but, as of yet, they have not found out how the weapons were smuggled on board the aircraft. Several of the passengers have informed us that the metal detectors and X-ray machines at the airport were not working when they entered the departure lounge at Banjul."

"Bloody typical Africans!" scoffed the Home Secretary. "They can never get their bloody act together!" Sir Hugh threw her a look that could have frozen boiling water on the spot.

"Be that as it may, Home Secretary. Somehow the terrorists smuggled these knives on to the flight and hijacked the aircraft. Of course, we have conducted initial interviews with nearly all of the surviving two hundred and forty passengers, but I'm afraid to say that most of them are suffering from extreme shock, as you might expect. We have been faced with a plethora of differing accounts about the hijacking and the subsequent events, and it has been quite difficult to piece together exactly what happened and the timelines involved."

"We understand the difficulties involved Sir Hugh," the Head of the Security Service MI5 spoke up. "You often get differing accounts from witnesses about any event, never mind an incident as traumatic as this must have been."

"Quite so. However, we believe that a constant theme has begun to emerge in the eyewitness accounts, and hopefully we will get a clearer picture as time goes by. It appears that at some time before midnight, whilst the aircraft was above London, some of the passengers decided to fight back and somehow they managed to overcome and kill all of the terrorists."

"My God!" said the Prime Minister. "That must have been a bloody affair!"

"It certainly was, Sir. There were several dozen casualties among the passengers, though thankfully only a handful of fatalities. Anyway, I digress. It also appears that at least one of the terrorists was a qualified pilot, as they seem to have tampered with the aircraft's autopilot and to have set it on to a different course. In fact the new course appears to have put the aircraft into a dive that would have resulted in the plane crashing into Buckingham Palace!"

There was a chorus of gasps around the table.

"Precisely, ladies and gentlemen. This attack was definitely aimed at our Royal Family. The passengers' action in retaking the aircraft from the terrorists led to the freeing of the aircraft's flight crew from captivity. They, in turn, managed to bring the aircraft out of its dive. Though only by the skin of their teeth. Apparently they still managed to knock some roofing tiles off the palace and snap the flagpole in two!"

"Is Her Majesty okay?"

"Thankfully, yes. She is upset of course, but unhurt."

"Bloody hell! That was a close call!"

"Indeed. This just happened to be the one night of the year when all of the Royal Family were gathered together to celebrate the Queen's official birthday in the palace. If the plane had hit them it would have wiped out the British Royal Family in one go!"

"My God!"

"What do we know about these terrorists, Sir Hugh? They appear to have been very well organised."

"At the moment we know nothing, sir. The bodies are of course being processed - fingerprints, photographs and DNA samples have been taken and the Yard's counter-terrorism unit is putting together profiles of the men for distribution amongst the security services. Hopefully we will be able to locate where the men came from and which organisation they belonged to. That is about all that we know at the moment."

"Thank you, Sir Hugh. Any questions?"

"Has any faction claimed responsibility for the attack yet?"

"No."

"What about the press, Prime Minister? Has a press release been offered to up to the vultures yet?"

"Not yet. My director of communications and I will be putting one together as soon as this meeting is over. Anything else? No? Okay. You all realise how close we have come to an all-out disaster! The Royal Family for God's sake! If it hadn't been for those brave passengers fighting the terrorists the whole country would have been in mourning today and our monarchy would have never been the same again!"

There was a chorus of "Hear, hear!" from around the table.

"Right. I do not have to tell you that this is the most serious attack against our country that has ever happened. You all know your jobs inside out and you all know what to do. I want to know what group of terrorists put this operation together. I want to know who they are and where they are! When we find out this information we will wipe them from the face of the Earth! Do I make myself understood?"

"Yes, Prime Minister."

"Good! I'm bringing this emergency meeting to a close, ladies and gentlemen. We will reconvene at six this evening. By then I want some answers! Good morning."

TWENTY-FOUR

17th June
Holborn Circus, London

The queue of people at the customer service desk in the Holborn Circus branch of HSBC ground to a halt as the news came onto the TV screen perched high above them. Everyone in the room seemed to freeze as they looked up and watched in disbelief.

"Good Afternoon. This is the BBC *News at One*, with Anna Ford and Darren Jordan. Today's breaking news: A Monarch Airlines passenger jet was hijacked by Islamic terrorists late last night en route for Gatwick Airport from The Gambia, in West Africa. The aircraft narrowly missed crashing into Buckingham Palace where the Royal Family had gathered to celebrate the Queen's birthday. There are no reports of any of the Royal Family being injured. We go now to Prime Minister David Cameron speaking at a news conference held half an hour ago outside number ten."

"Good afternoon, ladies and gentlemen. It is with a feeling of intense disbelief that I am informing you of the latest terrorist atrocity to affect the United Kingdom. In the early hours of this morning a direct attack upon the British Royal Family was made by terrorists who had hijacked a civilian airliner en route from West Africa, and who attempted to crash-dive the aircraft into Buckingham palace. Only the brave actions of some of the passengers and crew prevented a great tragedy from taking place. None of the Royal Family was injured. At the moment we do not know which terrorist faction is responsible for this despicable action, but we believe that they were composed of Islamic extremists. I can assure you that the security services of this great nation of ours will stop at nothing to discover who these perpetrators are, and I can doubly assure you that we will stop at nothing to wipe out this threat to our nation's monarchy. That is all for now, ladies and gentlemen. I will keep you updated on this grave situation. Thank you."

"And now we go to our royal correspondent, Peter Hunt, who is live outside Buckingham Palace. Hello, Peter. We understand that the Palace was damaged in this morning's attack, but that none of the Royal Family has been injured?"

"Good afternoon, Anna. Yes, in the last few minutes there has been a press release issued by the Queen's press office that has categorically confirmed that no member of the Royal Family has been injured by this attack. However, it goes on to say that Her Majesty is very distressed at how close this attack came to being successful.

If you look behind me at the top of the Palace you can clearly see the damage to the roof where the aircraft apparently scraped its belly as the flight crew fought to bring it out of the crash-dive. You can also see clearly that the flagpole has been neatly snapped into two. One might say that this is almost symbolic for our country, as the Royal Standard was at full mast at the time of this attack. However as you can see, it is not visible at the moment."

"Were there any other injuries at the palace that we are aware of?"

"Only one, Anna. As you may know, about four hundred people work in the palace, but fortunately most of these were not present during the early hours of this morning. From what we understand, a member of the Grenadier Guards, who was on guard duty at the Palace, was hit by a falling roof tile, but the news is that he has been treated at the local hospital and has suffered only minor bruising and cuts. He has already returned to duty."

"Thank you, Peter. That was Peter Hunt, our royal correspondent.

We now go live to our special news correspondent, Allan Little, who is outside the Emergency Department at the East Surrey Hospital where casualties from the hijacked aircraft are being treated. Hello, Allan."

"Good afternoon, Anna. I'm standing outside the Emergency Department where all of the injured passengers from the hijacked flight were brought for treatment by a fleet of ambulances in the early hours of this morning."

"Two hours ago a statement was issued by the hospital trust informing us that twenty-three passengers have been treated for their injuries so far. Most of them have received some form of knife wound, though a few had also been badly beaten by the hijackers. Only one passenger has been seriously injured. We understand that his identity is not yet known, but we believe he is a man in his early forties who sustained several wounds while tackling the armed terrorists. The statement goes on to say that he is in a critical condition after undergoing several hours of emergency surgery, and has been admitted to the Intensive Care Unit. According to one unofficial source within the emergency department his prognosis does not sound good, and he is unlikely to make it through today."

"A few minutes ago I managed to speak with one of the passengers who had just been released from the hospital."

"It was all crazy. These big African blokes were walking up an' down the aisle stabbing people an' 'itting them, even young women. I was terrified!"

"Were the hijackers armed in any way?"

"Yeah. They 'ad these big knives an' they stabbed anyone who even looked at them!"

"Did they say who they were or what they wanted?"

"It's bloody obvious ain't it! They were bloody Muslims. They were shouting about *Allah* an' other stuff that I couldn't understand. When the plane started diving I was bloody shakin' in me boots!"

"I understand that some of the passengers fought back and overcame the terrorists?"

"Yeah! There was this one bloke. He went at them like a loony. Didn't stop until he'd killed the lot of them! He's a bloody hero!"

"There was just one passenger who fought back then?"

"Nah. There were a couple of others who got stuck in and helped 'im out. But from what I could see, 'e was the one doing most of the fighting. He was covered in blood and screaming blue murder at them. I don't know who terrified me more; 'im or the terrorists!"

"Have you any idea who this man is?"

"Nah, never seen 'im before, but 'e was one hell of a fighter though. Went through the big black blokes like a knife through butter! I saw him at the end. He was lying on the floor and covered in blood. One of the passengers was treating 'im, but 'e looked like 'e was dead. I don't know what happened to him after that. It was bloody chaos when we landed at Gatwick! There were soldiers and policemen with guns all over the show. It was like something out of the movies."

"Did the terrorists kill anyone on board?"

"Yeah. There were some blokes sitting behind me who tried to fight with 'em earlier in the flight. But the terrorists beat them up and then they cut all of their throats! It was terrible! There was blood all over the show. I was terrified, I tell yer!"

"What injuries did you receive from the terrorists?"

"One of 'em slashed me across me face and me hand. I was only askin' for a drink of water for my missus!"

"Are you going home now?"

"Nah. The missus is still at Gatwick. I've gotta go an' pick 'er up an' talk to the cops again."

"Well, thank you for your time."

"That's okay, mate. That bloke is a bloody 'ero, he

is! I 'ope 'e makes it alright! He saved all our lives. A bloody 'ero!

TWENTY-FIVE

17th June
Bakau, The Gambia

For the hundredth time since they had landed in The Gambia the Irishman muttered under his breath:
"BeJaysus, but it's feckin' hot!"
Donnelly looked across dispassionately at his colleague and answered.
"Of course it is; we're in Africa."
"Smart arse. I could do with a feckin' drink."
"You've just had a cold coke. Just do your job and shut up."
"BeJaysus, but it's feckin' hot!"
Donnelly sighed in exasperation and returned his gaze to the compound at the end of the short road. The mid-afternoon sun blazed down on a scene that was as different from London or Belfast as you could imagine. The street was nothing more than a dirt road made of compacted orangey-red sand that undulated with dips and hollows. It led off from where their battered Land Rover was parked in the partial shade of a whitewashed wall of concrete blocks, down between a series of similar walls to where Paul Gray's compound lay at the end of the street. Interspersed between these walls, with their big gates of colourfully-painted sheet metal, were the trunks of a few massive white-flowered silk-cotton trees. The trunks were so wide that three grown men would not be able to touch their fingers together if they tried to encircle them with their

arms. The trees threw down significant patches of deep black shade across the road, and Donnelly found himself wishing that he had parked beneath one of them.

It was the people that walked the street or sat on makeshift wooden benches in the shade of the trees that were really different from anything that either of the men had ever encountered before. For one thing they were all black. Not a white face to be seen anywhere. The women seemed to come in two types - they were either sexy with lovely rolling buttocks beneath gently swaying hips, or they were literally massively fat. All of them were dressed in an array of brightly coloured long skirts, tops and strips of cloth tied around their heads. The men looked more westernised with worn and sometimes dirty jeans, trousers and T-shirts. Most of the people on the street ignored the vehicle with the two white men sitting in it, but gangs of kids kept bothering them, coming to the windows with big grins on their faces, holding out their hands and shouting.

"*Toubab! Toubab! Minty? Minty?*"
Several times both men had been close to losing their temper and they had tried their best to ignore the incessant pestering.

"BeJaysus, but it's feckin' hot! We stand out like a couple of spare pricks at a wedding so we do!"

"I tend to agree with you, but you saw what the place was like when the High Commissioner's driver drove us around Gray's compound. It's the same on every side. It doesn't really matter where we place ourselves, we're going to stick out like a sore thumb wherever we are. At least here we can see the compound's gates. If he uses his vehicle to get from place to place he'll have to drive down this road and use the gates to get inside and we'll see him."

"If he doesn't feckin' see us first."

"A chance we'll have to take, old boy. I don't see that we have any other choice really."

"Well how long are we going to sit here sweating our knackers off?"

"As long as it takes, old boy, as long as it takes."

"Ah well. That's something to look forward too then." He said with heavy sarcasm. "BeJaysus but it's feckin' hot!"

Donnelly sighed once again.

TWENTY-SIX

17th June
Redhill, Surrey

John Smith felt as if he was hovering. He struggled to get his thoughts into some sort of order but found that he couldn't. There were just fragments. Sometimes he dreamed that he was back in the interrogation block in Afghanistan, with the hated voice of that Russian bastard whispering in his ear.

"Tell us what we want to know John. Tell us what we want to know."

At other times he was fighting his way through a cloud of dust and airborne sand, the crack and thump of rounds passing his ears. Sometimes he saw the faces of his kids grinning up at him as he play-wrestled with them on the floor of his sitting room.

Occasional fragments of conversations came to his ears, but they didn't make sense to him.

"He must be one of the hijackers. Have you seen the scars on his body?"

"Of course I have, he's been proper sliced up!"

"No I don't mean the recent wounds. I mean the old scars. His body is covered in them. And he looks really mean too!"

"So would you if you had a six-inch slash down your face!"

"I don't care who he is or what he's done! He needs our help, so get back to work!"

A woman's voice, soft and caring, with a faint Australian accent.

"Just be still, love. Everything's okay. You're safe now. Try to sleep."

"I wish he'd stop calling out like that in his sleep. It gives me the willies!"

"How many times do I have to tell you lot to stand outside? I will not have guns in this room! Stand outside in the corridor please! Can't you see that he's not going anywhere?"

"Sorry, Doctor, it's orders. We aren't worried about him getting away, we're worried about who might come after him!"

"I don't care. I'm in charge of this man's health and I do not want guns in this room, so get out!"

"Okay, Doc, okay. We'll stand outside!"

"About time!"

"Hello? Can you hear me? Do you remember your name? Can you talk to me?" The Australian woman's voice again.

"He's still bleeding internally! Get me a chest drain, quick! Before we lose him again."

Smith felt himself drifting away into the darkness once more. He saw his sons Robert and Allan. It was his first Christmas leave spent at home in years and he and Anne-Marie had spent several hours the evening before putting together lego models for the kids. There were houses and a fire-station and a garage and a hospital. They covered half of the floor of the sitting room, there were so many. *The kids will love them*, he thought...

The sitting room faded, to be replaced by the noisy and dusty interior of a plane. Smith was sitting on the bench along one side of the fuselage, one of a long line of troopers laughing and shouting over the noise of the twin-engined props. He felt the heat of an African day swirling through the aircraft as the side door was pulled inward by a Rhodesian Air Force dispatcher and he shuffled to his feet along with the others. His body was weighed down with kit, his FN FAL rifle strapped tightly to his side. He lifted his right arm and placed his hand heavily on the shoulder of the trooper to his left as they turned and formed a line, looking up like all the others at the bright jump lights beside the open door.

"Red light...green light! Go! Go! Go!" shouted the dispatcher as he slapped the nearest paratrooper on the back and half pushed him out of the doorway. The line quickly shuffled forward until Smith found himself standing at the edge and looking down on the African bush brightly lit by the flaming orb of the sun high in the sky. *Jesus! The ground looks so bloody close!* he thought, as he felt the thump on his back and launched himself out and down...

Suddenly he found himself on the high slopes of a mountain. He was running forward, firing from the hip as he went. The ground around his feet was erupting in little spurts as the Soviet rounds hit. His breath was rasping in his throat as he gulped great gasps of freezing air into his lungs and his body was soaked with hot sweat beneath his padded *bushlat* as he forced his tired and shaking limbs to move him forward. He looked up and saw the smoking trail of an RPG rocket swishing through the air towards them. He opened his mouth to scream a warning and watched the rocket roar straight towards his mate. He saw him disintegrate in a bright flash of crimson gore and suddenly Smith was covered from head to foot in the hot red liquid, sharp with tiny slivers of bone. He could taste his friend's blood in his open mouth. He gagged and retched as he swallowed some of it down...

He was lying in a cold wet hole in the ground. He looked out through the screen of vegetation in front of him. He could plainly see the windows of a farmhouse and hear the voices of the little Irish kids playing outside it in the cobbled yard. He looked to the left and saw their father walking towards them. The Irishman grinned widely as the kids ran laughing to him, pleased that he was home at last. But Smith was grim. He knew that the bastard had just set off a bomb that had killed a dozen civilians in West Belfast, including kids just like his. He reached forward and slowly cocked his rifle...

"Just tell us what we want to know John. Everything will be alright. Just tell us what we want to know John."
"No! No! Please! Leave me alone! Nooo...!"

"Don't worry, David, it's just a nightmare. Just lie back. Everything will be okay." The Australian woman's voice again.

TWENTY-SEVEN

17th June
Downing Street, London

The Prime Minister looked tired. In fact they all did; it had been a very long day and it wasn't over yet. The atmosphere in the emergency COBR meeting was tense and irritable.

"Yes Sir, we have positively identified one of the dead terrorists." Sir Rupert Giles, Chief of the SIS looked down at his hand-written notes on the table. "He is a Palestinian by the name of Mohammed Saeed ibn Khalid al-Filasteeni. He has been a known player for about five years, formerly a member of the Palestine Liberation Organisation. The most recent information that we have on him is that he was unhappy with the Israeli/PLO treaty and left the organisation about twelve months ago. We have no further information about where he went or what he's done after this."

"Well I can tell you what he was doing last night!" snapped the Home Secretary.

"He tried to kill the Royal Family!" Sir Rupert looked coolly across the table at her.

"Obviously, Madam. What I'm trying to point out to the meeting is that he disappeared off the radar completely when he left the PLO."

"So we have no idea which faction or organisation he was working with?" the Prime Minister asked, shooting a warning look at the Home Secretary.

"Not at the present time, sir. We are currently mobilising every asset that we have in the North African region to find out."

"Why North Africa, may I ask?" asked the Home Secretary, though with less anger in her voice this time. Sir Hugh Metcalfe of the Metropolitan Police answered her.

"Initial autopsies on the other dead terrorists have revealed that they are of black North African origin, Home Secretary. It seems wise to assume therefore that the group has originated in that region, rather than in the Middle East."

"I see. Have you identified any of the others yet?" The PM again, his question directed at the SIS chief.

"No, Prime Minister. As I said a moment ago, we have every available asset in the region working on this, but thus far have had no luck in identifying the other terrorists."

"What about the Gambian angle? I realise that their security systems seemed to have broken down somewhat, but surely there must be some information forthcoming on the terrorists from there?"

"We are in close contact with the Gambian National Intelligence Agency sir, but quite frankly I don't hold out much hope. Their bureaucracy is a nightmare at the best of times and as for CCTV or any other modern technology in The Gambia, I'm afraid that they are almost non-existent." Sir Rupert paused for a moment.

"However, fortunately I do have a couple of assets presently in the country involved in another totally unconnected operation, sir. I will pull them off their current assignment and get them working on this independently of the Gambians. They are a resourceful pair and may be able to find out some useful information that the Gambians have missed."

"I'll send a few of my chaps from SO15 to help them if you don't mind, Sir Rupert?"

"That's fine, Sir Hugh. I'll inform them that they're coming."

"Good idea. I want to see the maximum amount of inter-agency cooperation on this."

The Prime Minister looked around the table at the haggard faces of the other COBR members. He made eye contact with his Director of Communications.

"Yes Bill, do you have something to add?"

"Just that we now have a much clearer picture of the events that occurred last night aboard the aircraft, Prime Minister, mainly due to the sterling work of the Met of course."

He inclined his head at the Chief Constable in acknowledgement.

"Information gathered from interviews with the surviving passengers has revealed that the aircraft was retaken from the terrorists mainly through the efforts of just one of the passengers, a man by the name of David Keller. Amazingly, he took on all of the hijackers almost single-handed and killed them all! This was an absolutely fantastic feat of courage and self-sacrifice but unfortunately he received several significant wounds during the fight and is currently in the Intensive Care Ward of the local hospital, where he is now in a coma."

He paused for a moment and looked around the table.

"I know that you have all been very busy with your various departments and agencies in trying to track down the origin of these fanatics, but have any of you watched a news programme recently?"

His gaze was met by gently shaking heads.

"I thought not. Well the news is full of the incident of course, especially the part played by David Keller and the pilots of the aircraft, who managed to pull it out of that dive, thank God!"

There were heartfelt murmurs of agreement at this.

"There is also a spontaneous public gathering outside the gates of the palace and along the Mall, and thousands, perhaps tens of thousands of people are making their way there to hold a candlelit vigil of thanks that the Royal Family is safe. Obviously the British public are appalled at this attempt to murder the monarchy, but it goes far beyond the shores of Britain. The news of the attempted attack has spread around the world like wildfire. All of the Commonwealth nations are experiencing similar public vigils of thanks, with literally millions of people gathering together in their capital cities, and the world's religious leaders are also getting in on the act. Everybody from the Pope to the Dalai Lama is holding special thanksgiving services, not only because the Royal Family has been spared, but also praying for the safe recovery of David Keller. His story has become an instant worldwide sensation. There are even hundreds of local *Imams* and other Islamic religious leaders joining in as a show of solidarity. It's truly amazing! I think that we've all underestimated just how much the British Monarchy is loved and respected around the world."

"Hear, hear!" the Prime Minister joined in with the rest.
He looked to see whether his Director of Communications had finished, then added:

"As the eyes of the whole world are upon us, it makes it even more imperative that we all do our jobs well. I can see that you are all tired though, so let's call a break and have a cup of tea before we continue. Thank you."

TWENTY-EIGHT

18th June
Bakau, The Gambia

Chris Donnelly closed his mobile telephone with an audible snap.

"Good news?" asked the Irishman.

"Depends on how you look at it? We've been temporarily pulled off the Smith operation."

"What? Why?" the man was flabbergasted. "I thought your Chief wanted Smith dead almost as much as I do?"

"He does, but apparently events have moved on quite a pace while we've been sitting sweating our balls off in this car. There has been a terrorist attempt to kill the Queen and the Royal Family, and the terrorists either originated, or passed through The Gambia. We've been pulled in to try and find out anything that we can on the terrorists' activities before they left the country."

"Feckin' hell! Does that mean that we let this murdering bastard walk free then? BeJaysus!"

"Don't worry too much, old boy. I'm sure we will get back on to it once the hullaballoo over this incident has died down. The Chief is still very keen to see this Smith problem dealt with. Meanwhile we must get back to the High Commission and try to get a handle on what to do next. Oh, and by the way, I want you to be on your very best behaviour and to keep your mouth shut over the next few days. We're going to be joined by a couple of officers from Scotland Yard's Counter-terrorism Unit, SO15. I just hope that none of them recognise you."

"Feckin' hell!"

"Precisely, old boy. Just what I was thinking!"

TWENTY-NINE

18th June
Redhill, Surrey

John Smith lay in his hospital bed. His breath was slow and regular, helped by a plastic airway that kept his throat open. From his arms sprouted a veritable plethora of tubes and wires that were attached to a variety of bleeping machines that regulated and monitored his condition. Although he looked to be simply sleeping, he was in a deep state of unconsciousness. His mind was full of dreams though.

He dreamt that he was lying in the baking sun, on a rocky, acacia-dotted hill, gazing down through the thorny bushes at a path below.

"I still dinna git it, John lad," whispered his companion, lying next to him on the hill. "How the fuck are we going to stop this lot from moving down the valley? There's only the two of us and there's bloody 'undreds of them wee bastards!"

His companion was a Glaswegian by the name of Andy. He was a Sergent Chef in the 2nd Parachute Battalion of the French Foreign Legion, now serving in the French Special Forces unit called the 'Commandos de Recherche et d'Action en Profondeur' or 'CRAP' for short (Deep Action and Reconnaissance Commando). The two of them were watching an entire battalion of the Libyan Army making their slow, deliberate way along the path at the foot of their hill.

"It's gonna be easy, Andy me old mate."

John smiled at him through the layer of dust and grime that caked his features.

"I learnt this trick from an old Sergeant Major of mine called Tony. Do you see how this path winds around our hill?"

"Yeah, sure. But that just means that when they get around there we'll have the bastards on two sides of us!"

"Exactly! We'll have the bastards just where we want them, and this is how we'll do it..."

He leant forward to whisper in Andy's ear.

Fifteen minutes later the long line of enemy soldiers had wound around the dogleg on the path below the hillside, so that they were now walking along on the path on two distinct sides of the hill. As the lead scout of the battalion began to leave the path and descend out of sight into the valley to the south of them, John Smith opened fire on the men below him from his new position. His rifle was set to automatic and he let off several bursts, taking down a few of the Libyan soldiers in the process.

When he heard the gunfire, Andy also opened up on the line of men below him on the other side of the hill. There was instant chaos as the startled troops instantly sought cover from his fire behind rocks, only to be dislodged by the shouted instructions of their officers and NCOs. Slowly the troops began to fire and manoeuvre their way up the hillside towards the spot that the enemy fire had come from. They ducked and dived as several more bursts of automatic fire picked men up as the rounds hit them and tumbled their bodies back down the hill.

John and Andy dived into their RV, panting and sweating after their fast withdrawal. They now had a grandstand view from a rocky perch on a nearby hilltop and looked down on the Libyan soldiers storming up the two sides of the hill that the two men had just vacated in such a hurry.

When the two groups came together on the top of the hill, their rate of fire increased in intensity as they each mistook the other group for the enemy. John and Andy lay there safely watching the Libyans shoot hell out of each other for a full half an hour before some bright spark realised that they were attacking their own men, and called a halt to the firing. By that time there were dozens of bodies scattered about amongst the scrub and rocks and John and Andy were desperately trying not to give away their own position by laughing too loudly.

"I've got to 'and it to yer lad! That was fucking marvellous! The silly bastards have well and truly fucked themselves! Great stuff John!"

"All credit is due to my mate Tony," he grinned back. "He was a fucking sly bastard and a great soldier! Now let's get the fuck out of here before those silly bastards cotton on to where we are. We can get ahead of them if we skirt the hills to the west. Then we can lay a few claymores to shake them up a bit more."

"Och. But you're a cruel wee bastard!"

"Well known for it, mate. Let's go."

The bright North African landscape faded into deep and empty blackness. Smith tried to move around and reach out with his hands but there was nothing there to touch, nothing to feel. In front of him, a face slowly emerged from the darkness and emptiness. It was a young black African. He had a handsome and smiling face in profile but then he turned to reveal the gaping hole of a huge exit wound dripping with bright red moist gore and the grey globules of his exposed and destroyed brain tissue. The African's smile disappeared and he looked accusingly at Smith as his face faded away to be replaced by another with the shattered face where a grenade had torn his flesh to bright red ribbons, and then another ruined face and yet another and another. A long line of torn and bleeding visages loomed before him - the faces of the people that Smith had killed in one way or another over many, many years of conflict and war and brutality. He tried to scream but even as he opened his mouth he knew that there would be no sound, only the faces, one after another and another...

THIRTY

19th June
Downing Street, London

David Cameron's Director of Communications laid a hand on the Prime Minister's arm as he sat eating his breakfast at Number Ten.

"We really must get some good exposure from this affair, David."

"In what way? We're already the talking point in just about every country in the world. How can we get more exposure than that?"

"Well, I think you ought to make a special visit to the East Surrey Hospital David, to see this Keller chap. It would be great PR, especially as he's a worldwide hero."

"Mmmm. I see what you mean. How is he by the way? Is he going to pull through?"

"It's still fifty-fifty. I spoke to his surgeon about half an hour ago. She said that he's in a deep coma. Her exact words were that his life was hanging by a thread."

"Bloody shame. I can't go to see him while there's still a chance that he won't pull through, can I? Let's hope he makes it, after all the man *is* a bloody hero for what he did on that aircraft!"

"He sure is David. I agree that you can't visit him immediately, but I've had a word with the CEO of the hospital trust, and as soon as Keller shows any signs of recovery he will let us know. It would be great PR for you," he repeated.

"Okay. That's agreed. Let's just hope that he does recover. We certainly owe him a favour or two for pulling our bacon out of the fire! I can't bear to think what might have happened if the entire Royal Family had been killed. The total collapse of the Government would have been almost guaranteed. There'd have been rioting on the streets of every town and city, murders and reprisals against the Muslim community. It would have been hellish!"

"Quite so Prime Minister, quite so. You've heard that several world leaders have nominated Keller for their highest awards for valour? The President of the United States has nominated him for the Congressional Medal of Honour, the Gambian President has nominated him for..." He had to look at the papers in front of him on the table. "...the 'Grand Officer of the National Order of the Republic of The Gambia'. Even the French President has nominated him for the Croix de Guerre, because there was a solitary Frenchman amongst the survivors!"

"Yes. So what? We'll put him forward for the Victoria Cross, of course."

"Are you sure that that is a high enough award, David? We don't want to be outdone by the foreigners, do we?"

"Well? What else is there? The Victoria Cross is the highest award for gallantry that we have!"

"Couldn't we award him two VCs, then?"

"Mmmm. I see what you mean. I'll talk with Her Majesty about it. Now let me eat my breakfast in peace!"

"Of course, Prime Minister."

THIRTY-ONE

20th June
Redhill, Surrey

"Where are you, John?"

"A long bloody way away, the further away from you the better!"

"Now, now, don't be like that, John. This is rather like old times."

"Bollocks, you prat. Why Harry? Why did you set me up?" Smith watched Harry bend closer towards the microphone.
In a low voice he answered:

"Because you know too much John, and you're unstable."

"Unstable? Of course I'm bloody unstable! It was you who made me this way with your bloody missions, you bastard! What did you expect? Did you think that you could just wind me up and point me in the right direction and that I wouldn't bloody well be affected by all of the sodding wars and the killing?"

"Now, now, old boy, don't get upset!"

"Upset? You set me up to face a life sentence for something that I didn't do and you didn't think I'd get upset, you bastard?"

"I am sorry, John. But you've got to understand that I couldn't just leave you as free as a bird to tell your story to whoever wanted to listen."

"You stupid twat. In all those years I'd never said a

word to anyone."

"Ah, but you're wrong, John. We knew about your visits to psychiatrists and the writing of your autobiography. For therapy wasn't it? Do you know what would have happened to HM's government if that had fallen into the wrong hands?"

"More to the point, what would happen to you. That's what you really mean, don't you, Harry?"

"Not at all, old boy, I'm just a tiny cog in a big machine."

"Bollocks, Harry! You're the head of the Increment. You've always believed that you were above the law, but you're not Harry. You're not untouchable."

Smith had been cradling the L42 Lee Enfield sniper rifle gently in his grip, slowly lining up for the shot as he spoke into the mobile phone that he'd taped securely in a nearby fork of the tree, so that he could use it hands-free. The long, heavy rifle felt good in his hands. The wooden stock and butt were polished from years of use and it was warm to the touch. It was a thing of beauty, this rifle. Yet in the right hands it was also a deadly tool, and John Smith knew how to use it. He had shot a lot of men with rifles just like this one. One more wouldn't bother him in the least. In fact he was going to enjoy this one.

He sighted the cross hairs of the telescopic sight on the spot between Harry's eyes. The torrential rain ran in rivulets down his face and body, but he didn't feel it. Every fibre of his being was concentrated on Harry's face. His mind flashed with images from the past, but he forced them aside. He breathed in, let half of his breath out and gently squeezed the trigger. He didn't hear the shot and hardly felt the rifle move in his hands. But he instantly knew that it had been a good shot as he saw Harry's head dissolve in a bright crimson flash of blood, snot and gore...

On his bed, Smith groaned. He body jerked as though it was him that had just been shot.

"Did you hear him say something?" a nurse standing by his bed asked another nurse who was checking the monitors.

"No, I heard him groan, that's all. Why, what did you think he said?"

"Oh, nothing. I must have been hearing things."

As she continued with the bed bath that she had been preparing for this scarily-scarred man in a coma, she couldn't help but think to herself: *Good riddance. I'm sure that's what I heard him say: Good riddance.*

She shrugged and carried on.

THIRTY-TWO

22nd June
Downing Street, London

"I have some good news, Prime Minister."

"About time, Sir Rupert! We seem to have been sitting on our hands and doing nothing for the past few days!"

"Hardly Sir, but I can understand your frustration at the current lack of progress."

"Well don't keep us all in suspense. Have you found out anything about the perpetrators of this incident?"

"Yes, Sir. That's the good news. My assets in The Gambia, in close co-operation with Scotland Yard's SO15 investigators, have retraced the steps of the terrorist leader, Mohammed Saeed ibn Khalid al-Filasteeni."

Sir Rupert nodded in acknowledgement across the table to the Chief Constable of the Metropolitan Police, Sir Hugh Metcalfe.

"Mohammed travelled into The Gambia from northern Senegal the day before the hijacking, using public transport all the way south from Dakar. Using CCTV footage from Dakar Airport (which luckily for us is probably the only airport in the West African region to be so sophisticated) we were able to identify the terrorist arriving on a flight from Algeria."

He paused for a few seconds, knowing that he had the unwavering attention of everybody seated around the table.

"Algeria, of course, has always been a hotbed of the international terrorist scene, so we have several assets already in place in the country. They have discovered that before Mohammed boarded his flight to Dakar he had just arrived at Algiers Airport on an internal flight from Tindouf Airport. This is in the extreme west of Algeria, close to the borders with both Morocco and Mauritania. Tindouf Airport is located just north of the town which bears the same name. The town is pretty small, with only about forty-eight thousand inhabitants, and apart from being the main town of the Algerian Province of Tindouf, it's pretty unexceptional. Apart from the fact that is..." he paused again, "...that there are several refugee camps located in the desert around the town."

He stopped to take a sip of water and looked down at his notes, enjoying the fact that the tension was becoming almost unbearable in the room as his peers and superiors hung on his every word.

"These refugee camps have served as a base for a 'National Liberation Movement' of Moroccans known as the 'Polisario Front' since the 1970s, allowing them to launch attacks against the Moroccan armed forces. However, the Polisario is not a terrorist organisation in the usual sense. Although they are fighting for the independence of Western Sahara and Morocco, they have renounced attacks against civilians and have fought their war using more conventional tactics. As a result they have had the unconditional support of the Algerian government for over thirty years."

He looked around the expectant faces.

"Of more interest to us is the recent establishment of a new, and much smaller 'refugee' camp to the east of the town of Tindouf, situated about half-way between two existing camps known as Aaiun and Asward. Satellite pictures of this new camp indicate that it has been in existence for less than twelve months."

"Ah," interrupted the Prime Minister, "that would tie in nicely with this Mohammed character on the Gambia flight, who disappeared from Palestine about twelve months ago!"

"Exactly, Prime Minister. Local intelligence leads us to believe that this camp is the headquarters of a new *Jihadist* movement led by another Palestinian called Abdullah ibn Nazid al-Filasteeni."

"Obviously a relative of Mohammed!" pointed out the Home Secretary, "they have the same surname!"

"I'm afraid not Madam," Sir Rupert's voice dripped with honey. "*Al-Filasteeni* simply means 'the Palestinian' in Arabic. The literal translation of his name is: Abdullah, son of Nazid, the Palestinian, and Mohammed's is: Mohammed Saeed, son of Khalid, the Palestinian. It's all very complicated, I know, Madam Secretary."

"Oh."

"This Abdullah was also a member of the PLO and he disappeared a month or so before Mohammed. I believe that Abdullah may be the leader of this new faction in Algeria, and that the new camp is in fact a terrorist training camp that is operating outside of the jurisdiction of the Algerians themselves!" he finished with a flourish.

"Excellent news, Sir Rupert! Excellent!" added the Prime Minister.

"What now?"

"I propose that we send a detachment of the Special Reconnaissance Regiment to get a close look at this camp, Sir. One of my assets who traced Mohammed's movements back from The Gambia is an ex-member of the SRR. He is already in Algeria and can join the army detachment to try and identify Abdullah on the ground."

"And if he does, what then, Sir Rupert?"

"That's when it leaves my hands, Prime Minister. Any action that we deem to take if he is identified is down to you, Sir."

He smiled at David Cameron and the Prime Minister beamed back.

"So it is! So it is!" he rubbed his hands together. "Let's hope for some positive news then!"

THIRTY-THREE

22nd June
Algiers, Algeria, North Africa

Chris Donnelly joined the Irishman at the table in the bar.

"You were gone a long time," said the Irishman. "I was beginning to think that I'd have to sit here all night on me own."

"Yes, sorry old chap. Sometimes it's hard to get a cab, even in a thriving city like Algiers."
Donnelly sat down and ordered a cold beer from a waiter.

"Any news from the home front?"

"Yes. I'm afraid that we are going to be parting company for a while. You've been ordered back to The Gambia."

"About feckin' time! Do I get to have a crack at Smith at long last?"

"I believe so, old chap. You're to report to a colleague of mine from the Increment. I'll give you the details when we get back to our hotel."

"Feckin' great! I was beginning to think that I was never going to get a go at him." The Irishman leant forward, his pale blue eyes blazing with hatred.

"He murdered my brother and I want to look into his feckin' eyes while I kill the son-of-a-bitch!"

"Yes, well as I said old chap, I believe that you *will* get the chance when you get back to The Gambia. Smith is still a very big embarrassment for HM's government, even though it's all been overshadowed by this latest terrorist incident. They still want to do everything in their power to get rid of Smith and sweep this whole mess under the carpet, so to speak."

The Irishman relaxed back into his seat, a smile playing at the corners of his mouth.

"What about you Donnelly? Will you not be coming back with me then?"

"Not yet. I've been given another job to do over here first."

"Well. Whatever it is, I wish you the best."

He called for another beer then leaned in again towards Donnelly.

"I understand that there's a very good brothel next door," he smirked. "I've been without a woman so long that I'm afraid my cock has forgotten how to behave! I don't suppose that SIS would fund a little visit there, would they? I fancy a bit of Arabian arse." Donnelly smiled back.

"I think I'll join you, old man. I'm sure that we could fiddle the expenses somehow. Perhaps we could put it down to a session of 'physical therapy'?"

"Bejaysus, but that sounds feckin' good to me Donnelly! Let's drink up and go then."

"Okay. Let's give it our best shot, shall we?"

Both men laughed as they headed towards the bar's exit.

THIRTY-FOUR

26th June
Near Tindouf, south-western Algeria.

Chris Donnelly had not always been a member of the Special Intelligence Service. Like many of his co-workers in the service he had an ex-military background.

Born in Doncaster in 1982, Donnelly had joined the First Battalion of the Royal Green Jackets in 1999 as a 2nd lieutenant, after completing his initial training as an officer candidate at the Royal Military Academy, Sandhurst. He had conducted his first overseas operational tour two years later at the young age of nineteen, commanding a platoon during UN peace-keeping operations in the bloody civil war in Sierra Leone. During this tour he had seen his fair share of death, destruction, misery and mutilation, and had had his first 'contacts' with an enemy that was high on drugs and tended to shoot first and ask questions later - maybe.

In 2002 his battalion was posted to Northern Ireland, where they witnessed the decommissioning of a consignment of the Provisional Irish Republican Army's illegally-held weapons. Even though hostilities between the IRA and the British government had officially ended four years previously with the signing of the 'Belfast Agreement,' the peace was still uneasy and Donnelly and his men were forced to use diplomacy to get themselves out of a few tricky situations that could easily have turned to violence.

The following year his battalion found itself posted

to yet another area of operations in post-war Iraq, as a part of 19th Mechanised Brigade. Donnelly was promoted to full lieutenant during this tour - and also killed his first man - a young gun-toting Iraqi terrorist during a shoot-out with his patrol in the suburbs of Baghdad. This was followed by yet another tour of Northern Ireland in 2004.

In 2007, a round of cost-cutting by the British government saw the Royal Green Jackets become the Second Battalion of the newly-formed regiment of 'The Rifles'. To reinforce the change they were moved to a new permanent base at Abercorn Barracks, Ballykinler, in Northern Ireland. By this time, Donnelly had grown frustrated with army life. He enjoyed being at 'the sharp end' as a young officer leading a platoon of equally young and keen infantrymen. However increasingly he felt that the lack of combat operations was leading him to lose his edge through a combination of boredom and complacency. He craved the excitement and adrenaline rush of combat and felt the need to fully test himself, something he believed he had not managed to do so far during his military career. Thus in 2008, only days after being promoted to captain (a rank that he envisaged would lead to a life of increased bureaucracy which he did not want), he applied for selection to the Special Reconnaissance Regiment.

The Special Reconnaissance Regiment, or SRR, is one of the newest regiments of the British Army. It was formed in April 2005, and together with the SAS (the Special Air Service Regiment of the British Army), the SBS (Special Boat Squadron of the Royal Marines) and the SFSG (the Special Forces Support Group, formed from a mixture of personnel from all of the UK's armed forces), the SRR is an integral part of the United Kingdom Special Forces, under the command of the Director of Special Forces.

The SRR has taken on the primary tasks of the now defunct 14 Field Security and Intelligence Company, once known as 'the Det' and the irony that Donnelly's present arch-nemesis, John Smith, had once served with distinction in the Det, was not lost on Donnelly. The primary tasks of the SRR include a wide range of highly classified activities including Close Target Reconnaissance (CTR), covert surveillance operations and intelligence gathering, mainly, but not strictly limited to, counter-terrorism activities. Prospective candidates for the SRR undergo the same gruelling nineteen week selection course that all other members of the UKSF are put through, with less than ten percent of volunteers passing the course, followed by a long period of further specialist training for the lucky few who have made it that far.

Donnelly not only sailed through selection, he excelled in it, showing a class of leadership and field skills that was way above the heads of his fellow candidates. In the years following his move to SRR he served constantly on operational tours in both Iraq and Afghanistan, earning himself a Military Cross for an act of 'exemplary gallantry' during one particularly dangerous operation against the *Taliban* in the deserts of Helmand.

It was while serving alongside members of the Special Intelligence Service in Afghanistan in 2012 that he was recruited into that most secret of all units, the Increment - a small highly-motivated unit formed of Special Force soldiers that carried out deniable operations against the enemies of Britain.

Now, in his early thirties, Chris Donnelly was the acting head of the Increment.

Less than two weeks after the failed attempt to kill the British Royal Family, Donnelly found himself holed up in a covert observation post with two members of his former regiment, the SRR. *Just like the old days* - he thought to himself as he wiped the sweat from his brow with the sleeve of his desert smock and peered through the optical eye-piece of his tripod-mounted AN/PEQ-1 SOF Laser Marker - a US-made hand-portable Laser Target Designator, or LTD. The observation post was dug into the almost featureless sand of the Sahara Desert, blending in so well with the surrounding landscape that someone could have passed within a few feet of it before noticing the patch of slightly different coloured sand where the three men lay hidden. They had been in this position for three days and nights - suffering in silence as the furnace-like heat crushed down on them. Swarms of flies seemed to penetrate every nook and cranny in their uniforms and constantly crawled over every exposed piece of sweating skin - driving the men slowly insane from the overpowering urge to get up and run away from them.

The large compound that Donnelly watched through his LTD, from their position about eight hundred metres away, showed no sign of life as the morning sun began to bake it. Yet Donnelly knew from his carefully logged observations over the past three days that about one hundred and eighty armed men shared the three dozen or so low buildings built of concrete and mud blocks. He had watched these budding terrorists as they were put through various training activities, such as firing their AK47 assault rifles on a makeshift rifle range to the north of the compound and sitting in on religious briefings under the eye of a fierce-looking bearded *Imam* in the shade of one of the buildings. Donnelly and the others had logged the position of the sentries placed around the compound and timed their changeovers, and had identified a sand-bagged bunker that was used as an anti-aircraft position. They had seen the sentries placed there occasionally lift up shoulder-launched surface-to-air missile launchers when they heard an echo of a civilian aircraft flying from the airfield in the town of Tindouf.

Beside Donnelly lay one of the men from the SRR, a trooper who had introduced himself simply as Buck when they had met in Algiers before moving south and into the desert about ten miles to the east of the town of Tindouf. Buck had said to him:

"And if you don't mind mate, we'll just call you 'Spook'".

Dan, the other SRR trooper, was quietly sleeping behind

them in the rear of the OP, as it was his turn for some 'downtime'. Donnelly had told the two SRR troopers that he had once served in the same regiment as them, but they didn't give a shit about what he had 'once done'. As far as they were concerned he had transferred to the bloody enemy and they had the typical mistrust that all Special Forces have for the 'spooks' of the security services.

Buck operated a very high definition video camera whose film was being fed back live via a satellite link to their masters back in the UK. Donnelly caught his eye and whispered into his ear:

"What the fuck is happening? It's been a whole night since we reported Target Alpha driving into camp. He could fuck off again before they get here!"

Buck looked back at him and grinned.

"Have patience, mate. They'll let us know when they make up their minds. You know what the head-sheds are like - it can take them a week to decide which hand to wipe their arse with!"

"True enough. Shit! I've had enough of this fucking place. And I hate these fucking flies! They're driving me nuts!"

Buck merely grinned again, and then quickly stuck out his tongue to snatch a fly that was crawling on his heat-cracked lips, drawing it into his mouth and chewing on it in an exaggerated manner.

"Just chill out, man," he said after making a show of swallowing the fly. "Mmm, they taste delicious!"

"You're fucking nuts!" spat Donnelly.

Buck just grinned in reply.

THIRTY-FIVE

26th June
Redhill, Surrey

John Smith is sitting in a room of a north London Social Welfare Agency. Behind a desk covered with piles of reports and manila files sits a fat middle-aged woman wearing half-moon glasses. She raises her eyes from the file she is reading and looks directly at him.

"I'm very sorry, Mr Smith, but after reviewing your case with my colleagues and my supervisor we can only agree that you have *supervised* visitation rights with your children once every month."

"Supervised? What does that mean?"

"It means, Mr Smith, that you will be supervised by a social worker for the two hours that you are allowed to see your two sons, in a *controlled* environment."

"So I won't be able to take them to the zoo or the park or anywhere else?"

"I'm afraid not. They will be brought to these offices for the supervised visit. There's a playroom down the hall that we use."

"And we'll be watched by a social worker all of the time?"

"That's correct, Mr Smith. A qualified social worker will be present for the entire visit."

"But why? I've never been a danger to my kids. Why should I have to undergo supervised visits for God's sake?"

The welfare officer sighed.

"As you are aware, Mr Smith, your ex-wife has levelled a complaint of mentally disturbed behaviour against you. She has told us of your criminal record and your stay in prison. She's also told us about your acts of violence towards her and your abuse of alcohol, and all of this has been corroborated by her mother."

"Her mother! I see."
Smith scowled.

"But this isn't the only reason for the supervised visits, Mr Smith. We have also noted that your ex-wife is verbally violent towards your children whenever you phone them. Therefore, in the interests of your children's safety *and* their proper development, we have decided that a properly structured, controlled visit under supervision is the only way we can fully protect your children, not only from potential violence from yourself but also against verbal abuse by their mother."

"Jesus Christ! You make it sound like any contact with me will damage my kids!"

"I'm afraid that that is the way that we see things at the moment, Mr Smith. Although you have applied to have normal visitation rights to your children through the courts, our report to the judge in charge of your case will conclude that you are a potential danger to their welfare given your current state of mind."

Smith sighed and his face fell as he thought about what the woman was saying. He knew just how strange he was feeling, knew about the sudden bursts of rage that he'd directed at his ex-wife and kids, knew that it was true that he'd taken to the bottle, and he knew too that he could explode at the slightest provocation. He impulsively made a decision.

"Okay. This is what will happen."
He raised his face again and looked directly at the woman, who automatically flinched at the rage glowing in his coal-black eyes.

"I will withdraw my court case against my ex-wife and I will stay away from my kids, even though it's going to break my fucking heart. I don't want her to shout and scream at them every time I call them up, or to have a bloody fit every time I see them. I'll walk away and leave them be. I'm going to break all contact with them."

His eyes suddenly flooded with tears and he caught a lump in his throat. The woman felt her own heart melting as she replied softly:

"I know that you love your children, Mr Smith, but maybe it's for the best that you withdraw yourself from their life, at least at the moment. Give yourself some time to get yourself together. Who knows? It's only a few years until they'll be old enough to make up their own minds. Perhaps they will decide then that they want to see you?"

"Yeah. Sure."

Smith stood up, visibly trying to contain his emotions.

"Thanks for your help. I'll see myself out."

He only just made it to the outside door before he broke down in sobs, his heart swelling inside his chest.

At Smith's hospital bed, one of the intensive care nurses looked down and saw the tears spreading down his face from his comatose eyes. She gently wiped them away with a tissue.

THIRTY-SIX

26th June
Downing Street, London

The Prime Minister sat at the head of the Cabinet Office Briefing Room table. Also present in the room are the Deputy Prime Minister plus the Prime Minister's Director of Communications, the Chief of the General Staff - the effective head of the British Army, the Chief of the Air Staff - the head of the Royal Air Force, the First Sea Lord - ditto the Royal Navy, and the Director of Special Forces – the man in charge of the United Kingdom's Special Forces. Also in the room is the Chief of the Secret Intelligence Service - MI6, and the Chief of the Security Service – MI5.
"Well, gentlemen, I've gathered you all here this morning because you have some decisions to make. As you are probably aware we have located the mastermind behind the recent terrorist attack on the Royal Family, Abdullah ibn Nazid al-Filasteeni. According to our very latest intelligence he is currently in residence at a *Jihadist* training camp in western Algeria, but how long he will remain there is unknown."
He paused to look around the faces of the very top men of the British Armed Forces and Security Services, and was pleased to see that they were hanging on his every word.
"I made a pledge to the British people that when I knew who was responsible for this atrocious and cowardly attack against our monarchy, I would take all necessary measures to wipe them from the face of the Earth. I did

not make this pledge lightly gentlemen, and wipe them from the face of the Earth is what I intend to do!"
This was met with several grins and nods of agreement from around the table.

"I have personally spoken to the Algerian President by telephone this morning. He is outraged that this terrorist movement is hiding in his country, and has promised us his absolute and utmost support in any measures we see fit to implement to destroy them. He has given me his word that, as of twelve noon today, all of the military assets in his country, and this includes the Algerian Army, Air Force and Navy, will be confined to their bases so that we can have complete freedom to operate militarily in his national airspace. As you can imagine, this is a hell of a big decision for him to make! It is only because of the perceived continuing threat to our monarchy from these terrorists, who have been operating freely in his country, that he has decided to virtually hand over all control of his country's sovereignty, albeit only briefly, to us. He has also offered to us the use of any of his ports, airfields or army bases that we may need for this operation."

"What I now want from you, gentlemen, is a working plan for the annihilation of Abdullah ibn Nazid al-Filasteeni and his followers. There is only a very limited time frame within which we can work, so I want the strike to take place tomorrow morning. I know that this leaves you almost no time at all to come up with a plan and to get your assets into place, and I know that this is a highly unusual order. But time is very short gentlemen, and I want this bastard! I also want the assault on this Abdullah to happen during daylight because I want it filmed. I want every terrorist in every country in the world to see, and to be aware of what is in store for them, if they dare to ever operate against us again. I also want every service within our Armed Forces, including the Navy, Marines, Air Force and Army to be involved, so that none of them will feel left out of this act of justified retribution."

"In, short gentlemen, I want these bastards dead

this time tomorrow. I want their camp to be levelled so that not one brick remains on top of another, and I want the whole world to see their dead bodies on their television sets! You've got twenty-four hours, the very best intelligence reports including satellite and aerial photos and 'eyes on' reports from the team on the ground, the finest armed forces in the world and the full backing of both the British and Algerian Governments. So get to it, gentlemen! We will never have this chance again!"

He rubbed his hands together and smiled at his deputy, Nick Clegg, as the men around him got down to work.

THIRTY-SEVEN

26th June
Redhill, Surrey

"Doctor Webb! The patient is showing signs of trying to breathe for himself. I think he's beginning to come round!

"OK, good! Let's get his intubation tube out and give him a chance."

Smith felt like he was hovering, but at least he was conscious. He opened his eyes for the first time since he collapsed in the aircraft.

"I think I've died and gone to heaven."
He croaked at the beautiful face looking down on him, his vocal cords feeling dry and sore.

"You must be an angel."
His attempt at a smile turned into a coughing fit, pain racking his lungs and pushing him up to a half-sitting position.

"Take it easy. You've had a tube in your throat to help you breathe so you're bound to be a bit sore for a while."
The beautiful face smiled gently as the woman's soft hands settled him back on to the bed. She wiped his brow with a cool cloth.

"You're lucky to still be with us, David."
David? thought Smith, *who the hell is David?* Then he remembered. *David Keller of course, I'm David Keller now.*

"Who are you?" he asked, "I think I've heard your voice before."

"I'm Doctor Linda Webb. I'm your surgeon. You probably heard me while you were unconscious."

"Oh!"

Questions flooded his head as he tried to move his head to look around, but the pain was too much for him. He lay still and closed his eyes again.

"Where am I? How long have I been here?"

"You're in the Intensive Care Unit of East Surrey Hospital. You've been here about ten days now, ever since you were carried off the plane at Gatwick."

"Oh."

"Do you remember what happened?"

"Vaguely. I was on a flight from somewhere. There was a fight. I can't remember much more than that."

"Well David, you are a hero. That's what all the news people are saying. You saved the lives of over two hundred passengers on the plane, never mind the Royal Family!"

"Royal Family? I don't remember......."

He started to slip back under, his mind floating away.

"It's okay David, just go back to sleep. Everything will be okay."

Her Australian-accented voice gently soothed him as he sank back into unconsciousness, her beautiful face filling his mind's eye as he drifted away. Then blackness overcame him once again.

THIRTY-EIGHT

26th June
Near Tindouf, south-western Algeria.

"OK control, wilco, wait out."
Dan looked up from whispering into his secure satellite handset. He spoke softly to Donnelly.
"They want confirmation that Target Alpha is still here."
Donnelly nodded in reply and fixed his eye to the optical scope of the LTD for what felt like the millionth time, scanning the terrorist compound about eight hundred metres away. The desert was beginning to darken with the sunset, the sand flaring to a beautiful pink hue. He blinked sweat from his eyes and focused on the farthest building in the compound. He took in a Ford pick-up truck and a brand new four-wheel drive Range Rover parked in front, then slowly scanned through the rest of the compound, picking out the shape of an Arab sentry having a quick sneaky cigarette away from the eyes of his superiors.
"Confirmed. Target Alpha's vehicle is still here and there's been no movement out of the camp since he arrived. So even though I haven't seen him since he went inside the building last night, he must still be here," he whispered back at Dan.
"Hello, Control. Confirmed. Target Alpha is still at our location over."
Dan listened intently for a few minutes then said:
"Ok, Control. Out"

"Well? What's happening?" asked Donnelly.
The SRR trooper ignored him as he reached back with his foot and lightly kicked at the sleeping form of Buck behind them.

"Wakey, wakey, rise and shine. Last one with his feet on the floor gets fifty press-ups!"

"Hands off cocks, put on socks," came the alert response of his buddy.
Seconds later Buck had wriggled forward into the already tight space at the front of the OP.

"What's up Dan?" he whispered.
Dan smiled.

"The boss has just been on the phone," he said. "The operation is going ahead at 0700 hours local time. They want us to maintain our position and film the whole of the main event so the folks back home can see what it's like to be a real soldier! Ground forces will be moving into our location in about two hours, and they'll make contact with us when they get here and give us our final orders."

"Bloody hell! Good stuff!" grinned Buck.

"They want the TLD trained onto Target Alpha's building before it gets dark, but not to paint the target until 06.45."

"OK, move over Spook, it's time for the professionals to take over. You can have a kip in the back while I sort the TLD out."
Buck began to push Donnelly out of the way so that he could get to the TLD.

"I hate to rain on your parade guys," snapped Donnelly, "but do they know that it'll be light at seven in the morning?"

"Of course they do," answered Dan.

"Obviously the head-sheds have decided that footage from a dawn attack will look better on the TV than just a load of flashing lights from a night attack. The TV butt-heads will be able to see what's going on for a start."

"And what about us? We're the ones that will be assaulting that bloody compound when everyone's already awake! Jesus! It'll be a nightmare."

"Not for us, pal. We're ordered to stay where we are and watch the fireworks. We're going to have ringside seats mate!"

"Wonderful," snarled Donnelly, as he moved backwards. "Just fucking wonderful!"

26th June
London

"Good Evening. This is the BBC *News at Ten* with Fiona Bruce and Huw Edwards. In tonight's news: Who is the mystery man that saved the lives of the Royal Family and the two hundred and forty passengers on the ill-fated 'Gambian flight' as it has become known? As hundreds of millions of people around the world gather for yet another night of vigil to pray for the recovery of David Keller, we ask: who is he? Tonight's programme also looks closely at the events of the terrorist outrage, and tries to determine whether our security services are at fault. Why was a crowded chartered flight allowed to be used as a guided missile in an attempt to kill the Royal Family? What more could the Security Services have done?"

"Also tonight we have exclusive footage from a BBC camera man's video of the fight between the terrorists and David Keller, taken from within the stricken aircraft itself. The film has been studied comprehensively by the police over the past days and only now has it been released to the public. We must warn you that this film contains scenes of extreme violence that may upset you."

"First of all though, we go live to our special news correspondent, Allan Little, who is outside the East Surrey Hospital, where hundreds of reporters from around the world have gathered to hear the latest news of David Keller…"

THIRTY-NINE

26th June
Redhill, Surrey

It was the pain that dragged John Smith back to consciousness again. A pain that was throbbing deep within his body with white heat.

"Hello, David. Are you okay?"

"Doctor Linda?"

"Yes, it's me. Can you open your eyes David?"

He tried, but he didn't seem to have the strength to perform even this little task.

"Jesus, but it hurts!"

"I know, David. I'm afraid that your condition is too delicate to use a high dosage of painkillers. I'm sorry."

He grimaced.

"You'd think I'd have got used to pain by now. How long have I been out this time?"

"It's been a few hours since you went to sleep again. Is there anyone I can contact for you? A friend or a relative?"

"No. There's no one - no one that would want to talk to me anyway. Have the police been to see me yet?"

"They've been here all along. There's an armed policeman on guard out in the corridor. No one else has come, but then you've been in a coma since you arrived here. I expect they'll send someone to interview you once you have recovered sufficiently."

"When they realise who I am, they'll come to take

me away."

"What do you mean? The police? What would they take you away for?"

"Not the cops, the spooks. They'll want to get rid of me."

His voice was hardly a croak now as he began to fade away again.

"David, can you hear me?"

"Yes."

"I don't understand what you're saying. What do you mean?"

Smith pulled himself back from the brink with a grunt of fresh pain. His eyelids snapped open and he stared at the woman's face above him. He felt a brief surge of strength coming to his battered mind.

"Do me a favour, Linda, get a pen and paper. I've got a message that I want you to give to someone. Please."

"Of course, David."

She went off to find a pen and paper and returned a few seconds later.

"Go on."

"It's to a man named Robert Smith, the son of John Smith. His number is..."

26th June
Rugby, Warwickshire.

An hour later the phone rang in a house in Rugby.

"Hello?"

"Is that Robert Smith? The son of John Smith?"

The woman's voice had a faint Australian accent.

"Listen, lady, if you're another bloody reporter, I'm not interested. It's all old news now and me and the rest of my family are sick and tired of you bloody vultures! We just want to get on with the rest of our lives in peace!"

"No, no, I'm not a reporter. My name is Linda Webb. I'm a cardiothoracic registrar at the East Surrey Hospital in

London. I have a message for you. That's all!"

"A doctor? What's happened? Has someone had an accident?"

"I've been given a message to pass on to you from a patient here."

"What patient? I don't know anybody in London. Are you sure you're not a reporter? If you are then yo..."

"I am not a reporter, Mr Smith! I'm a surgeon. I'm afraid that the person who sent the message did not want me to tell you who he is."

"I don't get it? What's the message?"

"He gave me your telephone number and asked me to tell you that there is a PO box set up in your name at the main post office in Coventry. He said that when you go there you will find a package addressed to you. In the package is a manuscript and lots of other documents. He said that once you have read it then you will understand, and that you and your brother Alan are to sell it to the papers, but not to accept anything under a million."

"This is crazy! A million what?"

"I assume he means pounds, Mr Smith, a million pounds."

"Jesus! What the fuck?"

"I'm afraid that's all there is. Would you like the number of the PO box?"

"I guess so. I still don't get it though!"

"Neither do I, Mr Smith, but I promised him I'd give you the message. The number of the PO box is ..."

FORTY

26th June
London.

Detective Constable Helen Wright was relaxing in her new London flat. She had come home late after another long fruitless day at the tiny office in the Headquarters of the Secret Intelligence Service at Vauxhall Cross.

    At first, when Alan Davies had chosen her to be his assistant on his secondment to the SIS, she had been thrilled and excited to be working with the Firm. Who wouldn't be? She had imagined that the Headquarters would be extremely glamorous and packed with James Bond types. Instead she had found it to be filled with grey men in grey suits pushing pens and polishing seats with their fat arses all day long. It was a bitter disappointment to her. Then she realised that it was working closely with Alan that was the real turn on. The infatuation that she had held for her boss at the Serious and Organised Crime Agency in Cambridgeshire had slowly developed into something more, something akin to deep love, she thought. But even that was wearing a bit thin now. He was bloody obsessed with tracking down and catching John Smith, and that was proving to be as tedious as the constant sexist remarks she was receiving from the other workers at the Headquarter's building. God, but she was getting tired of it all!

    She kicked off her shoes and sank into the old armchair facing the TV, a large glass of Scotch in her hands. She had just pressed the TV remote to catch the end of *News at Ten* when her mobile went off, startling the crap out of her. She looked down at the caller ID and saw Alan's name there, then automatically hit the mute button on the remote. What now? she thought, couldn't she even have five minutes of peace to herself?

"Hello?"

"Helen. Are you at home?"

"Yes, boss, I was just....."

"Switch the bloody news on!"

"I've got it on, boss. Let me turn the sound up." Her lower jaw slowly began to fall on to her chest as she watched the footage.

"Helen. Helen! Are you still there?"

"Yes, boss. I was just watching the video on the news. It's amazing! It's taken right inside that airliner with the terrorists!"

"I know. Look closely at the guy sitting next to the cameraman. The one with the goatee beard and the dark hair..."

"Yes. I see him. Why..."

"It's Smith, Helen! It's John bloody Smith!"

"Are you sure, boss? I only saw him for a second but he looks very different from Smith, or Paul Gray. Wouldn't we have heard if either of their names had shown up on the planes manifest? I mean..."

"Oh do shut up, Helen! It's Smith I tell you! And that's not all. Do you know what the man with the goatee is called?"

"How can I Sir, I've only just switched the TV on?"

"His name is David Keller!"

"What? David Keller? The hero who took on the terrorists and..."

"Exactly, Helen! David Keller is John Smith!"

"But Sir, he's a hero..."

"I know they bloody say he is, Helen! But I'm telling you that he and John Smith are the same man. Get your gear together right now. I'll meet you at the East Surrey

Hospital!"

"But Sir, it's..."

It was too late to argue. Davies had rung off. Helen looked down at the still full glass in her hand.

"Oh fuck it!" she shouted at the wall. "Why me? Why is it always me?"

She put down the glass in disgust and stood up, looking for her shoes.

26th June
Redhill, Surrey.

Fifty minutes later Helen met up with an excited DCI Davies at the main reception area of the East Surrey Hospital. They started on the long trek up several floors to the ICU Unit.

When they finally reached their destination it was to find a specialist firearms officer from Scotland Yard's SO19 barring their way. He was armed with a Heckler and Koch MP7 sub-machine gun slung across his chest and he watched them warily as they approached him along the corridor.

"Can I see your ID, Sir?" he called when they were still ten metres away.

Davies obliged by pulling out both his ID card and his Warrant Card.

"I'm DCI Davies of SOCA. This is DC Wright."

The firearms officer allowed them to approach and carefully studied their IDs. When he was satisfied he stood back, a smile on his face.

"Sorry about that, Sir. Can't be too careful. There have been a lot of journalists trying to blag their way in since the incident."

He indicated the room behind his shoulder.

"Is that the room where David Keller is?"

"Yes, Sir. I wouldn't try and get in there just now though. Doctor Webb is in there seeing to the patient and she's a proper Aussie firebrand, Sir. I don't think she likes policemen much."

"Really? Well never mind."

He pushed open the door and stepped inside. The ICU was dimly lit by overhead lights and there were shiny machines all over the place. Stuck in the middle of all this machinery and attached to it by numerous tubes and wires was the patient. Over to the left was a nurse emptying a catheter bag, and leaning over the patient, wiping his brow with a cool cloth, was a woman in a white coat. She looked up as they entered the room.

"Who are you," she barked at them, "and what are you doing here?"

As she straightened up Davies could see that she was a strikingly beautiful woman, probably in her late forties or maybe her early fifties. She was small in stature but very well proportioned beneath her coat.

"I'm Detective Chief Inspector Alan Davies of the Serious and Organised Crime Agency. My colleague is Detective Constable Helen Wright. Who are you Madam?"

"I'm Doctor Linda Webb. Chief Cardiothoracic Registrar of this hospital."

It was obvious to Davies that she could use her full title to intimidate just as well as he could.

"Now why are you here?"

"I believe that your patient is a dangerous and wanted criminal, Doctor Webb. I've come to arrest him on several charges including murder and terrorist offences. His name is John Smith, not David Keller."

He saw the momentary recognition that flickered across her face at the name of Smith and decided to keep on the offensive.

"I'm afraid that I'll have to ask you and your staff to vacate the room, Doctor. I will arrange to have the patient removed to a more secure hospital as soon as possible."

"Nonsense!" she barked back at him, her accent getting more Aussie by the second. "I do not care who or what my patient is, Detective Chief Inspector. He is just that - my patient. He will remain under my care so long as he is unwell. Do I make myself clear? He is not going to be arrested by you or anyone else, and he is certainly not going to be removed from this unit until he is well on the way to recovery! At the moment, he is only just hanging on to life by the tiniest thread. Any attempt to move him will almost certainly result in massive internal bleeding that will kill him."

Davies took an involuntary step back at the vehemence of the Doctor's retort. He stammered his reply to her.

"But you don't understand, Doctor. This is an extremely dangerous man! Your life and the lives of your staff will be in danger if I leave him here!"

"Really?" she returned to the offensive. "I have been led to believe that this man, whatever his name is, is a national hero! Didn't he just save the lives of the entire Royal Family and over two hundred fellow passengers by almost sacrificing his own? That doesn't sound like the type of man who would hurt the doctor or nurses that are treating him, does it?"

For once in his life, Davies was flummoxed and couldn't think of anything to say. He rapidly regained his composure though.

"Okay, Doctor. I will leave him alone for the time being, as I can see that he's too ill to attempt an escape. I insist on having a close look at his face though."

"Okay. You can have a very quick look, but then I must insist that you leave."

"Thank you, Doctor. We will."

Davies slowly walked forward, his heart beating in his chest like a bass drum. *Is this truly the man that he had been hunting for the last few months?* He prayed to God that he hadn't cocked it up again. Sir Rupert bloody Giles would be down on him like a ton of bloody bricks if he was wrong this time!

He made his way past the doctor, almost afraid to let his arm brush her as he passed. Then the moment of truth came upon him. He squinted down at the patient's face in the dim light, studying every contour. This was Smith! He knew it!

Suddenly the eyes of the man lying in the bed snapped open. He looked Davies full in the face from just a foot away, scaring the life out of the policeman, who again took an involuntary step backwards.

"Hello, Alan."
The man's voice croaked at him, barely audible against the thumping of his own heart and the blood coursing through the veins in his ears.

"Fancy meeting you again. Small world, isn't it?" the eyelids drooped down again, thankfully hiding the same coal-black eyes that constantly filled Davies's nightmares. He backed away quickly.

"That's him, Helen! It's definitely John Smith! We've got him by the balls at last!"

"Now get out!" the Doctor ordered, pointing at the door.
Davies left.

FORTY-ONE

27th June
Near Tindouf, south-western Algeria.

Chris Donnelly shivered inside his lightweight sleeping bag. *Nothing ever changes in the army*, he thought. *Mention 'desert' to the plonkers in the stores and they'll issue you with lightweight tropical kit. None of them know or care that it gets bloody freezing in the desert at night!* He pulled the sleeping bag as close around his face as was possible, to keep the warmth in.

It was a moonless night in the Algerian Sahara, and as black as a coal cellar under the camouflaged sheeting of the observation post. He couldn't see his hand if he held it up in front of his face. There was nothing wrong with his hearing though and a whole orchestra of faint noises assailed his ears. There was the constant swishing sound of billions of tiny grains of sand being moved by the slight breeze outside. It sometimes sounded a bit like the sea hitting a beach as small gusts of wind shifted the sand. Every now and then, his senses, prickled by the very real danger of his position, would pick up the patter patter of tiny scampering feet over the sand outside, perhaps made by a lizard or a large beetle. Occasionally he heard the faint excited whispering of the two SRR soldiers, Buck and Dan, from their position up in the front of the shelter. What he didn't hear was the approach of the soldier in the dark, or the camouflaged sheet being carefully lifted up at the back of the observation post. The first he knew of the soldier's presence was when the muzzle of an assault rifle was pressed hard into his forehead. He almost pissed himself at the touch of the cold metal, and froze.

"How are you, ladies?" came the softly-whispered greeting.

Donnelly felt the relief flood through him like a tidal wave.

"Jesus Christ, old boy! You scared the shit out of me! Who the fuck are you?" Although it was too dark to see, Donnelly got the distinct impression that the visitor was grinning.

"My name's Jim, mate. I'm the squadron Sergeant-Major of A Squadron, SAS. You can all relax now, the real professionals are here. We're digging in about a hundred metres behind you pansies."

"What the fuck are you digging in for? I thought you were going to hit the camp?"

"We are mate, don't yer worry about that. But first, the shit is going to hit the fan and I mean big time! There's enough ordnance coming down in the morning to blast the whole of this poxy place off the map! Your new orders are to dig in deeper where you are because you're going to be right on the edge of it in the bloody danger zone! Don't forget to paint Target Alpha's quarters at 06.45. Sweet dreams, ladies. I'll do my best to stop any of my lads from sneaking over during the night to steal a kiss from you girls! Oh, and by the way, the head-sheds have called this 'Operation Retribution', sort of fitting, considering the circumstances, don't you think?"

With that last parting shot the soldier slipped away as silently as he had arrived. Donnelly whispered urgently to the SRR guys:

"Did you hear all of that?"

"Sure did," came the reply. "Where did we put the fucking entrenching tools?"

FORTY-TWO

27th June
Near Tindouf, south-western Algeria.

At precisely 06.45 local time, as the sun started to rise above the distant horizon, Buck turned on the Laser Target Designator and 'painted' the building that the leader of the *Jihadists*, Abdullah ibn Nazid al-Filasteeni, was having breakfast in. The terrorist camp had been active for about half an hour, after being woken by the *Adhan*, or call to prayer at daybreak. Buck and Dan had watched as the majority of the camp's inhabitants spread out their woven prayer mats on a patch of flattened sand and prayed together. Abdullah led them in their prayers, showing himself outside for the first time since he had arrived at the camp around thirty-six hours earlier.

    Prayers over, the sentries had been changed and everyone else had retired for something to eat and a hot, sweet cup of green tea to welcome in the new day.

27th June
Downing Street, London.

At the same time back in England, COBR was filled to overflowing with the Prime Minister, his deputy and his principle aides, members of the Cabinet, armed force's Chiefs of Staff and prominent journalists. Even representatives of the opposition parties had been invited to witness how the might of the British Government can and will crush anyone who threatened them with terrorism. Everyone in the room sat on the edge of their seats in tense silence as they stared excitedly at the large screen that had been erected at the head of the table. It was filled with a large picture of the North African desert. The image was being fed live by the SRR boys in Algeria. The whole room seemed to be holding its breath while it waited for Operation Retribution to begin.

27th June
Near Tindouf, south-western Algeria.

The first wave of the attack comes at 07.00 hours local time. A flight of six RAF Tornado GR4 all-weather attack aircraft overfly the camp at a height of thirty thousand feet. They are so high that the terrorists don't even hear them coming. Two of the Tornados drop a batch of six Enhanced Paveway EPWII Laser-Guided Bombs that are guided precisely onto their target by the Laser Target Designator of the SRR team. The bombs, each packed with four hundred and fifty kilogrammes of high explosive detonate on impact with the building where Abdullah was last seen. The rest of the Tornados 'carpet bomb' the camp with twenty unguided General Purpose Bombs, each carrying five hundred and five kilogrammes of high explosive. Half of the bombs are set to detonate above the camp in 'airburst mode', to achieve the maximum fragmentation effect on the ground below. The other half are set to detonate on impact with the ground, to achieve the maximum blast damage to unprotected targets. The total of twenty-six bombs, carrying a combined weight of one thousand eight hundred kilogrammes of high explosive, obliterate the target building and all around it, virtually vaporising everything within their blast radius, sending a massive shock wave sweeping through the rest of the camp and for thousands of metres into the surrounding desert.

The six GR4 Tornados, which had been drawn from 12 (Bomber) Squadron, whose normal home was RAF Lossiemouth in Scotland, had been temporarily based at the Algerian Ain Beida Airbase, only about six hundred miles north-east of the target area. All six return to the airbase, unharmed, after they drop their deadly payloads.

The second wave of the attack hits the camp about two minutes after the detonation of the Tornados' bombs. Six TLAM Block IV Tomahawk Cruise Missiles are fired in three salvos, in quick succession, from the nuclear-powered attack submarine *HMS Astute* of the Royal Navy, positioned over a thousand miles away off the Algerian coast in the Mediterranean. The missiles hurtle out of the sky at over five hundred miles an hour. The Tomahawks are targeted to straddle the GPS co-ordinates of the camp's anti-aircraft defence position. Each of the missiles has a payload of four hundred and fifty kilogrammes of conventional high explosive and detonates within a few metres of the others, creating a huge smoke-filled crater where the sand-bagged bunker once existed. The surface-to-air capability of the terrorists is devastated with a huge hammer-blow that brings more death and mayhem from the morning sky.

The third wave of the attack sweeps in only a few minutes after the dust cloud caused by the first and second waves has begun to settle. This wave consists of eight Apache AH1 attack helicopters drawn from 656 and 664 Squadrons of 9 Regiment, Army Air Corps. The attack helicopters approach at medium altitude from the direction of Tindouf Airbase, where they had been temporarily grounded and refuelled during the night. The Apaches look like giant predatory wasps with bug-eyes as they sweep in over the desert sand, each firing their payload of eight Hellfire AGM-114N laser-guided missiles from a range of five hundred metres. They are targeted specifically at the remaining buildings spread around the camp, which they proceed to systematically destroy. The warheads of these missiles are known as 'thermobaric' or 'fuel-air' bombs, which produce a blast wave that is of significantly longer duration, and burns more intensely than conventional warheads. They are called 'enhanced blast weapons' by the Ministry of Defence.

At the same time as the Apaches dispatch their Hellfire missiles they undertake repeat launchings of CRV-7 unguided rockets from pods beneath their fuselage. Each Apache carries four pods with a total of seventy-six rockets, and when fired each rocket releases eighty five-inch tungsten darts or 'Flechettes' that can punch through one and a half inches of hardened armour, thus making mince meat of any unprotected terrorists that they hit. Finally, the Apaches use their 30mm Hughes M230 nose-mounted chain guns to mop up any other targets that they can see on their Forward Looking Infrared (FLIR) thermal cameras, such as fleeing *Jihadists,* firing thousands of High Explosive Dual Purpose (HEDP) rounds at a rate of six hundred rounds per minute into the debris where the camp had once stood. Each HEDP round is the size of a milk bottle and has an armour-piercing tip that explodes on impact like a large hand grenade, throwing out hundreds of red-hot pieces of shrapnel.

In total, the Apache attack helicopters stay on station above the camp for a mere twenty minutes before they too withdraw, unharmed, back towards their operational airbase.

Now it's the turn of the fourth and final wave of the attack to go in against the paltry remains of the terrorist camp. This is the 'ground attack' phase. About one hundred and ten highly-trained and highly-motivated men of A Squadron, 22 Special Air Service, close in for the final kill from the west. They are supported by over thirty men in two troops of the Special Boat Squadron of the Royal Marines acting as 'stop' groups to the north, east and south of the camp. The SAS had marched into position from Tindouf (about ten miles west of the camp) during the night, while the SBS had marched southwards from where they had been dropped along the N50, the only major road in the region - also about ten miles from the camp. Both groups of men consist of the finest Special Force soldiers in the world. For this mission they carry nothing but their personal weapons, lots and lots of ammunition, entrenching tools and water. As their shadowy figures rise from their hidden foxholes out in the desert and tactically advance through the cloud of suspended smoke and dust that covers the area of the camp, sporadic bursts of gunfire and exploding hand grenades are heard as they encounter - and overcome – the few surviving terrorists. Interspersed with these sounds are the harsh 'double-taps' of the ruthless soldiers putting rounds into the head of any bodies they come across, to make sure that they are definitely dead. "Take no prisoners" was the order that was passed on from high.

Operation Retribution has lasted less than one hour from start to finish. Every enemy building has been obliterated and every terrorist killed. Nothing has escaped the devastation and not one enemy terrorist has survived. Abdullah ibn Nazid al-Filasteeni and his fledgling *Jihadist* movement is no more. Not one British serviceman or servicewoman for that matter (as there were several involved in the operation) has sustained an injury of any sort.

Most importantly of all, the whole operation has been captured in wonderful Technicolor by the SRR team. The film is destined to be drastically edited and then flashed around the world within just a few short hours. It will stand as a grim warning to anyone who cares to follow in the footsteps of Abdullah ibn Nazid al-Filasteeni and try to terrorise the British.

"Try to kill us, and we will *definitely* kill you" is the message.

One of the Apache attack helicopter pilots taking

part in the operation was His Royal Highness, Prince Harry, the son of HRH Prince Charles and Diane, Princess of Wales, and brother to HRH Prince William, the future King of the United Kingdom of Great Britain and Northern Ireland. Prince Harry is a serving officer in the British Army and a fully qualified Apache pilot who has seen plenty of action in Afghanistan fighting against the *Taliban*.

Ironically, Harry had also been present at the private celebration of his grandmother's birthday in Buckingham Palace during that fateful night when the terrorists had attempted to crash the airliner into the building and wipe out the entire Royal Family.

The boot is on the other foot now.

FORTY-THREE

Monday, July 7th
Centre page spread of *The Sun* newspaper.

'Ex-SAS soldier, ex-MI6 agent and an assassin working secretly for the British government John Smith is the real-life equivalent of the fictional 007 – James Bond. And just like Bond he was licensed to kill.'
'John Smith is the real name of the man who has instantly become world famous for taking on eight terrorists single-handed on the 'Gambia flight' terrorist hijacking, and killing them all, thus saving the British Royal Family and over two hundred fellow passengers from certain death.'
'Here, in a manuscript written by Smith himself, and supported by hundreds of documents in the form of hotel receipts, aircraft boarding passes, car hire receipts and - most telling of all – false official documents and passports, we tell his amazing story...'

Saturday, July 12th
The Sun editorial

'Shocking Story'

'Just a few days ago, millions of people around the world were lighting candles for the recovery of John Smith. Religious leaders of all faiths were praying for this brave and courageous man and the world's political leaders were falling over each other in their hurry to nominate him for the highest gallantry awards that their respective countries could offer.'

'Now, after his exclusive life story has been serialised by *The Sun*, the majority of those same people, religious and political leaders have turned their backs on him amidst shouts of "murderer" and "assassin". John Smith has become a pariah almost overnight.'
Why? Is he not still the same man that put his own life in mortal danger to save the lives of others? Is he not now lying in a hospital bed, recovering from horrific injuries after having lain in a coma, from which it was thought he would probably never emerge again? Why has the attitude of the world changed so much?'

'Is it because he was once a courageous soldier and a spy? Or is it because he was then employed by his own government, at the time of his life when he was most vulnerable, to kill terrorists?'

'John Smith is a man of undoubted courage and ability who has sacrificed his whole life, his home and his family, to fight for the freedom and safety of the British people. He has been wounded in combat several times, been tortured horrifically, and fought for us in wars that most of us have never even heard of. Time and time again he has put his own life on the line for the people of Britain, and yet this is how some of them choose to repay him, by calling him a "murderer"'.

'*The Sun* says that it is about time we pulled the wool from our eyes and recognised that the terrorism, whether political or religious, that has ruled our lives for so long is evil, and that sometimes you have to use evil means to fight evil. If that involves asking for a good man like John Smith to do our dirty work for us and go out there and kill terrorists before they have the chance to kill even more of us, then so be it.'

'*The Sun* praises the former Prime Minister, Baroness Margaret Thatcher, for her own particular bravery in ordering the war of terror to be taken to the terrorists themselves. We salute the courage of John Smith and we thank him with all of our hearts for the hundreds, if not thousands of innocent lives that he has saved from death and mutilation at the hands of these terrorist scum.'

'In Denial'

'The British government is denying that any of John Smith's claims are true. Official spokesmen from the Secret Intelligence Service, MI6 and the Ministry of Defence have categorically denied that Smith was employed as an agent whilst serving in the Rhodesian armed forces, and say that he has never even served as a soldier in the British Army, never mind in its Special Forces. They have stated that "it is laughable to suggest that the British government or its security services ever employed John Smith or anyone else as an assassin.'

'David Cameron, the Prime Minister, has gone so far as to say that John Smith is a sad "Walter Mitty" character, which is even sadder because of his "recent heroic actions on the Gambia flight".'

'The Yard'

'*The Sun* today handed over the complete dossier of John Smith's claims to New Scotland Yard. Apart from the now famous manuscript of his life story, there were also hundreds of pieces of supporting documentation, including false passports and bank account details and dozens of Polaroid snapshots of Smith's alleged victims of assassination, taken at the scene of the killings by Smith himself as his "insurance".'

'There is also the taped confession of the barrister Steve Mackay, the Chief Prosecutor of Cambridgeshire Crown Prosecution Service, where he clearly states, (even if he gave it under torture), that he and other figures in authority in Cambridgeshire falsified evidence against

Smith and caused him to be unjustly put on trial for the abduction, rape and murder of eleven year old Mary Knightly last year.'

'*The Sun* eagerly awaits what the police have to say.'

'Just remember this, though: It's unwise to lie to us anymore. We deserve the truth.'

FORTY-FOUR

14th July
Redhill, Surrey.

"Hello. This is Linda Webb."
"Doctor Webb?"
"Yes, that's right. Who is this please?"
"It's Robert Smith, Doctor Webb. John Smith's son. Do you remember calling me a while ago?"
"Of course I do! How are you Robert? Can I help you?"
"I hope so, Doctor."
"Call me Linda, please."
"Okay, Linda. Do you mind if I put you on speaker phone? I've got my brother Alan with me."
"No, of course not."
"This isn't easy for us, Linda. I take it that you know that we haven't spoken to our father for a very long time?"
"Yes. I read John's story in the newspapers. It must have been very difficult for you."
"Yes, it has been. The thing is - we don't really know what to do now. We were paid one and a half million pounds by *The Sun* for our dad's story, but it isn't really our money. We want to give it to our dad. How is he?"
"Well, he's really poorly at the moment."
"We know, we've been watching the news, but there's been nothing about him for a few days. Is he still 'hanging by a thread'?"
"He is, yes. I guess that the news people are getting

bored with the story now. I'm afraid that your father suffered what we call a 'subarachnoid haemorrhage'. This is where there is bleeding into the subarachnoid space, an area between the membrane and the fluid surrounding the brain. This bleeding caused him to fall into a coma. Probably the easiest way to think of it is that your dad suffered a cerebral aneurysm, a form of stroke."

"How did it happen? Was it because of his fight with the terrorists?"

"I believe so, yes. Your dad suffered a massive loss of blood from several nasty wounds, and this probably led to the cerebral aneurysm. We operated on John and relieved the pressure on the aneurysm by inserting a catheter in the femoral artery of his groin and advancing it through the aorta and into the arteries that serve the brain."

"Bloody hell! Will he make it, Linda?"

"That's really hard to say. The normal chance of recovery for a person who suffers a subarachnoid haemorrhage is around fifty percent, but I'm afraid that in your father's case there are added complications."

"What sort of complications?"

"Well, for a start there's the undeniable fact that your father has suffered severe brain injuries in his past, probably as a result of his torture in Afghanistan. Even though your father has recovered from his comatose state he may well experience what we call delayed ischemia. This is where the blood vessels of the brain constrict and restrict the blood flow, which can result in increased brain damage. There are also the dangers of fluctuations in blood pressure, electrolyte disturbances, pneumonia or even cardiac decompensation. I won't lie to you Robert: any of these complications could end your father's life, and even if he does recover, the chances of him being able to live a full and active life are almost zero. I'm really sorry."

"That's okay, Linda. We sort of guessed that it was going to be like this. How long before you know whether he's going to make it or not?"

"Again, that's hard to say. We're monitoring his situation and medicating against the possible complications, but really your guess is as good as mine, Robert."

"Well thanks for being so honest with us, Linda. Would it help our dad if we came to visit him?"

"Oh yes, it would! That would be a wonderful idea! Please do!"

"Has he had any other visitors?"

"Too few, I'm afraid. There have been regular visits by the police of course, and a few of the passengers that he saved on the plane have managed to get to see him in spite of the heavy security around your father. But there have been no visits from your father's family."

"I'm not surprised. He's apparently got two older brothers, but we don't know who they are. We didn't even know that they existed until we read his autobiography. They probably don't even know that the 'John Smith' in hospital is their brother. He apparently changed his name when he came back from Rhodesia and no one alive seems to know what his real name is. It's a bloody nightmare. We don't even know who *we* are really."

"I'm really sorry for both of you. I'm sure that he loves you immensely - from the way that he wrote about you in his autobiography. It would be great if you could come and visit him."

"Okay, we'll think about it. Have you spoken to him much since he came out of the coma?"

"Yes, I am fortunate to have had a few short conversations with him, though he is very poorly and easily tires."

"What do you think of him?"

"To be honest Robert, I like him very much. He has a lovely smile and I still find it hard to believe that he is capable of the violence that I've seen on that video on the TV. I find him to be very nice and very gentle. I believe that he is a *good* man."

"Okay. Well thanks again, Linda. Perhaps we'll meet

you soon. Bye."
"I hope so. Bye."

FORTY-FIVE

14th July
Vauxhall Cross, London.

Sir Rupert Giles, Chief of the Secret Intelligence Service, gestured for Chris Donnelly to sit down in the chair in front of his desk.

"I must congratulate you on your successful part in Operation Retribution, Chris."

"Thank you, Sir. I was just doing my job."

"Of course you were, Chris. But you conducted yourself *very well* indeed, and you have upheld the fine traditions of the Service. Well done!"

"Thank you, Sir."

"So well, in fact, that I have decided to promote you. You are now not the *acting* head, but the *Head* of the Increment, and there will be a corresponding increase in your pay packet as well. A *considerable* increase."

"I'm grateful, Sir Rupert."

"Good."

The Chief, his good news dispensed, now leant forward in his chair and lowered his voice.

"Now we come to the bad news. I'm afraid that the recent publicity concerning the John Smith affair, despite the numerous assurances given to the media by the Government that he was never a part of this organisation, have rather fallen on deaf ears. Although Smith has become a pariah to most of the sensible people around the world, it appears that some of the tabloid press in this country have rather taken him and his predicament to their heart, and have even begun a campaign for him to receive a Royal Pardon for the murders and other crimes that he committed while he was on the run last year. It's hard to believe, but some of the newspapers are actually saying that he is a national hero who was forced into acting illegally by a conspiracy between the police and the Firm! Huh!"

Donnelly just smiled at his Chief, fully aware that all that he was denying was actually the truth.

"This leaves us in a rather sticky situation. We do not want this press campaign to drag on for years and to continue to erode the high esteem with which the Firm is held in government circles."

"I understand, Sir. I take it that you would still like my section to take care of this problem?"

Sir Giles paused before answering, his eyes boring into Donnelly's as though expecting a trick from his subordinate. Donnelly stared back, his face and eyes empty of emotion, as they always were when he talked to his Chief.

"Not in the way that we planned it previously, Chris. I take it that your Irishman is still with us?"

"Yes Sir. He's cooling his heels at a local hotel and still champing at the bit to get a crack at Smith."

"Good, he'll still get his chance. However, I'm afraid that the present circumstances will call for a slight change in our plans."

"In what way, Sir?"

"Originally, the Irishman was to have taken care of Smith and then to have joined the Increment, as an integral part of your team. I'm afraid that that will no longer be possible, Donnelly."

"Sir?"

"With all of the publicity now surrounding this case, it would be extremely foolhardy of us to allow the Irishman to survive his encounter with Smith. After all he is a known terrorist and used to be a hitman for the bloody IRA! It, *he*, would become an extreme embarrassment to us if any of his association with the service was to ever come to light at any point."

"I see, Sir."

"At the moment it would appear to be an understandable act of revenge for his brother's death at the hands of Smith, if the Irishman was to kill him. But I'm afraid that this would only be truly believable to the media if he was, for instance, shot dead by armed police after he has killed Smith."

"Yes Sir, I can see the logic in that."

"Good! Let's get this over with as soon as possible then. I'll leave the details in your hands Donnelly."

"Yes Sir, and thank you again for your continuing support, and the promotion, Sir."

"Nothing more than you deserve, Chris."

"Thank you, Sir."

FORTY-SIX

15th July
Redhill, Surrey.

"Good morning, John."
"Morning, Doc."
Dr Linda Webb breezed into the Intensive Care Unit, her intense beauty causing a momentary flutter on Smith's heart monitor by his bed.
"How are feeling this morning?"
"Okay, thanks Doc."
Smith's voice was still hoarse and faint, causing her to lean closer to hear him as she took his wrist in her hand and began to time his pulse. He caught just a whiff of her perfume in his nostrils, causing another brief flutter on his heart monitor.
"No, how are you *really* feeling, John?"
"Alright, you've got me," he grinned at her, "I'm feeling pretty bloody shitty to tell you the truth. Don't get me moaning though. Remember I'm an old soldier and we like nothing better than to moan!"
He coughed, wracked by a sudden spasm that brought just a hint of blood to his lips. Linda grabbed a tissue from the bedside cabinet and used it to gently wipe the blood and spittle from Smith's mouth.
"Sorry about that," he apologised.
"No need, John. You are still very poorly and it will be a long time before you are completely out of the woods."

"Well, as long as you'll still be around, I don't mind waiting."

"Hmmm," she smiled, searching his eyes with her own. "I have some good news for you today, John."

"Can't imagine what that could be? Not much of it going around at the moment."

"Well, I had a phone call from your sons yesterday." Smith perked up.

"Yeah. What did they say?"

"They're thinking of coming to see you, John."

"Oh."

His face fell. Linda showed her surprise at his reaction by arching her eye brows.

"Isn't that good news? I thought that you would be pleased?"

"I am, Doc, honest. It's just that..."

His voice trailed off.

"What is it, John?"

"Well, it's a little bit scary, know what I mean?"

"Scary? In what way? I don't understand."

Smith cast a look around the room, catching the eye of a nurse who was sorting some drug dosages out in a corner of the room. She quickly looked away from him. He looked back at Linda and gestured at her to lean closer. Then, in a barely audible whisper he said:

"Haven't you noticed the way that everyone is looking at me?"

He cast his eyes towards the nurse again, who studiously carried on sorting out the drugs, ignoring them both. Linda's own eyes followed his gaze.

"What do you mean, John?" she whispered back, her breath gently fanning against Smith's cheek.

"Everyone knows what I *really* am," he said. "I'm not some bloody hero, I'm a killer. I'm nothing but a pure bloody fruitcake. You can see it in their eyes when they look at me. They're all fascinated, but they're all scared shitless of me as well. Not one of them, except for you, can even hold my gaze for more than half a second."

"I see. Well, that's only to be expected, John. You are rather unusual, you can see that can't you?"

"Yeah, of course I can. What I'm worried about is that my sons will look at me and think about me in the same way. I'm worried that they'll just see me as a fruitcake, like the rest of these buggers. That's what really scares me."

"Well, that's understandable, John. All I can say is - just to be yourself. I'm sure that they will eventually see that you are the same dad that they loved when they were young."

Smith leaned back onto his pillow, exhaustion plainly showing on his face.

"Ah. But will they, Linda? Will they?"

His eyes fluttered for a moment and then he succumbed to sleep. Linda stayed where she was, staring at his lined face, still deeply tanned despite the hint of grey in his skin that showed his exhaustion. She felt the strength that was there in the firmness of his jaw and the set of his lips, but also saw the extreme vulnerability. She felt very privileged to have shared some of this man's deepest feelings and fears, and was strangely compelled by her closeness to him. She shook herself and dropped the hand that she was still holding gently on to the bed sheet. Then, all businesslike once again, she turned her attention to the bank of monitors and started to take notes.

Only she couldn't concentrate on her job. She'd only known John Smith for a short while, even shorter if she took into account the fact that he had been in a coma for most of the time, but already she had seen many of the different facets that made up the man. Unlike many of the men that she had known throughout her life, John was not shallow. *He's like an onion,* she thought. *Every time I speak to him I see a new layer of skin pulled back, revealing yet another layer of deeper feeling underneath*. She knew that he was capable of extreme violence. She had seen the video of his fight with the terrorists on the plane, as had millions of other people. Yet he had never shown a sign of that violence to her, not even a hint of it. He had a dry, dark sense of humour and could make her laugh over the silliest of things, yet he also had a sadness about him that ran deep through his persona. He was so strong and could appear to be as steady as a rock while everything flowed in chaos around him, yet at the same time he was extremely vulnerable and obviously felt ill at ease with what other people thought about him. Sometimes he would smile and he looked for all the world like a small mischievous boy, yet he could also be very serious and she could easily imagine that he would have been a very tough and professional soldier.

Linda Webb paused in what she was doing and glanced back at John Smith as he lay asleep on the bed. His face was peaceful and reposed as he slept the sleep of exhaustion. *He's so handsome, s*he thought, and smiled secretly to herself.

FORTY-SEVEN

Saturday, July 26
The Sun editorial

'Death *Fatwa* ordered by Iran'

"The news that a Death *Fatwa* has been issued on John Smith by Iran, has left many people confused as to the reason why."

"The exact wording of the *Fatwa* which is a legal pronouncement in Islam, and was handed down yesterday by *Ayatollah* Akbar Hashemi Khomeini, the Supreme Leader of the Islamic Republic of Iran, says: "The *Kufr* (an unbeliever) John Smith is a mercenary and must be killed. The death of this man is a religious duty. He has been paid by the infidel British Government to murder innocent Muslims.""

"Is this the Iranian's way of saying that the British Government was somehow aware of the attempt to wipe out the British Monarchy and had paid John Smith to stop it? Surely if this is true, would they really have set just one *unarmed* man against a gang of *eight* armed terrorists? If the Iranians really believe that this could be true, then they must also really believe that the British Government are just plain stupid? Who in their right mind would ever have bet against the terrorists losing in any such encounter?"

'Assassin'

"Or has the *Fatwa* been issued because Smith has admitted to being a former government assassin who killed terrorists? Surely this isn't the real reason for the *Fatwa* either, as Smith has clearly stated that he never killed Muslim terrorists, and that Islamic terrorism was unknown in his day. So how could he "murder innocent Muslims"?

"Indeed, John Smith actually fought alongside the *Mujahedeen* in their *Jihad* (Holy War) against the Soviet invaders of Afghanistan back in the 1980s. If anything, surely this would make Smith a friend to Muslims and not a man who should be killed as part of Islamic religious duty?"

'Hidden Agenda'

"Or has this *Fatwa* been delivered to sow confusion and doubt about the veracity of secret documents found in the terrorist camp of the *Jihadist* terrorist Abdullah ibn Nazid al-Filasteeni?"

"*The Sun* believes that it is no coincidence that this *Fatwa* against Smith has been issued the day after British security services released information that documents (recovered after Operation Retribution successfully crushed the terrorist movement in the Algerian desert), proved a direct link between Abdullah's *Jihadists* and the Government of Iran."

Does the Government of Iran have a hidden agenda to murder the Royal Family and thus bring an end to the British Monarchy? Do they really believe that such a dastardly cowardly act would make our country weaker?"

The Sun says this to the despotic leaders of Iran: "Remember guys: Operation Retribution showed the world just why there is a 'Great' in Great Britain. Don't mess with us."

FORTY-EIGHT

26th July
Redhill, Surrey

The two men who approached the main entrance to the East Surrey Hospital in Redhill looked nervous. They constantly cast about with their eyes as if they half expected to be pounced upon by a policeman or worse - by a journalist - at any second.

They were both in their late twenties and dressed alike in dark suits. It was obvious from the way that they carried themselves that they were not used to wearing suits and would have been happier in T-shirts and jeans, but for some reason both had independently come to the same conclusion that they ought to look their smartest for the reunion to come.

The elder of the two men was tall and stocky, his bright ginger hair cut short, and he sported a moustache and short goatee beard. The younger was slightly taller and thinner, though still powerful looking. He wore a pair of narrow fashionable glasses and had short-cut sandy blond hair.

Once inside the hospital foyer, they walked to the crowded reception desk and waited their turn in line. Eventually one of the staff behind the desk looked up at them. She was a young woman and very attractive. Her eyes widened slightly at the sight of the two handsome men in smart suits standing in front of her and she gave them her best smile.

"Hello, can I help you?"
The older man looked down at her, noting her reaction to them and feeling a surge of self-confidence where before he had felt totally nervous.

"I hope so," he smiled back. "We'd like to speak with a doctor that works here, if it's possible?"

"OK. That shouldn't be a problem. Is he expecting you?"

"Sort of, we said that we might come. Only the doctor is a *she*, not a *he*."

"OK. What's her name?"

"Doctor Linda Webb."

"Oh, the Australian doctor."

The woman's eyes widened even more. Obviously it was well known that this particular doctor had a very famous patient in the hospital. She blustered for a second or two.

"Let me just find her number...okay, got it. I'll ring her pager and ask her to call back to reception. Could I have your names please?"

The two men shared a brief look at each other.

"My name is Robert, and this is Alan."

They looked at each other again, and this time they both shrugged their shoulders as though they had come to a silent decision between themselves.

"That's Robert and Alan Smith. We're John Smith's sons."

The two brothers were eventually escorted from the reception area to Linda Webb's office by a security guard, who knocked on the office door, poked his head in and announced them. They went in and the guard walked off.

Linda rose from behind her desk with a huge smile on her face, reaching across to shake their hands.

"I'm so glad that you decided to come! Your father will be very pleased to see you!"

She cleared the stacks of manila files off two chairs and gestured for the brothers to sit down. Then she perched herself on the edge of the desk, looking down at them with a gentle and kindly smile on her face.

"I know that this is very hard for you both."
Alan cleared his throat, obviously still nervous, though put at ease somewhat by the warmth of the doctor's welcome.

"It *is* hard," he said. "We haven't seen our dad for years, not since we were young teenagers."

"Yes. He told me he hadn't seen you for a while."
Robert spoke up:

"We didn't have a clue about all this assassin business. We knew that he had been in the army of course, we can still remember him ironing his uniform in the living room - but he never really talked about it."

"I understand."

"Then after he left our mum, we used to see him at our grandparents' house, but we still didn't talk about his past, and granddad and grandma never mentioned it either. I don't think that even they knew what he had been up to."

"Then he went off to Africa and we didn't hear from him again for a long time," Alan added. "And *then,* to top it all, there was all the fuss when he got arrested for killing that young girl. The police came to our workplaces and grilled us for hours. It was very upsetting."

"I can only imagine what that was like for you both."

"The bloody journalists were the worst," Robert chimed in. "Once they found out where we lived they hassled us all of the time. It was a nightmare!"

"Well at least you know now that your father isn't a paedophile."

"Yeah, that's true, just a murderer and an assassin! And not just terrorists either; he murdered policemen and a judge and God knows who else!"

"I can see that you are both very upset by all this."

"Too right. To be honest we don't know what to think anymore."
There was a lot of bitterness and anger in Alan's voice.

"Well, if it helps you at all, please remember that your father is also a hero. He nearly died when he fought those people on the plane, and he saved the lives of a lot of other innocent people, including the Royal Family. Don't be too hard on him."

The brothers took in her soothing words and seemed to calm down. After a pause, Robert asked:

"How is he anyway? Is he past the worst?"

"I'll be honest with you both. It's hard to say whether he's past the danger point yet. Sometimes he appears to be getting better by the minute, while at other times he looks so poorly that I barely hold out any hope for him at all. This is one of the reasons why I am so glad that you've come. In many ways, it's a medical miracle that he has survived so far with the extensive injuries that he sustained during the hijacking, and I've come to believe that it was just his amazing will to live that got him through it. Pure bloodymindedness, if you like?"

"Yeah. That sounds like our dad."

"But over the last day or so John seems to have lost all hope and I'm beginning to feel that he is losing the will to carry on. Hopefully, seeing you two will help him get that back."

Linda paused. For the first time a look of uncertainty crossed her face.

"However, you have – unfortunately - chosen a very bad time to visit."

The brothers looked at each other.

"Why?"

"Well, John's got other visitors at the moment and I'm not sure what to do."

"Oh. Is it the police?"

"No, no. Nothing like that! It's someone else, someone rather special. I'm not sure that I'll be able to get you in to see your father, at least for while."

"Who is it then?"

Linda didn't answer Robert's query for a few seconds, and she seemed to be fighting some sort of internal battle with herself before she eventually spoke.

"Sod it!" she said. "Your visit is just too important to John. They'll just have to lump it!"
The brothers looked surprised by the anger in her tone.
"Come on, let's go up and see your dad!"

FORTY-NINE

26th July
Redhill, Surrey

Sean O'Connell was angrily pacing the floor of his hotel room. He was beginning to feel like a caged animal. Four days previously he had been left and ordered to stay in the room by one of Donnelly's henchmen. His patience was wearing thin. *Didn't they think he was up to the job anymore?* he thought. *Or have they changed their fucking minds now that the British bloody Empire has showed how feckin' great they are by knocking off a few badly armed Arabs with all of the might of their feckin' war machine?* He was well pissed off and steadily going more and more stir crazy. He nearly jumped out of his skin when he heard the knock at his door.

Grabbing a pistol from his bedside cabinet, he forced himself to take his time crossing the floor and to slow his madly beating heart. Standing to one side of the door, gun at the ready, he took a deep, calming breath.

"Who is it?" he growled, his teeth clenched together.

"Donnelly," came the curt reply.
Carefully, O'Connell turned the key and opened the door fractionally while he looked out. He recognised his Secret Intelligence Service mentor and threw the door open. O'Connell angrily gestured for the smugly smiling bloody Brit to come inside, before slamming the door closed behind him and locking it.

"About feckin' time! Where have you been you bastard?" he snarled at him.

"Now, now, old boy, where's your manners? Pissed off are we?"

"You'd be pissed off too if you'd had to spend four feckin' days in this bastard dump!"

He gestured around the small hotel room with its cheap furniture and battered TV.

"Prison was better than this feckin' place!" Donnelly followed his gaze.

"I can see what you mean, old boy. Not exactly the *Hilton*, is it? However, I am the bearer of good news."

"What? The Brit bloody Government has finally decided to declare that Northern Ireland is to be free of their Imperialistic rule and returned to its rightful people?" Donnelly smiled.

"No, I'm afraid that that will never happen. Not in our lifetime anyway. No, I bring to you news about the killer of your younger brother: a certain Mr Smith."

The Irishman couldn't help himself. He had to smile.

"So I'm going to get to kill the bastard after all?" he asked.

"Exactly, old boy. You and I are going to pay a little social call on Mr Smith at last."

"About feckin' time!" When?"

"Tonight!"

"Great stuff. How are we going to get close to him? He's surrounded by armed bloody rozzers I bet."

"Well. You know the old saying: 'If you can't beat them, join them'?"

"Yeah?"

"So how do you fancy becoming a policeman?"

FIFTY

26th July
Redhill, Surrey

The corridor outside of the Intensive Care Unit was packed with people: there were armed policemen looking like black-clad paramilitaries with their bulky body armour, helmets and goggles; several other police officers in more formal uniforms (both men and women, obviously of higher rank); and about half a dozen big, bulky men in civilian suits. Robert and Alan Smith stood nervously at the end of the corridor where they were eyed suspiciously by everyone else, while Doctor Linda Webb stepped forward.

"Who's in charge here?" she asked loudly in her best 'don't mess with me, I'm a doctor and an Australian' voice. There was a pause while several of the men and women looked at each other. Then one of the civilians stepped forward.

"I am," he said. "What can I do for you, doctor?" Linda stepped up to the man, grasped him unceremoniously by the elbow and began to talk to him intensely but so quietly that the Smith brothers could only catch a few words that she said:

"I know who's in there...no, I don't care...it's very important for...he's my patient..."
Eventually the man put a hand up to stop her.

"Okay, okay, Doctor. I'll ask. But that's all I can do. If they don't want to be disturbed, then that's it, okay?"

"Alright," she conceded reluctantly.

The civilian turned away from her, walked up to a door along the corridor and gently knocked on it. He opened the door and stepped inside.

Everybody was quiet for a few minutes. Robert and Alan continued to stand nervously at the end of the corridor while Linda smiled at them encouragingly. The police officers and civilians continued to stare suspiciously at the two men, the armed officers fingering their weapons. Then the door opened and the man who had said that he was in charge stepped back out into the corridor. He approached the three of them.

"Okay Doctor, they can go in," he smiled, "but I'll have to search them first."

"Great. Thank you very much for your help!"

"Not a problem, Doctor. I think that they would really like to meet Mr Smith's sons."
He smiled again.

"Okay, gents, if you don't mind just lifting your arms up for me?"
The man quickly and efficiently ran his hands over the bodies of the two bemused men. Robert finally got his nerve up to ask:

"Who the bloody hell's in there?" the man grinned at him and his brother.

"You'll soon see, son!"
Once their body searches were completed, the man led Robert and Alan over to the door, the police officers and civilians parting before them to the sides of the corridor. As he knocked gently on the door again, he turned to them.

"Now mind your language in there, lads. Don't go upsetting them, okay?"

"Okay," they mumbled in reply as a low voice beyond the door said:

"Enter."
The man pushed open the door. Then as the two brothers hesitated to go in, he said:

"Don't worry lads, you'll be fine. They don't bite".

He gently urged them forward.

"Not much anyway!" he added, almost too quietly to be heard.

When the brothers stepped into the room and the door was firmly closed behind them, the first thing that they saw was the figure on the bed. John Smith was lying on the bed, the lower half of his body covered by a hospital blanket. The rest of his body was swathed in numerous bandages. There were so many tubes and wires hooking him up to nearby machines that they had the immediate impression that he was some sort of insect caught up in a giant spider's web. Smith's eyes were open and staring at them, almost angrily. His jaw was clenched and he wasn't smiling like they had expected him to be, like they always remembered him. He looked thin and old and very, very frail. Both of them felt a lump rise into their throat as they stood there and stared at their father.

"Hello, Dad," said Robert, quietly.

"Hello, Dad. How're you doing?" said Alan.

Smith's face softened at hearing the concern in his sons' voices. The angry blaze in his coal-black eyes faded.

"Hello lads. I'm okay, thanks," he answered, his voice hoarse and weak.

At last a smile began to edge on to his battered face.

"It's good to see you."

"You too, Dad."

There was a slight clearing of a throat from the side of the room and both of the brothers, startled at the interruption, turned to see who had made the noise. For a second or two they were confused by what they saw, forgetting in the spell of the moment that there was somebody else in the room, somebody very important. For another few seconds, as they continued to stare at the two people sitting in chairs, they couldn't figure out what was happening and who these people were. They appeared to be just ordinary people, quite old, the woman in a long tan-coloured overcoat and matching plain headscarf, and the man in an old-fashioned tweed suit and with a flat cap on his head. Then it dawned on them both at the same moment and they were struck dumb.

The spell was finally broken by a gentle laugh from John Smith.

"Let me introduce you all," he said, pushing up the top half of his body from his bed and grimacing with pain. "These two young, handsome men are Robert and Alan, my sons."

There was obvious pride in his voice as he said this.

"Robert, Alan, please say hello to Her Royal Majesty, Queen Elizabeth and to His Royal Highness the Duke of Edinburgh, Prince Philip."

FIFTY-ONE

26th July
Redhill, Surrey

Linda Webb sat by Smith's bedside, looking at his sleeping face. They were alone in the room and Linda was holding Smith's hand in her own as she studied him. She saw him slowly emerge into wakefulness and then his eyes flickered open. For just a moment there was a small flame of fear in them before he realised where he was and recognised her.

"Oh, hi, Doc," he rasped.

"Hi yourself," she smiled.

"How long you been here?"

"Just a few minutes. My shift is about to end and I thought I'd call in and see how your morning has been. Did everything go okay?"

"Yeah, thanks. Well, sort of, anyway," he grimaced.

"It must have felt good to see your sons again?"

"Yeah it did. You should have seen their faces when they realised that the Queen and Prince Philip were here! They were flabbergasted! It was nice of the Royals to pop in and say thanks. Not everyone would have done that."

"Did you get much time on your own with your sons?"

"Yeah, thanks. HM and HRH just stayed on for a few more minutes, and then they left, warning my lads to stay 'hush hush' about meeting them here. They want to keep the visit secret, of course. They can't be seen to be hobnobbing with a murderer. Then me and the lads talked for about half an hour before they had to go. It wasn't easy though. Everything was a little bit stilted, if you know what I mean?"

"Well, you said itself John - a lot of water has flowed under the bridge. Just give it time and I'm sure that everything will work out in the end."

Smith grimaced again, shifting slightly on the bed.

"Are you in pain?"

"It never goes away, Doc. A bit like heartache."

He coughed, but at least this time there was no blood.

"We won't be seeing each other again. That was the one and only time that I'll see my sons."

"Why? I don't understand. I thought you would all get along fine once you got together. What happened?"

"Nothing happened, Doc. It did go fine. They wanted me to have the money that they got from The Sun for my story, but I told them to keep it. It's no bloody good to me where I'm going. Then we talked quite a bit about the past and they told me what they were up to these days. Alan even brought in some pictures of my two granddaughters. Can you imagine that? I'm a bloody grandad and I didn't even know it! Have a look over there."

He nodded slightly towards the bedside cabinet where there were a handful of photographs lying on top. Linda reached across and went through them slowly. They showed two sweet looking blonde-haired little girls pulling faces at the camera.

"Awww...they're gorgeous John. You must be so proud!"

"Yeah, I am," he smiled. Then his face fell. "Shame I'm never going to meet them, Doc."

"Don't say that, of course you will. It's only a matter of time."

"Ah, there's that bloody word again: time."

He gave her hand a squeeze.

"Time is one thing that I haven't got, Linda."

He smiled tenderly as he looked up into this beautiful woman's eyes.

"Even if I survive and get out of here, it'll only be to go to prison for the rest of my life. I'm a murderer, Linda. I murdered several people when I escaped from court and went on the rampage last year. As the Queen said to me this morning - I can be forgiven a lot of things because of what I did on the plane a few weeks ago, but I can't be forgiven for taking away the lives of other innocent people."

He coughed again, his body jerking in spasms from the pain. Then he smiled once more at Linda as the pain passed away as quickly as it had come.

"I guess I'm never going to get that Royal Pardon that *The Sun* wants for me."

"I'm so sorry, John."

"Don't feel sorry for me, Linda. I knew what I was doing when I killed those people. Okay, I happen to think that they bloody well deserved it, but I doubt that a jury will see it that way. If it ever gets that far, that is."

"Of course it will. You'll get better, I promise you."

"I've no doubt of that, Linda. It's not dying of my injuries that I'm worried about, girl. You've never lived in the same world as me, thank God. In my world there are lots of people who would love to see me dead and buried rather than have my day in court, where I can tell the entire world about all of their dirty little secrets."

"You mean the Iranians, with this *Fatwa* thing?"

"No Doc, they're the least of my worries," he laughed quietly. "It's my own bloody side that I'm worried about. The Secret Intelligence Service, the 'spooks' as we call them. They'll be the ones that come for me and I just don't have the energy to run away or to fight them anymore."

"Surely they can't do that, John? You've got police protection just outside the door. How could they even *get* in here?"

She looked alarmed. John squeezed her hand again.

"In my world there are lots of ways: kill the guards; pay one of the nurses to give me a fatal injection; blow the whole bloody hospital up and blame it on the Iranians. If they are determined enough to get me, then they will."

Linda didn't know what to say. He seemed so sure of what he was saying, he seemed almost resigned to it; and she knew in her heart that he was right - she didn't know his world. John Smith had lived most of his life in a world of war, horror, brutality, death and destruction. Even as a surgeon, Linda doubted that she had seen as much blood as Smith had in his lifetime. She felt her eyes filling with tears and wanted to tell this man that she had fallen in love with him, for she realised this now, and that she would do her best to make everything okay for him. But it was too late. His eyelids had fluttered down and he had drifted back into exhausted sleep again. She stayed with him for a while until a nurse came in to give him an injection. Then she wiped away her tears as she did not want anyone to see them and left.

FIFTY-TWO

26th July
Redhill, Surrey

"Wake up you bastard!"
Smith was shaken roughly by the shoulder. His eyes flickered wide open in surprise, then narrowed as he recognised who it was that had awoken him.
"Oh. It's *you*, you fucking idiot!" Smith spat out, his eyes now two blazing coals of pure rage. "I was wondering when you'd show your fucking face again. What the fuck do you want?"
Detective Chief Inspector Alan Davies smiled condescendingly down at Smith.
"Just checking up on you to make sure you're getting better, John, that's all."
"Super."
"After all, you've got to be fit and healthy to get sent down for life!"
Smith suddenly laughed, his good humour returning.
"You're a useless prat, Davies. You've no idea about what's happening around you, do you?"
"I understand enough to know that you will never ever get out of prison, Smith! You've fucked the police around too much. It's about time that you got your comeuppance!"
Smith relaxed, another smile playing on his face.
"Ah, what you really mean, Alan, is that I've fucked you around too much. What's up mate? Have I messed up

your career?"

Rage now flared in Davies's eyes and he could hardly control his voice.

"You fucking cunt! You've no idea what you've done to me! I had it *all* before you turned up. I was the DCI in charge of the Serious and Organised Crime Agency in Cambridgeshire. I was on the fast-track to promotion and I'd have probably made Chief Constable in another five or six years. And then you turn up in my fucking life!"

"As I remember it mate, it was the other way around. I was enjoying a quiet life when you and your fucking goons burst into my place and arrested me for something that I hadn't fucking done!"

"Bollocks, Smith, or whatever your fucking name is! You may have fooled the rest of the British people into believing that you were set up and that you're as pure and innocent as the driven snow, but I know different, you bastard. You're as guilty as fucking sin!"

Smith smiled again, his brain suddenly realising what had caused this late night visit from Davies.

"You've been moved sideways, haven't you mate? You hoped that catching me would get you back on the fast track to promotion, but they've moved you on to another unit haven't they? What is it - the dog patrol?"

He couldn't help but laugh softly at the look on Davies's face, which had turned the colour of a jar of beetroot.

"You bastard! You utter and complete bastard! You've ruined my life, do you know that? Completely ruined it!"

Smith was shocked by the strength of Davies's reaction. Jesus, the bastard was nearly crying! He almost felt sorry for the guy. Almost.

"But at least you'll be going straight to prison, you fucker. There'll be no new trial for you!"

Smith was taken aback by this barb. *What the hell does he mean, "no new trial"? Does he know that the spooks will try to top me? Is he a party to it?*

"You're not working for the bloody spooks now are

you? Are you in the Increment?" Smith couldn't quite believe that this straight-laced jackass would join the 'wet job crew'; but he had to ask anyway.

"There is no bloody Increment, you stupid little man."

"Oh, of course not. The Increment never existed, did it? That's what the bloody spooks want everyone to believe. Don't tell me that you believe them, Davies? Even you are not that naive, not after all that's happened."

"It doesn't matter what I believe or not. The fact is that you've already been sentenced to life in fucking prison, with no chance of parole. You're going away forever, you little fucker!"

"Sentenced? When? What for?" Smith was totally confused now.

What's going on? He thought. *Have I missed something?*

Davies looked very pleased with himself.

"You really don't know, do you?" he asked.

"Know what, you fucker, just spit it out!"

"15th October, last year. Don't you remember being in court for the abduction, rape and murder of little Mary Knightly?"

"Yeah, of course I remember." *Shit, I'm getting a bad feeling about this.* "I also remember escaping before they could sentence me."

Davies laughed at this.

"So? Just because you did a runner and went on a murder spree, it doesn't mean that the court just packed up and went home. After everything settled down, the jury was brought in and told the court that they had found you guilty. Unanimously, I might add!"

"But you *know* that the trial was a crock of shit. You know that I didn't do it!" Smith was exasperated now. "You were there in the Chief Constable's office when Harry admitted that he had set me up, and you heard the tape of what that bastard of a bent prosecutor said! He admitted setting me up as well, along with the fucking judge and your sidekick Price!"

"It doesn't mean a thing, you prick. You killed all of them, so there's no one left to help you and back up your poxy story."

"But what about the tape? Surely that proves that I was innocent?"

"Don't be a silly twat! You tortured Steve Mackay with a fucking electric drill! No jury in the world would ever believe what he said under duress like that!"
Davies was suddenly really enjoying himself.

"The judge sentenced you to life in your absence, with no chance of ever getting parole. You're going down, Smith. Like I said, for life!"

"Jesus! I'm going down as a fucking *paedophile*?"

"That's right mate, as a fucking *nonce*! Ha! Ha! It serves you right for fucking up my career. I hope the other inmates beat the fuck out of you every day, you miserable little wanker! You fucking turd! You shit-filled bastard cretin! The great John Smith is going down for life as a paedo! Ha! Ha! Ha!"
He was hanging right over Smith like a deranged ape, spittle flying from his mouth as he laughed and laughed at him.

"Oh for God's sake, Alan! Do shut up and start behaving like a man!"
This was a new voice, a woman's. Smith hadn't even noticed that anyone else was in the room, so focused had he been on his nemesis and his horrific news.

Davies was utterly taken aback by the tone of his assistant's voice as Detective Constable Helen Wright stepped forward and grabbed him by the arm.

"Let's go, Sir, before you make an utter and complete idiot of yourself."
Davies held back.

"But you know what this bastard has done to me!" his voice rose a few more decibels. "He's fucking ruined my career!"

"Oh for God's sake!"

Helen was on a roll now and wasn't going to stop. She had finally had an epiphany about the man that she thought she had fallen in love with. He wasn't the man she had thought him to be. He was a complete and utter wanker.

"Just fucking grow *up* will you. So you've been moved to the Child Protection Unit. It's not the end of the bloody world! Jesus! Look at Smith, he's been stabbed so many times that he'd leak if he drank a glass of water, and he's facing a lifetime in prison because he was set up by that twat Henry Price and the others. Yet you don't see him crying about it do you?"

Davies was at a complete loss for words, his mouth opening and closing like a stranded goldfish gasping for air, as Helen steadily pushed him towards the exit.

"We both know that he didn't kill that little girl. Isn't it enough that he's got to go to prison as paedophile without you rejoicing about it so much?"

As she gave him a final shove out of the door, Helen found time to quickly turn and give Smith a hard look.

"I'm sorry," she said.

Exhaustion was once again tugging at Smith's eyelids. He was finding it impossible to reconcile what he'd just been told, but his battered body still needed to close down and rest.

"Not your fault, love."

Smith and Helen shared a brief look, and then Helen and Davies were gone.

FIFTY-THREE

27th July
Redhill, Surrey

Aw, not again! was the first thought that entered Smith's head as he was roughly woken up by a shake of his shoulder. As he opened his eyes and looked around, he realised it must be some time during the night. The main lights of the unit had been turned off and there was just the relatively bright but eerie glow from the instrumentation of the intensive care monitors lighting up the room.

"Ah," he said when he saw the unwavering barrel of a pistol held up just a few inches in front of his face.
He took a deep breath, steadying himself, and then slowly let it out.

"About fucking time. I was beginning to wonder if you guys were ever going to turn up."
He closed his eyes again and relaxed, resigned to his fate.

"Get on with it then."

He had been expecting this moment for a long time. Not looking forward to it, but expecting it just the same. He had known all along that the spooks would rather have him as an embarrassing body than as a much more embarrassing live witness to their machinations. And then, of course, there was the equally compelling motive of revenge as well. Smith had killed two of their senior officers, one of them a former Chief of the Secret Intelligence Service, and

- the other one - Harry, the Head of the Increment. He had made them all look like bumbling assholes in the eyes of the public as he had set about his brief reign of terror and destruction last year. There was no way that they were ever going to let him get away with this. *Shame about Linda*, he thought as he lay there waiting to die. *She'll be really upset by this. I hope she gets over it quickly.*

"Fuck you, yer murderin' feckin' bastard! I'll kill yer when I feel like it, not when you feckin' tell me too!" Smith opened his eyes to see that the barrel of the pistol had been withdrawn. For the first time he could focus on the shadowy figure standing by his bed.

"Don't talk to him, old man. Just kill him," came another voice.

This one was short and clipped and definitely English, unlike the broad Belfast accent of the man nearest - the one with the gun.

"And fuck you too! I've been waiting a long feckin' time to kill this motherfucker. I'll take me own sweet time about it, so fuck off."

Smith could see both men more clearly now that his eyes were getting accustomed to the low light levels. Both of them wore the bulky body armour and black uniforms of armed police officers. Obviously they had used this disguise to get uninterrupted access to him. *For once the spooks have done a good job*, he thought to himself, unable to drop his own professional outlook even at the moment of his impending death. One of them, the English one, was still wearing his helmet and goggles and standing by the half open door to the corridor, looking out to make sure that they weren't disturbed. The other one had taken off his head gear and was glaring down at Smith, his face a mask of pure bloody hatred.

"So you're a paddy," said Smith, addressing the closer of the two men. "Now there's a shocking surprise!" he laughed gently. "I'm guessing that this is personal for you? Am I right?"

"Too bloody true, yer Brit bastard! I've been looking forward to this moment fer a long feckin' time!"

"So who was it then? Who did I kill? Was it family, or a friend?"

The Irishman stepped closer, bringing up the barrel of the pistol to point once again at Smith's face.

"Thomas O'Connell. Do you remember Thomas O'Connell yer murderin' feckin' bastard? I want to know why you murdered him?"

Smith closed his eyes. He was absolutely exhausted and in a great deal of pain from his wounds still. His brain felt like a big lump of damp cotton wool inside his head, but he did his best to concentrate. The trouble was, he admitted to himself with a feeling of utter regret, there had been so many of them over those few short years when he had killed mercilessly for the Firm. Too bloody many to remember all of them clearly.

"I'm not being a cunt," he said quietly, "but I didn't always know what their names were, mate. Give us a clue. When and how did I do him?"

The Irishman leaned down closer until his eyes were only inches from Smith's. Smith could see the red veins prominent in the white of his eyes.

"You poxy fucker!"

Suddenly the man whipped the barrel of his pistol hard against Smith's cheek with a crack that snapped back his head onto his pillow. The sharp blow opened up the stitches of the semi-healed slash down one side of Smith's face that had been given to him by one of the Muslim hijackers. Smith turned his face back to the Irishman's, spitting out a trickle of blood from his mouth.

"Fuck you too, Paddy!"

His eyes were blazing.

"Just get it over with! You'd be doing me a favour."

The Irishman pulled back slightly, breathing deeply and trying to get a grip of his anger. He didn't want this to happen too quickly. He wanted to take his time with this fucker and make him suffer for what he had done to his little brother.

"My name is Sean O'Connell. Thomas O'Connell was my brother," he said. "He wasn't even involved with the feckin' IRA, and neither was I until you murdered him, yer bastard!"

Smith sighed.

"Look mate, I'm sorry for your loss. I just don't remember anyone of that name. You'll have to give me a little bit more information before I can tell you why I topped him."

Sean O'Connell was taken aback by the calmness of the English assassin. For all of the years that he had feverishly thought about and planned for this moment, most of them while he had been rotting away in an English fucking prison, he had never in his mind's eye expected the Englishman to be so unafraid. He knew deep inside that Smith wasn't lying to him. He didn't remember killing his poor fucking brother.

"Feckin' hell!" he half-shouted in his frustration.

"Keep the fucking noise down and kill the bastard," Chris Donnelly snarled from across the room. "Get on with it before someone realises that there are no bloody coppers on guard outside his room!"

"I told yer before, mate. Shut the fuck up! I don't take bloody orders from you!"

"Of course you bloody well do, you silly bloody paddy! How else do you think you got this chance to revenge yourself on your brother's killer? Jesus, just get on with it, will you!"

Sean O'Connell looked down at his brother's killer.

"Tom was only seventeen years old," he began. "He was a good lad, even managed to get himself a job as an apprentice mechanic. He'd done his best to stay out of the bloody IRA, even though all of his mates were dodging and diving for them and wanted him to join up. He was going to get married a few months after you murdered him, to a lovely wee lass. She still hasn't gotten over losing the love of her life."

Sean's voice was dull and monotone as he related the facts of his brother's death.

"So when did I kill him?"

Smith could only imagine the heartache that O'Connell was going through. *How many brothers, sisters, parents and kids have I totally fucked up by murdering their loved ones over the years?* he thought. *Must be bloody hundreds of the poor bastards.*

"It was the 12th of August, 1985. Tom was leaving his house in Locan Street, just off Beechmount Avenue and the Falls Road in West Belfast. It was seven in the morning and he was on his way to work. You caught him just as he got to his garden gate and beat him to death with an iron bar. You smashed nearly every bone in his body but it still took him a couple of hours to die."

For the first time, his voice nearly broke from the grief that he had been carrying around bottled up inside him for all of these years.

"Nobody in the street heard or saw the attack. The person to find him bleeding to death on the garden path was his fiancée when she left for work a half hour after you'd beaten him."

He glared down at Smith, anger returning to his voice.

"He was only a kid! He didn't stand a chance against a bastard like you, did he? Do you remember him now, yer feckin' cunt!"

He pointed his pistol straight between the eyes of Smith, his finger slowly tightening on the trigger.

FIFTY-FOUR

27th July
Redhill, Surrey

John Smith lay perfectly still, his eyes tightly closed and his face screwed up as he tried to remember. He had killed a few IRA men by beating them to death, but for the life of him he couldn't pull up an image of this kid, Thomas O'Connell, in his mind's eye. Then it dawned on him. His eyes snapped open.

"When did you say he was killed?"

"Monday, the 12th of August 1985."

Smith looked Sean O'Connell right in the eyes. He was tempted to lie, to let this Irishman kill him. What did it matter in the end? He knew that his time was short no matter what he did, and it would be better than getting sent to prison for life as a fucking paedophile. Why not end it now and get it over with?

"It wasn't me," he said instead. "I was in South America for the whole of August 1985. I didn't even put a foot in England, never mind Belfast. In fact I was overseas for the whole of the end of that year. Sorry mate," he added gently.

Sean stared at him angrily.

"Don't lie to me, yer feckin' murderer!"

"I'm not lying, mate, I'm telling you the truth. It wasn't me that killed your brother."

Smith looked over to the Englishman standing by the door, who was now watching the pair of them closely.

"Ask him."

He nodded towards the spook.

"He's in the Increment right? He'll know that I wasn't in the country. Ask him."

"I've had enough of this fucking pissing around," snarled Donnelly.

He strode over to the Irishman and grabbed him by the front of his body armour.

"Just kill the bastard! Who cares if he really killed your brother or not, you silly twat! Just pull the trigger and have done with it!"

O'Connell looked totally confused. He stared into Donnelly's face, then back at Smith.

"You're telling the bloody truth, aren't you?" his voice was low and trembling, all of his assertions suddenly thrown to the wind.

"Yeah, mate, sorry. It wasn't me."

"Oh, for fuck's sake! If you won't get the job done then I will!"

Donnelly raised his MP7 sub-machine gun and suddenly Smith was staring right into the barrel of the Englishman's gun. He knew that his time had finally come and closed his eyes, waiting for the crack of the round leaving the barrel, wondering with his last thoughts whether he would feel anything or whether it would all be over too quickly. His last and final thought was of Linda.

Instead of the bang of the gun, there was a loud intake of breath. Smith opened his eyes in astonishment, hardly believing that he was still alive and breathing. Donnelly was frozen, the Irishman standing next to him with the barrel of his pistol jammed against the Englishman's cheek. O'Connell was fuming, his eyes blazing and his hand shaking with his pent-up rage.

"You've feckin' lied ter me all along, haven't yer, yer feckin' weasel? You knew all along that Smith had never even touched my brother, never mind killed him. Who was it that really did him in? Was it you, yer feckin' bastard!"

Donnelly raised a weak laugh at this.

"Of course it wasn't me! I was only three years old in 1985!"

"Yeah, I suppose you were at that. But yer do know who murdered my brother, don't yer?"

Donnelly's eyes were big and round behind the lenses of his goggles. He hesitated before answering.

"Okay, okay. So we knew that Smith didn't kill your brother. It's true that we knew he was overseas at the time and couldn't have done it, but we don't know who did, alright? It could have been anyone. They were bad times and people were getting murdered all over the place. It might even have been the IRA for all we know!"

"Shit! Then why did yer lead me on? Why did yer pull me out of feckin' jail to kill this motherfucker? Why didn't yer just do it yer feckin' selves?"

This time it was John Smith who laughed.

"It's obvious when you think about it. They've set you up as a patsy, mate."

"What do yer mean, a patsy?"

Smith sighed.

"Look Paddy, just think about it for a minute. The spooks want me out of the way, okay? But if they just have me topped there's bound to be loads of questions about who did it and why, right? The bloody press would be hounding the government for answers, the government would be hounding the Firm for the same answers. There'd be questions in the House of Commons and all sorts. In other words there'd be a right bloody fuss!"

"Yeah? So feckin' what?"

Smith sighed again.

"So think about it clearly. If it came out that I was killed by an ex-IRA man, in revenge for murdering his brother, then there wouldn't be half as much of a fuss, would there? It would all sort of make sense to everyone, right?"

"Yeah. I can see that. But how would everyone know that it was me that feckin' killed yer? I work for the

Increment. It's not as though they're goin' to hold their feckin' 'ands up and say 'It was feckin' O'Connell, but it's alright, he was working for us'."

"No, mate. That would never happen."
Smith looked straight at him, willing him to understand what he was trying to imply.

"Not unless you turned up dead by my bedside."

"What?" O'Connell stared back at Smith, and then he turned his blazing eyes back onto Donnelly as the realisation suddenly hit him. "You was going to kill me too wasn't yer? Yer feckin' bastard! All of this time training me up, and getting me even more riled up about feckin' Smith, and all of the time yer were just plannin' to bloody kill me after I killed him! That would tie in very feckin' nice, wouldn't it? A feckin' IRA hitman escapes from jail and kills the bloke who's a thorn in yer feckin' side! Feckin' perfect!"

With that outburst O'Connell finally gave way completely to his temper and smashed the pistol in his hand into Donnelly's face, clubbing him unconscious to the ground.

The Irishman stood there, breathing hard as he looked down at the slumped form of the Englishman.

"Bastard!" he spat, as he cracked his foot into the side of Donnelly's head.

"You feckin' lying English bastard!" he raised his pistol, ready to put a round through the prone man's face. "You've played me all along, you feckin' cunt, haven't yer!"

His finger began to tighten on the trigger in his blind rage.

"Hold on! Wait!" Smith rasped.

The Irishman threw him a glaring look, the hand holding the pistol not moving an inch. Smith tried to raise his arm to reach behind his own head, but he didn't have the strength. His hand slumped back down onto his bed cover, defeated.

"Use the pillow, mate. If you shoot him like this you'll have everyone in the bloody hospital running around like headless chickens! Use your brains, man!"

Sean O'Connell continued to stare at him for a moment or too. Then with a half-grin he said:

"Thanks. Yeah, that'll do nicely."

He reached behind Smith's head and none too gently yanked out one of the pillows from beneath him. Bending over he folded the pillow in two and put it against Donnelly's face, shoved the barrel of his pistol into it and pulled the trigger. There was a muted 'crack' and instantly the room filled with the smell of burnt cordite and scorched blood as Donnelly's head imploded to the low velocity round.

"Feckin' tosser!" he said, standing up and aiming another kick at the splattered head of the dead SIS man.

"That's better," whispered Smith, his strength at last beginning to leave him.

Sean turned back to him.

"And what shall I do about you?" he said. "You may not have killed my brother, but you're still a murderin' feckin' Englishman."

Smith managed to smile at him.

"Too true, Paddy, too true. Whatever."

Then he passed back into unconsciousness.

FIFTY-FIVE

27th July
Vauxhall Cross, London

Sir Rupert Giles was still at his desk at one thirty in the morning. He scanned through the notes of a briefing (about the damning evidence that had been found at the former terrorist training camp in Algeria) that he was due to give to the Prime Minister in a few hours' time. He was amazed that anything had been found at all, considering the devastation of the site after the hammering it had taken during Operation Retribution. But his technicians had sifted through the burnt and mangled wreckage of the place, bagging what bodies they could find for identification and searching for anything at all that would give them a clue as to how the terrorist leader, Abdullah ibn Nazid al-Filasteeni, had raised enough cash to get his faction of *Jihadists* funded. It was a miracle, but they had found the remnants of a sheath of documents, badly scorched but still readable, that had included bank statements and, even more surprisingly, copies of money transfers from the government of Iran to the terrorists. At last they now had definite proof that the Islamic state had funded the attack on the British Monarchy. *Wonderful!* he thought. *Now we'll have no problem getting more government cash to fund our own intelligence-gathering projects within Iran.* He almost rubbed his hands together at the thought of all the money that would be forthcoming to the Firm. *Of course, if some of that money finds its way into my own personal bank account, who would ever be the wiser?*

His mobile phone rang, startling him from his reverie. He looked at the caller ID. *Ha, Donnelly. Good, hopefully he'll have some more good news! This could turn into a great day!*

"Yes?" he answered the call. "I hope that you have some good news for me, Chris?" There was a pause on the line.

"I'm afraid not. Donnelly's dead."

Sir Rupert's mind went into instant overdrive. He knew a Belfast accent when he heard one.

"Is that you, Sean? What happened? Did Smith put up a fight?"

"No, Sir Rupert. Smith couldn't fight his way out of a feckin' wet paper bag. He's way too ill."

There was a touch of humour to the Irishman's voice that the Chief of the Secret Intelligence Service didn't like at all. He had a feeling of dark foreboding.

"I've found out the truth about your feckin' plan."

"What truth? What are you talking about, Sean? What plan?"

His own voice took on a wheedling tone that he fought to control. It was obvious that everything was suddenly going tits up.

"Your plan, Sir bloody Rupert! The plan that got me released from prison so I'd do your feckin' dirty work for yer. The plan that blamed Smith for my brother's death when he wasn't even on the right side of the feckin' Atlantic!"

"I don't know what you're talking about, O'Connell. Why don't you come into Vauxhall and we'll discuss it like civilised men?"

"What! Do yer think that I'm feckin' nuts as well as bloody stupid fer taking in all of yer feckin' lies! No way! I'm out of here and you'll never catch me, yer feckin' tosser!" Sir Rupert's voice suddenly took on a hard edge.

"Really, O'Connell? You really think that with all of the Firm's resources and manpower that we won't find you?"

"Oh, I've no doubt that you'll try your best, Sir Rupert. Meanwhile, why don't yer think about it the other way around?"

"What do you mean? The other way around what?"

"Maybe I won't run *too* far, Sir Rupert. Just maybe I'll come looking for *you* rather than the other way around, eh?"

With that the line went dead and Sir Rupert Giles sat there and stared at the mobile in his hand. He felt the hand of cold fear run up and down his spine.

FIFTY-SIX

27th July
London

"Good afternoon. This is the BBC *News at One*, with Anna Ford and Darren Jordan. Today's breaking news: A serving member of the Secret Intelligence Service, who had been heavily involved in the recent attack in Algeria during Operation Retribution, has been found dead at his home in Doncaster today. Local police were called to the scene in the early hours of this morning when a neighbour reported hearing a gunshot. A police spokesman, in a statement released to the media, has said that the police are not looking for anyone else in connection with the death."

"The statement also indicated that a suicide note had been left at the man's home".

"The Secret Intelligence Service, more commonly known as MI6, is the government service that originally identified the terrorist camp in Algeria. When contacted earlier today for a statement on the man's suicide, the service declined to comment, although one insider spoke to our reporter unofficially and told her that the man in question, who had previously been awarded the Military Cross during his service in the British Army, had only been a member of the service for a short time. He had been well-liked by other members of staff and they were shocked that he had obviously been hiding his deep depression from them so well".

"Other news today: The drop in bank loan rates..."

FIFTY-SEVEN

27th July
Redhill, Surrey

"Oh, John, I'm so glad that you're okay. What happened last night? I was extremely worried when I heard!"
Linda stood by Smith's bed, her face so concerned that John was almost tempted to tell her the truth. However, he had agreed with the police to lie about the early morning events, so lie he would. He would do his best to protect Linda from the unwholesome truth.
"It was nothing, love, just a couple of journalists that tried to break in and interview me." He patted her hand in reassurance. "I didn't even know about it myself until I woke up and one of the coppers told me."
"But I've heard rumours that there was a body found in the room!"
"Just rumours, Linda, that's all. Apparently one of the journalists was a little bit drunk and started a fight with one of the coppers. He got hit on the bonce, but they say that he'll be alright."
Smith tried to laugh it off, but it was hard for him to lie to this woman. He had learned to trust her with his life over the past few weeks, and he now knew that he had also fallen in love with her.
"The coppers want the whole thing kept quiet so that there's no comeback on them for not doing their job right. I don't mind. Everyone knows that they're all

plonkers anyway. No *new* news there!"
Linda didn't look convinced by the concocted story.

"But how did they get in here? There's always at least two armed policemen outside your door, especially since the Iranians issued that *Fatwa* against you!"

"Ah, that's why they want it covered up, love. Apparently one of the coppers had gone for a pee and the other bugger had fallen asleep on the job. The bloody journalists just crept past him. They were about to wake me up when the first copper came back from the loo and caught them at it. That's when they had the bit of a to-do. Like I said, I slept through the whole bloody thing!" He gave her what he hoped was one of his genuine smiles. "Anyway, forget last night, I'm afraid that I do have some bad news for you, Linda."

She stared down at him, looking at the sadness coming over his face, and felt a stab of dread hit her heart.

"What is it, John?"

"Well, they're going to haul my arse out of here to some secure prison hospital sometime later today."

"What! They can't do that! I'm your physician and there's no way that you're fit to be moved. You're still too ill!"

Smith smiled gently when he saw the fierce fire come into her eyes. But he had spent the last few hours having nightmares about what would have happened to Linda if she had been in the room when the two killers had turned up. She could have been hurt or killed. It was *his* idea to be moved, and the coppers had readily agreed to it.

"No, Linda. I've agreed to it. I'm a lot better now, thanks to you."

"But they can't take you away! It's not fair, what if I never see...," she broke off before she finished saying out loud what was really on her mind, and his too.

"It's okay, love, I know what you're saying."
He held both of her hands now, held them tight.

"Look, we both know that there's no future for us."
Smith felt a wound to his own heart open up as he saw her

face fall.

"I'm really sorry that we met in these circumstances. If things had been different..." This time it was him who left his sentence unfinished.

Linda stood looking down on him, and then suddenly she was in his arms and sobbing.

"Oh, John. Oh, John, I'll miss you!"

"I know Linda, I know. I'll miss you too!"

Even he was surprised to hear the words out loud. They clung to each other.

FIFTY-EIGHT

27th and 28th July
Winson Green, Birmingham

John Smith was transferred out of the East Surrey Hospital in an ambulance with a police escort of two vehicles, one of them an armed response vehicle. The authorities were taking no chances that he might escape from them again. He was sedated for the trip and unconscious for most of it, only stirring when the jolting and bumping along Britain's roads made the pain from his wounds unbearable. But he kept his mouth shut and didn't complain. He was in the system now and he knew that to show any weakness at all would mean that it would be used against him at some point. From now on he must grin and bear it. He had no choice.

    The trip from Redhill in Surrey to Her Majesty's Prison, Birmingham took several hours and the ambulance didn't reach the prison gates until the early hours of the following morning. Smith had passed out again by then, and missed all the excitement when he was eventually handed over to the Group Four Security (G4S) personnel who ran the prison. He was taken directly to the prison's healthcare centre and put into a bed.

    HM Prison, Birmingham, better known as 'Winson Green Nick' (as it's located in the Winson Green area of Birmingham, close to the city centre) is a Category B prison which holds nearly one thousand, five hundred remand and convicted male prisoners. It is run privately by G4S for the prison service. The old part of the prison is Victorian and was built in 1849, and still looks as bleak and unwelcoming as it has for the last one hundred and sixty years. However, a multi-million pound investment programme by the Prison Service in 2004 added extra accommodation wings, a new healthcare centre, educational facilities, workshops and a gym. Despite all of these improvements though, the prison still suffers from chronic overcrowding and a lack of resources and staff. A stay at Winson Green is still intended to be a harsh punishment for its inmates.

The morning following the transfer, Smith awoke to find himself in a great deal of pain. Some of his wounds had opened and were oozing blood, soaking through the bandages. Others just throbbed constantly. Linda had told him once that the pain was a good thing because it meant that he was still alive and that his wounds were slowly healing. At this precise moment Smith wasn't so sure about that. He just wanted it all to go away.

  He was in a small room in the healthcare centre, and the first thing that he noticed was the lack of the specialist monitors and equipment that had filled his room in the East Surrey Hospital. Here it was very basic; an IV flowing into his arm, carrying plasma and painkillers. The rest of the room was plain and empty, with a small washstand in one corner against the wall, one plastic chair, no windows and just the one wooden door. Smith sighed to himself. God knows how long he was going to be kept in this depressing joint. If the pain didn't kill him, then the boredom surely would. He made his mind up right then to get well and fit again as soon as was humanly possible. He would push himself to get out of this place as quickly as he could. He knew from his previous incarceration at the hands of Her Majesty that even being banged up in a cell for twenty three hours a day, with a convict for company, was infinitely preferable to this bloody nightmare. As it turned out he needn't have worried.

  His first visitor was one of the prison doctors. He was

a small Indian man whose grasp of English appeared to be good; it was just that his accent was so strong that Smith had to ask him to repeat everything he said three or four times before he could understand him. In the end he got the gist of what he was saying, which was that the healthcare centre was not set up to deal with long term medical care. The doctor couldn't understand why Smith had been sent there in the first place. Smith could though - he had had an inkling that this would happen to him. Essentially, he was being isolated and abandoned to the system. It was clear that he would soon be moved into the prison population whether he was fit and well enough or not. *Ah well*, he thought, *sink or swim time again*.

His second visitor confirmed it. It was mid-afternoon when the prison Governor walked into his room.

"Welcome to Winson Green, Mr Smith," the small dapper man said without a smile. "I trust that your journey from Surrey was not too odious? My name is Jeremy Bradsworth, and I'm the Governor of this prison."

"Super. The trip was fine thank you, I slept through most of it."

"Yes, so I was informed. I must say that everything about your transfer here is very irregular."

"Really?"

"Yes. I've worked at this institution for five years and I've never been ordered to take on a Category A prisoner before. Most irregular!"

He smiled at Smith for the first time and seemed to relax a little. He even pulled up a chair and sat down next to the bed, loosening his collar and tie as he did so.

"I don't really know what to make of it to tell you the truth, Mr Smith."

"In what way?"

The Governor paused before answering, getting his thoughts together.

"Well, first of all, Mr Smith, I have obviously heard all about your heroic act aboard the Gambia flight, as have most of the people in the world, I dare say!" he laughed gently. "Then, of course, we find out that you've been a spy, a soldier and a Government assassin! The Government has denied all of this of course, but just about everyone believes you, no matter what the politicians say. After all, no one ever believes a politician.

Then we find out that you are the same John Smith who escaped from court last year and caused such mayhem; and finally we are reminded that you were found guilty of the abduction, rape and murder of a little girl. It's all very beguiling, but also very confusing. Of course, I don't think that there is a person alive in this country who actually believes that you murdered that girl, and I'd even go so far as to say in private that most of us have come to the conclusion that you have been set up because of your past. However, you have been found guilty, and as far as the system - and this prison - are concerned then guilty you are, and you will be treated as such."

"I understand that."

"Good, because it will make your life so much easier if you accept that as a fact of life, and don't fight it all of the time!"

"I said that I understood, not that I won't fight it."

"Well, that's your choice, Mr Smith, but it won't help you in the long run. Even if you appeal, the due process will take several years, and there is no guarantee that you will be found not guilty."

"I understand that, too. But you're digressing from the question I asked. Why is it irregular for me to be transferred here?"

"Yes, of course, why indeed? You see, Mr Smith, there are several anomalies here. In the normal course of things a man with your extensive injuries should be in a prison with a fully-equipped hospital and not in a place such as this, which, as you can see, has only the most basic facilities. This is a healthcare centre and not a hospital."

"Yes, the doctor has just said as much."

"Indeed. The problem here is that I cannot authorise you to stay more than forty-eight hours in this centre. After that, you must either be transferred to a real hospital or placed within a cell, and I have been ordered by my superiors to put you amongst the general prison population, and not to transfer you away. Then, there is the fact that as a convicted murderer you should be at a maximum security Category A prison. Winson Green is a Category B prison, which means that we deal with the type of criminal who is less of a danger to the public, such as muggers, burglars, car thieves *etc*. I have never heard of a Category A prisoner being placed straight into a Category B prison before! It's a bit like putting the cat amongst the pigeons!"

"Well you don't have to worry about me, Governor. In the state I'm in I'm sure I won't be able to hurt any of your other inmates."

The Governor smiled weakly at Smith's joke.

"Glad to hear it. However, it's you that I'm more worried about, not the other way around, and for a couple of reasons. For a start you are a convicted paedophile, whether you and I like it or not. Convicted sex offenders like you are normally put under what we call 'Rule 45', which means that they are housed in a wing with other sex offenders and kept away from the general prison population. This is of course to stop 'nonces' (as paedophiles are known) being attacked by the other prisoners. Not that it always stops such abuse. The second reason is that it is well known that the Iranian government has issued a death sentence on you. What do they call it? A *Fatwa*?" Smith nodded. "Well, this prison gets all of its prisoners from the West Midlands region, and there is, as you may know, a high immigrant population within the area, including those of the Islamic faith. In fact, about twenty per cent of the prison population here is Muslim, although I'd guess that only about half of these are practising Muslims. As I understand it, this *Fatwa* issued against you calls for every good Muslim to attempt to kill you?"

Smith nodded again, suddenly feeling very tired and knowing where this conversation was headed.

"So you're going to tell me that despite Rule 45 and the *Fatwa*, you have been ordered to put me amongst the other prisoners regardless, yes?"

"Yes, indeed. As I said before, it's most irregular." Smith sighed.

"Not really, Governor. It's the Government's way of shutting me up. They want me to be killed by another prisoner. Whether it's for a religious reason or for any other reason doesn't really matter to the powers that be. I'm a problem that they want solved as soon as possible."

"But surely anyone can see what they are doing? The British public are not idiots. They'll see what's happening?"

"Of course, but even if they cared, what could they do about it? For that matter, what can you or I do about it? *Nothing*, is the answer. You've got your orders and I've got no choice whatsoever."

"But it's wrong!"

"Listen, Governor. I know that and you know that, but as far as the rest of the world goes, I'm afraid they just don't give a toss. I'm here, and I'll do the best I can to survive. That's all I can say."

"Well, for what it's worth, Mr Smith, I wish you good luck!"

"Super."

"I will of course do everything within my limited power to help you and to keep you safe. From what I've heard in the staff canteen, so will most of my officers."

"I'm glad to hear it, thanks."

"However, although most of my officers are trustworthy, and by the way a lot of them are ex-military as well, there are always the bad eggs. I'm afraid that I cannot oversee or control every minute of your stay here. I'm also afraid to say that a high proportion of my officers are Muslims."

"Super."

FIFTY-NINE

1st August
Winson Green, Birmingham

True to his word, the Governor had John Smith transferred out of the healthcare centre once his forty-eight hours were up. He was put into a cell on the third floor of 'A Wing', one of the older Victorian wings of the prison. The cell was small, just about big enough for the two beds that were in it, the toilet, (which had a waist high screen down one side) and not much else. Smith was lucky with his cell mate, who turned out to be a burglar called Gordon. He was chatty, but not *too* chatty, and definitely not a man who thought of himself as a hard case. In fact Gordon was quite chuffed to have a 'celebrity' like Smith as a cell mate, and while he did ask Smith lots of questions, (especially about the fight with the terrorists on board the Gambia flight, which seemed to fascinate him) he also appeared to have a sensitive side, and could tell when he needed to shut up and let Smith rest, which was often.

For his part, Smith was just glad to be out of the airless, stuffy room in the healthcare centre, where he had been going slightly mad. At least on the wing he had a window to look out of and someone to talk to when he wanted to. Physically though, he was still in a sorry state. His wounds were slowly healing, but they were extensive, with several deep stab wounds to his stomach, chest, back and left upper thigh, and even more gashes across his torso and one down his face where the terrorists had slashed him with their wickedly sharp knives. Most of the bruising he had sustained during that life and death struggle had faded. There were a few small sickly yellow patches that remained where the worst injuries had been. However, it was the constant pain that drained his energy and weakened him, keeping him awake at night and unable to lie down in one position for longer than five minutes at a time. He wasn't even able to walk yet and at meal times his cell mate was allowed to fetch his food from the canteen. Smith didn't complain though, as he knew that it was a miracle that he was still alive. He swallowed the few paracetamols that he was issued by the prison doctors to dull the pain and struggled on.

Smith had been in his cell for a week. It was late in the evening and Gordon was out of the cell for 'association' - the two hours when prisoners were allowed to gather and talk and either watch TV or play games such as pool together. Smith was alone in his cell, trying to read a paperback biography about the Kray twins that he had borrowed from his cell mate, in an effort to stave off the boredom. He was surprised when the cell door was unlocked and thrown open with a clang.

At the cell door stood three Asians, Pakistanis by the look of them, and obviously Muslims with their long beards and *Taqiyah*, or 'prayer caps' on their heads. They were all young, in their mid-twenties, and obviously fit and strong. They didn't attempt to enter the cell. They just stood there staring with hatred at Smith. He had pulled himself up to a sitting position expecting the worst, and stared back at them. He didn't show any outward sign of fear but inside his guts were churning.

One of the Pakistanis spoke, spitting his words out with a heavy Birmingham accent:

"You're a pig, Smith! One day we're gonna cut you open for murdering our Muslim brothers!"

Smith stayed calm and just stared back. He could see with relief that they weren't ready to make their move yet. He could also see a nervous-looking Asian prison officer standing behind the punks.

"So you're with them?" He directed his question at the officer, who glared back but didn't answer.

The others shuffled on their feet, keen to get away before they were caught.

"You're living on borrowed time, shithead! We're gonna get you sometime!"

Then they stepped back as the officer slammed the door closed.

Smith lay back down, exhausted even by this small effort.

Shit. He thought. *Shit*.

SIXTY

11th August
Winson Green, Birmingham

It was that visit by the Pakistanis, more than anything else, that finally make Smith decide that he ought to start getting fit again. He began by just trying to stand up, holding on to the bed for support, and then progressed to taking a few short steps. Gordon watched him as he pushed himself relentlessly, giving Smith words of encouragement. Gordon did not try to help Smith, especially after the first time when he had tried to help him and had been told to 'fuck off'.

In less than a week, Smith was walking a few paces up and down the cell with no support. He then started to take other exercise, stretching his muscles carefully so that his wounds didn't burst open.

Time passed slowly inside. There was a set routine to every day which never varied, and Smith, who was used to a lot of activity and variety in his day-to-day life, found it very hard to settle down. It wasn't just the fact that he was confined to his bed for most of the day because of his injuries. It was the lack of stimulation. He passed most of the days either reading books from the prison library (brought to him by Gordon), or talking with Gordon about a burglar's life (before he'd got nicked). His cell mate was still fascinated about Smith and asked him about his own life, but as ever the ex-soldier was reticent about telling him too much. *Trust no one* was forever his motto.

There was no privacy inside the cell either. It wasn't so bad when Smith went to the toilet as the way that the beds were arranged, with his opposite the door and Gordon's by the side of the door, there was always the waist-high screen between them. However, when Gordon used the loo there was nothing between the toilet and the head of Smith's bed. Still, this was nothing new to Smith as he had lived all of his working life amongst other men. What he found more disconcerting was that there was no way for the smell to dissipate, as the window only opened a little way behind its bars. However, Smith found that he soon got used to the smell of shit constantly pervading the air.

They also never knew when the cover that hung over the door's spy-hole would be thrown open and they would be stared at by a prison officer. It could happen at any time of the night or day, and Smith found this particularly galling as he liked his privacy. Whenever he heard the spy-hole cover being opened he would go very still and give it his hardest stare, intimidating whoever was behind it to shut it again as quickly as possible. It never really worked, but at least it gave him some satisfaction to believe he was fighting the system, even if only in a small way.

Today was going to be a major stepping stone, as he was going to attempt to leave the cell for the first time. He wasn't prepared to go the full hog and bound down the staircase to the canteen; just to take a short walk along the landing and back again, but it was a start.

The whole prison wing seemed to go quiet when Smith stood in the open doorway to his cell for the first time. Most of the convicts had not seen him at all since he had arrived at the prison, but he was still a celebrity amongst them. The prisoners were making their way along the landings and down the stairs towards the canteen to collect their breakfast trays, but they all paused and there were many craning necks as they tried to get a first clear look at the famous killer who had fought and overcome eight armed terrorists on his own. Smith ignored them all and concentrated on slowly limping from his door along the landing, conscious of the fact that his muscles and wounds were screaming silently with pain. He made it the twenty paces or so to the top of the first stairway and there he stopped, bending slightly forward as a particularly nasty spasm of pain wracked through his body, grasping on to the handrail for support. As he came out of the spasm he straightened and looked around for the first time, noticing that everyone had stopped to watch him. He looked into faces that had been made hard by hard lives, most of them admiring, but the Pakistanis' and the Somalis' faces were full of hate and loathing. He mentally shrugged and turned to limp back to his cell. It was then that the clapping started. One or two of the braver souls amongst the white inmates began to put their hands together slowly, ignoring the looks from the Muslim gangs intended to scare them into silence, and others soon joined in until the whole wing reverberated to the slow clapping, signalling their respect for the man and his heroism. Smith was confused at first, thinking that the slow handclap was a mark of hate for a paedophile on the wing, but as he glanced around at the grinning white faces he realised that they were saluting him. Some of them actually whistled and made friendly catcalls as he doggedly made it back to the cell door and almost collapsed against the doorway. Then everyone was on the move again to collect their breakfasts. The show was over. The cons that passed Smith in the doorway said quiet things to him, things like: "Nice one, Smudge, you showed them pigs a thing or two last year!" or "Good to see you, John, welcome to the nuthouse!" or "Watch them Pakis mate, they're after your blood."

  The Pakistanis and the Somalis did not want anything to do with Smith. They avoided him by using different landings and walkways, and crossing the wing to avoid passing near to him. Some of them glared at him and ran their fingers across their throats in the universal gesture that said 'We're gonna cut your throat'. By this time though, Smith didn't care. He was in agony and all he wanted to do was to lie down and drift into unconsciousness.

SIXTY-ONE

22nd September
Winson Green, Birmingham

Smith learnt a lot about the dynamics of the prison population by talking to his cell mate. The bosses on most of the wings were not the prison officers, as they liked to think, but the gangs of Somali immigrants. They were vicious thugs who controlled the smuggled contraband in the prison and dealt out rough justice to anyone that crossed them, being particularly adept at cutting them up with home-made blades fashioned from spoons. They had no respect for anyone but themselves and would intimidate the rest of the prisoners whenever they fancied. The contraband they dealt in consisted of everything from hard drugs to mobile phones. They called themselves Muslim but acted in a way that was contrary to the fundamentals of their religion.

    Next in line - and working as enforcers for the Somalis (who they were terrified of) - were the Pakistani Muslim gangs. They hated the white prisoners with a vengeance and had no respect for the country that had taken their parents in, professing to hate anything that was English, white or Christian. They relied on their large numbers to intimidate and control, always swaggering around in large gangs and doing their best to humiliate the white inmates. Although they were happy to tell anyone within hearing that they followed the Islamic faith, they were also the biggest users of smuggled drugs and booze in the prison.

The rest of the convict population were mainly white prisoners, most of them local to Birmingham. There were also several other ethnic and national groups present in small numbers, including Indian Hindus and Sikhs, a large contingent of West Indians, and even a few Irishmen. In the past it would have been the white criminal gangs or the Jamaican Yardies running the prison, but things had changed as quickly on the inside as they had on the outside. Now the whites and West Indians were subservient to the black Somalis.

According to Gordon, the Somalis had a fair few of the prison officers under their control, either through greed or through the intimidation of their families on the outside - by gang members who were free. These bent screws were the main source of smuggled goods within the prison.

From Gordon, Smith also learned how the inmates felt about him. It appeared that many of the prisoners believed that Smith had been set up as a paedophile, and while there were a few who really believed that he was a nonce, most of them didn't. It was the Somali and Pakistani Muslims who hated Smith though and there were always rumours that they were planning to knock him off - though all of them came to nothing, of course. However, Smith was well aware of how vulnerable he was to these gangs and he was very careful to stay away from them as he began to show himself more often outside his cell and began to build his strength up once again.

The preceding weeks had been hell for Smith as he slowly forced his ailing body to overcome its injuries, but he had made it and at last he felt well enough to book a session in the prison gym. He had to wait a few days after booking a gym time, but he used the delay to start doing a few press-ups and sit-ups in the confines of his cell. He was now able to go down the stairs to the canteen level without stopping for a rest, though the return journey took an immense amount of willpower to fight against the ever present, though gradually lessening pain. He was really looking forward to getting out of his cell and into the gym.

SIXTY-TWO

25th September
Winson Green, Birmingham

Today was finally the day. Before the allotted time for him to go to the gym arrived, Smith spent a full hour slowly stretching and warming up his muscles. Gordon was going to go with him, showing him the ropes and introducing him to the training staff. He still felt fascinated by Smith and his status amongst most of the other inmates had definitely risen by being his cell mate.

It was quiet and the prison wing was almost deserted as they were escorted by a prison guard called Sweeney along landings and hallways to the brand new gym. Most of the inmates, at least those wanted to, were off in other blocks catching up on the education that they had never had as kids, or working in one of the prison workshops. Sweeney was a grizzled old veteran of the prison service, now working for G4S. He was also an ex-squaddie, a former Coldstream Guardsman, and he chatted amiably to Smith about his own time in the forces as they ambled along, slowed down by Smith's unfitness and injuries.

"You know, the Governor's not a bad bloke," he said. "He's been getting us to keep an extra eye open for yer, to make sure that none of them Somali bastards 'ave a go at yer. He's even vetted the other prisoners that are going to be using the gym today, to make sure that there's no trouble, like."

"I'm happy to hear that."

"Yeah, not that yer'd have any trouble sorting 'em bastards out though, eh, being ex-SAS and all!" he laughed. Smith was in a good mood and indulged the old officer by laughing with him.

"That was a long, long time ago, mate!"

"Didn't stop yer from beating them bloody terrorists though, did it! Eight of the bastards. That must 'ave been a real rare fight. I saw a bit of it on a Newsnight show. That bit that was filmed by the BBC cameraman on board the plane. A hell of a job you did on 'em bastards!" Sweeney was enthusiastically full of praise and there was no guile in the man's words.

The mention of the cameraman brought back a flash of memory to Smith. He remembered how terrified the poor bastard had been when he asked him to get involved. *It looks like he made some money out his film after all!* This was the first that he had heard about the film though and it made him realise how isolated he had been since that night - and still was. Sweeney kept on talking as they walked along but Smith hardly heard what he said, for now his head was suddenly filled with memories of Linda. His heart ached even more than his body.

The prison gym was a lot better equipped than Smith had imagined it would be. There were numerous different types of multi-gyms, rowing machines, step-up machines, treadmills and just about every other kind of fitness machine that he could think of. Smith had never been one who relied upon gyms to keep himself fit in the past. During his army days, his fitness training had more often than not involved putting a large heavy Bergen on his back, and running for a few miles up a steep hill somewhere. *Still, beggars can't be choosers*, he thought. *I don't suppose that I'll get many opportunities to go for a road run while I'm in here!*

Even better than all of the kit though was the staff, who worked full time in the gym. They weren't prison officers. They were all professional fitness trainers, and they were more than happy to show John Smith the celebrity around and demonstrate how to use the various bits of equipment. The chief fitness trainer even sat down with Smith and worked out a training programme for him so that he wouldn't overdo it and open up his wounds again. After a couple of hours and the first decent workout that he had had for a very long time, Smith and Gordon left the gym and were escorted back to their wing, again by Sweeney, who had spent the time drinking tea in the staff room. Smith felt absolutely knackered but strangely happier than he had been feeling of late. He had been promised access to the gym every other morning for an hour and a half, and he supposed he was feeling good because he had something to look forward to at last. He would enjoy getting himself fit again.

For the first time since that fateful flight from The Gambia he allowed himself to think about escaping. *After all, I really don't want to spend the rest of my life in prison.*

His loud laugh earned him strange looks from Sweeney and Gordon, but he just grinned at them, feeling like his old self again.

SIXTY-THREE

27th October
Winson Green, Birmingham

Anybody who's ever had the misfortune to spend a spell in prison at Her Majesty's pleasure knows that it is real, heartfelt punishment. From the outside it often looks like prisoners are having an easy time of it. After all, being banged up with no work to do, all the leisure time you could ask for and three square meals a day, and all of it free, can sound pretty good to someone who has to struggle to make ends meet on the outside, working all day, every day, just to put food on the table. But the truth is that being locked up is hard: you have no control over your time; you are told what to do and when by complete strangers; you don't have access to your home or the things in it, or to your loved ones; time passes very, very slowly, and all you can think about is getting out. For Smith, who will spend the whole of his life in prison, caged like an animal, with no chance of parole, the thought of being free again is denied to him. This is it for the rest of his life, no reprieve. This thought alone can drive a person insane and anything that breaks the monotony of the endless time behind bars is welcome, even if it is talking to the police.

So it was that when Smith was scheduled to be interviewed by his favourite group of police officers, from the Serious and Organised Crime Agency in Cambridgeshire, he found that he was looking forward to it. He was escorted to an interview room in the visitors centre by three burly prison guards who had handcuffed his hands behind his back. They weren't taking any chances with Smith. His reputation as a killer was well-earned.

He was taken into a comfortable interview room, uncuffed, told to wait and asked if he wanted a drink of some sort. He asked politely for a cup of tea which was bought to him from a machine outside. It tasted like hot piss but Smith didn't mind. It was a treat to have a cup of tea at a point in the day that wasn't a routine meal time.

After half an hour or so of waiting in the room on his own, two police officers in civilian clothes finally entered. The first was a tall elegant woman. She was in her mid-forties and good looking - not plastered in make-up like so many of the younger women appeared to be these days - but with subtle colouring around her eyes and shiny lip gloss that accentuated her full lips and mouth. *I've been locked up too long already.* Smith thought to himself as he looked at the woman. *Even coppers are beginning to look sexy!* The man who followed her in was also in his mid-forties but there the similarity ended. He had a nose that had obviously been broken at some stage and was sprawled across a heavy-jawed face that looked hard and unforgiving. *Jesus*, thought Smith. *He looks more like a bloody criminal that most of the convicts in here do!* The woman sat down on the opposite side of the table from Smith, and barely giving him a glance she began to pull out a handful of manila files from her shoulder bag, and piled them up in front of her. The male copper sat next to her, his big frame making his chair seem too small for him as he openly stared with disdain at Smith. He sneered in return at Smith's smile, which gave the old soldier a small hint of pleasure. *This bastard's going to be easy to wind up.* He smiled at him again and sure enough he was favoured with a small grunt of displeasure, and pure hatred flashed into the man's eyes.

The woman finally finished setting her paperwork out and looked up at Smith, staring him full in the eye. He gave her a smile too but she totally ignored it.

"My name is Detective Chief Inspector Beverley Nicholls. I'm the officer in charge of the Serious and Organised Crime Squad, based in Cambridge. My colleague here is Detective Inspector Michael Thomas, also with SOCA."

Her voice was fairly soft and mellow but her eyes still showed nothing.

"I'm happy for you," Smith replied. "I guess that you're Alan Davies's replacement? How is old Alan? Enjoying his new role in life, I trust?"

"DCI Davies is fine thank you. And yes, he seems to be fitting in very well at Child Protection."

There was no hint of irony in her answer and Smith was impressed with her self control. He knew that she would appreciate that it had been Smith's actions that had forced Davies to lose his exalted position within the Cambridgeshire Police Force - the very position that she now held. Maybe she was grateful to him for showing Davies to be a prat and giving her a chance to prove herself, but Smith could tell that she would never let that show. He was beginning to like DCI Nicholls.

"So what can I do for you, Beverley? You don't mind if I call you Beverley, do you?"

"As a matter of fact I do, Mr Smith. You can address me as DCI Nicholls. I am not your friend and never will be."

"That's fine, then, Beverley, you can call me John," he said, deliberately beginning to bait her, "and how about I call your friend here 'knob head'?"

He indicated DI Thomas, whose face reddened at the insult.

"You'll excuse me if I don't kiss your arse though? I know that police officers are the same as every other group of people, with some good coppers, and some bad coppers. Unfortunately I've only met the bad ones so far."

"Whatever," she replied, instantly dismissing his words as though she didn't give a damn either way. "We are here to interview you about various crimes that were committed by you between the 15th and 28th of October

2013."

"Oh, super, that's interesting. What crimes were these then?"

She looked down at her pile of files and opened the top one.

"The first is the murder of two civilian prisoner officers in Peterborough Crown Court on 15th October 2013. We believe that you were involved in these murders?" Smith smiled again.

"That's right," he said calmly and quietly as though he didn't feel a thing about the fact that he had killed two people. "I killed them both."

For a split second DCI Nicholls carefully controlled demeanour slipped at the easy way that Smith had admitted to the murder, and then she regained control, though there was a hint of uncertainty in her voice as she carried on.

"So you admit to the murder of the two prison officers?"

"Of course, Beverley. I killed them both and I'm afraid to say that they probably didn't deserve to die, even though they had really pissed me off."

"What do you mean by that? Can you explain yourself more clearly?"

"Certainly," Smith took a second to get his mind together before carrying on. "I had just been put through a trial for something that I hadn't done. These two men were taking the piss."

She interrupted.

"How were they taking the piss? What did they do to deserve to be killed by you?"

"Well, looking back, not that much really. They were winding me up about being a paedophile and had just spat into my lunch, but I agree that that wasn't reason enough to kill them."

"Then why did you do it?"

Smith edged forward on his seat. He stared directly into DCI Nicholls' eyes and she felt herself involuntarily drawing back from this man. Suddenly his eyes, which just a second ago had been glowing and full of humour, were now the most frightening thing that she had ever seen in her life. The coal-black eyes stared at her, seeming to pierce directly into her mind. But it wasn't that that frightened her; it was that his eyes were empty of all emotion. They were like the eyes of a shark, a predator's eyes that held nothing in them at all. They were flat, cold and pitiless.

"I killed them because it was necessary to kill them. I wanted to escape. They had the keys to the cell and the cell block. I needed the keys. Simple."

He smiled at her but the smile didn't reach his eyes and she felt a shiver go down the full length of her spine. She knew that he would kill her right now if he wanted or needed to with the same efficiency and coldness with which he had killed the prison officers. There would be nothing that she could do to stop him. Suddenly she felt very, very afraid and vulnerable.

SIXTY-FOUR

27th October
Winson Green, Birmingham

John Smith had seen the fear in Beverley's face as he had recalled killing the prison officers. Suddenly he wasn't so keen to wind this pair of coppers up. He knew what a bastard he could be and how he could look to others, so he relaxed and sat back. DCI Nicholls' face reflected the relaxation of his body with relief.

"Okay," he said, "I'm getting bored with this. Let me make it easy for you."
He smiled at the woman copper again, but this time the humour *did* show in his eyes, and she breathed easy.
"You know what I really hate?"
"Go on, what?"
"Wankers who do something wrong and then won't admit it. Take for instance those bloody Muslims who trained themselves up as terrorists a couple of years ago. They even made their suicide videos before they got caught. Do you remember them?"
"Yes, I think they were from Birmingham?"
"That's right."
"What about them?"
"Well, they train themselves up, prepare a load of home-made bombs, make their bloody suicide videos, and then they get arrested and sent to trial. Then what do they do? They have the nerve to plead not guilty! I really hate people like that. People who haven't got the guts to stand

up in court and say 'Yes, we were prepared to bomb the fuck out of some innocent bystanders because we believe in our cause. We were prepared to kill ourselves too!' Why did they have to plead not guilty and try to get away with what they were preparing to do? Why didn't they just admit to it if they believe in their bloody cause so much? That's the type of wanker that I can't bloody stand! Gutless, spineless wankers."

"Okay. I understand what you're saying, but what's that got to do with you?"

"Well, I *do* have the guts and I *do* have the nerve to admit to what I've done wrong. I killed those prison guards because they were in my way and they were pissing me off. I wanted to escape and the only way out was to go through them. It's the same with the others that I killed last year. The prosecutor, the judge and the copper had conspired to send me down even though I was innocent. As far as I'm concerned they deserved what they bloody well got. I killed them too. It was the same with the Police National Computer and the National DNA Database. They were in my way and I also wanted to cause mayhem and confusion so that I could get away, so I blew them up. I admit it. It worked too - while I was out there killing and blowing things up, no one in the police or the security services could tell their arse from their elbow. No one knew where I would strike next or who my next target might be. I also freely admit that I shot Harry and his fucking ex-boss, and they bloody well deserved to die as well. Is there anything else that you'd like to know?"

DCI Nicholls was taken aback by the lack of vehemence in Smith's voice and the easy way that he had just admitted to the crimes that everyone knew he had committed. This was probably the first time in her career that she had met a criminal who didn't try to squirm out of his guilt.

"Will you put that down in a statement?"
"Of course I bloody will."
"Good. Is there anything else that you'd like to tell

us?"

"There's lots, love. Where would you like me to start? Do you want to hear about how I murdered dozens of bloody terrorists for Queen and Country?"

"Ah, you mean your *so-called* life-story that was published by *The Sun*? How you were an assassin for the British government? Ha!"

It was the first time that DI Thomas had spoken during the interview and his scorn was clear. Smith turned to him and again his eyes had gone cold. As Smith stared him, the Detective Inspector also felt the cold wriggle down his spine and the hairs at the back of his neck stand up.

"Listen to me *Detective Inspector*, and listen good!" His eyes bored into the DI's brain with freezing intensity.

"I've been fighting for Queen and Country and for people like *you* for most of my adult life. I've fought and killed the enemies of Britain in a dozen wars in just about every poxy corner of this rotten world. I've been shot, bayoneted and blown up for *you*, and *your* family, *your* friends and *your* way of life. I've been tortured to within an inch of my life by the best in the world at what they do, and I've been hunted by the toughest, most brutal people that you could ever imagine, and I've always won in the end. I've always come out on top. Do you know why? Because I'm the meanest, coldest and most brutal son-of-a-bitch that you'll ever meet in your life. While you were getting into your nice, warm and cosy bed at night, while you were cuddling up to your missus and feeling as though nothing bad could ever happen to you, *I* was out there making sure of it. *I* was the man that gave up everything to fight for *you*, including my own missus and my kids. *I* was the one that stared death in the face every day of my life to make sure that *you* could sleep safely at night. *I* was the one that risked everything by killing the bastards that would have taken everything from *you* if they'd been given half the chance. Me, and others like me. Do you understand?"

He leaned forward, his eyes suddenly blazing.

"I'm the one that made sure you could sleep safely at night and without fear. The only thing that you've got to fear now is that I don't ever get out of this prison. Because if I do, I might just come looking for you, and believe this asshole: if I ever do take it into my head to come looking for you, then there is absolutely no one and nothing on this earth that can stop me. I'll track you down no matter where you run to and I will find you no matter where you hide, and when I do I'll kill everyone that you've ever loved and destroy everything that you've ever owned before I finally stick a knife between your ribs and take your life away from you. Look deep into my eyes, asshole, *real deep*, and tell me to my face that you don't believe me."

SIXTY-FIVE

10th November
Central London

The one thing about the security services, thought Sean O'Connell, *was that no matter how good they thought they were, (and in this case they were* very *good), they were still human; and humans always make mistakes.* O'Connell had tailed Sir Rupert Giles, the Chief of the Secret Intelligence Service, for six days now and realised that he was a real stickler for routine. He always set out from his big fancy house in Chelsea at the same time every morning. He always drove his own Mercedes car and was followed by an unmarked Range Rover containing his two bodyguards, and he always stopped on the way to work to eat breakfast in the same restaurant near Piccadilly. It was just the sort of stupid routine that a man in his position *shouldn't* have. His bodyguards had also settled into a routine that mirrored their master. Two of them followed him from his home to SIS Headquarters at Vauxhall Cross. They always drove in the same car, the same distance behind him, along the same route every day. *But they're only human*, O'Connell thought to himself. *It's easier to get into a routine than to try and vary everything all of the time, especially when you have a hard boss like theirs - a man who likes to do things his own way.*

Sir Rupert also parked his car in the same car park every morning when he went to eat his breakfast, leaving one bodyguard behind to watch the vehicles while the other escorted him into the restaurant. That would have been safe and okay, but the bodyguard who was keeping an eye on his master's car was only human too. Every now and again he would take his eye off the ball while he slipped to the car park entrance to grab a quick fag and buy a newspaper off the stall on the street. *Human, but stupid,* O'Connell thought.

It took Sean one minute and thirty-five seconds exactly to attach his small package beneath the SIS chief's car, just about the same length of time that it took for the useless bodyguard to light his cigarette up and open the morning newspaper to the sport pages.

SIXTY-SIX

10th November
Winson Green, Birmingham

At last, after months of solid, hard, muscle burning training, Smith was beginning to feel like his old self again - physically as well as mentally. The pain from his wounds was just a vague memory to him now, though the fierce scars carved into his body from the terrorists' knives would always be there as a reminder of those few short minutes that had changed his life forever. Smith tried not to dwell on the past too much - though it wasn't easy when you were banged up in a tiny cell all day, every day. He filled his waking hours with anything he could to keep the memories at bay such as reading, talking to his cellmate or playing card games with him. It was only at night-time when he was asleep that he couldn't stop the memories from flooding into his mind.

One thing that kept him busier and busier during the long days was his 'fan' mail. At first he had only received a few letters each day, but as time went by his celebrity status in the outside world saw those few letters grow into a daily half a mail bag. As a matter of course the prison officers opened all the letters and parcels received by prisoners. They said that they didn't read them, only opening them up to search them for contraband, but Smith could imagine some prison guard sitting in the mail room, probably just as bored as the prisoners were, looking through the mail and getting off on the raunchy letters sent by horny girlfriends and wives.

Smith's fan mail was an eclectic mix. There were hate letters of course, from sad fuckers all over the world who called him a murdering bastard or an evil assassin. They wanted him to die a slow and agonising death like all the poor fuckers he'd ever knocked off. At first he had read these for the novelty factor, but after a while they began to get boring and he just threw them to one side after reading the first line. *No imagination*, he thought. *They all sound the bloody same.* Then there were the letters from the Bible bashers, hoping that he had seen the light now that he was in prison and would take up the worship of God to help him get through what lay ahead. *No fucking chance! If there is a God, he must be a right bastard to let the world go on as it is!* There were also letters from the passengers, or relatives of the passengers who had been on board the Gambia flight. These were invariably praising him and thanking him for saving their lives from the terrorists. They were written by people who obviously just couldn't get rid of their own memories of being on that fateful plane, and needed to let it out in some way. Smith read all of these and as time went by and a few of them kept writing to him, he began to recognise their handwriting even before he opened up their letters. In a weird way it was like belonging to other people's families on the outside, and he learned how their children were doing at school or how their jobs were going or what new cars they'd just brought. It gave him a good feeling deep down to know that these people were alive and able to get on with their normal lives, entirely due to him. It was pure feel-good factor and he really looked forward to receiving them. He even wrote back to them occasionally.

Then there were the weirdest letters of them all: the love letters. Women (and a few men as well) from all over the world wrote to Smith declaring their love for him. They ranged from 60 year old Latin-Americans to Japanese teenagers, and from thirty stone women with enough fat on them to feed a starving African village for a month, down to skinny women who looked more like anorexic whippets. There were black girls and white girls and girls from India, China, Malaysia, Germany, Sweden, England and Canada - it was like a bag of Liquorice Allsorts. Smith had never ever experienced anything like this in his life before. The letters ranged from a simple declaration of undying love to very detailed explanations of what they would like to do to him if they got into bed with him. Some of them sent soiled panties for him to sniff or pictures of themselves in the nude, doing to themselves what they'd like him to do to them. There were even a few DVDs from sex-crazed women.

Smith just couldn't believe it. Okay, if he'd met one of them and she was an old girlfriend, then fine; but undying love from complete strangers who had only ever seen his picture on the TV? These were seriously deranged women who were obviously in need of some sort of professional help. Of course, on the other hand, he was only a bloke, and some of the fantasies that the girls had about him got to him in the place where some women like to tell men that they keep their brains. It didn't help being banged up with only a load of hairy-arsed men for company either.

The best of the sex letters he shared with Gordon and they had a good laugh. He even allowed him to take the best of the best with him when he went out on association in the evenings, so that his friends could read them too. In prison you find your entertainment where you can.

There were a handful of letters that Smith wouldn't share with anyone though, including one or two from his sons, Robert and Alan. There was even a handmade card, with a few photos, from his granddaughters, sent to him for his birthday. The card had a drawing in crayon of a horse in a field, with a bright sun behind it. He attached it to the wall above his bed with sellotape, so that it was the first thing that he saw when he opened his eyes in the mornings and the last thing he saw before lights out at night-time.

There was also a pile of letters from Linda, and Smith would sit there for hours and read them over and over as she talked about her life at the hospital, her family in Australia and a million other little things that made him feel closer and closer to her. She had quit her job at the British hospital in disgust at the way that Smith had been treated by the authorities and after a short visit home to Oz she was now looking for a job some place – anyplace - else. He kept her letters in a shoebox under his bed and wrote back as often as he could.

SIXTY-SEVEN

11th November
Winson Green, Birmingham

Today was another big day for John Smith. He had been informed by the Prison Governor, during one of his regular rounds that he would be allowed to join the other prisoners on his wing for association that evening. He would be given the relative freedom of being able to mix with the other prisoners in the TV and games rooms for two hours. The Governor also warned him to be careful. There was no doubt in the Governor's mind that the rumour mill inside the prison would be in full swing and that the Muslim Somalis and Pakistanis would learn of his being allowed to join them before it actually happened.

"Don't get drawn into a fight, Mr Smith. Be under no illusion that I will stop this privilege if there is any trouble."

"Super," replied Smith.

Association took place every evening between the hours of eight and ten o'clock. Approximately eighty prisoners incarcerated in the wing were released from their cells and allowed to mix with each other on the ground floor. They could sit and talk and buy hot or cold drinks from vending machines, or play pool or table tennis, dominoes or card games, or they could watch TV or a DVD in the TV room, or smoke cigarettes in the confines of the smoking room. It was the highlight for men who were kept cooped up in their cells for a large part of the day, but it was also a privilege that could be denied to any of them at the drop of a hat if they caused trouble. Of course, where there were men who were locked up for breaking the law, trouble was bound to happen, and there were often arguments and occasionally fights amongst them. They seldom amounted to much though, and the prison officers tended to leave the men alone and maintain a small unobtrusive presence during association time. The prison authorities recognised that they had to allow prisoners some freedom to relieve the tensions and frustrations of being locked up away from their families and loved ones.

As eight o'clock drew nearer, Gordon was getting very excited.

"Hey, John. You're gonna love it, mate. There're loads of the guys that want to meet you. They've been looking forward to it for months! You're famous, John!"

"Super," was his only reply, but inside he was really looking forward to a bit of a change as well. Gordon was fine as a cellmate, but he probably wasn't someone that Smith would choose as a mate on the outside. The guy was a petty criminal and had lived a sheltered and uneventful life compared with Smith. They didn't have anything in common except for the fact that they were locked up together in the same cell. Smith wondered whether the rest of the prisoners would be cut from the same cloth.

"Watch out for them Somalis though. They stabbed Leroy last night, you know that big Jamaican on the first floor?" Smith shook his head. "Oh yeah, sorry, you ain't met him yet 'ave yer?"

"What did they stab him for?"

"He bought a quarter of Moroccan Black off them last week."

When he saw Smith's questioning look he added:

"That's cool stuff man, good canabis resin. Then he reneged on the deal. He was supposed to give them five packs of Golden Virginia tobacco in exchange, but he short-changed them and only gave them four. He said that he was skint and couldn't afford the other pack of baccy until next week. The Somalis got him in the showers and three of 'em held him down while one of 'em carved up his back! He's in a right old state! Still, 'e shouldn't have short-changed the Somalis, man. They're mean fuckers!"

"Hmm," was Smith's reply.

The younger prisoner's face lit up as he decided to change the subject.

"The guys really loved that DVD that you lent them last week. Those two lesbian birds were really going for it, giving each other some lezzy lovin'".

Gordon ground his hips in a faintly comical impression of a sexual act, causing Smith to wonder, and not for the first time, if the guy was still a virgin. Smith had given Gordon one of the home-made DVDs that had been posted to him by two girls who had written and said that they wanted a threesome with him when he got out of prison. *Just shows how dumb they are I suppose*, he thought. *Don't they realise that I'm supposed to be in nick for life?*

He hadn't watched the DVD himself as he didn't have access to a TV or a DVD player.

"Even those fuckin' Pakis were glued to their seats and watching it with big round eyes! They were goin' around afterwards sayin' that it was a load of typical Western Christian filth, but they sat and watched it all the way through anyhow! Boy, those lezzies were hot!"

"Yeah, okay Gord. I get the message mate. I heard you pulling your bloody plonker all night afterwards."

"Fuckin' too right, mate. They were a horny couple of lezzies. You should *definitely* go and fuck them when you get out of here!"

"Shut up Gordon. I'm in here for *life*, with no chance of parole, remember?" Smith snapped at him, and not for the first time during his time in the nick.

"Oh yeah, sorry mate. I forgot."

He was so contrite over his *faux pas* that Smith instantly felt sorry that he had spoken so sharply to him. After all, he was only a kid.

"I'll tell you what, Gord, when you get out I'll give you their address so that you can go and get fucked by them, alright?"

"Cool!"

Smith knew that Gordon would never have the nerve, but what the hell?

Everyone's gotta have their fantasies, right?

SIXTY-EIGHT

11th November
Winson Green, Birmingham

It went very quiet as John Smith and Gordon stepped off the stairwell and on to the ground floor of A Wing. The long concourse was full of convicts sitting around tables in small groups. Smith paused for a few seconds to take it in, his eyes roaming from group to group, searching out the potential troublemakers and seeing what was what. Most of the men who were nearest the stairwell were either Pakistanis or Somalis. They stared at him with undisguised hatred and several of the Somalis spat out gobbets of phlegm on to the floor as a sign of their distaste. Behind and through them Smith could see the white convicts sitting at the farthest tables. He felt rather than saw Gordon stiffen with fear at his side and heard him say "Shit!" under his breath. Smith could see that he'd have to run the gauntlet of hatred before he could reach the men behind. He didn't give a toss.

He stepped forward, aiming between two of the tables to one side of the most direct route through the throng, tables that held about a dozen Somalis between them. He wanted to see what they were capable of if they weren't shown the deference that they were used to from the other prisoners. Gordon reluctantly followed him, trying to stay as close as he could to the big man he had learned to like and trust.

Smith confidently walked forward, his eyes searching

out those of his self-declared enemies, looking them all in the eye for a second before passing on to the next one.

If looks could kill, he mused. *I'd be deader than a dodo right about now!*

His hard face with the fierce scar split into a grin at his own joke. He had no way of knowing it, but that grin scared the fuck out of the black men in front of him, though they tried their best not to show it.

As he approached the space between the tables, Smith saw that some of the men were sitting with their legs arrogantly outstretched across the gap, and they were in his way. He fixed his hardest stare on the eyes of the closest and saw the flicker of fear deep within the Somali's eyes. Smith grinned again, but this time it wasn't at a joke to himself - this time even the Somali in question could tell it was in joyful anticipation of violent conflict. *Fuck, this man is crazy!* he thought, about half a second before he pulled his feet out Smith's way, though he tried to do it as nonchalantly as he could so that he wouldn't lose too much face. Smith's eyes darted across to the next in line and had the same effect. He strolled between the tables with Gordon so close behind him that he was almost tripping up over his own feet. All was going well, until one of the Somalis, a little more courageous than his compatriots, gobbed a mouthful of phlegm which landed with a splat on Smith's upper right sleeve. Smith stopped in mid-stride and Gordon bumped into his back. The big man pushed his cellmate past him with an irritated movement that sent the smaller man almost tumbling past the Somalis table, and then he turned and once again ran his eyes from man to man. In his mind he now knew that most of these so-called gangsters were just cowards. He had seen it in their eyes and their faces. They were typical bullies, arrogant and nasty when in a group, but shitting themselves when they were caught alone. Only one of the Somalis showed a bit more backbone when he met Smith's stare with a half-smiling sneer. Smith went directly to the man, who was slim but strong looking, wearing a bright red T-shirt with

'Liverpool FC' sprawled across the front in bold white letters. Smith stopped in front of him and bent down slightly so he could see into his face as he continued to fix the man with his eyes. Without saying a word he stuck out his right arm and in slow controlled movements he wiped the phlegm from it on to the man's T-shirt. He could see the anger and the shame welling up in the man's eyes but Smith didn't stop until he had wiped away all of the disgusting mess. Then calmly he turned and continued on his way. The Somali was incandescent with rage behind him, but glancing around at his comrades he could tell that no one was prepared to back him up and not one of them had the guts to meet his gaze. He stayed put and let the rage bubble up in his breast.

As Smith walked towards the tables holding the rest of the lags one of them began the slow handclap again. He was quickly joined by others until the whole ground floor was thundering to the sound of clapping and cat-whistling and shouting. Smith grinned in pleasure at seeing the welcome and as he continued through the men thronging around him to a table at the rear he was slapped on the back so many times that it began to hurt.

"Fuckin' well done, mate!"
"Goddamn pigs, you showed them!"
"Nice one, mate!"
"Good to see you at last!"
"Bastard Somalis. I thought you'd had it there, pal!"
"Cowardly little toerags!"

SIXTY-NINE

11th November
Winson Green, Birmingham

Things gradually calmed down after the tense start to the association period. Smith found himself busy chatting with cons as they paid quick visits to his table and told him what a hero he was, not only for fucking with the Somalis and the terrorists on the plane, but especially for messing around with the fucking coppers when he was on the loose the previous year. They loved him and held him in awe for that. After all, the coppers were the lifelong enemies of most of these men, and there was not one of them that couldn't have told you a true story about real police brutality, lies or corruption.

For his part, Smith was just glad to be out of his cell and amongst a bunch of normal blokes again. The attention was getting on his nerves a bit but he knew it wouldn't last and sure enough most of the lags slowly drifted back to their own tables and mates. After twenty minutes or so, Smith was left with the company of only half a dozen men.

"I always said that 'em bloody wogs ain't half as hard as they think they are," said one man who had identified himself as 'Smiler'.

"True, but you've never 'ad the bottle to have a go at them, 'ave you Smiler?"
This was from a big ginger-haired thug known unsurprisingly as 'Ginger' or 'Ginge' for short.

"Fuckin' too right, Ginge. I ain't no bleedin' 'ero

like old Smithy 'ere."
His answering grin and the easy banter between the two men showed Smith that they were old friends.

"We were in the car-ringing game together after we left the bleedin' army," added Smiler. "Frank over there," - he indicated another man sitting at a nearby table, - "he used to nick the cars, I'd do the business on 'em, grinding off the old engine plate numbers and that, and old Ginge 'ere was our enforcer if the clients decided not to pay up. We 'ad a good deal goin' until some bastard grassed us up to the pigs. Fuckin' shame. We got five years each."

"What regiment were you in?" asked Smith.

"RCT."

"Yeah," added Ginger, grinning from ear to ear. "Royal Corps of Tosspots."

"That would be *transport*, not *tosspots*," reproved Smiler. "I was a full screw and this itinerant was a bloody private. You can tell can't yer?"

"So you made sergeant then, Smithy?"

"Yep. Not that it ever did me much good."

"Is it true what we read in the papers, like?" asked another convict who hadn't introduced himself.

"Which bit?" asked Smith with a feeling of *déjà vu*, as he'd already been asked the same thing at least half a dozen times during the evening.

"The bit about the SAS and that. Was you really in the SAS?"

"Afraid so mate."

"Bloody 'ard bastards 'em," interrupted Smiler. "Remember that time at Catterick Ginge? When 'em SAS blokes got in a fight with the fuckin' monkeys and 'ammered 'em?"

"That wasn't the SAS, yer daft bleeder. They was a bunch of bleedin' Paras!"

"Same thing ain't it. They're all bleedin' loonies anyway!"

Suddenly he seemed to realise who he was with and what he had just said, and glanced quickly at Smith to see whether he'd caused offence. Smith grinned back at him to allay his fears.

"You're right," he said "We're all bleeding loonies. In my day they used to say that a Para was just a SAS man with his brains kicked out!"

That got a good laugh from around the table, just as Smith had hoped. Despite their obvious criminality, these guys were the 'salt of the earth' - the army that he had known had been filled with blokes like these.

The Somalis and Pakistanis had been unusually quiet after their encounter with Smith earlier, though they still glared at him whenever he made eye contact with them. It was getting close to the end of the association period when Smith noticed that the Muslims all seemed to have gathered around one table in a large group. He couldn't make out what they were doing as they were all too close to each other, but he could hear faint voices from a radio. Suddenly there was a loud shout of triumph from the group, followed by excited chatter and the chanting of *"Allahu Akbar! Allahu Akbar!"* as the Muslims began prancing around and waving their arms in glee. Some of them looked over at Smith and the other prisoners, making their familiar 'you're gonna have your throat cut signs'. No one seemed to know what had started the Muslim chanting of "God is Great!" and their obviously joyous celebration, until one of the white convicts came over to Smith's table.

"They're all happy because some big knob with MI6 got himself blown up by a car bomb," he said. "I just heard it on the radio news."

Smith's ears pricked up at this.

"Who was it that got killed? Did they say?"

"Some twat with a posh name. I think they said he was the chief or something." Then he added. "That bloody Muslim *Al Qaeda* or whatever they bleeding call themselves, phoned in to a newspaper and claimed it was them what did it. Only the bloke that called the newspaper had an Irish bleeding accent. The pigs can't figure it out

and they're saying on the radio that it might mean that the bloody Muslims and the IRA have joined up together. That's all we bleeding need!"
Smith was silent for a while, his memory suddenly filled with the image of the angry ex-IRA killer, Sean O'Connell, as he put a bullet into the SIS man's head at the hospital. Then he surprised everybody in the room by laughing out loud and slapping his thigh.
    "Good old Sean!" he shouted. "Bloody good for you mate!"
He laughed so hard that tears came to his eyes.

SEVENTY

3rd December
Winson Green, Birmingham

Time continued to pass slowly for the hundreds of men locked away from society inside Winson Green nick. Smith carried on joining the other prisoners on A-Wing during the association periods and slowly began to get to know most of the non-Muslim men better. He was surprised to find out how many of them had served at some time or other in the British Armed Forces. They came from a lot of different regiments. The big turbaned Sikh called Daljit Singh Bohgal, or 'bogroll' to his mates had served for fifteen years in the Army Air Corps as a technician before getting sent down for fraud. There was also the only other guy on the wing who was ex-Special Forces like Smith, a big bloke who had served for six years in the mob, two of them with the Special Reconnaissance Regiment. He had lost it in a bar brawl one night and ended up getting jailed for six years for manslaughter when he punched another bloke too hard and killed him. He would have been done for murder if his brief hadn't convinced the court that he was suffering from severe PTSD from his time spent with the regiment in Iraq. Smith worked it out one day and reckoned, apart from the Somalis and the Pakistanis, that at least forty percent of the prisoners had done some time in the Army, Navy, Marines or Air Force. It was a frightening figure if you thought about it deeply enough. Why was there such a high proportion of ex-servicemen in the nick? Was it because many of them had been affected by their time in the forces? Or was that just a load of old bumph?

Smith was left alone by the Muslims and gradually, as time went by, there was a subtle change in the interactions between the Muslims and non-Muslim prisoners. Before, the Somalis and Pakistanis had definitely ruled the roost, because of the high numbers of Pakistanis and the viciousness of the north-eastern Africans, but things began to change in the way that the non-Muslim prisoners reacted to their bullying tactics. More and more of the non-Muslims, given confidence by the way that Smith had showed the Muslims up and the fact that they had still not retaliated against him, began to stand up to the intimidation that was meted out to them. More and more of them stood their ground and told the Pakistanis to fuck off and leave them alone, though only a handful of them had the nerve to stand up to the Somalis - they were still the top dogs and ran the prison with an iron hand.

      Smith was treated as a hero, and though he tried to shrug it off with a smile and a quick joke, he found that more and more of the prisoners began to come to him for help and advice when they were in trouble, hoping that he would sort it out for them. This trouble could be anything from a silly argument about someone cheating in a game of backgammon to a growing conflict between two groups of men who each thought that the other group had fiddled them out of some cigarettes which had been used to pay for some contraband booze. The prisoners looked up to Smith, for reasons that he just couldn't fathom out himself, and they sought out his no-nonsense and non-partisan judgements on their conflicts. He knew that he had always had a cool head and could also usually tell if a bloke was lying or telling the truth - although not always. He also knew that his past achievements were, for want of a better term, quite extraordinary, but for the life of him he couldn't figure out why anyone in their right mind would come to him to pass judgement on their problems. Even more surprising to him, once he had reluctantly given his verdict, the prisoners would accept it completely. Smith was totally flummoxed by this.

SEVENTY-ONE

23rd December
Winson Green, Birmingham

Smith woke up when the door to his cell was opened with a typical clang. For a second he didn't know where he was and he felt a momentary panic until his head cleared. It was exceptionally early and the lights in A-Wing had not yet come on. He could see an almost ghostly figure standing at the cell door, illuminated by the dim light of a flashlight behind it. Instinct and adrenaline instantly kicked in as Smith bunched his muscles and prepared to jump up and fight.
"It's okay, Mr Smith. It's only me, Sweeney."
The grizzled old prison officer, late of the Coldstream Guards, stepped into the cell and recognising the man, Smith relaxed - though not entirely - as there was something shifty about the way the prison officer looked and his voice was a harsh whisper.
"I know it's unusual, but the Governor wants to see you immediately. Me and PO Lakely 'ere 'ave been told to take you down to his office, and to keep it quiet like. The Governor doesn't want anyone else to know."
"What's up, Sweeney?"
"I'm not supposed to know, but I reckon there's going to be some trouble with the Somalis. Get dressed and we'll take you down."
Smith got out of bed and began to put his prison uniform on.

"What's with the Somalis then?"

"You'll find out from the Governor, Smithy. Like I said I ain't supposed to know."

Fifteen minutes later Smith was ushered into the Governor's office in the newest part of the prison. He was surprised that the office was so small and cosy, as he had imagined that the office of a prison governor would be large and sumptuous. The reality was a spartan room, with just a simple desk and plain chairs. His escorts were thanked by the Governor and then asked to stay outside until he was finished, at which time they could take Smith back to his cell. Then, with the door closed behind Smith, Jeremy Bradsworth asked him to sit down on a chair while he perched himself on the edge of his desk.

"Good morning, Mr Smith. I'm sorry about all the cloak and dagger stuff, but I dare say that you of all people are used to it!"

The Governor smiled at his quip. Even this early in the morning he still looked dapper in a smart suit and tie.

"Morning, Governor."

Smith's reply was bland, but he couldn't hide his anticipation from the sharp-eyed Governor.

"I expect that you'd like to get straight down to business and find out why I called you down here?"

"Sounds good to me."

"Okay then. I am not unaware of what has been happening on A Wing in the last few weeks, Mr Smith. I know that you confronted the Somali gang on the wing and caused them to lose face. I am also aware that there has been a change in attitude towards the Somalis by the non-Muslim prisoners."

He paused for a moment and leaned forward.

"In all honesty, John, I am not entirely unhappy about this change in the situation. I have been fully aware of the Somalis hold over several of my less-than-trustworthy-officers, but until now I have never had the opportunity to curb the way that these gangs appear to have taken over much of the prison."

He stood up and stepped behind the desk. Smith decided to keep his mouth shut until the Governor had finished.

"I am also aware that the rest of the prisoners have begun to look upon you as some sort of leader, John, and again I am not unhappy about this. You appear to have a shrewd head upon your shoulders and I'm pretty sure that you have helped to calm down several minor incidents that could have easily become a lot worse if they had been left to fester. Even minor problems can blow up out of all proportion when men are locked up for so long."

"True," Smith admitted, wondering exactly where this was all going.

"Unfortunately though, there still remains the problem of the Somalis and to a lesser extent the Pakistani gangs. You made them lose face John, and even though they have been quiet until now, you can be sure that they have not forgotten and have certainly not forgiven you for that!"

"No, I don't imagine that they have," Smith agreed with a smile. "But why have you dragged me down here, Governor? All of this is pretty obvious, if you don't mind me saying?"

"Of course it is John, of course it is. I've 'dragged' you down here because there has been a new and rather astounding development. It appears that one of the Pakistani gang members on A-Wing has decided to inform on his friends and the Somalis. He has spoken to me in private about an attack that will be made upon you later today!"

Smith was a little taken aback by this, but he hadn't been born yesterday.

"That's interesting, Governor, but how do you know that this informer is telling you the truth? How do you know that he isn't trying to pull the wool over your eyes and setting us both up for something else?"

"Well I can't be sure, of course. Like you say, this could be part of some other plot. I've got to admit that I was very sceptical myself at first. But then I pulled the man's file and guess what I found?"

"Go on, enlighten me."

"Well, it turns out that the Pakistani involved actually served for eight years in the British Army! He was a sergeant in the Royal Regiment of Fusiliers!"

The Governor was so pleased with this revelation that he actually banged his hand on the table.

"How about that then!"

Smith stayed silent for a minute. He was confused by this. One of the Muslim Pakistanis was an ex-soldier? He knew that he shouldn't be too surprised, as there were plenty of Muslims serving in the British Army, just as there were lots of Jews, Hindus, Sikhs and Catholics and just about every other religion that you could think of. But why would the man turn informer on his mates?

"I know what you're thinking, Mr Smith," said the Governor. "Why has he turned informer? Well I asked him that very question and he told me that it was because your appearance on the wing had reminded him of other loyalties that he had once felt, especially towards his fellow soldiers. I've got to say that the fellow appeared to be telling the truth. It's certainly true that he is taking a big chance in talking to me. I believe him, John."

"Okay. I guess it does have the ring of truth to it. If it is true, what do you want me to do about it?"

"Ah, I was hoping you'd ask me that." The Governor grinned at Smith. "Let me give you the gist of what he had to say first..."

SEVENTY-TWO

23rd December
Winson Green, Birmingham

Association was almost at an end. The TV room had been packed while everyone had been watching a porn film about the Russian Queen, Catherine the Great, on a cable TV channel. Smith, Ginger and Smiler were sitting in the first rank of plastic chairs, along with young Gordon, who was full of praise for the film as the ending credits came on.
"Jesus. That Catherine loved her nookie, didn't she!" he exclaimed. "I wouldn't have minded being one of her footmen!"
Smiler nudged Ginge with his elbow.
"Reminds me of that bird who used to run that cafe down in 'ammersmith. She was a right goer an' all."
"Yeah! I remember 'er. She 'ad the biggest tits I've ever seen. Did you ever get off with 'er Smiler?" the big man asked, grinning.
"All the time, Ginge, all the time! She could suck a tennis ball through a hosepipe!"

The four of them had been so enthralled by the gorgeous Russian Queen and her sexual antics with both men and women that they hadn't noticed that the Somalis and Pakistanis had gradually been moving in on the TV room behind them. They had forcibly but quietly taken control of row after row of sitting men, gesturing silently for them to get out while they moved forward to intimidate the next row. As the TV screen went blank at the end of the association period, Smith and the others stood up and stretched their stiff backs.

"Don't reckon I'll be able to sleep after that," grinned Ginger. "I'll 'ave to 'ave a wank or I'll never get any shuteye!"

"Well just do it quietly. I'm too fuckin' old to 'ave to listen to you wanking all night long," laughed Smiler. His laugh died in his throat as he turned with the others to make their way out.

"Oh shit!" he said when he saw that the darkened room behind them was filled with grinning Muslims, the gang of Somalis at their head. There had to be at least twenty-five of the bastards and most of them were carrying some sort of home-made weapon, from the bottom section of a metal bed leg through to sharpened spoon handles.

"Fuck me!" exclaimed Ginger, as the four of them slowly stepped back from the mob in front of them. "We're in deep shit!"

The Muslims edged forward. Even though they vastly outnumbered their enemies, they were still nervous, especially when they saw the grin that came on to John Smith's face. They knew he was a killer and they were building up their nerve to get stuck in.

"We're gonna cut you up, you motherfuckers!" snarled the Somali that John recognised as the one who had gobbed on him before.

"Yeah. You fuckers gonna die, man!" growled another Somali. They continued to edge forward, weapons held out in front of them. The Somalis hadn't earned their reputation as vicious thugs for nothing.

John Smith, the grin still on his scarred face and his eyes blazing with the anticipated joy of a fight, stopped edging backwards. He was close to the far wall and almost nonchalantly he stuck out his hand and flipped a switch on the bank of light switches beside him. The back of the room flashed into brightness as an overhead light came on, followed by more lights as he continued to flick the long line of switches.

"Come and get it," he growled at the black faces in front of him.

The Somalis had closed in, the more numerous Pakistanis pushing them onwards from behind, and they were just about to leap forward into the attack on the small group of men in front of them when, there was suddenly a loud commotion at the entrance to the TV room behind them. There was a lot of shouting and the sound of fists hitting flesh.

"Okay, boys!" Smith shouted over the heads of the Somalis, in a drill-sergeant's voice that could be heard across a windy parade ground. "Remember. Don't kill any of the bastards! Just kick the shit out of them!"
With that he pulled out a wooden chair leg from where it had been hidden under his sweatshirt and leapt forward. He smashed the long piece of wood downward on to the left collar bone of the loud-mouthed Somali in front of him who howled in pain, as the crack of breaking bone sounded like a pistol shot in the air. Ginger and Smiler grinned at each other as they also pulled out a couple of metal bed legs from where they had hidden them. Then with screams of vengeance they followed Smith into the fray, followed only a few moments later by the more nervous but suddenly very angry Gordon. As they laid about them the sounds of fighting grew even louder as dozens of non-Muslims laid into the Pakistanis from the rear. The Muslims didn't know it, but this was a classic ambush that Smith had set up all afternoon through whispered conversations passed on from one man to another.

The ex-squaddies amongst the prisoners on A-Wing hadn't realised it before but, with the arrival of John Smith in their ranks, they had once again become a unit. They had all been through the same blood, sweat and tears in the forces. It didn't matter what colour they were, what religion they believed in, what regiment they had served in or for how long. It didn't even matter if they had never actually fought for their country, although many of them had, in Bosnia, or Northern Ireland, Iraq, the Gulf, the Falklands or Afghanistan. The main thing was that they had spent time living with other men like themselves and had shared the same hardships and tough discipline. It didn't matter whether they were young or old - the Army, Navy, Air Force or Marines had always been a lot more than just a job to them. While they had served they had lived and breathed for their regiment, ship or squadron. It had been their life. Now, at last, they were getting back some of that feeling of comradeship that each of them, whether they knew it or not, had missed so much once they had hit the dirty pavements of civvy street.

They had also been abused and intimidated throughout their prison sentences by these vicious thugs who thought that they were so much better than they were. These Africans and Pakistanis who had been welcomed with open arms into this great country, and had shit on their hosts by taking to a life of crime as drug-pushers and pimps, thieves and muggers, murderers and rapists.

Now these fuckers were going to pay the price for their arrogance as years of frustration and anger were about to be let out in one short orgy of violence.

The Muslims were getting hammered from the front and rear and as the fighting grew more intense they were being pushed into a tighter and tighter group in the middle of the room, where they found that they didn't even have the arm-room to raise their weapons to defend themselves. Their morale collapsed entirely as the other prisoners waded into them with kicks and punches, head-butts and swinging chair and bed legs. They didn't stand a chance. It was well-deserved vengeance for years of their bullying and intimidation, by men who all had one thing in common. They had all, at one time or the other, been trained to fight by the best army in the world: The British Army. And they loved it.

SEVENTY-THREE

10th August
Snittersfield, North Warwickshire

It was getting on for twilight when the Land Rover pulled to a shuddering stop in the small lay-by.
"Are you sure this is the place?" said the big man sitting next to the driver.
"Have another look at the instructions if you want, Nigel, but this is the only lay-by along here that's got a gate and a track going into the wood."
The driver sounded irritated. It had been a long drive and they had taken several wrong turns on the way.
"Look, lads," piped up a voice from the back seat. "Just have a look at the lock on the gate. If it's the right one it'll be a bloody combination lock, for Christ sake!"
"Okay! Okay! I'll have a quick butchers."
The big man opened his door with a sigh and stepped out.
"I'll give you the thumbs up if it's the right one."
Two minutes later they could see him grinning and giving the sign as the last of the summer sunlight began to dip behind the trees. The driver banged the gears into reverse, drove back a couple of yards and then forward again, nosing the front of the Land Rover through the gap as the big man pulled the gate open.
"Looks like he gave us the right combination for the lock then."
"Of course he did! You know he wouldn't let us down."

"Yeah, I know. But he did warn us that he hadn't been here for a while. It might have been changed or something."

The driver edged the Land Rover onto the tarmac surface of the track to give big Nigel room to swing the gate to and lock it again.

"Bit bloody creepy this place, ain't it?"

"You're just a woosey."

"Fuck you too."

They drove on into the dark, the headlights picking up the weird shape of trees and bushes closing in on the track as though they were living things.

"What's the instructions say again, Nigel?"

"Keep driving until we come to a fork in the track, then go right and there's a massive big oak with a bird box on it that almost blocks the track."

"Righty-ho. Roger that."

Five minutes later, after a sharp right turn at the fork, they came to what could only be the tree, with a huge trunk several feet across.

"Bloody hell, that's a big 'un! I was reading about this place. Apparently all of the bloody trees were cut down by the RAF during the last war. They used this place as a big ammo dump. That's why there are tarmac tracks everywhere."

"What, you mean that tree's only seventy years old? Jesus!"

"Alright, stop it with the history lessons, will you, Matt. We've got to pace off twenty paces to the east of the tree and then ten north. Me and Darren will take the spades. You and Billy walk down the track and set up OPs in case some bugger decides to take a walk in the dark and bumps into us. Have you got the torches, Darren?"

"Here you go Nigel, you take the small one and I'll keep the rechargeable. Remember not to wave it about. We don't want some local seeing strange lights in the woods and giving the Old Bill a tinkle!"

"Okay, smart arse."

The big man and the driver disappeared into the woods, pacing off the distance from the tree while Matt and Billy quickly made their way in opposite directions along the track.

It was hard going through an area of dense bramble, and after tripping over a small sapling and nearly ending up on his backside, Nigel decided to use the torch. They paced off the distance east and then the ten paces north, coming to what the feeble torchlight showed them was a small clearing.

"Right. X marks the spot I guess. We'd better get digging."

The two men stripped off their combat jackets, and jammed the torch into the fork of a branch so that its faint light illuminated the ground. Then, grabbing a spade each, they started to dig into the loamy soil. The going was easier than they had thought it might be, as there weren't any large tree roots in the ground and the soil was still damp from a rain shower earlier that day. It was only fifteen minutes later that Darren was rewarded with a quiet clang as the spade banged down into something solid. Both men threw their spades to one side and began to use their hands to scoop out the soil. Pretty soon they had unearthed a four feet long metal box. They tucked their hands under the edges and pulled the box up, setting it on to the ground next to the hole with a grunt of effort.

"This is fucking heavy!"

"Too right."

They took a minute to get their breath back from the hot and sweaty work of digging, and then Nigel retrieved the torch and they had a closer look at the box.

"Here's the lock. Did you bring the jemmy with you, Darren?"

"Yeah, got it here, mate. Back up and give us some room."

Darren jammed the end of a small crowbar into the space made by the lock's hoop and gave it a sharp tug. He was rewarded by the ping of the lock snapping open.

"Here we go then. Keep your fingers crossed, Nigel." He opened the hasp and pulled sharply on the lid, which gave way with a slight screech of un-oiled hinges and the patter of loose soil falling onto the ground. Both men bent forward to look inside.

"Jesus fucking Christ Almighty! Will you look at that."

The weak light from the torch shone onto several Heckler and Koch MP5 sub-machine guns, each of them well wrapped up in plastic sheeting and sealed against the damp with gaffer tape. Darren reached in and pulled out one of the packages, revelling in the familiar weight of the firearm.

"How many are there?" asked Nigel, reaching in to pull a package out.

"Six that I can see, mate. Look here, under the guns, there's half a ton of fucking ammo as well!"

"Great! Let's hump the whole box back to the Lanny."

Replacing the two guns they closed the lid and each took an end of the metal box.

"I'll walk backward mate but don't go too fast or I'll end up arse over tit!"

They carried the heavy box towards the Land Rover, occasionally cursing as a long strand of bramble with its barbed hooks scraped across their shins or hands, or when they nearly lost their footing.

Half an hour later, four weary but happy men sat in the Land Rover as it made its way northwards along a country road. They had filled in the hole before they left the wood and retrieved all of their tools. The large metal box could be heard bouncing around in the back as they drove along.

"This is it, boys. It won't be long now and we'll be rich men! Piece of piss, this!"

"Don't get too excited. I know that the guns have given you a hard on, but there's a long way to go yet."

"Nah. It'll be no bother. All we gotta do now is rob a shit-load of stuff off the bloody army and then kidnap the royal fucking couple. Like I said, piece of piss!"

The men all laughed together.

SEVENTY-FOUR

10th August
Winson Green, Birmingham

"Are you sure that that is all you want, Mr Smith? I can get you a good deal on anything – crack, coke, heroin, morphine. I have a very good supplier."
It was association time and Smith was holding court on the ground floor of A-Wing, sitting at one of the tables with Smiler, Ginger, young Gordon and a few other prisoners. He looked up at the Pakistani prison officer standing nervously in front of the table.
"I've told you before, Radish..."
"It's *Ramesh*, Mr Smith..."
"That's what I said, *Radish*."
His simple joke brought out a few smiles around the table.
"Just watch my lips and listen to what I say. Now that we run things here on the wing, we don't agree with smuggling in the hard stuff anymore. Got it?"
"Yes, Mr Smith. None of the hard stuff."
"Finally. What we want is cannabis resin, or pure bush, but make sure it's none of that fucking 'skunk' stuff, okay? Apparently it sends you bloody paranoid."
"Okay, Mr Smith, no skunk."
"And for fuck's sake make sure you get in at least six bottles of bloody brandy. We don't care if it's only the cheap stuff, but no more whiskey. Do you understand, Radish? Whiskey tends to bring out the worse in some folks."

At this point he gave Ginger a stern look.

"Whiskey makes some people fight all the bloody time..."

Ginge looked back sheepishly, nursing a bright blue and yellow bruise beneath his left eye.

"...only they're so pissed that they lose!"
Everyone laughed out loud at this one, everyone except Ginger, who just grinned weakly.

"Do you want anything else, Mr Smith?"

"Er, yeah. Hold on a minute...," he looked down at the 'shopping' list on the table in front of him. "...Tomkins on the second landing wants one hundred *Marlboro* cigarettes for fuck's sake. Apparently they've stopped selling them in the canteen and he can't be doing with any other brand. Oh...and Gordon here would like another porn DVD, preferably one with some *bondage* in it!"
This got another good laugh as Gordon's face turned a bright red.

"Perhaps you'd better make that *two* porn DVDs, Radish! He's a growing lad and he's been reading *Fifty Shades of Grey*! And make sure we get your best price for it all, okay, Radish?"

"Yes, Mr Smith, I always give you my best price, Mr Smith!"

"Of course you do, Radish. Of course you do. Off you go then."
As the PO walked off, Smith looked around at the others and said quietly:

"You know I can't get over the fact that he was the screw that opened my cell door and let them Pakistanis threaten me when I first got here."

"Yeah, and now he works for us!" said Smiler.

"Only because you got them bastard Somalis off his back eight months ago, Smithy. Apparently he was being threatened by them all the time. They told him that if he didn't bring their stuff in, they'd rat on him to the Governor."

"Yeah," said Daljit, the big turbaned Sikh. "He's got

a young family on the outside and he knew he'd be sent to prison if he was caught."

"Why did he get into it in the first place, the silly sod?" Smith asked.

"They threatened his family. There's a small gang of Somalis that live in the same street and they said that they'd pour petrol through his letterbox and burn them up. Those old houses are a firetrap. They wouldn't have stood a chance."

"Jesus! Do we know if they're still being threatened? I wish we could do something to help them."
Smith grimaced and Daljit smiled at him.

"Are you sure that you want to? After all he *is* a Muslim."

"I've got nothing against Muslims, mate. The vast majority of them are okay. It's just the few wankers that fuck it up for the rest of them. Like these fucking Somalis - they reckon they're Muslims but they just use the religion as an excuse to be nasty bastards. Young Ramesh doesn't seem to be so bad. If I could help his family, I would."

"Well, in that case, maybe I can help."

"How's that then, Daljit? You're a Sikh. Why would you help a Muslim family, especially one from Pakistan?"

"At heart, all Sikhs are warriors," Daljit replied, grinning. "Good warriors should always help those that can't help themselves. Besides, I cannot abide those Somalis - it's about time that they were run out of my neighbourhood."

"Okay. How are you going to do it, then?"

"We Sikhs are warriors, but our young men are living in the real world. They do not get a chance to fight like we did when we were young. Maybe it's time that some of them learned how to flex their muscles and be bloodied. My brother is visiting this week. He is a good man - I will get him to organise things."

"Excellent!" exclaimed Smith, slapping Daljit on the back. "I'm glad you're on our side!"
The big man turned his dark eyes on to Smith's and grinned

again.

"So am I! Although you would make a worthy enemy, John!"

Smith grinned back.

"I wouldn't be too sure of that, Dal. If I saw a bunch of your mob coming after me over a hill, I'd run a bloody mile, mate!"

They all laughed. But Daljit thought to himself. *I doubt that very much John, very much indeed!*

SEVENTY-FIVE

12th August
Swinton Barracks, Wiltshire

It was about two in the morning and there was a cold wind blowing, even though the previous evening had been hot and balmy. The armed guards at the entrance gate to Swinton Barracks were wrapped up warm in their combats but the wind still plucked at their exposed faces and tried to squirm up their sleeves with its cold tendrils.

The barracks were usually home to 22 Engineer Regiment but at this point in time all three of its Armoured Engineer Squadrons, the Headquarters and Support Squadron, the Light Aid Detachment from the Royal Electrical and Mechanical Engineers were on deployment in Afghanistan. Their important work in Helmand Province in support of ISAF (the International Security Assistance Force) included route proving and clearance as an integral part of the Counter-Improvised Explosive Device Task Force. This is not, as you may well imagine, one of the safest jobs in the British Army, but the Royal Engineers are a tough, no-nonsense bunch of men and women who are not shy of placing themselves in danger to save others, including Afghan civilians.

However, the engineers were not at home and the barracks was almost empty except for a guard force made up of Ministry of Defence Police and a platoon of bored infantrymen on detachment from a county regiment.

The two army Land Rovers approached the main gate

situated just west of the small town of Perham Down from the direction of Tidworth. The bored soldiers on the gate heard the distinctive sound of the Lanny's cross-country tyres on the road a long time before they saw the vehicles themselves, and had smartened themselves up a bit in case they contained one of their officers. It could easily be a snap inspection by that bastard Captain Lansdale - he'd really got it in for them after catching one of the guys drunk on duty last week. They wouldn't put it past the wanker to turn up this early in the hopes of catching someone else. He was an out-and-out cunt.

Luckily, when the Land Rovers pulled up, it turned out that it was only a corporal and three privates from 1 Logistic Support Regiment, Royal Logistic Corps. A relieved guard commander directed them to park up and sign in at the guardroom.

The logistics corporal sauntered into the guardroom and across to the counter.

"Morning, miss," Nigel said to the female MOD police officer, giving her a big smile. "I believe you're expecting us. We're from 1 LSR, come to pick up some kit from the stores."

The woman smiled back at him, glad of anything to break up the monotony of her nightshift. It had been the most boring job of her life since the engineers had gone off for their stint in Afghanistan, and she missed the easy banter she had had with them when they were at home in the barracks. She looked through a pile of paperwork in front of her on the counter.

"No, there's nothing here about you."

"Bloody typical, if you'll excuse my French," he laughed. "Those plonkers in RHQ probably forgot to send the fax through."

"1 LSR? I thought you boys were based in Germany? What are you doing over here, then?"

"Yep, Princess Royal Barracks in Gutersloh, a right bloody dump, I can tell you! We're off to Afghanistan next month and we're part of the advance party, staying at Abington for a couple of weeks before we go. We're supposed to be picking up some weapons, ammo and explosives to keep the Afghans awake. They should have bloody well let you know we were coming!"

"Well, you know the army. Never gets anything right."

"Too true. What am I going to do now though? It's been a long bloody drive and RHQ won't be up and running until nine at the earliest."

The woman looked at the soldier in front of her. He was a big man, but handsome in a tough macho way. She liked his easy manner, but especially his twinkling blue eyes.

"I'll tell you what, corporal. I wouldn't normally do this but seeing as you boys are off to Afghanistan I'll make an exception in your case. Here's a map of the barracks..." She handed him a photocopy of a road map and quickly drew a circle around one building on it.

"...this is the main stores. There should be a store man on duty there but you might have to wake him up! I know it's the middle of the night but make sure you follow the road signs and keep to the one-way system, alright? Otherwise I'll get a telling off from my boss if there's any complaints made. Okay?"

"Thanks, love, you're a star! Don't worry, we'll behave ourselves."

Nigel gave her another big smile.

"Let's have a look at your ID card and I'll get you to sign in."

"Okay love, no probs," he said as he pulled out a perfect forgery of a force's ID card from his breast pocket. "I owe you one. Perhaps I could take you out for a drink sometime?"

She blushed, and then flashed her left hand at him, showing him the gold wedding ring around a finger.

"Sorry, love. I'm already spoken for!"

"Shame!" he said, and he meant it.

She wasn't a bad looker at all.

When he had finished signing in, Nigel went back out into the cold and up to the Land Rovers. Matt, Billy and Darren were huddled around the back of one, out of the wind and having a sly smoke, behaving just like any soldiers anywhere in the British Army.

"Alright, corps?" Matt asked.

"Yeah, no problem, worked like a charm, especially the bit about going to Afghanistan, just like you said it would Billy."

"Yeah, they just can't resist a bloody hero mate."

"Right, put your fags out and we'll go through the gate. I want to be out of here before any of the bloody officers wake up."

"Okay, Nigel."

"Hey, that's bloody *corporal* to you!" he grinned.

The rest of it went like a dream. The four men drove through the silent, deserted roads of the barracks and parked up, and then the 'corporal' woke the duty store man up with a loud banging on the door to the main stores. The store man was only a young lance jack (a lance corporal) and he did what every good soldier does when faced with a man of higher rank to himself - exactly as he was ordered to do. Nigel gave him a forged requisition order for the kit that they wanted, and off he went to get it bit by bit. As he returned to the counter with each piece of equipment, the rest of the lads carted it out and put it in the back of the Land Rovers while Nigel played his part of corporal faithfully - doing none of the carrying and fetching but instead helping himself to a mug of the store man's tea and putting his feet up in his chair. RHIP as the old army acronym goes: 'Rank Has Its Privileges'. Once they had the technical stuff loaded up, the store man unlocked the separate armoury, ammo stores and explosives lockers and counted out exactly what they wanted.

When the Land Rovers were full and they had everything they needed, the corporal got the store man to put the kettle on so that they could all have a hot brew and a break, while he went through the required paperwork and signed everything out. The British Army always works to a set routine, and the team knew that if you stuck to that routine and did nothing out of the ordinary then no one, especially a lowly lance jack, would ever get suspicious of them. Having a brew and a laugh with the man once they'd finished the hard work of carting all the kit about was just another facet of the army way of doing things.

The team was back on the road by half past four. It would probably be days before anyone at the deserted camp realised that they had been scammed, and by then the team's objective would already be known to the authorities, just as they planned. Only one item on their list of kit had not been in the stores.

"It's a shame they didn't have any bloody tasers; we really need those," said Matt as he struggled to strip off his uniform on the back seat of the lead Land Rover.

"I know, mate," replied Nigel. "I didn't really think that they'd have them though. They're not a bit of kit that the army needs."

"Where're we gonna get some, then? You can probably order them over the internet from the States, but they'll take bloody ages to come through and there's always the chance that the Customs boys will pick them up before they get to us. We haven't got the time to fuck about; we're on a tight schedule."

"The boss thought this would probably happen, so we worked out a backup plan just in case. I think you'll enjoy it, mate."

"What's that, then?" Matt's interested was piqued.

"We'll just have to mug a few coppers!"

"Brilliant! Some of them always carry tasers. Nice one, Nigel. Just wait till I tell Billy and Darren. They'll get a hard on when they find out we're gonna mug some pigs!" Both of them laughed then.

"Nice one!"

SEVENTY-SIX

12th August
Lozells, Birmingham

At about the same time that Nigel and his team were setting out from Swinton Barracks in Wiltshire, another group of men were hiding in the shadows of a house on a side street just off Lozells Road, in Birmingham. The leader of this group of men was as large as Nigel in stature, but there the resemblance ended. This particular man was dark-skinned and wore a *Dastar*, a Sikh turban, around his head, and had a long grey beard. He turned to the other Sikh men who accompanied him, all considerably younger than he was.

"Have you called your white friend again, Adeeb?" he asked the man nearest to him.

"Yes, Ajai, he's on his way. He should be here in a few minutes."

"Good, let's get into position then."

Ajai looked intensely into the faces of the younger men around him.

"Remember what my brother Daljit said. You will be drawing your *Kirpan* to prevent violence from being used to harm defenceless people. We have tried hard to get the Somalis to quit their drug-dealing and I warned them last night to leave our area, but they laughed in my face and threatened me with violence. They are evil men, so I am sure that our God will look down upon our work this morning with favour. Prepare yourselves."

The young Sikh warriors fanned out into the street silently, moving like dark shadows in the blackness.

A few minutes later a skinny young white man dressed in jeans that hung around his backside, and a backward-facing baseball cap, walked into the street. At a hiss from his friend Adeeb he went into the shadows.
"Hi, Mike, thanks for coming out."
"No probs, Adeeb. Everybody in this street hates these fuckin' Somalis. Are you really gonna sort 'em out?"
"Yep!"
"Cool! What do you want me to do then?"
"Just go up to door and tell them that you want to buy some drugs. When they open the door to take your money make sure that you don't get in our way, okay?"
"Cool. Want me to go now?"
"Yes please, Mike."
"Okeycokey, see yer in a minute mate, good luck!"
"Thank you."

As Mike banged loudly on the heavily-reinforced steel door of the Somalis' crack house, he surreptitiously glanced around to see if he could see any Sikhs hiding in the darkness, but he couldn't see anyone at all. Then the small spy-hole in the door opened and a heavily-slurred voice called:
"What you want?"
Mike felt distinctly nervous and alone. Adeeb had been a good mate since they'd been at school together, but he hoped he wasn't going to let him down now. These Somali bastards scared the hell out of him. He swallowed back his fear.
"I wanna score, man," he said loudly.
"You got money?"
"Yeah, man."
"Let me see."
Mike held up a twenty pound note to the spy-hole.
"Okay. Want crack?"

"Yeah, man."

"Wait."

As he waited, Mike very slowly began to inch backwards from the door until he was about five feet away. He jumped nervously when the spy-hole flipped open again and an eye appeared at the hole. Then he heard the distinctive sound of locks being turned, bolts being slid back and security chains being released.

The second that the door was opened enough to show a scarred black face in the doorway, there was a rush of bodies past Mike and the air was torn apart by the blood-curdling screams and war cries of the Sikhs as they smashed into the door and into the hallway beyond.

Mike was scared stiff as he stood outside the house, listening to the sounds of violence coming from inside. It seemed like hours, but was probably only a few minutes until the first of the Sikh men, the older man with the grey beard, came back out of the doorway. He was dragging out a Somali man by his hair, holding his ceremonial sword at the African's throat. The Somali's face was ashen with fear and blood-stained from a smashed nose.

"Don't continue to fight me, young man; it will do you no good," Ajai said calmly, shaking the man like a terrier shaking a rat.

He was soon joined by the other Sikhs, who dragged out five more blood-stained Somali men, and then escorted out a sobbing red-eyed white girl. Mike, much to his surprise, recognised the girl.

"Angie? Is that you, Angie?" the girl just sobbed in reply. "What the fuck are yer doing here?"

"They...they raped me!" she sobbed again, absolutely distraught. "I've been here for days...they..."

"It's okay now, Angie," said the young man as he put his arms around her. "Yer Mum and Dad thought yer'd run off. They didn't know that these bastards had got yer!" He glared with hatred at the captive Somalis on the overgrown lawn. Ajai looked at the battered face of the girl and back at the open door of the house.

"Adeeb," he said, "start a fire inside and burn the house down!"

He was angry now, and forced back the African's head that he still held by the hair, so that he could stare him in the face.

"You will watch now as we burn down your filthy house, with its evil drugs and dirty money still inside! If I ever see your face again I swear that next time I will burn down your house with you still in it! Do you understand?" The Somali blubbered an affirmative, trying to nod his head in the man's hard grip but unable to.

"Good. Now watch while we burn it down and pray to your God that we don't come looking for you again!"

SEVENTY-SEVEN

14th August
Winson Green, Birmingham

John Smith started the day with an early summons to the Governor's office, delivered to his cell by a grinning Sweeney.

"What's it about this time, Sweeney?"

"Haven't got a clue, Smudge."

"Then why are you grinning like a bloody Cheshire cat?"

"What me? Grinning? No way!" the prison officer said while another grin split his face. "Come on, John. We don't want to be late. You'll enjoy this, mate!"

"Enjoy what? I thought you said you didn't know what's going on?"

"I don't mate."

"Hmmm..."

When Smith arrived at the Governor's office he was let inside quickly by his escort and the door closed behind him. To his surprise, the Governor wasn't there, but there was a handful of other prisoners sitting around the office, none of whom he recognised. For a crazy moment his survival instinct went into overdrive and he prepared to fight and kill. *Was this a setup? Had the Governor been bought? Were this lot going to try and knock him off?* It took a full minute to calm down his surging adrenaline before he realised that the men were just sitting there looking at him and showing no sign of aggression. They, of course, had no idea what had just happened, as Smith's face and usually calm outward demeanour hadn't changed a bit, apart perhaps, from a narrowing of those cold, coal-black eyes.

"Who are you lot then?" he asked the room in general, his gaze going over the men in front of him one by one.

There were six of them. The first on the left was a tall West Indian with dreadlocks, next to him was an Asian guy, probably an Indian Hindu by the look of him. Next to him were three white guys, all in their mid-forties and clean-cut. The last man on the right was another Indian, a turbaned Sikh. One of the white guys, a short but powerfully built blond headed man, was the first to answer.

"My name's Pete Barnes," he said in a well educated voice, "but it doesn't really matter what our names are. All you have to know is that we all have something in common with you, Sergeant Smith."

"Oh yeah? And what would that be?" *What indeed?* he thought. *What the fuck is going on here?* "And that would be *Mr*, by the way, not sergeant."

"Okay, *Mr* Smith it is then. I'm from B-Wing, and these other gentlemen are representatives from the other wings of this wonderful prison. We are all, despite appearances..." and here he grinned at the tall dreadlocked West Indian, "...ex-servicemen. All of us are ex-army to be exact, except for poor old Johnny here." He indicated another blond haired guy to his right.

"Johnny was in the RAF Regiment, but we don't like to talk about it. I'm sure he'll get over it one day."

"Piss off, woodentop!"

"Thanks, Johnny...typical bloody rock-ape!"

"Alright. Enough. So you're all ex-squaddies then. What the fuck does this have to do with me and why are we here?"

"Well, Mr Smith. It's all around the prison that you have taken control of your wing from the gangs, and have set up a sort of council amongst the lags."

"Yeah, that's right."

He was silent for a moment, thinking to himself *This is beginning to make sense now*.

"Has the Governor spoken to any of you?"

"Not officially," said the Indian, "but he did invite us into his office one by one and told us about what's been happening on A-Wing. He said that since you set up this 'council' there has been hardly any violence, and absolutely no intimidation on your wing."

"Yeah!" interrupted Johnny. "The Governor said that you had banned any hard drugs coming in and just kept to the soft stuff. He said that things had really settled down on A-Wing and everybody there was a lot happier now that those Muslim twazaks had been given what for!"

"But of course," added Pete Barnes, "the Governor didn't say that he was condoning what you have done, nor your 'council'. In fact he didn't really say anything at all apart from giving us the bare facts. It was almost as if he wanted us to make up our own minds."

"Yeah. He's a fucking sharp one for sure. He doesn't want to be seen to be condoning this sort of thing, but on the other hand, if all of the wings managed to overthrow their bloody gangs, and then set up similar councils to yours, and if all of those councils just happened to be run by ex-military guys..."

Johnny left it to hang.

"Okay. I get it. The Governor wants *us* to run the prison from the inside, *not* the Muslim gangs, because then he'll have a quieter and much happier bunch of inmates who will behave themselves."

Smith had to smile. *He certainly is a bloody sharp one!*

"Right. If you're all willing to do this, then we'd better work out how. It looks like the army, and the RAF...," he nodded towards Johnny, "...will be taking over the whole prison! So let's try and do it without too much bloodshed, shall we?"

"Wait a minute, Mr Smith," said the tall West Indian.

"If we're going to do this, we have to have a name for the brothers, man."

Smith thought for a moment and then he smiled again, looking around the expectant faces in front of him.

"Why don't we take a leaf from your book then," he said, looking up at the tall black-skinned man. "Why don't we call ourselves the 'Brotherhood'?"

"Yeah man, that's cool!"

Suddenly everyone was excited and chipped in.

"The *Brotherhood*! I like that!"

"Yeah. We're all brothers in the forces right? Cool!"

"Brilliant!"

Even Smith was suddenly caught up in their excitement and the possibilities presenting themselves.

"Okay. The Brotherhood it is then. Right, let's get down to work..."

SEVENTY-EIGHT

14th August
Enfield, London

Nigel and Darren sat in an old battered BMW estate, Nigel in the front passenger seat and Darren behind him in the back seat. Nigel was scrutinising the wing mirror on his side, which was angled so that he could clearly see the pavement of the side street behind them.
"Okay Darren, here they come. I can see Matt and Billy behind them. About two minutes to go."
"Roger that, Nigel."
They waited tensely, the early morning sun making the interior of the car uncomfortably hot and sticky. The palms of their hands were sweaty. Darren was constantly monitoring the rest of the street while Nigel kept his eye on the four approaching people.
"Thirty seconds."
"Roger that, the street is still clear."
"Twenty seconds."
"Ten seconds, prepare to move."
Hands were wiped on thighs to get the sweat off and moved to the door handles.
"Roger that."
"Standby...standby...standby...go! Go! Go!"
They quickly opened their doors and stepped out on to the kerb, pulling down their balaclavas to cover their faces. At the same time, Matt and Billy, who had been strolling along some fifteen feet behind the two yellow high visibility

jacketed police constables that they had been tailing, also pulled down their balaclavas. Only in their case they faced out, away from the coppers, and watched the empty street. Nigel and Darren raised their short-barrelled Heckler and Koch L104 baton guns. The surprised looks on the police officers' faces made Darren laugh out loud.

"Goodnight pigs!" he growled as both he and Nigel fired at almost point-blank range. The 37mm four-inch-long L21 solid plastic baton rounds smashed into the police officers at lower chest level, throwing the big men backwards on to the pavement, stunning them completely. Their standard-issue stab-jackets saved them from serious injury but didn't stop them from being knocked unconscious by the sheer force of the baton rounds hitting them.

Nigel and Darren stepped forward, leaned down over the prone bodies and quickly slipped the X26 Taser guns from their pouches on the coppers' equipment belts. Darren couldn't resist a not-too-soft kick into the face of one of the coppers.

"Eat shit, fuckface!" he snarled.

Darren *really* didn't like the police.

"Okay, guys!" shouted Nigel, smiling beneath his balaclava at Darren's antics. "We've got them. Bug out!"

The whole ambush had taken only a few seconds to complete. The four men jumped into the BMW, and Matt gunned the engine and drove away with a squeal of burning rubber on tarmac, leaving behind the two unconscious policemen lying on the ground like so much trash. Half a mile farther on they abandoned the stolen BMW and split up on foot, just normal guys making their way in the big city. In thirty minutes time they would meet up to go through it all again, using another vehicle that would be stolen by Matt. He was ex REME (Royal Electrical and Mechanical Engineers) and there was no vehicle on Earth that he couldn't break into, drive, or repair (as long as he had a stick of chewing gum, a six-inch nail, an elastic band and a very big hammer).

As Nigel strolled through the early-morning rush hour crowds he thought *Two down – two more tasers to get, and then we'll be ready*. He felt the thrill of the adrenaline rushing through his system as he went through the plan in his head. He loved this shit.

SEVENTY-NINE

16th August
Winson Green, Birmingham

The attack, when it came, came from absolutely nowhere. There had been no prior indications, no prior intelligence - it came straight out of the blue. John Smith had just left his cell to begin the association period, and was strolling along the landing towards the head of the stairwell, his head full of ideas and plans for the Brotherhood, not really paying attention to the prison around him.

    The Pakistani had been a few yards behind him, like Smith who was making his way to the stairwell to go downstairs. He'd timed it perfectly, and only had to extend his strides slightly in order to rapidly close in upon the Godless infidel, which he did very smoothly, desperate not to draw attention to himself until the moment to strike came. Slowly he let the blade that had been hidden up his right sleeve slide down into his hand, keeping it straightened by his side so that no one could see it. Everything was perfect.

    Unfortunately he hadn't banked on the Pakistani prison officer standing on the opposite landing. Ramesh had been doing his rounds of the wing when he had seen John Smith leave his cell. He had paused for a minute, thinking hard. The relief that he had felt when he had learned that the Somali gang that had been intimidating his neighbourhood for the past few years, had been driven out, was intense. His wife had cried her eyes out when she had described the scene from that night to him - police cars and fire engines filling the street with their flashing lights, and the Somalis' crack house burning fiercely in the darkness. She had heard one of the policemen laugh about the smell of burning cannabis which hung heavily in the air, joking that they'd all be stoned by the time they finished this job. It wasn't until the day after, when the former crack house had been nothing more than a smouldering ruin, that the rumours had started. One of their neighbours had heard some screaming and shouting during the evening of the attack and had risked a quick look out of his bedroom window. He had clearly seen the Somali gang held prisoner on the unkempt lawn in front of their house by a group of huge turbaned Indians who could only have been Sikhs. A few other people had seen them too and suddenly everybody in the neighbourhood had been talking about how the Sikhs had routed the Somalis and sent them packing, then burned down their house with everything, including their drugs and money, still in it. People who knew the Sikhs personally asked them quietly if the rumours were true, but were met with nothing more than silence and smiles. Nobody would admit to the attack but everyone knew who had done it. The Sikhs that lived in the neighbourhood suddenly found themselves very popular indeed. They were told to keep their cash in their pockets when they brought groceries at the Hindu-owned corner shop. The local Irish car mechanic gave free services on the cars owned by Sikhs. Prayers for their good health and fortune were said at the local Mosque by the Pakistani Imam.

    Ramesh couldn't prove it, but he knew that John Smith had had something to do with the attack on the Somalis. Him and that big Sikh that he hung around with - Daljit. One of his snouts on the wing had told him that the Brotherhood had organised the attack specifically to get rid of the Somalis who had been intimidating and threatening Ramesh's family, but he couldn't understand why. After all, he had been the one who had unlocked Smith's cell door soon after he had arrived on the wing, so that some of his fellow Pakistani Muslims could threaten Smith. Surely the man hadn't forgotten that? Why would he want to stop the intimidation that had left his wife fearing for her life and too frightened to even go out on the street? Why on Earth would a white Christian man care enough about him and his family to help him? Ramesh was totally confused. He watched Smith as he walked along on the opposite landing. The man walked like a big rangy cat, like one of the tigers that had once lived in Ramesh's home country a long time ago, but which he had only ever seen on the TV. Smith had long loping strides that could eat up the miles, and despite his advancing years, which were indicated by the greying hair and the deep lines on his face, he was still fit and athletic enough to put to shame many of the younger men in the prison. More than that though, there was something else about him. There was a looseness in his walk and the set of his shoulders that spoke of a man who was totally self-contained and confident in himself. John Smith smiled an awful lot and could be very easy-going, but Ramesh had seen the video of him taking on and killing those eight black terrorists who had been armed with long wicked knives. He had seen the rage and hatred in Smith's eyes and had heard his animal-like snarls as he had taken the men's lives and totally ignored his own awful wounds. Ramesh had felt the hairs rising on the back of his neck and had felt a deep-rooted fear take hold of him as he had watched this same smiling, laughing man butcher his enemies on that plane. He just couldn't figure out this man named John Smith at all.

    Something about the Pakistani man walking quickly behind Smith caught Ramesh's eye. He appeared innocent enough, but there was something...what was it? Then he caught a tiny glint of shining metal in the man's right hand. That was it! He was hiding something in his hand! Ramesh didn't stop to think. He just opened his mouth and roared out a warning:

    "John! Behind you! Watch out!"

A normal man would have heard the warning and frozen on the spot while his brain took precious milli-seconds to register the shouted message, wonder whether it was intended for him and then think of a way to react. By this time a normal man would have been writhing on the landing floor with the six-inch sharpened handle of a dessertspoon sticking in his back while his life-blood gushed out of the wound. But John Smith was not a normal man. From the age of eleven he had started the long road to train his body to react to danger and attack without conscious thought. First of all in the sweat-filled training rooms of Kung Fu Masters and Tai Kwon Do and Karate black belts, then from the age of sixteen in the tough no-nonsense environment of the British Army. He had lived a long life of brutality, pain, fear and death where only the quick and the ruthless survived. He had survived through horrors of undercover life in Northern Ireland, the terror of fighting the Soviet Army in the bleakness of Afghanistan and through a dozen other wars and conflicts around the world. He had killed so many men that he couldn't remember them all, except in his nightmares. Where he had fought there had been only two kinds of soldiers: the quick and the dead - and John Smith was very much alive.

Even before Ramesh had ended his warning, Smith had whirled around, taken in and registered the man behind him who had a look of pure hatred in his eyes, saw the glinting blade striking towards his stomach and reacted to the attack in a lightning movement. He deflected the blade to the side by sweeping his left arm across his front and catching and pushing the Pakistani's arm up and away. At the top of this swing, and still held in position firmly under the wrist by Smith's moving arm, the Pakistani's arm was stretched out, elbow facing upwards and the blade still in his hand. Smith's right arm flew up so fast that it was nothing but a blur of movement - too quick for the eye to register. Then it smashed back down on to the Pakistani's exposed and vulnerable elbow joint with such force that the arm snapped with an audible crack and the blade dropped to clatter on the steel floor of the landing with a clang. He didn't know it but the Pakistani had attacked John Smith in the precise way that allowed for one of Smith's favourite counter-moves, a move that Smith had practised over forty years, time and time and time again, until he didn't even have to think about it at all. His body had developed a muscle memory after the millions of repetitions of the move that allowed it to react to that particular mode of attack automatically and without conscious thought.

    The only other sound in the now silent wing was the ear-piercing howl of sheer agony that escaped the Pakistani's lips as his arm was snapped almost in two by the force of Smith's counter attack. Even though Smith had disarmed and disabled his attacker in less than two seconds he wasn't finished. Smith drew back his right arm in readiness to launch it forward and finish it with the man's death. His hand flew forward...and then stopped an inch from the man's throat. Smith stared hard into the Pakistani's eyes. He saw the pain and fear that had replaced the hatred, saw that his attacker was absolutely helpless in his hands, and then he smiled his terrifying feral smile into the man's face. With a swift movement that belied his age he grasped the man at throat and groin, grimaced with effort as he lifted his body up and above his head, slightly staggered under the weight as he stepped to the landings railing and with a grunt threw the body over the rail into the emptiness beyond. The Pakistani screamed in terror as he felt himself begin the fall to the ground floor of the wing three floors below, but it was cut short as his body hit the net suspended a few feet below the railing. Smith leaned over the railing and laughed out loud as he saw the floundering figure of the Pakistani bouncing helplessly on the net. It had been put in place many years ago to stop prisoners from committing suicide by throwing themselves off the landing. *I bet that scared you!* he thought to himself. Then he turned to see who had shouted the warning from the opposite landing that had saved his life. He saw Ramesh the Muslim prison officer looking on in absolute amazement, with his mouth still hanging open from giving the shout. Smith nodded at the man in acknowledgement and thanks, then turned and carried on to the stairwell as though nothing unusual had happened at all, his mind already switching back to the thoughts that he had been having before he had been so rudely interrupted.

It was only after the alarm bell had brought a dozen prison officers running to the scene, and the would-be assassin had been retrieved from the safety net, that another prisoner approached John Smith. Smith was sitting on the ground floor with his friends, who were laughing and joking about the racket that the Pakistani had made every time someone touched his broken arm while the officers removed him from the net. The prisoner leaned in close and whispered into Smith's ear:

"I had a good look around his cell and found a lot of *Jihadist* stuff John, just like you'd expect with a bloody Muslim extremist like him! The most interesting thing was this though."

He produced a page that had been torn from a magazine at some stage, and unfolded it so that Smith could read it clearly.

"It's a bloody magazine article from that bastard in Iran. He's offered a reward of half a million quid to any Muslim who carries out the *Fatwa* against you!"

Smith read the article carefully. *That explains that then,* he thought. *I'll have to watch every Muslim very carefully from now on. That's a lot of bloody money on my head.*

"Okay, thanks Tom, you've done well, mate. Let the others read it now. We'll have to think about this and what we can do to guard against it."

"Gotcha, John. Half a million bleedin' quid eh? That's a lot of bloody dosh!"

"Cheap at half the price!" laughed Smith, not feeling quite as funny as he tried to sound. "Fucking

cheapskates!"
Tom laughed with him, amazed at how calm and collected this man was, and only a few minutes after someone had tried to stick him proper! *He's got a thousand times more courage than I'll ever have,* he thought to himself as he passed the folded article across to Smiler. *But I wouldn't want to be in his shoes. No way, José!*

EIGHTY

22nd August
Coombe Abbey, Coventry

Coombe Abbey Hotel is a beautiful four-star hotel situated in five hundred acres of parkland in Coombe Abbey Country Park, located on the outskirts of the City of Coventry. The Abbey itself was founded by Cistercian monks in 1150 and the grounds were designed by Lancelot 'Capability' Brown in the eighteenth century. This world famous landscape architect contructed a huge lake (by damming the Smite Brook which flowed through the land), which is now populated by the largest heronry in Warwickshire. He also created wild-looking woodlands, marshes and open fields in the grounds. The country park is used by thousands of local people for recreation, especially during the weekends or Bank Holidays.

The hotel itself is located in the former abbey and country house, and is a beautiful mixture of old arches and cloisters converted into modern rooms which retain the magic of a time gone by.

Barbara Mitchell was an overweight nineteen year old lass who lived in the Binley area of Coventry, just a few miles down the road from the hotel. She had worked as a receptionist in the hotel for eighteen months, long enough for her not to be overawed by the sumptuous elegance of the arched reception area any more, nor with the VIPs who occasionally stayed at the hotel. However, earlier tonight she had been completely tongue-tied when she had had the job of welcoming Prince William and his lovely new bride, formerly known as Kate Middleton (both now known as the Duke and Duchess of Cambridge), to the hotel. Their stay was to be brief and very informal as they prepared for an official visit to Warwick Castle the following day. Even so, the paparazzi had still managed to sneak into the grounds during the day, though they had all been rounded up by the local police and escorted from the park, which officially closed to the public (including the paparazzi, to their disgust) at dusk. The photographers had therefore missed the arrival of the Royal Couple, who had been whisked up to the hotel entrance and quickly escorted inside by an armed detachment from the Royal Protection Branch, SO14, of the Metropolitan Police. Barbara had been allowed about thirty seconds to say hello to the Duke and Duchess before handing over the room keys to one of the protection officers. In return she had received a radiant smile of thanks from Kate and a quick grin from the handsome prince; this had set her heart fluttering and made her very happy indeed.

  The evening had quickly settled back down into the normal hotel routine. Barbara wasn't exactly busy, as there were only a few guests staying. She spent a lot of the next hour daydreaming about the world-famous glamorous young couple who were only a few hundred feet from where she sat and worked. If only *she* could meet and marry a handsome prince like William. How her life would be different! No more boring evenings sitting behind the reception desk of this bloody hotel.

  Her daydreams were interrupted by the arrival of the Johnstons, a young couple and their carers who had been staying in the hotel for the last two nights. It was so sad! They were so young! What a tragedy that they had both been crippled in the same car accident. She smiled at the couple as one of their carers, a nice young man with a lovely smile, collected their room keys. Then she watched sadly as the two young people in their wheelchairs were pushed into the ornately-gated lift. *They're on the same floor as William and Kate,* she thought. *I hope that they get to meet them. That would be a nice surprise for those poor people.*

Barbara turned back to her computer screen as the lift doors shut.

EIGHTY-ONE

22nd August
Coombe Abbey, Coventry

You'd think - wouldn't you? - that something like kidnapping the Royal Couple would be very difficult indeed; whereas in reality, as long as you've got a few things going in your favour, it's actually not that difficult at all. These few things include good intelligence, such as where the couple will be and when, and how much security they will have with them as protection. Then there's having a good plan and the ability to stick to it when the shit hits the fan as well as the right weaponry and the trained manpower to use it efficiently. Lastly, of course, without which all of the above is absolutely useless: is having the balls, guts, bottle, bravery, audacity or whatever else you want to call it, to carry the kidnapping out.

     Finding out where and when the Duke and Duchess would be was probably the easiest of the things to do. It was simply a matter of logging on to the internet and searching, and being patient. Just about everything you could ever want to know can be found somewhere on the worldwide web if you look hard enough. The Royal Couple's visit to Warwick Castle was well publicised. The fact that they would be spending the night at Coombe Abbey Hotel was harder to discover, but a little slip in an interview given by a friend of the Couple started the trail that led there. An additional discreet telephone call to the hotel's manager, pretending to be a member of the couple's entourage confirmed the fact quite simply.

Getting the right equipment for the job had been quite difficult, as you've already read. But even this, with prior knowledge about how the British Army operates and its standard operating procedures, can be fairly easy if you're determined and bold enough.

The plan's preparation was down to the men's boss. It was a full and detailed plan, dealing not only with what the men should do if everything went okay, but also with what they should do if it went unexpectedly wrong at any stage. That the team would be able to carry the plan out even if the shit hit the fan was never in question. Each team member was well motivated, excellently trained and above all else, had nothing to lose. They would do it no matter what.

As for having the courage - each of these men had been tried and tested in combat, fighting for their Queen and country. They had proved themselves to be as brave as lions and each of them would rather die than let their comrades down.

As it happened everything went very smoothly and according to the original plan. Matt and Nigel were the two men pretending to be the crippled Johnstons' carers. Darren pretended to be Mr Johnston, and Billy who to his dismay had quite a girlish face (especially with the addition of a long blond wig) pretended to be Mrs Johnston, both of them in wheelchairs. They had been staying at the hotel for the previous two days, going out a few times each day to let the hotel staff get to know them. It was a matter of luck that their room was in the same cloister of the hotel as the Royal Couple, but they would have carried out the plan regardless. It just happened to make things easier. That evening still in character they left the lift, with Matt and Nigel pushing Mr and Mrs Johnston in their wheelchairs. As they approached the armed police protection officer on duty outside the Royal Couple's room, they were so convincing that he actually said "Good evening" to them with a smile on his face and stepped back against the wall to allow them room to get by. The smile vanished as Billy lifted up the brightly-woven blanket that covered 'her' crippled legs and let him have it with a X26 Taser gun into his own unprotected legs. Two small, barbed, dart like electrodes, which were connected to the gun by conducting wires, were propelled from the gun by small compressed nitrogen charges and lodged themselves in the policeman's right thigh. A huge electrical discharge surged down the conducting wires causing instant neuromuscular incapacitation, which, while not lethal, disrupted the man's ability to control his own muscles. He collapsed in a heap against the wall without a sound, and was instantly jumped on by Nigel, who disarmed him and had him gagged and tied up in about thirty seconds.

Next the team got ready to assault the rest of the protection officers in their own room, which was adjacent to the Royal Couple's room. Billy reloaded the cartridges on his taser gun and the guys positioned themselves on either side of the door. Then Billy, still in his wig and make-up, knocked on the door. An officer inside looked out of the spy-hole and saw a girl in the uniform of a chambermaid outside the door.

"Yes? What do you want?" he asked pleasantly from the other side of the door.

"A gift from the management, Sir," said Billy, in his most girlie-like voice (which was pretty damn convincing, once again to his intense dismay). "There's some food and drink, and some DVDs to help you pass the time, Sir."
The door opened on to the eager face of the protection officer.

"That's very decent of..." he started to say, until Billy's taser darts hit him in his thigh and he slumped to the ground, helpless. Nigel followed up immediately, jumping over the prone man into the room with his taser gun ready, followed straight away by Matt and Darren. Within a minute they had disabled the remaining two protection officers inside the room with their own tasers and were busy tying them up. It was all over so quickly and quietly that no one else in the hotel knew that it had happened. Once the three coppers were tied up, the team quickly pushed the wheelchairs, with the first copper occupying one of them into the bedroom. Matt then pulled off his Barbour jacket, revealing a dark suit underneath, and took the place of the copper on duty outside the Royal Couple's bedroom. To anyone else's eyes, had anyone else been there to see it, everything was back to normal.

Ten minutes later Billy was knocking, again in his guise as a chambermaid, on the adjacent bedroom door. Prince William himself answered, having peeped through his own spy-hole and been reassured by the sight of a Royal Protection Officer standing by the girl looking down the corridor. As he opened the door William looked into the barrel of a 9mm Browning pistol, which was unceremoniously shoved into his face, and was told to back off into the room. The Duke and Duchess of Cambridge, both of them shocked beyond belief, but as calm and unflustered as they could be in the circumstances, were quickly knocked unconscious by the judicious use of chloroform-soaked pads to their faces. They were loaded on to the two wheelchairs, a hat pulled low over the Prince's face and Billy's blonde wig covering the dark hair of the Princess, and wheeled out to the lift by Nigel and Matt, once again pretending to be the Johnstons' carers. They pushed the inert couple out through reception, Matt giving Barbara Mitchell his handsome smile as they went, and called out that they were going into Coventry for a meal at a restaurant and would hopefully see her again before she went off duty.

  Outside the two men pushed the couple in the wheelchairs to their stolen Chrysler Voyager, with its orange disabled badge prominently displayed in the windscreen. The car was parked close to the hotel reception entrance in a disabled parking bay. The men lifted the couple from the wheelchairs and placed them carefully into the back seats of the car, fitting their seat belts to them. Then they folded up the wheelchairs, put them into the boot of the car and climbed into the front seats. All of the time they were being watched by two bored firearms officers sitting in a local police Armed Response Vehicle in the car park. They were another part of the protection team for the Royal Couple - supposedly still inside the hotel. Nigel started up the Chrysler, reversed carefully out of the parking bay and drove off smoothly into the evening.

Upstairs in the hotel, Darren and Billy would take turns at pretending to be Royal Protection Officers outside the Royals' bedroom until night came. Then they would silently leave the hotel via a fire exit whose alarm system had been bypassed by Darren, the team's electronics expert. They would disappear into the night, tab it a couple of miles to another stolen vehicle which they had parked up previously, and then they would make their way north to rendezvous with the other half of the team and their very important captives.

Everything had gone like clockwork, just as the boss had planned.

EIGHTY-TWO

23rd August
Winson Green, Birmingham

It was evening again, and the two hour association period was underway, with the prisoners of A-Wing sitting and talking, as per normal, on the ground floor of the wing. John Smith was at his usual table along with Smiler, Ginger, Daljit and Gordon. They were talking seriously about the threat to Smith from Muslim fanatics who fancied claiming the half a million pound reward from the Iranians for his death. They were interrupted by Sweeney, the prison officer, who uncharacteristically ran across the floor to their table. He was breathless when he arrived and had to take a few seconds to get his breath back before speaking.

"Smudge! I've just been sent down urgently from the Governor's office. The cops are 'ere, and they want to talk to you!"

Smith looked up at him, his face impassive.

"Slow down, Sweeney. What cops? What do they want?"

"I don't know what they want, Smudge, but they've got the top brass with 'em! Lots of silver braid on their 'ats!"

Smith smiled at Sweeney's excitement.

"Well, that's fine, Sweeney, but I'm busy at the moment. Tell them to make an appointment for some time during the week, and I'll see them then."

"What? Make an app...Smudge! It's urgent! They want to see you now!"
Smith was not impressed by the prison officer's pleading. With a hint of irritation in his voice, he said:
"Look Sweeney, I spend most of the bloody day locked in a tiny fucking cell, mate. Association is my only chance to get to talk to anybody except Gordon here. Now go away and tell the fucking coppers that I'm not interested in talking to them, there's a good chap."
With that, he turned away from the exasperated prison officer and continued talking to his comrades. Sweeney stared incredulously at the back of Smith's head, then turned on his heel and ran back the way he had come. Smith turned to watch him go, grinning to himself. To Smiler he said:
"It must be important if they've sent the top brass down."
"Yep, it must be."
"God, I hate fucking coppers!"
"You and just about everyone in here, John!" Smiler laughed.
"Too true blue!" he clapped his friend on his shoulder. "Anyway, where were we?"

Twenty minutes later Sweeney reappeared on the ground floor of A Wing, but this time he wasn't on his own. He had a group of about fifteen prison officers following him. They marched across the floor towards Smith's table and the whole wing went so quiet that you could have heard a pin drop, as about eighty inmates looked at them with hostility on their faces. The group of prison officers came to a halt in front of the table.
"Bloody 'ell Smudge!" said Sweeney. "You've really pissed off the coppers now, mate! They've sent us down 'ere to take you up to the Governor's office whether yer want to go or not!"
Smith's face was calm but his eyes were blazing as he looked the small group of prison officers over.

"Really? And what will you do if I refuse to go, Sweeney? Are you guys prepared to take on the whole wing?"

He gestured around him at the glowering faces of his comrades. Many of them had left their own tables now and were slowly converging on the prison officers. From the look of them they were spoiling for a fight.

"Now don't be like that, Smudge!" said Sweeney. "You know that I don't want any trouble." He was looking at the prisoners nervously. "But the Governor wants you and if we have to fight to get yer then we will!"

Smith went quiet for a minute, considering his options, as the prisoners continued to slowly converge on the group of prison officers. Finally he stood up abruptly.

"Okay, Sweeney. I'll go with you. But only because the Governor wants to see me, not because of the fucking coppers."

Sweeney almost laughed with relief.

"Thank you, Smudge. Thank you!"

"What are we hanging around for then? Let's get a move on! We can't keep the Governor waiting!"

EIGHTY-THREE

23rd August
Winson Green, Birmingham

The Governor's small office was crowded almost to overflowing when Sweeney finally showed John Smith inside. There was the Governor himself, with three or four policemen in uniform, and as Sweeney had said, they were definitely highly-placed officers with plenty of silver braid on their caps. There was also an army officer with the red collar tabs of a staff officer, and two other men, in dark suits. At the sight of the 'suits' the hackles on the back of Smith's neck began to rise. *Spooks*, he thought. *What the fuck are spooks doing here?* The Governor dismissed Sweeney from the gathering, and as the door closed behind the prison officer he leant across his desk and shook Smith by the hand.

"Nice of you to agree to join us, Mr Smith," he said ruefully, a smile threatening to break out on his face. "I'd introduce you to our guests here, but I'm afraid that I don't know any of their names except for Chief Superintendant Charles here."
He indicated a stocky black policeman who didn't extend a hand to be shaken, but was instead glowering at Smith. Smith smiled back sweetly, just to annoy the policeman.

"Shall we sit, gentlemen?" the Governor asked the room in general, and there were a few moments when everyone shuffled around, trying to place their chairs so that they faced the Governor's desk. Smith found himself sitting between the army officer - who turned out to be a Brigadier - and one of the suits. He nodded at the staff officer.

"Evening, sir."

"Evening, Sergeant Smith."

"That's *Mr* Smith, sir," he corrected him.

The old soldier just smiled at him.

"Not any more, *sergeant*."

Before Smith could get his wits together enough to counter this, Chief Superintendent Charles cleared his throat.

"Gentlemen," he began, addressing everyone in the room, "as the rest of us are already aware of the situation, this is just to bring Mr Bradsworth and Smith up to speed."

John just couldn't resist annoying the policeman again.

"That's *Sergeant* Smith to you, Chief Superintendent."

The Brigadier had to clear his own throat to prevent himself from laughing.

"Please carry on," Smith added.

The senior copper glowered even more furiously at him.

"As I was saying, this is to bring you up to speed on a very serious situation. You have both signed the Official Secrets Act, I take it?"

Both Smith and the Governor nodded in acknowledgement.

"Good. Then I will inform you that everything that you hear in this room is covered by that Act, and nothing, I repeat nothing, is to be passed on to anyone outside of this meeting. To put the situation into a nutshell: Yesterday evening at approximately 20.00 hours, their Royal Highnesses the Duke and Duchess of Cambridge were forcibly kidnapped from a hotel in Coventry."

He paused to let this sink in. The Governor gave an audible gasp at the news and his face reflected his shock, but Smith's face maintained his impassiveness, though his eyes narrowed a little.

"The kidnapping was not discovered until early this morning when the Duke and Duchess failed to attend their breakfast. The Hotel staff then discovered that the armed officers of the Royal Protection Group, who had been assigned to protect the Royal Couple were tied up in their room. They are currently being interrogated by counter-terrorism officers of my department, SO15."

"Why are they being interrogated?" asked the Governor.

"To ascertain whether one or all of them were in league with the kidnappers."

"Oh. Is it possible that they had something to do with it then?"

"At this stage it appears unlikely, but we are trying to cover all possibilities and eventualities. The initial reports from the protection officers indicate that between two and four assailants disabled them using tasers, somehow drugged the Duke and Duchess, and then smuggled them out of the hotel last night disguised as wheelchair-bound guests."

"Was anybody injured?" asked Smith.
The Chief Super reluctantly answered him.

"No, as far as we can see no one was injured apart from the Royal Protection Officers, who were temporarily disabled with the tasers."

"Okay, do you have any idea who the kidnappers are?"

"We do not, at this stage, have a clue as to the kidnappers' identities or why they have kidnapped the Duke and Duchess. However, they did leave a note behind, pinned to the suit lapel of one of the protection officers."

"So? What did it say? Have they made any demands?"

"The note was handwritten, and it was short and to the point. It indicated an Ordnance Survey grid reference in Derbyshire's Peak District, approximately equidistant between Manchester and Sheffield. The note informed us that we would find a field telephone at the site, with which we could contact the kidnappers directly."

"So?" Smith was irritated at the police officer's reluctance to tell him exactly what had happened.

"A local police unit was dispatched to the site

immediately and found the field telephone. I personally then flew by helicopter to the site and spoke to the kidnappers, at precisely 11.00 this morning. A male spoke to me on the phone and informed me that the Duke and Duchess were safe for the moment."
He paused again, reluctant to go on.

"Look Chief Superintendent. I don't know why I'm here, and I don't know what's going on or what the bloody hell this has got to do with me, but if you don't give me the full picture I might as well pack up and go back to my wing. Spit it out man!"
The policeman glowered again at Smith. It was obvious that he didn't like mixing with a convicted criminal, especially an animal like Smith, never mind sharing state secrets with him.

It took the Brigadier to eventually break the silence.

"For God's sake, Chief Superintendent! Get a grip on yourself, there's a lot more at stake here than your ego."
He turned to Smith.

"The upshot is that the Duke and Duchess of Cambridge are being held prisoner in a cave in the Peak District."

"A *cave* sir?"
Brigadier smiled at his look of incredulity.

"Yes, sergeant. A bloody great hole in the ground appropriately called the 'Giant's Hole', which apparently carries on underground for several kilometres. It's a pot-holer's paradise, or so I have been informed by the chairman of the local Cavers' and Pot-Holers' Association, with underground rivers, several different levels and huge caverns all over the show. In other words it's a bloody nightmare to assault!"

"I can imagine, sir."

"The field telephone that the Chief Superintendent has talked about is a basic army job, attached to a communications line that goes into the cave. We can't tell how far the buggers are in the system or even whether they're there at all. We are totally blind. The duty CRW squadron of the Special Air Service Regiment have sealed off the entire area of course, and boys from the Special Reconnaissance Regiment, with help from MI5...," he nodded at the suit sitting on the other side of Smith, "...are also providing technical assistance, but at this stage no one really has a clue about where we go from here."

"So what about me, Sir? Why have I been dragged into this? It's not as if you haven't got enough wannabe heroes who will be happy to make a name for themselves rescuing the future King of bloody England! So why get me involved?"

"It's not our choice to make, sergeant."

"I don't understand, Sir?"

"The kidnappers have asked for you to be the negotiator between them and us. They asked for you by name."

"But why, Sir? What the bloody hell do I have to do with any of this?"

"They told us that you are the only person that they can trust."

Smith looked at the Brigadier with astonishment on his face. Then abruptly he stood up and started to make his way to the door. Surprised, the Brigadier shouted out at him.

"Where do you think you're going, sergeant?"
Smith gave him a hard look over his shoulder but didn't stop moving.

"This has got fuck all to do with me, Sir!" he spat out. "I'm going back to my fucking cell, where I'm going to get me head down. Why should I give a toss about you lot, or the Royal bleeding Couple!"

"But what about your duty as a former British soldier?" shouted an angry Brigadier in reply.
Smith stopped.

"A British soldier?" he laughed. "I *used* to be a British soldier, Sir. I fought for my country in more wars than I can fucking well remember and put my life on the line for Queen and Country more times than these fuckers..."

He looked around the room at the spooks and police officers

"...have had hot fucking dinners! And where did it get me, Sir? Eh?"

He spread his arms wide to take in their surroundings.

"I'll tell you where it got me, Sir! Locked up for life at Her Majesty's pleasure for something that I didn't fucking well do and with no chance of parole! Begging your pardon Sir, but *fuck* you, *fuck* the British fucking army, and *fuck* the Royal bloody Family! I'm going to bed!"

With that he pulled the door open, stepped out and slammed it shut behind him.

EIGHTY-FOUR

23rd August
The Peak District, Derbyshire

It was getting dark and chilly on the foreboding limestone hills of the Peak District. A few miles west of a small village called Castleton, on a minor road that was so small that it didn't even seem to have a name, a group of army Land Rovers shared a small car parking area at the bottom of the valley with several police cars, ambulances, a fire engine and a lot of scattered sheep shit. The major in command of A Squadron, 22 SAS Regiment (the duty 'Counter Revolutionary Warfare' Squadron), looked across the top of his Land Rover's bonnet into the face of his senior warrant officer, Squadron Sergeant-Major James Goode. The light had faded fast but they were 'tactical' so there were no torches to fuck up his night vision, and he could see the Sergeant-Major's craggy features quite clearly in the darkness.

"Did you hear the latest news, Jim?"

"No, Mike, I've just got back from checking over our lads' positions. What did I miss?"

"Nothing much, just that John Smith has refused to become involved. Apparently he told the Brigadier and the coppers to fuck off!"

The major chuckled quietly to himself.

"Bloody typical!" said the Sergeant-Major. "I've never met the man, but after he sold his story to the bloody tabloids, I lost all respect for what he did to those bloody hijackers on that plane!"

"Ah, but I heard a rumour that he never received a penny for his story. Apparently all of the dosh went to his two sons."

"Well, even if that's true, I still don't trust the bloody man. After all, he worked with the spooks, didn't he? He's not really a Regiment guy at all."

"Sorry to disappoint you again Jim, but I knew him quite well back in the eighties. He was the best bloody soldier I ever met."

"Really, sir? You knew him?"

The Sergeant-Major couldn't resist asking, interested in spite of his negative feelings for Smith.

"Yes. We were on a mission together in Afghanistan, when the Soviets were there." Jim leaned forward to hear his officer's low voice better.

"I was just a young officer with a brick between my ears where my brain should have been!"

They both chuckled at this one as they both knew plenty of officers that would still fit that description.

"I was nominally in charge of a small team that was aiding the *Mujahedeen*, but of course it was Sergeant Smith who was really in charge. He was about the same age as me but he'd already seen enough action to write more than a few Andy McNab novels. He was a tough bastard and he knew his stuff. I could tell you a few stories about those days, Jim!"

"I'm sure you could, Sir."

The officer didn't realise it, but he had just gone up in the Sergeant-Major's estimation. Jim was an old veteran of many a shooting war himself, including the recent Operation Retribution in Algeria, but he had heard stories about what a bastard it had been in Afghanistan during the time of the Soviet involvement there.

"What the hell is going to happen now then?" he asked. "It'll really piss the kidnappers off if Smith refuses to be their negotiator."

"Ah. Apparently our esteemed colleague Chief

Superintendent Charles (he ignored the snort of derision by his Sergeant-Major at the mention of the policeman's name) has already told the kidnappers the bad news."

"So what happened?"

"They've told the Chief Superintendent that he's got twenty-four hours to persuade Smith to join the show, or they'll shoot the hostages, starting with dear old Katie."

"Fuck me!"

"Precisely Sarnt-Major! It looks as though the proverbial may indeed hit the fan."

"Do you think he'll do it, Mike? Will Smith join us?" The officer pondered this for a few moments.

"I'm sure of it, Jim. Despite being a right old bastard, the John Smith that I knew couldn't resist a bit of action. I'll bet he's just holding out to piss everyone off, and I can't say I blame him after the way he's been treated by the Government."

"Are you sure Mike? Afghanistan was a hell of a long time ago? Smith might have changed an awful lot since then?"

"It's always possible, Jim. But I've got a feeling in my water that Smith will join us eventually. Despite all of his bluster, and despite everything that's happened to him, I just can't see him being happy to be the cause of our future King's demise. He'll join us, I'm sure of it."

"Well I fucking hope so, Sir!"

"Don't be too enthusiastic about it, Jim."

"What do you mean, Sir?"

"Wherever Smith goes there's bound to be some real shooting! Trouble follows him like a bloody magnet!" he chuckled again.

EIGHTY-FIVE

24th August
Winson Green, Birmingham

"So why me then, Sir? I just don't bloody understand it!" Smith was sitting on the bed in his cell with the Brigadier, who was looking around the small room with interest. Gordon had been moved on when the old soldier arrived.

"Only they know that, sergeant. They've told us it's because they trust you to tell them the truth and be straight with them, but you know as well as I do that people like this are total fruitcakes. The real reason could be because they fancy you, or because you're a bloody celebrity now, or it might be because they want to carry out the *Fatwa* and earn themselves half a million pounds! Christ knows what they want!"

"You're a fat lot of help, Sir, if you don't mind me saying."

"Actually I do, and I still haven't forgiven you for telling me to fuck off yet!"

Smith laughed at the old git. The Brigadier was okay; he was a proper soldier's soldier.

"Look Smith, I can understand that you're a bit annoyed at what has happened to you..."

"Annoyed? You're having me on aren't you, Sir? Why would I be a bit annoyed? The bastards only took my life away in an attempt to keep me quiet. They only fitted me up with the abduction, rape and murder of a teenage girl and got me sent down as a fucking *paedophile* for life. Why would I be annoyed at that, Sir?"

"Yes. But you did go out and cause a bit of a nuisance as well. You murdered people and blew things up, Smith!"

"Of course I bloody did, Sir! If they'd done it to you, would you have sat on your arse and done nothing about it?"

"I'd have got myself a good bloody lawyer, sergeant!"

"Well I did that, Sir. He's called Lee Enfield!"

"Very droll, sergeant, very droll. This is getting us nowhere. Are you going to help us or not, Smith?"

"Of course I bloody am, Sir. I just didn't want to make it too easy for that fucking chief superintendent, the stuck-up prat."

The Brigadier let out an exasperated sigh.

"Well I can't really disagree with you there, sergeant. The man is a prat. Well, I'm glad you're on board at last. I'll go and tell the rest of them the good news. Then we'll have to sort out the logistics for our move up to Derbyshire. I don't suppose that they'll want you on the loose with no security!"

He stood up and moved towards the cell door, and then paused to look around the cell once more.

"Don't go anywhere, will you Smith?"

"Oh, very droll, sir, very droll!"

The old soldier grinned as he turned and banged his fist on the door.

"Okay, you morons! You can let me out now! He hasn't bloody murdered me - yet!" He turned and grinned back at Smith again, who despite himself grinned back at the old bastard.

Half an hour later and Smith and the rest of them were on their way. He was leaving the confines of Winson Green Prison for the first time in thirteen months, and his only regret was that he didn't get a chance to say goodbye to his mates, though he had left a brief note on Gordon's bed wishing them all good luck if he should never see them again. He had made some good friends amongst the lags during his time there.

Of course, Smith wasn't allowed to just walk out of the prison on his own. Chief Superintendent Charles had insisted that he be handcuffed and surrounded by enough security men to man a small army, though at least the Brigadier had made sure that they were *military* policemen, rather than civilian coppers. That sensible precaution made Smith a lot happier and easier to handle. With his typical army banter, he was laughing and joking with the 'monkeys' within a few minutes, much to the chagrin of the Chief Superintendent, who seemed to think that Smith should be chained up and gagged, as well as handcuffed. Smith didn't help the situation by constantly winding the policeman up.

Smith was flown, with his security team and the others who had been at the prison, to the Peak District in Derbyshire aboard a Royal Air Force *Chinook* helicopter, where they landed next to a small car parking area located in a steep valley. Inside the car park and flowing out on to the fields around it were two dozen army Land Rovers, police cars, civilian ambulances and a fire engine. There was also a huge white truck with 'Mobile Incident Control' stencilled on its side in large black letters. Smith was bundled from the chopper and led into the mobile control room, leaving his security team outside.

The 'Giant's Hole', Smith learned on the briefing he was given by the Brigadier in the control room, is a well-known cave system in Derbyshire's Peak District, and is very popular with pot-holers and caving enthusiasts. The entrance to the cave lies on land owned by Peakshill Farm, and is located to the west of Castleton, a small village that is a magnet for tourists visiting the national park, especially during the summer months. The actual entrance to the cave lay about three hundred and fifty metres east of the car parking area where the mobile control room was located, and the field telephone that Smith had heard about was placed prominently on a large rock to one side of that entrance. Army signallers had attached another length of communications line to the telephone, so that it now rang directly through to a handset located in the mobile control room. This was the only way that the kidnappers had contacted the authorities so far, and the other end of the land line ran directly into the cave system. It was presumed that the Royal Couple were being held somewhere below the ground in the cave, though this had not been verified so far.

Smith was introduced to the major, who was the officer in command of the SAS CRW teams The Brigadier turned out to be Brigadier Clarkeson, the Director of UK Special Forces. Smith was astonished to find out that he knew the major in charge of the SAS.

"Hello, John," said the officer when they were first introduced. "Good to see you again."
Smith looked closely at the grizzled major, obviously a veteran of many campaigns by the look of the seamed lines on his leather-tanned face. It took him a few moments of concentration before a flash of memory hit his brain - a memory of a fresh-faced young Rupert in the mountains of Afghanistan thirty years earlier.

"Bloody hell! Is it you, Mike? What the fuck are you still doing in uniform after all this time?"

"You know how it is, John. Nowhere else to go and nothing else to do. I keep putting in for extensions to my service and the army keeps accepting for some reason!"

"Christ, but it's been a long time since we last met. I never did get the chance to thank you for your recommendation for the Distinguished Conduct Medal."

"No worries, John, you more than deserved it. The mission was a success thanks to your skill and bravery. If I'd had my way the gong would have been gazetted."

"Yeah well. We both know that that will never happen. But thanks anyway, and I'm glad that you got out of that hell-hole alive. Although it sounds like we've swapped one bloody *hole* for another, doesn't it?"

"Yes. This Giant's Hole is a bloody nightmare. You'll get a briefing from our local caving expert after this and he'll explain exactly what we're up against. First of all though, I'll let you into the picture about what my chaps have been up to since we arrived yesterday in this God-forsaken valley."

The SAS major went on to describe the forces that had been detached for the mission. There were two full troops from A Squadron, plus his Squadron Headquarters, which amounted to a total of just thirty-six men, most of them long-serving members of the regiment. He also had a brick of four men from the Special Reconnaissance Regiment and various other attached technicians from the 'Box' (MI5). On top of this he had been allocated two companies of a regular army infantry battalion of the Rifle Regiment, numbering about three hundred men. The infantry were being used to seal off the valley at both ends and to provide a thinly dispersed outer perimeter around the area, mainly to keep out any sightseers that might turn up. A Squadron were providing a much closer inner perimeter around the cave itself, especially at the cave entrance to prevent a mass break-out of the kidnappers, if it ever came to that. Two SAS bricks of four men each, were currently getting their equipment together to enter the cave system via another nearby cave system, and an old mine located elsewhere in the valley which linked underground to the Giant's Hole. They were tasked with making cautious approaches to the rear of the Giant's Hole system and then to stay in position in case an assault, or a diversion, was needed from their direction. Some of the team members were from Mountain Troop of A Squadron, and they were very experienced rock-climbers. Most of them had also pot-holed at one time or another. The other team members were from Boat Troop and were skilled divers. They were considered essential to the mission as there were several sections of the cave systems that were under water.

The four-man brick from the SRR were currently trying to figure out a way of getting an 'eyes-on' the kidnappers, but this was proving extremely difficult due to the nature of the ground. They had managed to sneak some very sophisticated and sensitive microphones inside the entrance to Giant's Hole, but so far they hadn't picked up any direct sound from the kidnappers in the caves, because there was too much interference from ambient noise, which came from dripping and running water. Apparently a stream ran directly into the cave entrance itself and along the nearest passages, and there were other streams within the cave system. It hadn't helped that it had rained quite a lot locally over the preceding couple of weeks and there was a higher than normal level of water entering the cave.

Most of the civilian police had been removed from the immediate area of the caves and were helping the Rifles to man the outer perimeter. A few senior officers were a part of the mission's command and control element in the mobile control room. Chief Superintendant Charles, who was the commander of New Scotland Yard's Counter-terrorism Unit, SO15, was in command of the police element, and he was in direct contact with the Home Secretary, while Brigadier Clarkeson, who was in overall command of the operation, was in constant touch with the Prime Minister. Up to this point though, the politicians were thankfully staying aloof from the situation and letting the police and military decide what to do on the ground.

A decision had been made at the highest level (which included input from the Royal Family themselves) that the kidnapping of the Duke and Duchess was to be classified as top secret. There was already a 'D Notice' in place to legally curb any media interest in the situation that was bound to arise at some stage or another. For now a deception plan had been instigated that informed the media and the public that a full scale joint exercise between the civil authorities (including the local ambulance service, fire brigade and police) and the military was underway in the valley.

After the detailed briefing by his old comrade and the Brigadier, Smith was introduced to a nervous-looking local man who had intimate knowledge of the Giant's Hole, Oxlow Cavern and Maskhill Mine underground systems. He outlined in detail the underground passages and caverns, using a hand-drawn map to clarify certain points, and described the conditions that could be expected underground. Smith quickly came to the conclusion that Mike was right. This was a bloody nightmare. The combined cave systems stretched underground over several kilometres and included dozens of passages, some of which were dead ends and many of which could only be traversed by skilled climbers. There were several sumps, underground streams, rivers and canals, and only a handful of caverns. The kidnappers had chosen the perfect spot in which to set up their base.

One notion worried all of them though. This was the thought that even though the kidnappers could easily control all of the various routes into the cave systems, at the same time they had left themselves no escape route. They were trapped like rats in a barrel.

EIGHTY-SIX

24th August
The Peak District, Derbyshire

By two o'clock in the afternoon Smith had been fully briefed by just about everyone except the milkman, and everything was in place for him to make his first contact with the kidnappers. Even a Metropolitan Police negotiator was on hand to help Smith with advice when he communicated with the people who had abducted the Royal Couple.

Smith was as nervous as hell when he rang through, surrounded as he was by senior army and police officers who were going to hang on his every word. However, as usual, nobody would have been able to guess how anxious he was. Outwardly his posture was relaxed, his face impassive, his voice calm and his hand as steady as a rock.

The field telephone was answered almost immediately by a male voice, which was amplified for everyone to hear in the mobile control over a loudspeaker.

"Yeah? What do you want? I hope that you've got Smith."

"I'm here, mate."

"Is that really you, John?"

"Yeah, it is. But only my friends call me John. *You* can call me *Mr* Smith, unless we already know each other?"

"No, I've never had the pleasure, Mr Smith, though I've seen you on the TV, of course."

"Super."

"Yeah. Did you know they had a Panorama programme on the TV about you last week? They interviewed lots of people who knew you at work and had served with you in the army, and apparently you're a right hard case! It was an interesting programme, especially the bit where New Scotland Yard admitted that the file that had been passed on to them by *The Sun* had gone missing, and with it all, and I'll quote them here, 'the so-called evidence that you had committed numerous assassinations for the British Secret Intelligence Service'! Did you know about that, Mr Smith?"

Smith looked across at the Brigadier, who simply raised an eyebrow.

"No. I didn't know that Mr...what do I call you?"

"You can call me 'Staff'. After all, that was my rank in the British Army, staff sergeant."

"Okay, Staff. Let's not waste any more bloody time on pleasantries. It's pissing down out here and I've got a nice warm cell waiting for me back in Winson Green. What is it that you want?"

There was a pause on the other end of the line.

"Justice. That's all we want; justice."

"What do you mean? Justice for whom?"

"You were in the army for a long time and look at how you've been treated after serving your Queen and Country? Well, you're not the only one. There are literally thousands of ex-servicemen who have been treated like shit by the Government and the Ministry of fucking Defence! There are hundreds of soldiers who have been killed, and thousands of ex-servicemen who have been wounded during their service, and even more who have mental illnesses brought on by the things that they've been forced to do or by the horrors that they've seen, illnesses like Post Traumatic Stress Disorder or severe depression. How many of them have received no treatment at all? How many of them have seen their families disintegrate around them because they couldn't re-adjust to life in civvy street, and how many of them have committed suicide? For example, did you know that there are hundreds of veterans who are homeless and living on the streets with nowhere else to go? Do you know how much a wounded soldier receives in bloody compensation? Next to bloody nothing! He or she has to rely on bloody charity to even get the right treatment and rehabilitation! Yet poor old Iraqis or Afghans that are accidentally injured during our operations are given bloody millions and MOD employees who stub their toe on a crack in the pavement get hundreds of thousands in compensation! This is what we want, *Mr* bloody *Smith*! We want justice for our comrades, and if we don't get it then the successor to the throne of bloody England and his pretty wife are going to be shot! Do you understand what I'm saying?"

The kidnapper's voice had been rising in pitch and timbre until he was almost shouting with barely suppressed rage. Smith paused for a minute or so before answering, looking around at the faces of the coppers and squaddies in the mobile control room. He recognised a mixture of emotions plainly reflected back at him, ranging from the arrogant hatred on the face of the Chief Super, through to a look of 'Yeah! Go for it!' on the face of an old signal's corporal. Finally he answered the kidnapper, his voice low and gravelly.

"Yeah. I understand what you're saying, Staff. I understand only too well. But before anything else happens I want to know that the Duke and Duchess are safe and well. I want to be able to speak to them. Do *you* understand?"

"Yeah, I do. I'll call back in five minutes and you can ask them yourself. By the way, in about thirty seconds you will hear some explosions on those fancy microphones that you've put into the entrance of the cave. We're blowing up the connecting tunnels to Oxlow Cavern and Maskhill Mine."

With that the line went dead.

Mike looked around at the others and summed it all up for

them in one word:
    "Shit."

EIGHTY-SEVEN

24th August
The Peak District, Derbyshire

One hundred and ninety-six metres inside the Giant's Hole cave system, and over one hundred metres below the surface of the Peak District National Park, is a large cavern known as the 'Base Camp Chamber'. The cavern can be accessed from the entrance to the system via a descending set of large, easily negotiated passages. You do have to stoop low in a few places though to duck beneath the millions of tons of rock that forms the roof above your head. It is quite an impressive cavern, eight metres long by three metres wide and nine metres high, with a stream entering the chamber from the right. Beyond the Base Camp Chamber another roomy passage approximately eleven metres long leads to the next equally impressive cavern 'Boss Aven', and way beyond that is yet another cavern, two hundred and fifty six metres from the entrance, 'Garlands Pot'.

    The interior of the Giant's Hole cave system is normally pretty wet, with the constant drip, drip of water playing as an accompanying sound to the echoes of your feet as you make your way further underground. However, after a few weeks of constant rain and drizzle the drips have been replaced by the gurgling rush of running water. It cascades down the sides of Base Camp Chamber and joins the bubbling flow of the stream that enters the cavern from the Upper Stream Passage, and eventually disappears into a deep sump closer to the entrance. The cavern is so wet that the kidnappers' electronic equipment has to be housed inside the double skin of a small tent erected on the floor of the chamber - just to protect it from the moisture-laden air and keep it dry. Inside the tent, Darren, the team's electronic expert and an ex-member of the Royal Corps of Signals, constantly watches the pictures transmitted to a series of monitors from the small, unobtrusive infrared cameras that he had installed earlier along the cave system's passages. They are only cheap cameras, purchased from a magazine over the internet, and originally intended to protect people's homes from burglars. But they make very effective remote sentries as well, and their pictures are transmitted back to the monitors via ordinary household co-axial cable - the sort most television aerials use. All members of the team take turn to watch the monitors and make sure that they won't be surprised by an incursion of Special Forces troops. This was how Nigel had known that the SRR had already placed some listening devices within the cave's entrance, as he and the rest of the team had watched them while they did it.

Sitting outside the tent, protected from the worst of the cascading water by an overhead awning that they have fixed in place above them, the rest of the team relaxes on collapsible canvas chairs. They are dressed in worn, dirty combats, wearing dark balaclavas to hide their faces. Next to them are the Royal Couple, their hands and feet tied to the arms and legs of their chairs. They are not gagged and certainly, apart from the constant damp, are not entirely uncomfortable. The couple and the team have talked to each other quite a lot so far during the time that they have already spent underground together, and surprisingly they have all got on despite their differing circumstances. HRH Prince William is, of course, a serving officer in the Royal Air Force, where he pilots search and rescue helicopters, so the team is not surprised that they have much in common with him and that they can share a laugh and a joke. The

Duchess though, is from an entirely different and much wealthier background than the council estates and reform homes that the team have grown up in, yet she is also very likeable and appears to understand the dark sense of humour, so common in members of the armed forces. Within this short space of time, both of them have impressed the hard-bitten ex-soldiers with their calmness and bravery. They just wish that they could have met under slightly less challenging circumstances.

"Okay, William, it's almost time to make the call," says Nigel. "Remember to tell them that you are both well and that we have treated you okay. Do not though, under *any circumstances* tell them anything else, such as how many of us there are, where we are or what we're armed with, okay? I don't want to get rough with the pair of you but I will if I have to, okay?"

"Don't worry, I understand."

"Good. Just keep it short and sweet."

Nigel wound the handle on the field telephone quickly and was rewarded with the sound of ringing. The phone at the other end of the line was picked up promptly.

"Smith here."

"Hi, Mr Smith. I have His Royal Highness Prince William for you. Do not attempt to question him on anything tactical. I'll be listening in, okay?"

"Super."

"Okay. Here he is."

He held the phone next to the Prince's ear while he leaned in close to hear what was said.

"Your Royal Highness, are you there?" asked Smith.

"Yes, I am. Is this John Smith?"

"It certainly is, your Highness. We're all very relieved to hear your voice. Are you and your wife okay?"

"Yes thank you. We're both fine. We are being treated okay."

"That's good to hear, William."

"Thank you for what you did before, Mr Smith."

"Before?"

"On the Gambia flight. It was a very brave thing to do, and I for one am very glad that you are as good as you are at what you do! I hope that my grandmother passed on our thanks to you for saving our lives while you were in hospital?"

"That's no bother at all, your Highness, and yes, she did pass on your thanks." Smith was slightly embarrassed by the thank you and was relieved when the voice of the kidnapper replaced the Prince's.

"I agree with the Prince," said Nigel. "It *was* a very brave thing to do, which is one of the reasons that we chose you to be our intermediary, Mr Smith. We believe that you still have some *honour*, something that is sadly very lacking in many people these days. We hope that you will be straight with us?"

"Oh I will, don't worry. I happen to believe in the 'justice' that you appear to be fighting for, Staff. Of course, just as long as you understand that I will kill you if I'm given the chance?"

Nigel laughed out loud.

"Of course! That goes without saying, John! I know the score, as do my colleagues. What is it that they say - no gain without pain?"

"I couldn't have put it better myself, Staff," Smith chuckled. "Now let's get down to business. What is it that you want exactly?"

"I'll make this easy, John. First and foremost we want the Prime Minister himself to stand up and announce to the country on a national news programme that the Ministry of Defence is going to build a new hospital. This will be a hospital that is dedicated purely to treating both the physical and mental injuries of servicemen and women acquired while serving their country, giving them the best medical care that can possibly be had. Then we want him to announce to the country that the compensation paid out to wounded servicemen is going to be *tripled*, and that there will also be a substantial increase of - at least one hundred per cent - in the pension given to dead servicemen's spouses, of whatever gender, and that it will *not* be means tested or affect any other state benefits that they are entitled to receive. Then we want six million pounds sterling to be electronically transferred to a bank account in Ecuador, the details of which I will give you tomorrow afternoon. If all of these demands are met with by tomorrow evening at 22.30 hours, the Duke and Duchess of Cambridge will be released unharmed. There will be no negotiation on any of these demands. If the Prime Minister fails to stand up on national TV and tell the country about these changes, or if the money is not paid into the bank account, we will kill the Duke and Duchess. Do you understand, Mr Smith?"

"Yes, I understand."

"Good! We will require independent verification that the demands have been met in full, because, as I'm sure the techies from MI5 have already told you, we are unable to monitor the TV news from our current location. I will contact you tomorrow afternoon with the details of how and when this verification will be made, as well as with the bank details. One more thing Mr Smith..."

"Carry on."

"...if we so much as smell a single soldier entering the caves, all bets will be off immediately and we will kill the Duke and Duchess. Have you got that?"

"Loud and clear."

"Good! Make sure that your masters understand it as well. I've grown to like William and Kate, but I will not hesitate to kill them both! Good night, Mr Smith."

The line went dead.

EIGHTY-EIGHT

25th August
The Peak District, Derbyshire

The night passed quickly but not without a great deal of heated debate and exchanges amongst the men manning the mobile control room in the Peak District. Arguments were passed back and forth about what they should do, and various scenarios were bandied around about how they could rescue the hostages, but nothing came of it. They all realised that they were caught by the short and curlies *and* bent over a barrel. There was nothing that they *could* do. Eventually, Chief Superintendent Charles passed on the kidnappers' demands to the Home Secretary, and Brigadier Clarkeson passed on the same demands to the Prime Minister, both of whom took the news quietly and without argument. Their questions about whether the hostages could be rescued within the required timescale were met with negatives: there was no way that troops could get down into the caverns unobserved (the SRR boys had already spotted the cameras in the passages) and carry out an assault one hundred metres below ground without getting the Royal Couple murdered.

    John Smith had simply left them all to it and gone to bed inside a campervan that had been driven up there for that purpose, so he missed most of the feeble and downright eccentric assault ideas that had been passed around. They ranged from pumping sleeping gas into the caverns through to drilling a hole down through the solid bedrock and dropping onto the kidnappers from above. Of course, nothing that they came up with was in any way practical. Smith knew it was a hopeless scenario, as did the kidnappers, the Brigadier and the SAS major. No one could think of a way of getting at the kidnappers without putting the lives of the Royal Couple in mortal danger.

Back in London, at yet another emergency meeting in the Cabinet Office Briefing Room, the Prime Minister passed on the demands of the kidnappers to his colleagues and was met with stony silence. It was obvious that he would have to make a stark choice: he could either meet the kidnappers' demands, and appear on national TV, an appearance that he would never be able to back down from without losing considerable face and probably his position at the head of the Government, or he could refuse and be personally blamed for the death of the hereditary successor to the British crown. It was a lose-lose situation whichever way you looked at it. The COBR meeting broke up after only an hour and everyone who left knew that the choice was down to the Prime Minister and to him alone. There wasn't a man or woman there that envied him that choice or his position.

Finally, it took a chance comment by Mrs Cameron as the couple prepared to go to bed in the early hours of the morning to brighten up the situation.

"So what if you meet the kidnappers' demands? OK, it will cost the exchequer several million pounds for the hospital, increased compensation and the ransom, but if the great British public never find out about the kidnapping or the danger to the Duke and Duchess, you will just be treated as a national hero. After all, nearly everyone in the country agrees that our service people have been given a hard time. If you are seen to lessen that, and to help them more, everyone will love you!"

It took a few minutes of careful consideration for her comment to sink in, but the more that the Prime Minister thought about it the more he agreed with her. Of course, he *would* be treated like a hero! Why on Earth hadn't he thought of it before? He went to bed a far happier man than he had for quite a while.

In the morning, the Prime Minister immediately got the media machine of the Conservative Party moving. The message that he sent out to the TV stations and newspapers was that he would be making a huge policy-changing statement on the BBC news that very evening. He was buzzing with delight and the media buzzed with him, wondering what the hell it could all be about?

EIGHTY-NINE

25th August
The Peak District, Derbyshire

At five o'clock in the afternoon the expected call came from the kidnappers. Smith reacted fast and answered within seconds.

"Hello, Staff."

"Hi, John."

"What are your instructions?"

"Okay. First of all here are the details of the electronic bank transfer. Six million pounds to be transferred to the *Banco del Pichincha*, using the INTERNEXO system. The account number is: 048 356 7209. The money must be deposited in the account by seven o'clock our time. Do not bother to trace it as we have a system in place that will instantly begin to divert the money around the world the moment it arrives, though I've no doubt that you'll try to."

"I'd say that that was a given."

"Hmm. Well hopefully our system will beat your experts, but we shall see. Anyway, the most important part of our demands will be met by the Prime Minister's speech on national TV. Has he agreed to do it?"

"Yep. He's going to give the speech live on the Ten O'clock News tonight."

"Really? Just like that?"

"Yeah. Apparently you've only pre-empted a policy change that he was going to put into place anyway."

"Bollocks! The lying bastard!"

"Yep, I agree. But what does it matter to you so long as he does it?"

"True enough. We'll need independent verification that he's given the speech and that the money has been transferred before we release the Duke and Duchess."

"Yeah, you mentioned that before. How's that going to run?"

"Well, I want you to take a trip to a pub called The Castle, which is in Castleton. It's along Castle Street funnily enough. Buy yourself a pint and sit down in the lounge and watch the news on the TV. I don't suppose that that will be too much hardship considering where you've been for the last year"

Smith chuckled and looked around the control room. The look of distaste on Chief Superintendent Charles's face made him grin and chuckle again.

"No Staff, that won't be too hard at all. I don't have any cash but perhaps the coppers will buy me a pint!"

He grinned again, this time looking directly at the Chief Super, who could only scowl back at him.

"Good. I thought that that might cheer you up. At 22.30 exactly you will receive a telephone call on the pub telephone from a colleague of ours. She will have monitored the bank account in Ecuador to make sure that the money has been transferred and everything is okay, and she will also have watched the Prime Minister's speech on TV. If everything is fine and the PM has met all of our demands she will give you a single code word and then hang up. It'll do you no good trying to trace the call as it will be from a pay-as-you-go mobile and our colleague will dump it the moment she breaks contact with you."

"Super. What happens then, Staff?"

"Then Mr Smith, we will get the chance to meet face to face. I want you to come into the Giant's Hole. Just follow the main passageway to where we are holding the Duke and Duchess. Once here, you will give us the code word that verifies that all has gone well and in exchange we'll give you the Royal Couple, unharmed. You'll be a hero all over again, Mr Smith."

Smith looked around the faces in the control room. This was a new twist that none of them had expected. He saw the Brigadier nodding at him.

"Okay, Staff, that seems to be okay with everyone here. You've got a deal."

"Good. I look forward to meeting you."

"Same here, Staff. There's just one thing that's bothering me?"

"Oh? What's that?"

"How are you expecting to get out of there in one piece? Surely this isn't a suicide mission for you guys, especially not with a big fat ransom waiting to be spent?"

There was silence down the line for a moment or two before the kidnapper answered.

"That's our business, Mr Smith. Whatever will be, will be."

"Super. I'll see you guys later then."

"Just one more thing, Mr Smith..."

"Yeah..."

"Don't try any of your fancy tricks when we meet, John. There's enough plastic explosive in these caves to bury all of us so deep that no one will ever be able to dig us out, and that includes the Duke and Duchess."

"No worries mate. In-and-out, that's my middle name."

"Glad to hear it, John. Catch you later."

"Super."

Smith turned again to face the others as the phone went dead.

"Right," he said, "has anyone got any ideas about how I can kill the bastards without getting me and the Royals blown to kingdom come?"

His tone was light but his coal-black eyes were hard and unforgiving. There was more than one person in the control room that felt a cold shiver pass down their spine as Smith looked at them.

NINETY

25th August
The Peak District, Derbyshire

Smith enjoyed his pint of lager; it was the first one he'd had in quite a while and despite all of the excitement of the last day or so he was feeling very relaxed. The Castle was a lovely old-fashioned pub, though it was pretty quiet tonight. Smith sat in the lounge surrounded by his entourage of military policemen, now all dressed in civilian clothes. Most of the monkeys were also nursing a single pint as they watched the large flat-screen TV on the wall with attentive faces. The Prime Minister was doing a first-class job of turning a nightmare scenario into a vote-winning success.

"...So let me end by saying to you all that the Conservative Party and the Government of the United Kingdom deeply value the sacrifices that have been made by our servicemen and women. With the change of policy that I have outlined here, we will do everything within our power to ensure that they are treated as fairly and as well as possible. We also acknowledge the enormous sacrifices that the spouses and families of those who have been killed in the service of our great nation have made. These policies will ensure that no one who serves our country in time of war or peril will ever want for proper care and attention again! Thank you for listening."

"That was Prime Minister David Cameron speaking live from outside Number Ten Downing Street........"

The rest of the commentary was drowned out by a heartfelt cheer from the group of military policemen.

"About fucking time!"

"Good on yer, Cameron!"

Smith smiled as he watched their beaming faces. Even though they were all a part of the incident in the Peak district, not one of them knew about, - or had made a connection with the promises made by the Prime Minister and the drama that was going down only a few short miles away up the valley. He doubted whether any of this would ever find its way into the public domain - it was just way too sensitive. If the British people ever found out that the darling Duke and Duchess of Cambridge had been kidnapped and held to ransom or that the Prime Minister's obviously popular about-turn in policy was not done for the reasons that had been given to them, then there would be hell to pay and heads would roll. Such a disclosure would probably bring down the Government and force a General Election. No, he was sure that all of this affair would be neatly swept under a carpet and laid to rest. And that of course, probably meant him as well. He doubted if he would be allowed to live after this was over. *Ah well,* he thought. *What's new?*

Smith kept his eye on the wall clock and at a minute to half past ten he got up and went to the bar, being watched carefully by his minders. The strident ring of a telephone cut through the hubbub and the barmaid reached behind her to snatch up the receiver.

"Hello?" she said. "Who? Hold on a second, love." She cupped her hand over the mouthpiece and looked up, straight into the eyes of John Smith.

"That's for me," he told her, reaching across the bar and gently prising the phone from her hand.

"Smith, here."

There was a slight pause and then a woman's voice said very clearly "Cold fish." The receiver hummed as the line went dead. Smith handed the phone back to the startled barmaid, winked at her and turned to the sergeant in charge of his escort.

"That's it, mate. Let's go."

He turned towards the exit, all thoughts of relaxation gone from his mind as he began to contemplate what was to come. He felt the first tightening of his stomach muscles in anticipation.

"Okay, Sergeant Smith, you know your orders. I don't have to go through them again. Get in there, tell them what they want to hear and get out again, and don't forget to bring the Duke and Duchess with you!"

The Brigadier grinned at Smith.

"And don't go causing any bloody trouble, do you hear? I know that you want to kill these bastards almost as much as I do, but your orders are to be meek and passive. There is to be no last minute rescue attempt or heroics. In and out. Plain and simple!"

"Roger that, Sir, I promise to be a good boy."

"And we'll have no more of your bloody cheek! As soon as this is over you'll be put back into that bloody prison where you no doubt belong!"

"Yes, Sir, thank you, Sir, and I've enjoyed working with you too, Sir!"

The Brigadier relented a little and patted Smith's shoulder.

"Good luck, John. Be safe."

"Thank you, Sir. I'll be on my way then."

He turned and left the control room. A four-man brick of the SAS were waiting for him and even in the dark he recognised the tall figure of Major Mike.

"Hello, John. We're going to be your escort to the cave's entrance."

Smith smiled.

"Couldn't ask for better, Sir," he said.

They walked off into the night.

NINETY-ONE

25th August
The Peak District, Derbyshire

The SAS team dropped back and went to ground as Smith approached the entrance to the Giant's Hole. He had taken a walk up there earlier in the day to have a look at the place, and he had to admit that it did look fairly impressive with an entrance at least fifteen metres wide and ten metres high, with a stream flowing directly into it. That was during the daylight though. At night in a moonless sky, it just looked plain spooky. As he clambered down the rocky path to enter the cave Smith flicked on his LED head-torch to light the way forward. All he needed now was to slip on his arse and break an ankle and the whole thing would go to pot.

   He paused for half a second on the threshold, took a deep breath to steady himself and stepped down and into the cave. Just inside there were the remnants of an old gate which he carefully avoided. His head-torch lit up the passage ahead; it was wide and roomy and echoed loudly to the sound of the stream bubbling over rocks down its centre. Water was everywhere; it cascaded down the walls, dripped from the roof and lay on the rocky ground in little pools. Outside the night had been quite balmy, but as soon as he stepped over the threshold Smith felt a distinct and unpleasant drop in the ambient temperature. He shivered as he moved forward slowly, pausing only to wave at one of the kidnappers' cameras that his torchlight picked out, attached high up on the right hand wall.

The passage remained roomy for a little while before Smith found that he had to stoop where the roof came down low. This happened a few times as he walked deeper into the cave, until eventually he came upon another passage that led off to the left. He could see that the co-ax cable for the cameras led off down this passage, so he used his common sense and turned left and away from the stream. *They'll be in this direction, in one of the big caverns.*

After going up a step, the passage became higher again and he could walk forward easily. The tunnel then began to descend rather steeply, and to make a well defined right-hand turn before levelling and straightening out once more. Looking ahead he could see that he would have to stoop again further up, but even more importantly, he could see the glimmer of lights in the near distance. He kept going, every nerve in his body seemingly on fire and ready for the famous 'fight or flee' response as the adrenaline surged through his veins. For the first time he realised just how naked he felt without the comforting feel and weight of a rifle or pistol in his hands, especially as he guessed that the guys up ahead were armed to the bloody teeth. He walked and feigning nonchalance searched the walls and roof of the passage, swinging his head-torch back and forth with what he hoped were casual movements. It wasn't long before he realised that the kidnappers hadn't been bluffing. There were clumps of plastic explosive jammed into all sorts of nooks and crannies along the whole length of the passage, joined together by detonation cord. If it all went up, then this bloody cave would become his grave. *That's a cheering thought.*

About a hundred metres from the junction, having stooped down low a few times to get by, Smith had his first clear view of the kidnappers. Three of them were waiting to meet him as he walked into the bright light at the entrance to the Base Camp Chamber - all of them were dressed alike in combats and balaclavas. There were two tall, big men and one a fair bit shorter, with a body so slender that Smith first thought it was a woman. He changed his mind though when the slender kidnapper grabbed him with fingers like a steel vice and roughly slammed him against the wall at the end of the passage.

"You know the score, mate. Assume the position while I search you."

Smith did as he was ordered, opening his legs and arms and leaning forward until he was resting just on his toes and fingertips. Despite himself, he was impressed by the slender man's quick and efficient body search. *This one's a pro.*

"Okay, Smith, you're clean. You can stand up now."

He turned to face the three men, all of whom were holding Heckler and Koch MP5 sub-machine guns, their barrels pointing unwaveringly at his stomach.

"Hi lads, nice place you've got here," quipped Smith as his eyes roved around the lighted chamber in front of him. "Mind if I come in?"

He stepped down and into the large cavern before any of them could answer, taking in the tent with a luminous glow lighting it from within. *Probably their camera monitors.* Then he saw the Royal Couple sitting on a pair of canvas chairs, noting that their hands and feet were free, though he couldn't fail to see the tell-tale red marks that showed they had been tied until recently, probably until he was within sight of the cavern.

"Your Royal Highnesses."

He stepped forward again, neatly side stepping one of the kidnappers so that he had an unobstructed view of the hostages.

"I trust that you are both okay and that these *cretins* haven't hurt you in any way?"

William and Kate both had to smile at the sheer audacity of this man, faced as he was by three desperate men holding guns.

"Yes thank you, Mr Smith."

The Duchess was the first to answer.

"We are both fine thank you. Have you come to take us back to civilisation?"
Her voice was surprisingly calm and well-modulated and Smith found himself impressed once again.
"I sure have, Ma'am."
"Not so bloody fast, Smith. There's something you ought to say to us first!" bristled one of the big men, with a voice that Smith instantly recognised.
"Hello, Staff. So we finally get to meet in person." He smiled easily at the man. "I suppose that you want the code word then?"
"Don't piss about, Smith! Have you got it or not?"
"*Cold fish* is what your young lady told me, Staff."
All of the kidnappers visibly relaxed at the word. The one known as Staff clapped both of his comrades on the backs and then gave the tent a kick.
"Did you hear that, Darren?"
"Yep!" came a happy reply from inside the canvas. The big man turned on Smith.
"Did you see it with your own eyes?" he asked eagerly. "Did the PM himself stand up and give us everything that we asked for?"
Smith smiled again in recollection.
"He sure did, Staff! And he managed to take all the credit for the idea himself, the crafty bastard!"
He joined the kidnappers in their relieved laughter.
"We don't give a toss!" Staff said. "He'll never be able to back out of it now that he's said it on national TV!"
"That's true. Well done. You've improved the lot of every serviceman and woman in the country, and their families."
Smith gestured at the Royal Couple.
"Well, we've kept our part of the bargain, now it's up to you to keep your part." The kidnappers' laughter suddenly faded away. The big man known as Staff lifted the sub-machine gun in his hands and pointed it directly into Smith's face.
"Ah," he said. "I'm afraid that I lied to you about

that bit, Mr Smith."

NINETY-TWO

25th August
The Peak District, Derbyshire

Smith's voice cut through the sudden silence. If ever there was a sound that was cold and cruel enough to make goosebumps stand out on your flesh, it was his voice at that precise moment.

"What do you mean? I thought we had a deal? We've done our bit, now it's your fucking turn."
The big kidnapper shuffled on his feet, embarrassed but not repentant.

"We're not fucking stupid, Smith. What do you think will happen to us if we hand over the hostages?"

"The same thing that was always going to happen to you, you *prat*. You're either going to get shot or you'll go to prison. It's your choice. You didn't think that you could embarrass the Government like this and then walk away scot free, did you?"

"What we want is a helicopter to get us away from here!" the other big kidnapper piped up. "So fuck off out of here Smith and go and tell that to your fucking bosses!"

"And what about the Duke and Duchess?"

"They're coming with us. If there's any funny business we'll kill the fucking pair of them!"

"Bollocks, you prat! There's no way on earth that that lot out there will let you waltz out of this bloody cave with the Royals! Do you think they're fucking stupid?"
He glared at the kidnappers.

"We had a *deal*. If you stick to it I'll do everything I

can to help you. But if you blow it now you're all fucking dead men!"
Smith was as angry as fuck.
"Just do as you're told!"
The big kidnapper stepped forward to jam his gun barrel into Smith's chest and it was then that Smith made his move. He struck out at the man like a snake, his right hand raking down the kidnapper's face and reaching for his eyes like an animal's claw while he grabbed the barrel of the MP5 with his left hand and pushed it to one side. The kidnapper howled with the searing pain in his eyes and automatically his finger tightened on the gun's trigger. The noise of half-a-dozen 9mm rounds being fired sounded like a whole battery of cannons going off in the close confines of the cave and all hell broke loose. Smith swore as he tugged the gun from the blinded kidnapper's tight grip and reversed it, but was too late to get a clear shot at the other two men as they dashed into the cover of a big rock sticking out from the wall of the chamber. Instead he turned slightly and sprayed a quick burst through the canvas of the tent and heard an encouraging scream as the rounds hit the fourth kidnapper who was still inside. Moving very fast indeed Smith stepped forward and grabbed the Duchess by the arm.

"Quick! We haven't got much time! Move yourselves!" he screamed, physically propelling her towards the cavern's entrance behind him.

Staff suddenly poked his head out from behind the rock and sent a short burst of rounds their way. Thankfully they were too high to catch them. Smith responded with a burst of his own forcing the kidnapper to duck out of sight. Smith then quickly gave the blinded and still screaming kidnapper a belt on the head with his gun, which dropped him like a stone to the ground and put him out for the count. Then he knelt down and swiftly withdrew three more magazines for the MP5 from the man's pockets.

"Right! The exit is that way!" he said to the Prince. "In a hundred metres you'll come across a junction. Take the right hand turn and follow the stream. That'll take you right out of the cave. Move!"

"But what about you?" said the Prince. "There's hardly any cover in here. You won't stand a chance!" Smith grinned at him.

"Just get your missus out of here, William. It's you two that matter, not me! Go on, move! Kate *needs* you, Sir!"

The young Prince looked him straight in the eye for half a second and said "Thank you John" before he turned and stumbled into the dark of the passage to follow his wife.

"Here!" shouted Smith, as he threw his head-torch after the Prince. Then he turned back and sent another quick burst of 9mm rounds at the rock hiding the kidnappers.

"Come and get it you bastards!" he screamed.

NINETY-THREE

25th August
The Peak District, Derbyshire

William and Kate moved as quickly as they could through the passages of the cave system. The bright beam from Smith's head-torch helped to light their way but they still stumbled over rocks and slipped on the water-soaked ground. For the first five minutes they could hear the staccato bursts of sub-machine guns firing behind them. However as they turned the corner and made their way along the main passage the sounds of the continuing conflict were drowned out by the noise of the rushing stream. They were both cold, wet, and exhausted after their ordeal, But they kept going as fast as they possibly could, holding on tightly to each other.

It was a full twenty minutes before they finally stumbled up the step at the caves exit and out into the warm, pitch-black night.

"Stand still!" the shouted command made them freeze to the spot. "Down on the ground! Move it! Spread your arms and legs! Now!"

They felt - rather than saw - several shadowy figures emerge from the darkness around them and nervously obeyed every shouted command. Instinctively they knew that there was more than one gun barrel pointed directly at them, and that the men behind the guns would instantly shoot to kill if they weren't obeyed. The Duke and Duchess sank to the ground and did what they were told without question. They felt hands roughly and efficiently searching their bodies for weapons. Then a dull red light was flashed into the Prince's face for half a second.

"Fuck me! It's the Prince!"

Another light flashed into Kate's face and then the same hands were gently helping them to their feet and guiding them away from the danger zone outside the cave's entrance. William suddenly pulled to a halt, peering into the darkness at the face of a soldier that he knew was there but couldn't quite see. His voice was almost breathless.

"Stop! Give me a weapon. I've got to go back and help him! Smith's holding them off on his own!"

He was gently and insistently pushed forward again.

"No! You don't understand! He doesn't stand a chance in there, I've got to go back and help him!"

The voice of the soldier by his side was quiet and firm, and very sad.

"I'm sorry, Sir, but I can't let you go back in there."

"He saved our lives! Don't be so bloody stupid, man. We've got to help him!"

"I know. But the cave is wired to blow. John will have to take his own chances, Sir. He knows what he's doing."

Just as the brave Prince was deciding to make a grab for the soldier's weapon anyway and damn the consequences, the all-enveloping quiet of the still night was split by a tremendous crack, followed by a tumultuous roar that grew and grew in intensity until it deafened everyone standing outside the cave. As they turned instinctively towards the source of the sound they caught a glimpse of a dull red flash from deep within the cave followed immediately by a huge cloud of rock dust that spewed out of the cave's entrance and caught them all in its embrace. The rocks beneath their feet shuddered and bucked as more explosions erupted deep within the ground and they staggered away, coughing and spluttering as the thick dust made its way into their mouths, noses and eyes.

Finally, after what seemed an age, the deep rumbling and crashing of millions of tons of collapsing rock slowly ceased and the huge dust cloud began to settle. The Giant's Hole had disappeared and everyone inside had gone with it. It was the end of John Smith. The Duke and Duchess of Cambridge, future King and Queen and the United Kingdom of Great Britain and Northern Ireland, wept for the wasted life of the man that they had met for only a few brief seconds - seconds that they would remember for as long as they lived.

NINETY-FOUR

25th August
The Peak District, Derbyshire

The rain of the previous few weeks had finally cleared and a bright autumnal sun shone down on the beautiful hills and valleys of the Peak District National Park. The mobile control unit, army, police, ambulance and fire brigade vehicles had packed up and returned to their respective bases and stations. It was as though the hubbub and excitement of the last few days had never had happened. There was a delightful peace and quiet to the scene that was only broken by the sigh of the wind and the distant melody of a singing skylark high up in the sky.

Brigadier Clarkeson and Major Mike stood on their own at the site that had once held the impressively large entrance to the Giant's Hole. There was no longer a hole, just a jumble of loose rocks, some the size of small cars littering the hillside. Above them were huge expanses of disturbed and sunken ground where the millions of tons of collapsing bedrock had caused earth slides and sink holes to suddenly appear on the ancient landscape. The two old soldiers had been standing in comradely silence for a while, but at last the Brigadier spoke:

"It's a real shame. I hadn't known Smith for long but he seemed to be brave and honourable man."

"He was that, Sir. He was also the best bloody soldier that I've ever known. I owe my life to him several times over from when we fought together in Afghanistan."

"As do the Duke and Duchess of Cambridge."

"Any news on them, Sir? Are they okay now?"

"Well, they're both upset that Smith sacrificed his own life to save theirs of course, but they're both young. They'll get over it eventually, as we all will."

"Is it true what I heard about them, Sir? That the Duchess is pregnant?"

"It certainly is! Let's hope it's not a boy, eh? They'll probably call him John and we could do without another Prince John in our Royal Family!"

They both smiled at the feeble joke.

"Oh, I don't know, Sir. They could do a lot worse than to name their baby after a man like John Smith."

"Yes. I suppose you've got a valid point there."

They fell silent again for a while, contemplating the enormity of the event that had almost happened on this spot.

"I don't suppose that we'll ever know who the kidnappers were?"

"Probably not, major. I don't think that there will ever be an investigation into this affair. It will be consigned to the 'never happened' file, at least for our lifetime. Everyone involved is just too relieved that it's all finally over. And let's face it, the bloody Government has come out of this as heroes and no one there will be sad to see the end of John Smith. He's been a thorn in their backside ever since he escaped from prison a couple of years ago."

"What will they tell the Press about his disappearance? Even they can't ignore a figure like him vanishing into thin air. There's bound to be questions asked."

"Oh, I'm sure that they'll come up with some cock-and-bull story to cover it all up. They're politicians after all, and lying is what they do best!"

"Too true, Sir."

The SAS major indicated the ground in front of them.

"I don't suppose that they'll try and dig up the bodies, sir?"

"Not a chance in hell, major!"

"I thought not, Sir."

The two soldiers stood in silence for a few more minutes, each wrapped up in their own thoughts and memories of the man that was known to the world as 'John Smith'. A man whose real identity and name would never be known now.

Then they turned and began to make their way down to the valley floor and their waiting Land Rover.

EPILOGUE

30th September
Brussels International Airport Lounge, Belgium

Nigel, Matt, Darren and Billy sat around a table in the airport cafe, drinking coffee and talking to each other in subdued voices.
    "I still can't get over it you know. I'm a rich man!" Darren said quietly. "In fact I'm a fucking millionaire!"
They all grinned at his excitement and shared in it.
    "One million, two hundred thousand pounds! Each! That's a hell of a lot of dosh. Did you know that if you took it all out of your bank, even if it was in the largest denomination notes that they have, you'd hardly be able to lift it up and carry it!"
    "What are you going to do with your cut, Nigel?" Darren asked the team leader eagerly.
Nigel's face was split by a huge grin as he answered.
    "I'm gonna transfer two hundred thousand to a bank in *Rio de Janeiro*. Then I'm gonna spend the bleedin' lot on whores! Did you know that Brazil has some of the finest-looking whores in the whole world, and there are thousands of them! I was in prison for way too long without any nookie. I'm gonna shag myself stupid!"
    "What you gonna do when you're *shagged* out then?" There were a few chuckles at Matt's feeble joke.
    "Well, I think I'll probably waste the rest on booze and women!"
They laughed out loud at this one.

"I'm gonna go to Brazil as well," said Billy nervously.

"You going to get yourself some women as well then, Billy?"

"Nope. Ladyboys."

The others fell silent, their mouths gently beginning to fall open as they stared at their friend. Finally Nigel spoke up.

"Ladyboys? You mean like *chicks with dicks*?"

"Yep."

"But you'd have to be *gay* to go with a ladyboy mate! I mean...they've got cocks!"

"Yep."

Billy tilted his chin, holding his head up as he stared his friends down. The silence was once again broken by Nigel, who laughed, grinned and slapped the slender young man on the back.

"I always thought that you were as bent as a nine-bob note! I'm glad you're *gay* mate. After all, *I'm* as happy as a fucking dog on heat!"

They all laughed at this one and then they all clapped Billy on the back and grinned at him.

"You bloody woolly wufter!"

"Pansy!"

"Nancy boy!"

Their good natured humour and easy acceptance of his ultimate 'coming out of the closet' put a huge grin on Billy's own face.

Matt checked his watch.

"The boss should be along in a minute," he said.

They looked around and were rewarded by the sight of a tall, lean man walking through the concourse towards the café. They would recognise the boss anywhere.

"Here he comes now. What the bleeding hell is wrong with his face?"

As he came closer they could see that the man had a large white bandage covering one half of his face, including one of his eyes. Eventually he reached their table, pulled up a chair and plonked himself down.

"Aye aye!" quipped Nigel and they all smiled at the

joke, though they still all looked concerned. "What the fuck have you done to your face, John?"
John Smith smiled back at them.

"Just a bit of plastic surgery. That fucking scar that the terrorists gave me was too obvious. Everyone and his fucking dog's uncle have seen pictures of me with that bloody great scar down me face! The surgeon says that he's got rid of most of it and there will only be a small thin white line left. It's as sore as a mother's nipple though!"

"Aww. It's a shame you got rid of it, mate. It made you look as hard as nails."

"Nah! He should have had his whole face done so he wouldn't scare little kids with his ugly mug anymore!"

"Hey!" Smith chuckled. "You know that you can't improve on perfection! Leave me alone!"

"Talking about being hard..." moaned Matt. "You nearly knocked my block off when you belted me with that MP5 John!"

"Yeah. Sorry mate, I had to make it look realistic though!"

"Jesus!" added Billy, with feeling. "I never thought that they'd fall for it you know. I was sure that the Duke and Duchess would figure out we were using blanks!"

"Nah! It was too dark and too scary. I reckon that their minds told them to see just what they expected to see. It worked like a fucking charm!"

"It sure did! It was lucky that we rehearsed it so many times when we were all banged up in Winson Green though."

"Luck had nothing to do with it," said Smith. "Do you remember the six 'Ps' from basic training?"

"Yeah, I do..." answered Billy "...'Prior Preparation and Planning Prevents Piss-poor Performance!'"

"Correct, Billy, and we all played our part to perfection."

"It was lucky that Nigel knew that secret way out of the cave though."

"Nah," said Nigel. "Remember, I was born in

Castleton, just down the road from the Giant's Hole. I've been pot-holing and diving in that cave for bloody years, even before I joined the SRR. It was obvious that all of that water had to leave the cave somewhere. I found the way out about ten years ago. I just forgot to tell anybody else, that's all."

"I'll tell you what though, it was bloody freezing in that underground river."

"Huh!" laughed Smith. "It was alright for you lot. At least you had wetsuits on under your combats. I had to go in with just my prison uniform on. We were down there in that bloody river for so long I was sure that my cock would drop off with the bloody cold!"

"I know what you mean, mate. It was only an hour or so, but I was scared shitless! I thought me bleedin' oxygen bottle was gonna run out and I was gonna bleedin' drown down there!"

The five men all laughed with relief, taken back to that moment when they were plunging along in the water of the underground river, hemmed in with millions of tons of solid rock. There had been no other way out for them but to keep swimming forward with the flow of the current. It had been pretty fucking scary and that's the truth.

"It was your plan that made it all work though, John" said Nigel, being serious for once.

"Yeah," they all piped up at him.

Smith grinned at them.

"What are you going to do now then, John?"

"Well, a certain gorgeous woman that I know wrote to me in prison to let me know that she has got a new job up in Norway. I thought I might drop in on her there and see if we can't make a go of it together."

"Is this the bird from the hospital in Surrey that you told us about?"

"Yeah."

"Does she know that you're still alive, then?"

"Not yet. I thought I'd surprise her!"

"Bleeding hell! You'd better wait for a while then."

"Why?"

"If you turn up with that bleeding bandage on your face you'll scare her half to death!"

"Yeah! She'll have a bleedin' heart attack!"

"That's okay. She's a doctor ain't she?"

After another fifteen minutes of happy reminiscing and banter, John Smith looked at his watch.

"Well guys. I'm going to be taking the long route to Norway – by train. I'll have to go now if I'm going to catch it."

He looked around at the faces of his friends and smiled.

"Remember that e-mail address I gave you and make sure you keep in touch. You never know, we might have some more fun and games together in the future!"

The team sadly shook hands and hugged the tall lean man.

"Good luck, John."

"Yeah, I hope it works out for you, mate."

"Give her one from me!" Nigel was the last one to hug him and his final words summed it up for all of them.

"Thanks John, for everything. You've given us our lives back, mate."

He stood back, straightened himself up and threw up the smartest salute of his life.

"It's been a privilege and an honour to know and work with you, Sergeant Smith!" John felt a lump rise up in his throat and for the first occasion in a very long time he felt the burn of tears threatening. He looked at all of their faces for one last moment.

"Ditto," he said.

Then he straightened his shoulders, took a hard grip of his overnight bag, turned on his heel and walked off to begin a new life.

Author's note

I have certainly enjoyed writing this book. Unlike the first John Smith novel *One Heartbeat a Minute*, which, to a certain extent was tied down to actual historical happenings and events, in *Public Enemy* I have really had the opportunity to let my imagination go wild, and it has been great fun. I just hope that you enjoy reading it as much as I have enjoyed writing it!

That said, there are some real locations that I have used in this book too, including Abuko Nature Reserve in The Gambia, where I had the pleasure of living for eight years, and the Giant's Hole cave in the Peak District. Some of the characters I have used are real too, so I'll mention my two sons, my granddaughters, and my mates Paul Gray, Matt, Nigel, Darren and Daljit. I hope that they all recognise themselves and that I haven't done them too great a disservice. Dr Linda is alive and well too, only in real life she's even tougher and more beautiful than I make her out to be in the book!

This isn't the end, and John will be back in even more adventures. You can't keep a man like Smith down for long. There will always be plenty of other baddies for him to kill, and more good people for him to help, as long as the world keeps spinning.

I would like to take this opportunity to thank each and every one of my readers for buying my books, and my special thanks go to those of you have given me such great feedback about *One Heartbeat*. Every time that a new review is made by a reader it encourages Amazon to keep advertising the books to other readers, so please keep them coming in! You can also become a friend of John Smith (22 SAS) on Facebook. Just look him up.

Even when these books were only a twinkle in the author's eye, both Linda and I decided that a significant amount of our royalties would be donated to *Combat*

Stress, the veterans' mental health charity, and we have stuck to our promise. They have already received one cheque from us and hopefully there will be many more in the future. So thank you too for helping this little-known charity make a difference to the welfare of some of the extremely brave men and women who have served our country so well and given so much. I never in a million years believed that my stories would be liked so much by so many people! Thank you all.

Craig William Emms
January 2013

Also available by Craig William Emms: the first John Smith novel.

A John Smith short story

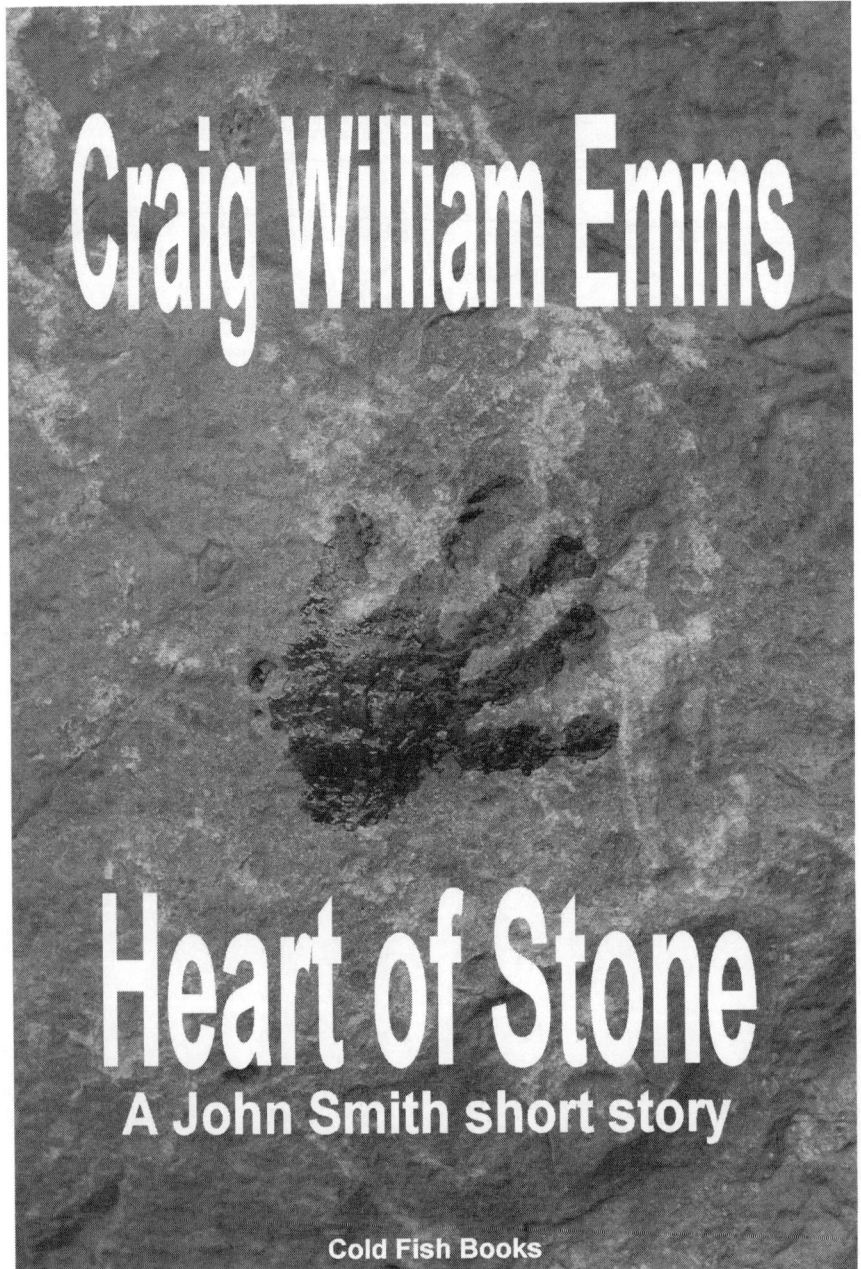

Printed in Great Britain
by Amazon.co.uk, Ltd.,
Marston Gate.